KEVIN CROSSLEY-HOLLAND

AT the CROSSING~ PLACES

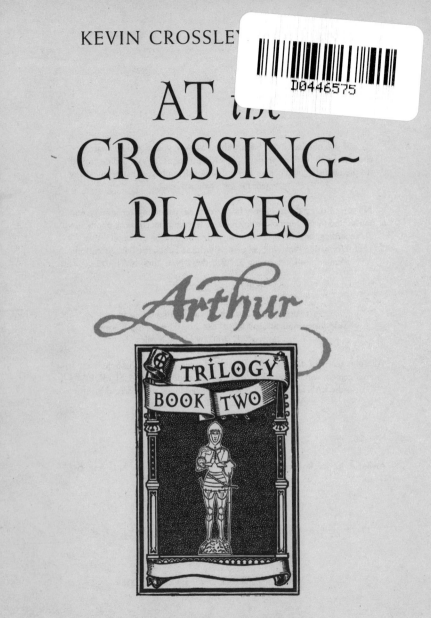

Arthur

TRILOGY
BOOK TWO

SCHOLASTIC INC.

New York   Toronto   London   Auckland   Sydney
Mexico City   New Delhi   Hong Kong   Buenos Aires

ISBN 0-439-26599-1

Text copyright © 2002 by Kevin Crossley-Holland
Title page woodcut copyright © 2002 by Christopher Wormell
Maps copyright © 2002 by Hemesh Alles

All rights reserved. Published by Arthur A. Levine, an imprint of Scholastic Inc.,
by arrangement with Orion Children's Books, London, England. SCHOLASTIC,
the LANTERN LOGO, and associated logos are trademarks
and/or registered trademarks of Scholastic Inc.

Arthur A. Levine Books hardcover edition published by Arthur A. Levine Books,
an imprint of Scholastic Inc., October 2002.

12 11 10 9 8 7 6 5 4 3   7 8 9/0

Printed in the U.S.A   40

First Scholastic paperback printing, October 2004

for linda —
with love

BALK
BALK
BALK

OTHERSIDE

HEADLAND

RIVER CLUN

HIV

SHEEPFOLD

FORD

TO OFFA'S DYKE & WALES

N

W   E

S

FALLOW FIELD

TR

GLEBE

The Manor of HOLT

Holt Castle

Agnes the Wise-Woman

Stables

Rhys the Stableman

East Yard

Bakehouse

To Bryn & Verdon

Headland

Balk
Balk
Balk

South Yard

Armoury

Barns

Cluneside

Track

Robert

To Clanton & Caldicot

Kennels

Sayer the Kennelman

Herb Garden

Orchard

Wilf

Donnet

Common Grazing Land

Pigsty

Ford

Butts

Crofts

Knighton

Crofts

Crofts

Haket the Priest

Church

the characters

AT HOLT

LORD STEPHEN DE HOLT

LADY JUDITH DE HOLT

ARTHUR DE CALDICOT, aged
14, author of this book

RAHERE, the musician and
jester

MILES, the scribe

ROWENA, the first
chamber=servant

IZZIE, the second
chamber=servant

GUBERT, the cook

TANWEN, the chamber=servant
from Caldicot

KESTER, her baby son

ANIAN, the kitchen boy

CATRIN, his twin sister,
the kitchen girl

ALAN, the armorer

RHYS, the stableman

SIMON, the messenger

SAYER, the kennelman

HAKET, the priest

AGNES, the wise=woman

ROBERT, a villager

WILF, an old villager

DONNET, a villager

PIERS, a villager

ABEL, a villager

AT GORTANORE

SIR WILLIAM DE GORTANORE

LADY ALICE DE GORTANORE

TOM, Sir William's son,
aged 15

GRACE, Sir William's daughter,
aged 13

THOMAS, a freeman and
messenger

MAGGOT, his wife

PEG, Lady Alice's
chamber=servant

FULCOLD, the cook

AT CALDICOT

SIR JOHN DE CALDICOT

LADY HELEN DE CALDICOT

SERLE, their son, aged 17

SIAN (PRONOUNCED "SHAWN"),
their daughter, aged 9

NAIN (PRONOUNCED "NINE"),
Lady Helen's mother

OLIVER, the priest

SLIM, the cook

GATTY, the reeve's daughter, aged 13

LANKIN, the cowherd

JANKIN, Lankin's son, a
stableboy

JOHANNA, the wisewoman

RUTH, Lady Helen's chamber=
servant

OTHER

MERLIN, Arthur's guide

RHODRI, the horse=breeder at
Quabbs

TUROLD, the armorer from
Ludlow

JACOB, the moneylender

MIRIAM, his daughter

SIR WALTER DE VERDON, twin
brother of Lady Judith de Holt

LADY ANNE DE VERDON

WINNIE DE VERDON, their
daughter, aged 12

EDIE, Lady Anne's chamber=
servant

KING JOHN'S MESSENGER

DAW, a messenger

LADY MARIE DE MEULAN
(MARIE DE FRANCE)

HUMBERT, prior of Wenlock

BROTHER AUSTIN

BROTHER GERARD

BROTHER ALMUND

BROTHER CRISPIN

GIB, one of the constable of
Wigmore's men

THIBAUD (PRONOUNCED
"teebow"), count of
Champagne

COUNTESS BLANCHE, his wife

MILON DE PROVINS

MILON DE PROVINS'S MESSENGER

SALMAN, a Muslim trader

JEHAN, Milon's farrier

in the stone

SIR THEW=HIT (SIR PELLINORE
   BY ANOTHER NAME)

BORS, king of Gaul

BAN, king of Brittany

THE KNIGHT OF THE
   BLACK ANVIL

QUEEN GUINEVERE

LEODEGRANCE, king of Cornwall,
   her father

CADOR, duke of Cornwall

SIR GARLON, the invisible knight

SIR HERLEWS DE BERBEUS

PELLAM, king of Listinoise,
   Garlon's brother

LADY DIONISE

ARIES, the cowherd

SIR SOURLOUSE OF THE
   FOREST

SIR BRIAN OF THE
   ISLES, his brother

LOT, king of Orkney

MORGAUSE, wife of Lot, Arthur's
   half sister

SIR MILES

GRIFLET, a squire

NIMUE

SIR BLAMOURE OF THE MARSH

LADY SARAIDE, his wife

LADY ANNA (MORGAUSE IN
   DISGUISE)

THE KNIGHT OF THE
   RED LANDS

THE KNIGHT OF THE
   BLACK LANDS

LYNETTE

LADY LYONESSE, her sister

HUON, Beaumains's servant

THE RED KNIGHT

SIR GRINGAMOUR, brother of
   Lynette and Lyonesse

SIR URIEN, husband of Morgan
   le Fay

SIR DAMAS

ENID, Sir Erec's wife

COUNT ORINGLE

LIONORS

THE GREEN KNIGHT (SIR
   BERTILAK OF THE HIGH PEAK)

SIR BERTILAK'S WIFE

ELAINE OF ASTOLAT

HOWELL, duke of Brittany,
   Arthur's cousin

THE DUCHESS OF BRITTANY

THE GIANT OF THE MOUNT

PERCEVAL, a Welsh boy

BLANCHEFLEUR

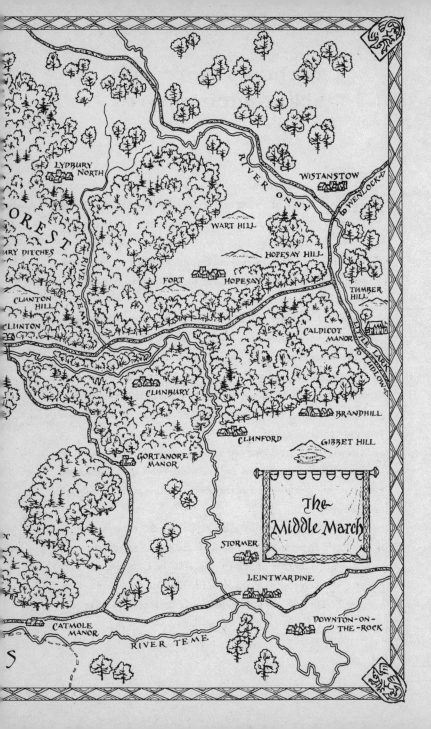

AUTHOR'S NOTE AND ACKNOWLEDGMENTS

A NUMBER OF PEOPLE HAVE GENEROUSLY GIVEN ME ADVICE on specific matters: Thérèse Ballet-Lynn on the identity of Marie de France, David Crombie on cartography, Donald Davis on Jewish beliefs and customs, Anne Holland at the Ludlow Tourist Information Centre on Clun Castle, Maddy Léget and Anne Marzin on the history of Provins, and Simon Puttock on the organization of chapters.

Jeremy Flynn has continued to educate me in aspects of early medieval armor, Matthew Francis introduced me to the legend of the Butterfly Bishop, Fiona Fraser lent me books, and Lawrence Sail led me to Arthur's mother's ring, while my father and elder daughter, Peter and Oenone Crossley-Holland, have made helpful textual suggestions. I'm so grateful to all of you and to Helen Flanagan and Annabel Plowden for your word processing skills.

Hemesh Alles has drawn two attractive maps. Students of Shropshire will see that Holt Castle and the manors of Caldicot, Catmole, Gortanore, and Verdon stand on the sites of existing medieval buildings or their ruins.

My British publishers, Orion, are supporting this trilogy with great skill and style. In Judith Elliott, I have a friend and editor/publisher with an incomparable eye for the whole as well as the particular, and I am deeply grateful to you; to Fiona Kennedy for your finesse with world rights and sensitive editorial help; to Tamsin Curror for your flair with publicity; to Alex Webb and Jane Hughes; and to our maestro, Anthony Cheetham, himself a medievalist.

Nicole Crossley-Holland, a distinguished and humane scholar, has worked through my drafts with a fine-tooth comb and made very many invaluable suggestions, large and small. Any factual inaccuracies are mine, not yours, and I am greatly indebted to you for giving me such guidance and time.

My wife, Linda, and I have had many valuable discussions (often while walking) about this book's issues and ways of enacting them, while as teacher, she has blue-penciled my drafts with "the impatient eye of a twelve-year-old." We have shared the pressures as well as the pleasures, and your belief in the author is rather more than he deserves. To you this book is dedicated.

BURNHAM MARKET

APRIL 12, 2001

◆　◆　◆

In readying this text for American publication, I have made a number of changes as a result of my editor Arthur Levine's imaginative and very helpful suggestions. I am most grateful to him.

MARCH 14, 2002

CONTENTS

AT *the* CROSSING~ PLACES

ice and flames

HE FIRST DAY OF MY NEW LIFE BEGAN WITH ICE AND
ended with flames.

As soon as I woke, I was wide-eyed awake. Under
my badger-skin it was warm, and for a little while I
lay still as a huntsman in a covert. I stared around me at the high
hall where I have slept and woken almost every day of my life. I
tried to wake my brother and sister by making faces at them. I listened for a moment to my grandmother Nain snuffling, and one of
the hounds groaning and grinding his teeth. Then I leaped up. The
whole world was waiting for me.

When I unbolted the hall door and tugged it open, the ice in
the jambs clattered down. Then I saw Gatty. She was standing beside the mounting block with my horse Pip. I had to look twice because she was dressed in dirty sacking, sparkling with frost, and all
I could see were her large river eyes and one fair curl.

"Gatty!" I exclaimed.

"Jankin said I could."

"How long have you been here?"

Gatty ignored my question. "The biggest saddlebags we got,"
she said.

I kicked at the shards and thorns of pearly ice and, barefoot, I
walked out and slapped Pip on the rump.

"You look as if you've been here half the night," I said.

Gatty lowered her eyes and shook her head dumbly.

"Oh Gatty! When I reach Jerusalem, I will send you a message. I'll try to."

Gatty stared at the ground. "Don't matter," she mumbled.

"It does matter," I said. "We're friends."

"Can't be," Gatty replied. "Not with the likes of you."

"But we are. We rescued Sian when she went through the ice, and we separated the bulls, and drove off the wolves together. Didn't we?"

Gatty sniffed. "You could load up," she said.

"Nobody's awake yet."

"I can help, can't I?"

"You're frozen."

"When are you coming back?" Gatty demanded.

"Three years," I said. "Two, maybe."

Gatty shuddered and hunched her shoulders.

"Go on, Gatty," I urged. "Get out of this cold. I'll see you before I leave."

Gatty looked at me. She gazed at me as gravely as the painting of Mary on the church wall, and her long eyelashes flickered. Then she turned away.

Nain and my brother and sister and Ruth, our chamber-servant, were still asleep, so I hurried back across the hall. Avoiding the fourth and fifth steps, and the ninth and tenth, the ones that always creak, I ran up the staircase and along the gallery to my freezing writing-room.

That's where I've hidden my seeing stone since Merlin gave it to me last summer. We were up on top of Tumber Hill when he unwound this saffron bundle. Inside it was a flat, black stone, my obsidian, just a little larger than the palm of my hand, deep as an eye of dark water, and it flashed in the sunlight.

"Until the day you die, you will never own anything as precious as this," Merlin told me. "But no one must know you own it, or see it, or learn anything about it."

Merlin is right. My seeing stone is my other world. My guide. My echo. I can't leave that behind!

I pulled the stone out of the gap in the wall and ran back downstairs. I went straight out to Pip and jammed the saffron bundle into the very bottom of one of the saddlebags.

All morning I was very busy. I cut reed scabbards for my quills and shaved acorn stoppers for my ink bottles, and I wrapped my valuable parchment pages in shaggy towels. I stuffed my saddlebags with writing materials and clothing. In my wooden chest, which is going to be sent after me, I laid more clothing, my new flight of arrows, my ivory chess pieces, and my mail-coat. Then I went round the village, and found Merlin, and Oliver the priest, and Jankin, who was mucking out the stables, and took my leave of them; but Gatty and her father, Hum, weren't in their cottage. After that, I set up the board for the Saxon-and-Viking game, and showed Sian how to play one more time. Then I had a rough-and-tumble with Tempest and Storm, our running-hounds, and Storm tore my right sleeve, so Ruth had to mend it. And then I decided to take my own practice-sword with me, and my brother Serle said in that case I ought to clean it properly, otherwise Lord Stephen would be sure to notice and it would reflect poorly on him and my father. But he didn't offer to help.

We were still eating dinner when Lord Stephen's rider, Simon, arrived to escort me to the castle at Holt and my new life as Lord Stephen's squire.

I've met Simon before. He's very thin and his cheekbones are so sharp they look as if they might shear through his skin. He usually looks rather melancholy, but I like him because he has a very long upper lip, like a horse, and makes quiet jokes, mainly against himself.

"Simon!" exclaimed my father — my foster father, that is. "You look like a snowman. Come and eat with us."

"Thank you, Sir John."

"I hope your ride has given you an appetite," my foster father said. "You look as if you could eat a horse."

"I am a horse," said Simon in a hollow, dark voice, and his upper lip looked even longer than before.

Although I've wanted to be a squire so much, and for so long, it still felt painful to be leaving Caldicot. I think Sir John knew that, and as soon as he had said grace after dinner, he walked across the hall and picked up my traveling cloak and whirled it around my shoulders.

Then I embraced everyone — Sir John and Lady Helen, who held me to her so tightly I thought I would burst, then Serle, and Sian, and Nain on her two sticks.

They all came out of the hall to wave us goodbye.

Sir John looked up at me in the saddle. "Do you remember what I told you on New Year's morning?" he asked me quietly.

"I think so."

"I told you I'm proud of you. I told you that who we are isn't only a matter of blood; it's what we make of ourselves."

"I do remember," I replied.

"And I said that you, Arthur, are fit to be a king."

With that, Sir John slapped my left thigh, and Pip started forward. I heard Tempest and Storm barking. I heard my family calling out, wishing me a safe journey, wishing me joy, wishing me peace, wishing me Godspeed.

So Simon and I crunched away into the snow, which wasn't falling so much as circling us and blowing upwards. When I turned round in the saddle, everyone was still standing outside, silent and waving. When I turned round for a second time, they had gone. Gone as if they had never been. Snowflakes on my eyelids, my checks; the huge blurred hulk of the manor house, patient and grey; nothing else.

I looked around me for Gatty: I kept looking for her. Day after day of fieldwork, barnwork, stablework, and half the time she's hungry. I'm sure she had been waiting for hours in the dark. I hoped she was somewhere warm.

As we rode away from the manor, we passed Joan and Will and Dutton dragging back deadwood from the forest. I pulled up and greeted them, and they wished me good health.

"You tell Lord Stephen what I said," Joan instructed me.

"What was that?"

"At the manor court. I can't even pick up deadwood and I get fined. He's so high and mighty, but he wouldn't live that rich except for us."

For a while, Simon and I rode side by side down the track that leads west through Pike Forest. But before long, the forest closed in around us, and I felt like a hare caught in a trap, snagged and dragged back by everything I was leaving behind. I kept thinking about all the things that have happened during the first few days of this new century.

On New Year's Day, Sir John told me I could be a squire. He said he'd arranged for me to go into service with Lord Stephen at Easter. When I heard that, I leaped up and embraced him. But no sooner had he told me this than he shocked me by saying that he and Lady Helen are not my true parents, my blood-parents. They're my foster parents. But I've lived with them since I was only a few days old, and I'll always think of them as my mother and father.

Then Sir John told me my blood-father is his own brother, Sir William de Gortanore. He's vile and violent. Worse than that, he's a murderer, and I don't want to see him again.

And my blood-mother . . . who is she? I don't even know who she is, or whether she's still alive. I don't know where she is, but I'm going to find her.

And then, after all this, Lord Stephen sent word to say that he wanted me to come not at Easter, but in three days' time. He had decided to take the Cross. We're going to join the crusade that Fulk, the friar, preached about when he came to Caldicot last autumn. So that may mean there won't be time to meet my blood-father . . .

I must have been thinking about these things for a long time because, when I looked around me, we were already passing the forest hamlet of Clunbury.

We reined in, and I drank a few mouthfuls of milk from Simon's gourd.

"Slow going in this weather," Simon said. "We must push on or the dark will overtake us."

This tenth day of January, it has been one of those days when it gets dark before it gets dark, and then by the time we neared Clun there was very little light left.

"Lord Stephen told me to get back ahead of you," Simon said. "Follow this track. Just before you come to an open field, there's a track up to the castle on your right."

With that, Simon cantered off, while Pip and I continued to pick our way along the snowy track, stepping over branches that had fallen across it, wading through hidden pools of mud and mush.

Holt Castle is on top of a small, steep hill, and as I was riding up to it, a rider came dashing out of the courtyard and across the drawbridge. Down the hill towards me pelted the horse and rider, and the horse was whinnying and neighing. Down the hill they came: sliding, slithering, forelegs splaying, the rider yelling — desperate and yelling — and the horse almost wailing, and then I saw the rider was a girl, and the hem of her cloak was on fire.

Orange flames! Blue flames! The girl's cloak was alight, and her horse's belly and flanks were scorched and smoking.

As they careered towards me — the girl helpless, her horse wild — I swung Pip round to meet them sideways and braced myself.

We were hurled to the ground. Pip snorted, he trumpeted, and but for the blanket of snow, I would have broken every bone in my body. At once I scrambled up and staggered through a drift. I dragged the girl out of her saddle. I pulled her down into the snow, and heaped it over her legs, her feet and legs, right up to her hips.

The girl's horse, meanwhile, just dived into a drift; it writhed and wriggled, and neighed pitifully.

I looked at the girl. And she looked at me. She had a blaze of red-gold hair, tied back at the neck, and tawny eyes the color of horse chestnuts.

I gave her a hand and pulled her up, and she blew out her pink cheeks, and smiled.

"He bolted!" she exclaimed.

"You were on fire. Your horse's mane was burning."

"Poor Dancer," said the girl.

"Are you all right?"

"I think so," said the girl, brushing away the snow from her legs and feet, and inspecting herself. "My cloak's ruined. And your nose is bleeding."

"What happened?"

"I don't know. Before I left the hall, I was sitting beside the fire with my uncle."

"Who's that?"

"My uncle? Lord Stephen, of course! The fire was spitting and crackling, and one of the cinders must have caught inside my hem. Who are you, anyhow?"

"Arthur," I said. "Arthur de Caldicot."

"Arthur!" cried the girl. "The new squire." She shook herself. "And I'm Winifred. Winifred de Verdon. You may call me Winnie."

Together we walked our poor horses up the steep path and across the drawbridge, and then we tied them to the mounting block in the courtyard. Winnie led me through the storeroom and up the circular stone staircase to the hall. She threw open the hall door, and there I saw Lord Stephen de Holt and Lady Judith and his whole household waiting to greet me.

Lord Stephen took one look — at the snow and filth and soot smeared all over us, Winnie's scorched cloak, my bleeding nose — and then, seeing that neither of us was seriously hurt, he burst out laughing.

Not Lady Judith, though. She is a whole head taller than Lord Stephen, and she bore down on Winnie and buried her in her arms.

"Arthur —" announced Winnie, wrestling herself free, "Arthur saved me. Me and Dancer. Otherwise, Dancer would be ten miles away, and I'd be smoke and ashes."

When Winnie had explained, Lord Stephen gave me a curious, lopsided smile. "Well, Arthur," he said, "what use is chivalry if it doesn't begin at home?"

Lady Judith looked down the beak of her nose and then she smoothed Winnie's blaze of red-gold hair. "I warned you not to leave so late," she said. "Now you'll have to stay here tonight." And with that, Lady Judith put an arm round Winnie's shoulders and ushered her out of the hall and up the second flight of stairs.

I am writing this by poor candlelight, crouched in one corner of the hall. Instead of my grandmother Nain and Serle and Sian and Ruth and Tempest and Storm, my sleeping companions tonight are Simon, and Miles the scribe, whom I met at our manor court, and Rahere the musician, and Rowena and Izzie, who are both chamber-servants, and they're all asleep.

There's so much more to write, about Lord Stephen and Lady Judith, and about Winnie — she's a year younger than I am, and Lord Stephen says she comes to Holt quite often. I want to write about this castle, and everyone here, but I can't stop yawning.

Today I have crossed from ice to flames.

AT THE READY

F I MAKE MY HAND INTO A FIST AND PLANT IT ON THIS
ledge with my curled little finger at the bottom and my
thumb at the top, partly tucked in, I can see four levels.
This castle is like that. The bottom level is the
storeroom, and above that is the seven-sided hall. From there, another circular flight of steps leads to the third level, my middle finger, which is Lord Stephen and Lady Judith's private chamber —
they call it their solar. The fourth level, my index finger, consists of
six little rooms, each of them triangular, and each leading out of
the seventh room, which is at the center and has the stairwell in it.

Lord Stephen has given me one of these rooms for myself, and
this is where I'm to study and practice my writing. He says my
brother Serle used the same room when he served here as a squire,
and on warm nights Serle sometimes slept up here.

My writing-room at Caldicot has three plaster walls, and it's
tucked right under the roof-thatch. Little birds fly in and out
through the wind-eye, and beetles and spiders and flies and cater-
pillars are busy in the thatch, so it's almost like being in a nest. This
room's not as friendly as that, because all the walls are stone, but
it's quite light, and I can sit on the ledge under my lancet window
and look right into Wales. Offa's Dyke, which separates England
and Wales, is less than five miles from here.

Below me, I can see the castle courtyard. And below the courtyard, there's a grassy bank so steep that it would be impossible to attack the castle from this side.

Beyond that, I can see the South Yard and the cottages and crofts of the people who live on Lord Stephen's manor; I can see the archery butts and, far below me, the drawn bow of the dark river, which half-surrounds this castle.

"Does everything here look very strange?" Lord Stephen asked me at dinner. "Well, it's when things look strange that we see them most clearly."

I've noticed one of the floorboards in my room stops short of the outer wall. When I raised it, I saw that the joist had a hollow in it, and that's where I've decided to hide my seeing stone. I don't think anyone will find it there.

I couldn't see anything in my stone at all when Merlin gave it to me — not to begin with. Nothing but my own reflection: my sticking-out ears and blob nose. But after I'd looked into it a dozen times, and polished it, and warmed it in the palm of my right hand, I began to see deep into it. I watched the white dragon of England fight the red dragon of Wales, and saw King Uther fall in love with Ygerna, wife of the duke of Cornwall. I saw the mysterious hooded man help Uther by giving him drugs to change his appearance so that he looked like Ygerna's own husband. I saw Ygerna giving birth to their baby son, and how he was put out to foster parents when he was only two days old.

In the stone, I'm myself but not myself: I'm a boy who looks like me, and talks like me, but is not me because he knows magic, and has fought his murderous uncle and killed him, and has ridden with his father and brother to a tournament in London.

I watched my namesake gallop to the churchyard of Saint Paul's and pull the sword from the stone. Arthur has proved he is the king of all Britain. To begin with, most of the earls and lords and knights of the country refused to accept him because he was a boy. He was thirteen, like me. But then the hooded man addressed the crowd in his voice of thunder: "I tell you all, you men of Britain: Arthur is Uther's blood-son, the trueborn king of all Britain. Arthur's time has come!"

In the stone I heard the townspeople of London cheering and shouting, I saw them waving their cudgels. I saw all the great men of Britain reluctantly get to their knees and swear allegiance.

"I will be just to rich and poor alike." That's what Arthur-in-the-stone told them. "I will root out evil wherever I see it. I will lead you by serving you and serve you by leading you as long as I live."

Merlin gave me my stone, my other world, and because he knows magic, he was waiting for me inside the stone until I recognized him. He is the hooded man, I know he is, but when I challenged him he turned my words on themselves.

"But who are you?" he asked me. "And who are you to be? That's what matters. . . . Anyone without a quest is lost to himself."

I have been wondering whether serving as a squire is a quest.

Finding my true mother . . . that will be a quest.

Taking the Cross. Perhaps that will be the greatest quest of all.

Yes, this castle is like a fist. Upright and tight and knuckled. It's at the ready. And so am I.

ARTHUR'S MOTHER, YGERNA'S SON

RTHUR IS RISING OUT OF MY STONE TO MEET ME; HE is breaking the dark water.

And now I see where I am: the same great hall where King Uther feasted and fell in love with Ygerna, consulted with his dukes and earls, and handed down laws. Here he lay prostrate with pain after he had been poisoned by the Saxons, and tried to sit up as he was dying, crying out that he had a son, giving him God's blessing, calling on his son to claim the crown.

A door opens at the far end of the hall and a woman walks in. I recognize the gentle slope of her shoulders and her slender arms, pale as stripped willow. I can see the color of her eyes, violet as the first wood-violets in March. It is Ygerna, my own mother.

Now Sir Ulfius stands up and rudely steps right in front of the queen.

"Here she is," he shouts. "The rotten root! The black flower!"

Ygerna doesn't flinch. Like a woman who has learned to expect pain, she looks sadly at Sir Ulfius, then lowers her eyes and quietly listens to him.

"If this woman had told the world about her son," Sir Ulfius growls, "her son by King Uther, we would never have been leaderless for so long. The Saxons harassed us, we fought one another, and all the while this woman, this queen, remained silent."

Ygerna gently shakes her head.

"Isn't it true?" Sir Ulfius bawls. Then he rips off his right glove and throws it at the queen's feet. "If any man here thinks otherwise, let him say so, and I'll cross swords with him."

"Sir Ulfius," Queen Ygerna replies, "how could I tell you what I did not know myself? I have not seen my son since the day he was born. King Uther gave my baby to the hooded man, and he carried him away to foster parents."

"If that is true," says Sir Ulfius, loud and accusing, "the hooded man is even more to blame than you."

"I gave birth to my first son," Ygerna says in a low, steady voice, "but I do not even know his name. I do not know where he is or what has become of him."

Now I see the hooded man, and yes, he is Merlin, as he always has been. He walks down the hall and he and the queen stand face to face. "Ygerna," he says in his dark voice, "I told you once that everything has its own time."

Merlin takes the queen by the right hand, and leads her up the hall until she's standing right in front of me.

My own mother! I could reach out. I could touch her . . .

Now Merlin takes my right hand. Gently he lays Ygerna's hand over it.

"Ygerna," he says, "this is your son, Arthur. Your son." Merlin's eyes shine silver as sunlight on slate. "Arthur," he says. "This is your mother."

Merlin takes a step backwards. Everyone in the great hall falls back into shadow and silence.

For one moment, for thirteen years, for time beyond time's

hurt, Ygerna and I gaze at each other. My own blood-mother. Her own son. We are feasters, we are tremblers, inside-out somersaulters, we are dreamers waking, strangers, red-eyed and dissolving.

Needles of silver rain, fat drops of golden rain, pricked and burst inside my seeing stone. They began to rinse and blur everything.

Then my stone went blind. I crouched over my story. My eyes stung with tears.

knight and squire

 DREW IN MY BREATH.

"Yes," said Lord Stephen. "The hanging."

We stood side by side, and gazed at the enormous wall hanging. It must be fifteen feet long and ten feet high. The top half is divided into small squares, each of them beautifully embroidered with scenes of brightly colored people, animals, birds, buildings, flowers, trees. In the square in the uppermost left corner, a small boy is walking through a dark wood, hand in hand with his mother and his father.

"And this," said Lord Stephen, waving at the bottom half of the hanging, which was just plain linen, "is the part of the story still untold."

"Which story, sir?"

"The part still unlived," said Lord Stephen. "You must ask Lady Judith to tell you all about it. It's her work."

"She sewed all this?" I exclaimed.

"Rowena helps her, of course," Lord Stephen said. "Now! This is our solar, and it serves the same function as your chamber at Caldicot. Here, I can talk to people in private, and Lady Judith and I sleep in the inner room. And then the third room's up those steps."

"The third room?" I asked.

"You haven't heard of the third room!" said Lord Stephen, smiling. "That's where your right hand shouldn't know what your left hand is doing."

"Oh!" I exclaimed. "At Caldicot we call it the latrine."

I'm not sure whether Lord Stephen knows I'm left-handed, and whether he'll mind as much as my father. Perhaps it would be better not to tell him for the time being.

"Sit down, Arthur," Lord Stephen said, and then he padded down to the far end of the solar and back again. He is only a small man, and I'm already taller than he is. He's quite stout, too, but he holds himself upright and stands very still.

"Well!" he said, standing with his back to the fireplace and lacing his pudgy hands over his stomach. "I must thank you, Arthur, for agreeing to come and serve as my squire."

"Sir," I said, "it's what I most wanted."

"I liked your manner at the court," Lord Stephen said. "The way you asked for guidance when I was trying that man for theft . . ."

"Lankin," I said.

"Yes, you asked for guidance, but then you made up your own mind. There are far too many sheep in human clothing."

"And wolves too, sir," I said.

Lord Stephen smiled. "Now!" he said. "You won't find much difference between your duties as a page at Caldicot and those here as a squire. I suppose your brother has told you about everything."

I stared at the rushes on the solar floor.

"No, I thought not," said Lord Stephen. "Well, I'll expect you to dress and undress me, as you did your father. . . ." Lord Stephen hesitated. "Sir John, I mean. And then you must learn to arm and unarm me. I'll expect you to carve before me at table, sometimes to serve me. Do you know how to carve?"

"Not yet, sir. I know the words."

"Good," said Lord Stephen. "Words, yes! I want you to study with Haket, my priest. Read with him each afternoon. Practice your writing each day. In addition to this, I've asked Rahere to teach you to sing and dance. You may think you've never heard a man talk so much nonsense, but Rahere's nonsense sometimes makes very good sense."

Dressing and undressing; arming and unarming; carving and serving; reading and writing; singing and dancing . . . I kept wondering why Lord Stephen hadn't mentioned the crusade.

"All in good time, Arthur," said Lord Stephen, and he raised his right forefinger. "I can see you're impatient, but you can't run before you can walk. You must practice your Yard-skills, and above all your swordplay. Use the pel every day, and then practice your gymnastics. Then run round the courtyard three times in your mail-coat."

"I will, sir."

"Skills, strength, and stamina," Lord Stephen said. "You're going to need them all."

"When will we go, sir?" I asked eagerly.

Lord Stephen shook his head. "I'm sorry you have to practice on your own," he said. "Maybe you'd like to join forces with Tom for a few days."

"Tom!" I exclaimed.

"It's all right," Lord Stephen said warmly. "I know he's your half brother and Sir William de Gortanore is your blood-father. Sir John and Lady Helen have told me your history."

I could feel the blood rising to my face.

"There's nothing to be ashamed about," Lord Stephen said.

I am ashamed, though. I'm ashamed of my father. I don't know whether he cared for my mother at all — and I know he murdered her husband.

"Nothing at all," Lord Stephen went on. "Many excellent young squires have been born out of wedlock. Sir John and Lady Helen are fine foster parents. Isn't that true?"

"Yes, sir."

"I've heard Sir John say that bravery means facing and accepting the truth." Lord Stephen took a couple of steps toward me. "I agree with him. Sir John and I want you to go and talk to Sir William. As his son."

"But I thought . . ." I began. "I thought we were going to join the crusade."

"There's plenty of time for you to go over to Gortanore before that," Lord Stephen replied. "What you may think or feel about Sir William is beside the point. He's your blood-father and he's responsible for your inheritance. It's your duty, and in your own interest, to meet him and talk to him."

"It's worse than you think, sir," I said in a low voice.

"What's always worse," said Lord Stephen briskly, "is worrying about things rather than doing them. As soon as you're well settled in here, I'll arrange for you to visit Gortanore. Now, then! The crusade!" Lord Stephen stepped up to me and put his right hand on my shoulder.

"There's a great deal to do and a great deal to look forward to, before we can think of leaving. Sir John wants that Ludlow armorer . . . what's his name?"

"Turold," I replied.

"Yes, he wants Turold to measure you up and make your armor, though I can't think why. It's bound to upset Alan, my armorer, and he could do it just as well. And then we must find you a warhorse."

"A charger!" I exclaimed.

Lord Stephen took a step backward and screwed up his eyes. "A holy war can't happen all at once," he said. "It's a huge undertaking. Thousands of knights, thousands of squires from all over Champagne and France and Flanders. Only a few from England though, more's the pity! Think of all the horses! The armor and the clothing. The ships. The food. So, where to begin? We begin here at home: We build up our strength, we perfect our fighting skills, we prepare our armor and weapons, we train our horses. Yes, and we pray to God. From this day on, you, Arthur, have your duties as a crusader, and together we must forge a lasting bond." Lord Stephen smiled. "And then," he told me, "you and I must travel to Champagne or Flanders and take the Cross."

"I see," I said doubtfully.

"You must be patient," said Lord Stephen. "A crusade is not as simple as riding to Ludlow."

"But we are going to the land oversea," I said. "To recapture the Holy City?"

"That's certainly our aim," Lord Stephen agreed. "Our eventual destination. But there are many ways of reaching Jerusalem, and each way is tough and dangerous. We stand on the threshold of the very greatest adventure of our lives, you and I."

"I can't wait, sir," I said.

At Caldicot, everyone will be asleep. Tanwen in her cottage, carrying Serle's baby . . . Merlin and Oliver . . . In their chamber, Sir John, Lady Helen . . .

I know they care for me, but aren't they glad, really, now that I've gone away? Doesn't it make everything easier for them? Serle is. He has never liked me; he's always wanted me out of the way.

So where do I belong? Not at Caldicot any longer, and not at Gortanore.

I do trust my aunt, Lady Alice, and I know she trusts me, because she told me her suspicions about Sir William. But he doesn't like me at all. I think he may really have meant to wound me when he tested my swordplay before Christmas.

I'm thirteen, and Sir William has never once shown he cares for me. He must know Sir John has told me that I'm his son, but he hasn't sent me a message. Not one word . . .

If I have a home anywhere at all now, I suppose it is here with Lord Stephen. A knight needs his squire. So perhaps it's for the best that I'm going away, hundreds of days, hundreds of miles away from Caldicot and Gortanore and the March.

5

RAHERE'S
WELCOME-SONG

EFORE SUPPER, LORD STEPHEN SUMMONED HIS WHOLE household to the hall.

"I've asked Rahere to compose a welcome-song for Arthur," he said.

Hearing this, Scriff, the midden-dog, yelped and tore round and round, chased by all the fleas that inhabit him.

"Gubert!" barked Lord Stephen. "Get that beast out of here, or I'll have him skewered!"

When Rahere looked at me, I saw his eyes are not quite the same color: One is sky-blue, the other bluish green. He lifted his pipe — the one attached to a cow's horn — and mooed a melody, and then he sang:

> "Welcome Arthur! Welcome to this motte.
> Let this hall be home from home at Caldicot,
>> And less smoky than tonight. *Eia!*
>
> Your clothes don't fit, your shoes look tight.
> Your blob nose got punched in some fight,
>> And your ears stick out. *Eia!*
>
> I've heard you're going to take the Cross,
> But first you need armor and a horse,
>> And far better skills! *Eia!*

Thirteen years young! You impatient colt!
We'll put you through your paces here at Holt,
    And break you in. *Eia!*"

Rahere's long fingers danced on the pipe, and his bright notes dappled the gloomy hall.

"Welcome, Arthur! Welcome to the squire,
Who will set many a young girl on fire,
    And then save her. *Eia!*"

"*Eia! Eia!*" shouted everyone in the hall. We all laughed, but then I found myself thinking about what Rahere left out. My mother . . . and having to talk to my father. Anian and Catrin hurried down to the kitchen and brought back three jugs of ale and a platter of cream cheesecakes, one for each of us — but they didn't taste as good as the ones Slim makes at Caldicot.

6

ARThuR'S
CORONATiON

S SOON AS I RAISED THE FLOORBOARD IN MY ROOM
and grasped my precious stone, I saw that I was
sitting on the anvil from which I had pulled the
sword. And this anvil was resting on a huge block
of dressed marble, with gold lettering cut deeply into it:

> HE WHO PULLS THIS SWORD
>
> OUT OF THIS STONE AND ANVIL
>
> IS THE TRUEBORN KING OF ALL BRITAIN

But the stone and anvil are no longer in the churchyard of Saint
Paul. They're in the sanctuary of a huge church I've never seen
before.

To my left stands my mother, her almond face pale in the
gloom, and to my right stands Merlin with his floppy hood swept
back, and beyond each of them there are forests of winking candles. The archbishop of Canterbury stands in front of me, and
three priests are serving him. One grasps the archbishop's golden
staff, and one nurses the royal scepter as if it were a baby. The third
bears a scarlet cushion like an open Mass book, and on the cushion
lies a crown of red Welsh gold.

In his left hand, the archbishop is holding a small earthenware pot. He dips his king-finger and middle finger into it, then draws them out, shining. He reaches forward and makes the sign of the cross on my forehead.

"*Vivat! Vivat!*"

One thousand voices. The calls and cries of all the great men of Britain and their ladies reverberate around the great church. They rise above themselves. They swarm around me like memories and promises.

"*Vivat!* Let him live! *Vivat! Arthurus rex!*"

The archbishop raises the crown from the scarlet cushion. He steps towards me again and holds the crown above my head.

I close my eyes. My eyelids are like moths, weightless and trembling.

Now I can feel it. The hoop around my head. The crown. It is my power, my gold guardian; but I am its prisoner.

"*Vivat! Vivat! Arthurus rex!*"

Once more the knights and ladies cry and call out. In their voices I hear long-suffering, imploring, and relief. I hear hope and prayer, I hear bridling and envy and anger, I hear intention and joy.

Now the second priest gives the archbishop the royal scepter, and as he places it in my right hand, I see its stem is ornamented with two beasts. Two dragons, hopelessly entwined, like honeysuckle and bindweed. One has a diamond eye, one a ruby, and their scales are tiny tiles of emerald and amethyst.

Merlin raises his speckled hands, and in his grand, dark voice, he calls out: "King Uther's son! Queen Ygerna's son! Arthur, the trueborn king of all Britain! We have been leaderless, bending our knee to the Romans, succumbing to the Saxons. We have fallen out amongst ourselves, we have fought one another. But Arthur's time has come. Britain's time has come. At this feast of Pentecost, let each earl and lord and knight in this church step forward, one by one by one, and swear his king allegiance."

At once a whole army of shawms and trumpets strikes up. They blare and bellow and slice through the gloom. They welcome the bright day to come.

Sir Pellinore, Sir Lamorak, and Sir Owain, and now the Knight of the Black Anvil: Each knight names himself, kneels before me, and swears to be my liege man. The spade-faced knight and the copper-colored knight, Sir Balin, Sir Balan . . .

And now Sir Ector comes forward, my own foster father, with his son, Sir Kay. Together they kneel. I know my father's right knee often hurts him, so I place my left hand under his elbow to support him.

"Sir Ector," I say, "when you first knelt to me, I said you will always be my father. I told you that if ever I became king, you could ask me for whatever you wished."

"You did, sire," says Sir Ector.

"And you replied, 'Only this. Kay is your foster brother. When you become king, honor him.'"

Tears are glistening in the corners of my father's eyes.

"Rise, Sir Ector!" I say. "Rise, Sir Kay!" And now I rise myself, and call out clearly: "Sir Kay! Before God and all these great men of Britain, I name you the foremost man in this country. I appoint you my steward."

Sir Kay and Sir Ector bow and back away from me, and now Sir Baudwin kneels to me, and I name him constable of Britain. Sir

Brastias kneels, and I give him the Northern command, leader of all men loyal to the crown living north of the River Trent. Now Sir Ulfius! I don't like him much. He insulted my mother, Ygerna, and accused her of failing to reveal my name. Merlin says it's wise to hold a man like him at court where I can keep a close watch on him, so when he kneels and gruffly swears his allegiance, I put Sir Ulfius in charge of the royal household, and name him my chamberlain.

When each and every man in the church has sworn me his allegiance, I embrace my mother, and then I turn towards Merlin. Merlin looks at me, smiling and unsmiling, and then says in a low voice, so quietly that only I can hear him: "A king! But what kind of king?"

"A thousand men have sworn oaths to me," I say, "but I am lost in the forest of my life."

"True," says Merlin, "some men here in this church of Westminster are against you. They may have sworn you allegiance, but they'd still gladly stab you in the back. But other men here, brave men, loyal men, would sacrifice their own lives to save their king. Petitions, pardons, and punishments; but worse, far worse, trickery and infidelity, the dark drumroll of war: There's no avoiding them. They're the sharp stones on the path of a king. But friendship and loyalty, love and adventure, defending the weak, feeding and clothing the poor: Arthur, these also will be part of your story."

"But how?" I ask.

"You are not alone," Merlin replies. "I helped your father, Uther, and three kings before him. You are the king who was and will be. For a while I will help you."

deeper than words

N MY WAY DOWN TO THE STABLES LATE THIS AFTER-
noon, I was thinking about Arthur-in-the-stone. To
begin with, I actually believed I was him and he was
me. But then I saw him doing things I could never
do, and now he has pulled the sword from the stone and been
crowned at Westminster.

But to see Arthur reunited with his mother fills me with hope
in my quest for mine, and to hear Merlin cautioning Arthur about
Sir Ulfius reminds me that things contain their own opposites.
Where there is loyalty, there can also be betrayal. My whole life is
changing, and in a way, my patient stone is showing me all the different parts of myself.

When I looked up, I recognized her at once. She was limping
and still a long way off.

I ran down the hill and slithered to a stop right in front of her,
in almost exactly the place where Winnie collided with me.

"Gatty!"

Gatty looked at me. Her nose was red, her eyelids were orange,
and she'd dragged her lower lip against her teeth so often that it
was puffy and raw.

"How did you get here?"

Gatty sighed and looked at her feet.

"You've walked here?"

"Mmmm," murmured Gatty, as if she were mumbling in her sleep.

"From Caldicot?"

Gatty dragged her lower lip against her teeth again and closed her eyes.

"But how did you find the way?"

"Didn't," muttered Gatty.

"When did you leave, then?"

"Yesterday."

"Yesterday!" I cried. "You slept in the forest?"

"Got up a tree."

"The wolves!"

Gatty shrugged. "Wanted to see for myself, didn't I."

"But . . ."

Gatty's eyes were shining and turbulent, like the Little Lark in flood.

"Does Hum know?"

Gatty shook her head. "No one," she said.

"They'll think you've been caught in one of Macsen's snares. Or a wildman has carried you off into the forest."

Gatty brushed her sore eyelids and half-smiled.

"Well, you can't go back tonight," I said.

Gatty took a step toward me, but then she grasped her right knee and grimaced, so I put my left hand around her waist and helped her up the path. "I don't know exactly what to do," I said, more to myself than to Gatty. "Warm food . . . somewhere to sleep. I could ask Gubert . . ."

"Don't matter," Gatty said in a numb voice.

"No," I said uncertainly. "I'll have to tell Lady Judith. Lord Stephen's away at Knighton for the manor court, so I'd better tell Lady Judith."

Lady Judith was in the hall with Rowena and Izzie, embroidering a square for her wall hanging. As soon as she saw us, she rose and drew herself up to her full height, and eyed us fiercely, like an indignant bird when someone comes too close to her nest.

I told Lady Judith that Gatty is our reeve's daughter and that she'd walked from Caldicot, all the way; I explained how Gatty saved Sian when she went through the ice, and separated our bulls, and stopped the wolves from taking more than one of our sheep, and then I said she just wanted to see Holt for herself.

I don't know quite what Lady Judith was thinking, though, because her face was expressionless and she didn't ask any questions.

"Well!" she said, when I'd finished. "We can't have one of Sir John's tenants freezing to death."

"She slept up a tree last night," I said.

"Like a bear cub," Lady Judith said tartly. "And that's what she looks like in all that hairy sacking. Izzie! Take this . . . what's her name?"

"Gatty," I said.

"Take Gatty down to the kitchen. Tell Gubert to give her something. Then bring her back up here and find her a bolster."

"But where will she sleep, my lady?" asked Izzie.

"Here," replied Lady Judith.

"Here!" exclaimed Izzie, and she screwed up her face, and led Gatty out of the hall.

Lady Judith looked at me and smiled grimly. "I see you inspire great loyalty, Arthur," she said.

"I didn't know," I mumbled. "I mean . . ."

"Lord Stephen is going to have to keep a close eye on you," she said. "Winnie last week! And now this Gatty! Who next?"

By the time Gatty and Izzie had come back up to the hall, Lady Judith had already wished me a peaceful night and retired to her solar. Gatty yawned and pulled the sacking off her head; her fair curls gleamed in the candlelight. Then she yawned for a second time.

"You haven't seen half," I said. "I'll show you in the morning."

Across the fire, Gatty looked at me, worn out, wistful; then she buried her face in her bolster.

I had planned to show her my writing-room, and creep into Lady Judith's solar and show her the wall hanging. I was going to take her down to the dark river because there are stepping-stones right across it, and you can see big trout suspended and gliding just under the water's skin. And I wanted to ask Gatty about her and Jankin's betrothal, and whether Lankin was still against it, and everything else that's happened at Caldicot. It's already ten days since I left.

But when she woke up this morning, Gatty had a fever. Her blood was too hot and her nose was streaming, and she said she had a knife in her throat. She just lay by the hall fire and kept shuddering.

Lady Judith instructed Izzie to boil fennel and mullein and dill in wine, then add a little horehound, and strain it all through a linen cloth.

"Drink it warm," Lady Judith told Gatty. "It will clear the foggy smoke in your nose and throat, and wash away the harmful slime." Then Lady Judith glared at me. "This is all most irregular," she said. "She'd better stay here today."

Before midday, I heard rolling cartwheels, and when I ran down to the courtyard I saw Jankin arriving with Easy, our old affer, and my wooden chest.

"Jankin!" I called. "She's here! Gatty's here!"

"Gatty!" exclaimed Jankin, quite amazed. And then he hugged me. "Everyone's searching for her. The barns. The millpond. The forest. Some people thought she'd been caught in a snare. . . ."

"I knew it."

"'Little runt! Stupid reckling!' That's what Hum keeps saying."

"She slept in the forest."

"She didn't," said Jankin.

"Two days in Pike Forest," I said.

"The clucking clinchpoop!" said Jankin, grinning.

"She is," I said. "And she's a crock of mucus. She's got a fever."

"Where is she, then?"

I pointed over my shoulder.

"What? In the hall?"

"And Lady Judith's looking after her."

Jankin shook his head and whistled.

"What about your father, then?" I asked.

"No change," Jankin replied. "He says he'll see Hum dead before I marry his daughter. Can I go up?"

"I will first," I said, and I ran up the circular steps to the solar, and informed Lady Judith of Jankin's arrival.

"Behold the Hand of God!" Lady Judith exclaimed, and she crossed herself. "He can take Gatty back to Caldicot."

"Jankin and Gatty want to be betrothed," I said.

"They'd better get on with it, then," Lady Judith said, "before some bear snaffles her for breakfast. Make sure Jankin gets something to eat."

Gubert gave Jankin bread and three collops and a draft of milk. Then he unloaded my chest and carried it up to my room, and after that we went off to find Rhys in the stables. He let us have a big bundle of wheat straw and some dry sacking, to make a bed for Gatty in the cart.

"Better than walking," I said.

"You ever ridden in a cart?" Jankin asked me. "Bruises every bone in your body."

Last night Gatty was too tired to talk, and this morning she felt too ill to talk. But what would we have said anyhow? We never say much, Gatty and I.

I stood on the back of the cart and stared down at her.

"You got the sky on your shoulders," she said quietly.

"What do you mean?"

Gatty half-smiled and looked up at me, unblinking.

"Well, you've got stars back in your eyes," I said, "so your fever's cooling."

Jankin was sitting on the front edge of the cart, and he flicked his whip without touching Easy.

"We're off," he said.

"I wish I were coming too," I said. "I mean, it's all right here . . ."

"Lonely?" asked Jankin.

I could feel tears welling up behind my eyes and I swallowed. "But there's going to be time to come back to Caldicot. Before the crusade. I think there is."

Then Jankin flicked his whip again; the old affer started forward and I jumped off the cart.

For a while I watched as they bumped and rattled down the track, but Gatty didn't sit up, and Jankin didn't look back.

8

Beautiful and Horrid

UT OF MY CASE I LIFTED NEW ARROWS, NINE OF THEM, their silken flights made from the feathers of Lord Stephen's peacocks. Then a spare hempen bow-string and my old leather bracer. Three purple tunics. A linen bag bulging with my ivory chess pieces. And several pairs of drawers and hose. Underneath all this was my house-cloak, with a piece of parchment in one pocket.

I recognized Sir John's simple writing at once. "Here is an old friend," he wrote, "as beautiful and horrid as we all are. Keep him with you, and he will watch over you. Try the other pocket!"

I did, and the burnt orange tile was in it — the one Sir John bought last year from a peddler. It has a man's face on it, shaped like an upside-down pear. His brow is broad and his eyes wide apart, but his jowls taper and his little beard is pointed. Spiny leaves sprout out of his open mouth and nostrils and ears, but what's even more strange are his eyes. Sometimes they look kind, sometimes angry, and wherever I stand in my room, they're always looking at me.

They make me think how I am only a little lower than the angels; but they also make me feel little better than a hideous beast. Beautiful and horrid. Both. How strange that is.

Although Sir John can read, he has never learned to write properly, and from the way he forms his letters, you'd think he was a young boy. I suppose that's one reason he has made me work so hard at my own writing lessons with our priest, Oliver.

This is the first time he has ever written me. His letter makes me very proud, but it makes me lonely too.

I haven't got any friends here at Holt, and when I think about meeting Sir William as my father, and searching for my mother, and learning how to serve Lord Stephen as he expects, I sometimes feel afraid.

9

Blue rain,
white Bandages

ORD STEPHEN AND LADY JUDITH HAVE BOTH GONE TO the manor court at Verdon. But I wish they had asked me to accompany them, because then I would have seen Winnie again.

I couldn't practice my Yard-skills because it rained all day, and as Haket is sick, I didn't have my lesson with him either. I was quite pleased about that because I don't like Haket half as much as Oliver; there is something strange about him, and I can't work out exactly what it is. I did try to talk to Rahere in the hall, but he was very melancholy, and just sat beside the fire with his head between his hands.

"Go away!" he said. "It's raining blue inside my head."

So I went up to the solar and kept Rowena company while she stitched a new panel for the wall hanging, and she told me that when she and Lady Judith went to the fair at Chester last year to buy colored silks, they saw a woman in a cage who was born without hands.

"But her toe joints were so long and loose," Rowena said, "that she could thread a needle with them, and stitch. She was just as nimble with her feet as I am with my hands."

I remembered how Gatty and I had planned to go to the fair at Ludlow, where there's a woman with three breasts, and then I saw Gatty sadly gazing up at me from her straw bed in the cart.

"What's troubling you?" Rowena asked.

"Nothing," I said. "Too much."

"You sound like Rahere."

For a while I thought, and Rowena stitched. "If God loves us all the same," I said, "why doesn't He treat us all the same?"

In the dusk the rain eased and I went walking. All the snow has melted into pools and mud poultices, except for the white bandages along the hedgerows.

10

WARHORSE

HEN LORD STEPHEN AND LADY JUDITH RODE BACK
from Verdon, they brought Winnie with them.

"I told her we're going to find you a warhorse," Lord Stephen said, "and she wants to ask
the breeder about Dancer's burns. Anyhow, I didn't think you'd
mind a little company."

I grinned.

"Now, Arthur, go and tell Rhys we want to ride over to the stud
farm tomorrow."

"Is he coming?" I asked.

"Of course," said Lord Stephen. "Rhys is a fine judge of horses.
Without him, we wouldn't be able to understand a word the
breeder was saying."

At dawn, the air was as keen as a newly honed knife, and the
sky forget-me-not blue. The four of us rode out of Holt, following
the river Clun, heading west.

To begin with, we rode four abreast, but then Winnie kicked
Dancer and I followed her, and we raced each other for several fur-
longs, and I won.

When we drew up, Winnie blew out balloons of white breath.
"The last . . ." she gasped, "shall be first . . . and the first last."

"What do you mean?"

Winnie stared at Pip and widened her chestnut eyes. Then she narrowed them.

"What are you doing?" I asked.

"Jading Pip."

"What's that?"

"Stopping him from moving. I'm going to fix him where he is."

"You can't do that."

"I did once. I froze Dancer."

I dug my heels into Pip and he ambled forward, innocent of Winnie's designs. Then I turned round in the saddle. "You're a horse-witch!" I shouted.

Winnie laughed and trotted up alongside me again.

"Is it true?" she asked. "Is Grace de Gortanore your sister?"

"Who told you that?"

"My mother."

"She's my half sister," I said. "Sir William's our father. But I only found out a few weeks ago."

"So you can't be betrothed to her," Winnie said.

"Who said I wanted to be?"

"No one," replied Winnie. "Why? Did you?"

"I can't, anyhow. She's my half sister. Tom's my half brother."

"Tom," said Winnie, and she smiled a little, secret smile. "Come on! Let's have another race!"

After about an hour, we rode up to a huge earth-bank running from north to south, and although I've never seen it before, I recognized it at once.

"I can't think why King Offa bothered to build it, whoever he was," Winnie said. "No dyke would keep the Welsh out of England."

"It would," I said, "if it were manned and defended."

"Impossible!" said Winnie. "It's more than one hundred and fifty miles long. Anyhow, my father says fighting Wales is like trying to hold a slippery salmon. Not even the Normans could, and they planted castles all over the country, and married Welsh women. . . ."

"That's what my father did. . . ." I said. "Sir John de Caldicot, I mean."

"What about your mother?" Winnie asked. "Is she Welsh? Who is she, anyhow?"

At this moment, Lord Stephen and Rhys rose up. The stableman stared up at the earthwork and gave a loud sigh.

"*Sais!*" he growled, to no one in particular.

"What does that mean?" asked Winnie.

"Saxon," I said. "Bloody Saxon! My grandmother says that."

"He can't say that," protested Winnie.

Lord Stephen smiled at his niece indulgently. "Saying is usually best," he observed.

After this, I rode for a while with Lord Stephen. With his straw-colored, mud-spotted cloak gathered tightly around him, he looked like a large speckled egg.

"Yes," he said, "it's true the Welsh are our enemies, and it's only thirty-three years since they defeated us in the Berwyn Hills. But I admire them."

"Why, sir?" I asked.

"For being what we English are not," Lord Stephen said. "The way they honor the power in each and every thing: each leaf, each stone . . ."

"That's what my Nain says."

". . . and for their singing voices; their hoard of stories. But you know all this. Lady Helen's mother was married to a Welsh warlord."

"I know," I said. "And she's told me about the Sleeping King, the King Without a Name . . ."

"Look over your left shoulder," said Lord Stephen.

I looked and saw a hill, its heather almost black, its dead bracken pale gold.

"Weston Hill," announced Lord Stephen.

"Weston!" I cried. "That's where he's sleeping . . . there or Caer Caradoc. Until the day he wakes and marches out and forces the Saxons back into the sea."

Lord Stephen screwed up his eyes and nodded.

"Do you believe that, sir?" I asked.

"I don't disbelieve it. What about you?"

"I don't know," I said. "But isn't it best to believe, unless it's impossible to do so?"

"That's a very good answer," Lord Stephen said. "And there's another thing I admire the Welsh for: their horse-breeding. Come on! You'll see."

At Duffryn, there was a ford. After crossing the Clun, we rode southwest, and about three miles farther on we came to the stud farm at Quabbs.

What a sight! The palfreys in one paddock, the mountain ponies with their sweeping tails in another, the sumpters and other pack-horses in a third.

Two sheepdogs rushed out to meet us, furiously barking, their eyes on fire. They were followed by two dwarf dogs with legs so short they looked as though they'd been sawn off; their stomachs were almost sliding along the ground. And following them was a smiling man with pink cheeks and a tangle of white hair.

"Rhodri!" called Lord Stephen. "God's greetings! I'm glad to see you."

After we had dismounted, Rhodri broke into a tumble of words that sounded halfway between speech and song. Then he noticed Dancer's burns, and at once Winnie launched into an explanation.

"Wait a while, Winnie," said Lord Stephen.

"But . . ."

"First things first! Rhodri, this is my squire, Arthur de Caldicot, and he's looking for a great horse. A young destrier!"

Rhodri smiled and his blue eyes danced with light. He beckoned us to follow him and led the way round the stone farmhouse to the paddock behind it.

There they were, on the far side of the field! Broad-browed and wide-muzzled, deep-chested and lustrous — three young princes.

As soon as they heard us, all three pricked up their slender ears, but while the two black colts quietly stood their ground, the third trotted towards us with an enquiring look. A friendly look! His eyes were like ripe damsons, and a silver-white star shone on his forehead; his coat was the color of a horse chestnut as it breaks out of its spiky shell, gleaming like silk. I gazed at him, he gazed at me, and that was the moment we made up our minds.

Lord Stephen smiled. "Love at first sight!" he said. "Well! Instinct is often right, but it needs the support of reason."

"I'm absolutely sure," I said.

"Let's find out more about him, then," Lord Stephen said. "And more about the others as well."

Rhodri told us that all three colts were three-year-olds, and the black ones were half brothers while the chestnut was born to the same mare as Dancer.

"Not only that! The same stallion covered her both times," Rhodri told us. "So this chestnut here and Winnie's mare are brother and sister."

I looked at Winnie and she grinned at me.

"I don't want a black colt," I said. "Not really. Witches sometimes disguise themselves as black colts. Anyhow, look at this chestnut! How light-footed he is. And look at his long fetlocks. He's the one!"

Rhys untied from around his waist a length of sisal marked at intervals with dark red spots; and while Rhodri held the chestnut, Rhys measured the distance from the point of his shoulder to his withers, and across the broadest part of his chest, and from hip to hip across his loin, and from his cantle, just above his lovely silver-white star, to his swishing dock.

Then Rhodri and Rhys strolled over to measure the black colts, and Winnie followed them.

"Whichever beast you choose," Lord Stephen said, "you must think of him in two ways. He's a piece of equipment, and like all your other equipment he must be well made and strong and a good fit. But a destrier is also your friend. He'll travel with you, sometimes sleep next to you. If you cherish him, he'll protect you and even lay down his life for you." Lord Stephen put his hand on my right shoulder. "Arthur, the choice is yours."

"But . . . the cost," I stammered.

"Sir William will pay for your new suit of armor," Lord Stephen replied, "and Sir John will pay for your mount. And since you're my squire, I will be paying for your horse's upkeep. Very expensive! Destriers like oats."

"Which colt would you choose, sir?" I asked.

Lord Stephen smiled and licked his lips. "Let's hear what Rhys and Rhodri have to say, shall we?"

We listened to pedigrees, and listened to measurements; we listened as Rhodri described each colt's character; then he saddled them, and I rode each of them round the paddock.

"You're sure?" said Lord Stephen.

"Quite sure," I replied.

So then Lord Stephen and Rhys and Rhodri began to bargain. They pointed at one another, their voices rose and fell; in the end, they agreed on a price and shook hands.

My brain circled in the blue air somewhere above my head, and my heart thumped in my chest. And at last, after Rhodri had given Winnie an ointment for Dancer's burns, we all remounted and turned away from Quabbs.

Rhodri walked alongside us, stroking and patting the chest-nut colt.

"What is he saying, Rhys?" I asked.

"Keep him on an easy rein," Rhys replied, "and keep talking to him. Reassure him. You're taking him away from his home."

"What's he called?" I asked. "I haven't even asked you that."

Rhodri shook his head. "No name," he replied. "You name him. He's been waiting for you, Arthur."

"I will," I cried. "I'll find out his name."

"Very good," said Rhodri, and with that he buried his pink cheeks in the chestnut's mane and turned back towards his farmhouse.

Overhead, a red kite spread its drooping tail. Buzzards wheeled and dipped, and every mouse and weasel and stoat for miles around quaked in its burrow hole.

"You're a ford-jumper!" I told my chestnut. "You're a hoof-weaver and a trailblazer! You're a heaven-leaper!"

Away to the south, there was a little lake between two black hills. Under the ganging clouds, it looked ruckled and bitter.

"Beautiful yet sinister," Winnie said.

"Nain told me a story, a true one, about a lake like that," I said, and at once I could see us all sitting on the benches and floor at Caldicot, and I longed for us to be riding back there so I could show everyone my chestnut colt.

"What happened?" asked Winnie.

"A young woman lived in the water and a stableboy married her . . ."

But then Rhys began to chant in Welsh, and I asked him what he was singing.

"An old song," he replied. "A battle song:

> Youthful and strong-limbed,
> With a heart for combat,
> A quick, thick-maned stallion
> Between a young man's thighs.

Look at his shivering blade!
His dark cloak, silver braid . . ."

That's how the little lake looked when the January afternoon sun punched a hole through the clouds: a battle-blade, shivering; a dark cloak edged with silver.

excalibur

DON'T LIKE THAT MAN'S FACE," WINNIE SAID AS SOON AS she saw my clay tile. "He's watching me."

"He's beautiful and horrid," I said.

"No," said Winnie. "Just horrid!"

When I showed Winnie all the sheets of parchment covered with my writing, she was amazed.

"You wrote all this?"

"I have to practice each day," I said. "Haket the priest tells me what to copy out."

"I'm glad I don't have to read or write," Winnie observed.

"But sometimes I just write what I want to write."

"Want to write!" repeated Winnie, wide-eyed. "What about?"

"Anything," I said. "Yesterday. Tomorrow. I want to write about my colt. What he looks like and everything about him. I want to find out his name."

"Winnie!" boomed a hollow voice from far below.

"I wouldn't like to work up here," Winnie said. "Nothing's happening."

"Everything is," I replied.

"What do you mean?"

"Winnie!" boomed the hollow voice again. "Are you coming?"

"I'd better go," said Winnie. "Aunt Judith's a buzzard!" Then she looked at my tile-man again and stuck out her tongue at him.

As soon as Winnie had clattered down the stone staircase, I raised the short floorboard and lifted my precious saffron bundle from the hollow in the joist. In the palm of my right hand I held my cool dark stone, my shining obsidian, and I covered it with my left hand until I felt it begin to grow warm. . . .

Arthur-in-the-stone. Merlin. Quietly waiting for me.

"Merlin," I say. "I have no sword."

"You have the sword in the stone," Merlin replies.

"I can't quest with that. It's far too heavy."

"That's easily solved," says Merlin. "I know of a sword fit for a king."

Now Merlin and I canter side by side, we ride up a valley between dark hills and come to a lake. The water's like a sheet of silver, a metal mirror gazing up at the drifting clouds.

A hand rises from the lake, grasping a sword. A hand and then an arm dressed in rich white silk.

"Ah!" says Merlin. "There's the sword I was thinking of."

A misty wreath . . . a floating wraith . . . a beautiful young woman glides across the water.

"The Lady of this Lake," Merlin says quietly. "There's a huge rock at the bottom and inside the rock a cavern as fine as any palace, and that's where she lives. When she comes over here and talks to you, ask her to give you that sword."

Almost at once, as if she has heard Merlin's words, the Lady comes gliding across the skin of the water.

"Lady," I say, "whose sword is that, held high above the water?"

"Mine, sire," replies the Lady.

"I wish it were mine," I say. "I have no sword."

"If you'll give me whatever I ask for," the Lady of the Lake says in a low, husky voice, "you may have it."

"You have my word," I reply.

"All right!" says the Lady. "You see that little boat there? Row yourself out and take the sword and its scabbard from the hand. I will ask you for what I want at the right time."

"I will row you out," Merlin says to me.

As we come close to the outstretched hand and arm, Merlin ships his oars, and I grasp the sword by its crossguards, the sword and its scabbard. At once the arm and hand vanish. They sink into the waiting water.

I cradle the sword across my lap, and Merlin rows us back to the bank.

"What strange patterns on this blade," I say. "They're like woven water."

"*Ekk!*" Merlin exclaims. "*Ekk! Kss! Ka!* There's nothing watery about those sounds. The name of your sword is Excalibur."

"Excalibur," I murmur.

"Which do you prefer, the sword or the scabbard?"

"The sword, of course," I say. "That's like asking whether I prefer a person or his clothes."

"And that shows how much you have to learn," replies Merlin. "This scabbard is worth ten Excaliburs. Wear it wherever you go, and even if you're wounded, you'll never shed a drop of blood."

who's the winner?

AST NIGHT, WINNIE AND TOM AND I SAT AND SWUNG
on the lowest branch of my climbing-tree on Tumber
Hill, and it dipped so low that the underside scraped
the ground.

"I dragged a long ladder from the hay barn," my half brother
said, "and propped it up against the manor wall and climbed up on
to the roof and plugged the vent."

"You didn't!" hooted Winnie.

"The whole hall filled with smoke," said Tom, happily.

"When Sian went through the ice and almost drowned," I said,
"I bellied out and helped to save her."

"Everyone's done that," said Winnie scornfully.

"There are iron hooks under the high bridge at Gortanore,"
said Tom, "and I crossed the bridge on the underside, dangling and
swinging from hook to hook."

"Sir William and I crossed swords," I said, "and he wounded me."

"That's true," said Tom, "and once I was so angry with my father, so furious, that I shouted at him and told him to apologize."

"That's really brave," Winnie said quietly.

"I've seen the Sleeping King in the heart of the mountain . . ."
I announced.

"You mean magic?" asked Winnie.

". . . and I've pulled the sword from the stone. Anyone can if he knows how."

Tom scratched his left ear with a twig. "You're too clever for me," he said.

"You're strange, Arthur," said Winnie, frowning and smiling at the same time.

"Who's the winner?" demanded Tom.

"I don't know yet," said Winnie.

That was when I woke up.

mulched

 HEN I WENT OUT TO THE YARD THIS MORNING, the armorer was there. He's tall and bony, with watchful black eyes.

"Alan!" I exclaimed. "What are you doing here?"

Without really smiling, Alan parted his lips and pulled them back a little, so that he looked like a wolf. "I'm going to watch you. And parry with you," he added, rather threateningly.

First, I practiced my sword strokes against the pel. I can thrust all right, but each time I whack the post with a side stroke, my right forearm aches, and there's a stab in my right shoulder where Sir William wounded it.

"Too light," said Alan.

"What?"

"Your sword."

"Too light!" I cried. "It's too heavy. It makes my muscles ache."

"That's the idea," snapped Alan. "You little runt. You suppose the Saracens will feel sorry for you? You suppose they'll kiss it better and send you back home?"

"Of course I don't."

"Kiss my arse they will!" said Alan. "You're a milkweed!"

"I'm not," I said hotly.

"Your brother's twice as strong."

"Serle's not my brother," I replied, raising my voice.

Alan looked down his nose and pointed his little black chin beard at me. "So I've heard," he said slyly.

"What?"

"And you won't last long on crusade. You'll get . . . mulched!"

After this unpleasant conversation, Alan watched me with his dark eyes as I practiced my somersaults and headstands and cartwheels, and swung from the ring suspended from the old oak tree, and walked along the raised, narrow plank, and he made me feel more and more uneasy.

"Child's play," said the armorer. "Now, what about the quarterstaff?"

The staff's at least two heads taller than I am. I reached up with my left hand and down with my right hand, and gripped it.

"The other way round," Alan said.

"I'm left-handed."

Alan bent down, picked up the other staff, and suddenly leaped at me. I was taken completely by surprise, and as we crossed staffs, my left heel caught the ground. I tripped and fell on my back.

Alan pounced on me. He planted the quarterstaff across my neck.

"*Pax!*" I croaked.

Alan glared down at me. "Pulp!" he muttered.

"*Pax!*"

"I'll . . . mince you."

"Why? What have I done?"

Alan's beard was full of spit. "I'm not good enough," he growled. "Is that it?"

"What . . ." I began. Then I coughed and began to choke, and Alan slightly relaxed the pressure on my neck.

"Is that it? Is it?"

"I don't know what you mean."

"Why him?"

"Who?"

"The armorer from Ludlow. Turold."

I gripped Alan's staff with both hands and levered it away. Then I sat up, gingerly fingering my neck, while Alan squatted beside me.

"I didn't choose," I said. "Sir John did. Turold made a new helmet for him last year."

Alan sniffed and stood up. His eyes were dark slits. Then he turned and stalked away.

Alan will tell Lord Stephen I'm not a good swordsman, and it's true I'm not much good at tilting at the ring either. I might be, though, if I were allowed to use my left hand. I wish squires needed to be good at archery, because I'm good at that — I can even beat Sir John.

I know Alan is upset because Sir John didn't choose him to make my armor, but he almost strangled me. I can't tell Lord Stephen, though. He might think I'm too weak and not really able to look after myself.

I'm not a milkweed! But will I be strong enough when we're crusading? I'll have to fight grown men. Men like Sir William — except he's not a Saracen!

Once, when I went to Gortanore, Sir William showed me the shield of a Saracen he had killed. It was circular, and at the center was a man's face with glaring eyes and wild hair and a long, curling mustache. His mouth was open, as though he were yelling terrible threats or bloodcurdling cries. . . .

If I were at home — at Caldicot, I mean — I could talk to Merlin about all my worries, or even to Oliver. I could go and give Gatty a hand, or elbow-wrestle with Howell and Jankin, and play with Sian. But here there's no one like that. Only my chestnut colt, and I haven't taught him how to talk yet.

It's already three days since Winnie went home.

"When are you coming to Verdon?" she asked. "You can ride over with Lady Judith."

"I'll ask Lord Stephen."

"I'll tell him I want you to come," said Winnie. "Arthur, you know your writing?"

"Yes."

"When you write what you want?"

"What about it?"

"Will you write about me?"

sir thew-hit

HEN I STARED INTO MY STONE, I SAW KING ARTHUR
and Merlin riding together.

"I'm as bad as my brother," says Arthur-in-
the-stone.

"Why?" asks Merlin.

"I've forgotten my sword. Kay did that once."

"Arthur!" says Merlin in his dark voice, and he reins in. "I told
you to wear Excalibur and its scabbard wherever you go."

"Well, we can't go back now. I'll be all right in this armor."

"And at your coronation," says Merlin, "I told you that however
many men swear oaths of allegiance to you, others will be against
you. Britain has been without a king for so long that many men
have taken the law into their own hands."

"You said I need to be seen amongst my people."

"And to prove yourself with adventures," Merlin adds. "Not just
to hold court."

King Arthur and Merlin ride side by side until Merlin's palfrey
begins to make very strange sucking and gurgling sounds.

"He's thirsty," says Merlin. "I'll catch up with you."

Merlin rides down to the riverbank, and three fishermen
scramble to their feet.

"Come on!"

"Get him down!"

"On his back."

While Merlin yells for help, two of the fishermen pinion him with their stout rods across his shoulders and his shins, while the third goes fishing in Merlin's pockets.

As soon as Arthur hears Merlin shouting, he gallops back to the river, and the three men yell and throw themselves in the water.

Arthur's destrier stamps on the bank and whinnies.

"Let them be!" says Merlin. "They've got little enough except for their own lives."

"If I hadn't heard you," Arthur says, "you would have been a dead man."

"Not at all," Merlin replies. "I can save myself when I want to. You are much nearer to your death than I am to mine."

"What do you mean?"

"Work it out, Arthur," Merlin says.

"You mean I'll die young?"

"I didn't say that," Merlin replies.

Under the midday sun, Arthur-in-the-stone and Merlin ride on. They enter a beech wood and there, in a glade, is a canvas pavilion with a huge armed knight sitting on a tree stump outside it.

"Don't tell him who you are," Merlin says.

The knight stands up. "You cannot pass," he says. "Not before you joust with me. And yield to me."

"Who are you?" asks Arthur.

"That's for you to find out," the knight replies. "You can call me Thew-Hit."

"Sir Thew-Hit," says Arthur, "let us pass in peace. This is the king's highway."

"The king!" scoffs the knight. "The wart! The milksop!"

"You're breaking the law."

"What law?" demands the knight. "The king's as green as a beech leaf. I make the rules round here."

"Then I'll make you change them," says Arthur.

"You!" snorts Sir Thew-Hit. "How old are you? You're as pretty as a newly minted penny."

"Test me, then," says Arthur.

"Test you!" says Sir Thew-Hit. "I'll deface you!"

"I have no lance."

"You can have as many as you need," the knight replies. Then he bellows like a bull, and at once a squire comes out of the pavilion carrying two lances.

Sir Thew-Hit mounts, and he and Arthur-in-the-stone ride away to opposite ends of the glade, and when they charge back toward each other, I can hear their saddles creaking, their armor clinking and scraping, the soft *thud-thud* of hooves on beech mast.

Each of them aims well, right into the heart of the other's shield. Each of them splinters his lance.

"Many young men begin better than they end!" Sir Thew-Hit calls out. Then he roars again, and his squire emerges from the pavilion with two more lances.

For a second time, they trot away to the opposite ends of the quiet glade, in and out of shadow and sunlight; they charge at each other and shatter their lances.

"Few knights survive a third end," Sir Thew-Hit says.

When they charge at each other for a third time, Sir Thew-Hit's lance hits the very center of King Arthur's shield, and his destrier rears up. He throws the king right over his crupper.

The knight stares down at Arthur-in-the-stone; he squints at him fiercely through his visor. "Swords!" he says in a cutting voice.

"I have no sword," Arthur says.

"No sword?" scoffs Sir Thew-Hit. "Are you a knight at all?"

The squire walks across the glade from the pavilion and proffers Arthur a sword, and at once Arthur raises his shield.

"You little fool!" Sir Thew-Hit growls. "You think you can fight me on foot?" Then he levers himself out of his saddle, swings down, and faces his king.

Arthur's strokes are light, but each time Sir Thew-Hit swings his sword, Arthur thinks it may shear right through his armor. He throws himself at the knight, and their helmets crack against each other. Blood trickles down from the crowns of their heads over their faces.

Sir Thew-Hit and Arthur raise their swords again. They flash and hiss, and Arthur's sword fractures.

Sir Thew-Hit stares at the pommel and hilt in Arthur's hand.

"Well, now!" he says. "Either surrender and beg for your life, or else die."

"I'll never surrender to a lawbreaker," says Arthur in a low voice.

With that, he leaps at Sir Thew-Hit. He catches him off guard and topples him, and tries to hold him down. But he can't do it; the knight's as strong as Wayland the Smith. They wrestle on the ground and the knight pinions the young king.

Roughly, Sir Thew-Hit drags off Arthur's helmet and draws his dagger. . . .

"Wait!" calls Merlin.

"I'll slit your throat," the knight growls.

"Stay your hand," says Merlin. "If you kill this young man, you'll be putting our whole kingdom in jeopardy."

"Why?" asks the knight. "Who is he?"

"King Arthur," says Merlin.

The knight glares down at Arthur through his visor. His eyes are like troubled wasps, angry and afraid. He raises his dagger again.

But at once Sir Thew-Hit's eyelids begin to droop. He sighs and the knife drops from his hand, and he falls over sideways.

"Rise, King Arthur!" says Merlin, smiling and unsmiling, pulling Arthur-in-the-stone to his feet.

"You haven't killed him with your magic?"

"He's asleep, that's all," Merlin replies.

King Arthur stares down at Sir Thew-Hit. "Because I've fought him," he says, "I respect him."

"You need this man and men like him," Merlin says. "He's only taken the law into his own hands because England has been lawless for so long. Many knights have done the same."

"Why did he try to kill me, then?"

"He was afraid you'd have him put to death for threatening you."

"Who is he?" asks Arthur-in-the-stone. "What is his true name?"

"Sir Pellinore," Merlin replies.

"Sir Pellinore? I didn't recognize him."

"We all go by many names," Merlin says.

At this moment my seeing stone began to silvershine, as glass shines when the rising sun looks sideways at it. Merlin and Arthur-in-the-stone grew dawn-pale, and then they disappeared.

the armorer
from Ludlow

O BEGIN WITH, ALAN WAS VERY POLITE. HE ASKED
Turold about his long ride from Ludlow and the
new helmet he had made for my father. Then he led
him across the Yard, and as he opened the armory
door, a large rat raced out.

Alan kicked at it. "Get out!" he snapped. "Who invited you?"

While Turold began to measure me up, Alan leaned against the
door. He watched us with his blackberry eyes and picked his chin-
beard, and although he didn't say a word, I could tell he was becoming more and more resentful.

"Now then!" Turold said to me. "What about your helmet?"
His face is quite wizened, and when he concentrates, all the lines
and cracks in it gather and deepen. "The same as Sir John's?"

"You mean with vents?"

Turold smiled. "Without vents, you wouldn't be able to breathe.
Would he, Alan? No! I mean flat-topped or round-topped?"

"Flat-topped!" exclaimed Alan. "What kind of a helmet is
that?"

"The most recent. The armorers in London are making them."

"I see," Alan said bitterly. "London! Ludlow! What's wrong
with round-topped?"

"Nothing."

"And sword strokes glance off flat-topped, do they?"

Turold pursed up his whole face.

"So what stops a man's skull from cracking open each time he's hit?" Alan demanded.

"You're an awkward customer, aren't you?" Turold said calmly.

"And you," said Alan, "are an interference. What does it all cost, all this newfangled nonsense?"

"Are you paying, then?" Turold asked.

"I knew it!" shouted Alan. "Double the price! Half the protection at double the price!"

"Alan!" I said. "Please!"

"Are you mad?" said Turold. "If I overcharged, I'd get no work."

"I've heard about you," said Alan, his voice bitter as a sloe. "You and your armor."

"Alan! Stop it!"

"It's junk."

"That's enough!" I said, firmly and quite loudly, and I felt as if I were listening to someone else speaking.

Alan narrowed his eyes at me. Narrow as the dark sight of a helmet.

"Leave us alone," I said hoarsely.

First Alan spat on the floor at our feet. Then he turned on his heel and slammed the armory door behind him.

Turold raised his eyebrows, and his forehead was a mass of wrinkles. "Very good, Arthur! Very good."

I swallowed. "I was afraid to begin with," I said. "I still am."

"Keep well away from him," Turold said. "That's my advice.

Now then, if you do choose the flat-topped, you'll need a leather cap, of course . . ."

After Turold had completed all his measurements, I took him up to the hall to meet Lord Stephen.

"My armorer made you welcome, I hope," Lord Stephen said.

"In his own way," replied Turold in a dry voice.

"He did not!" I exclaimed.

Lord Stephen listened and kept blinking. "Jealousy is a deadly sin," he remarked. "Worse than pride or gluttony. Worse than avarice or sloth. It eats the guts of whoever suffers from it." Lord Stephen gave Turold a little one-sided smile. "Well! I did rather expect Alan would be upset, but that doesn't excuse his discourtesy. You're our guest. . . ."

"I've heard worse," Turold said.

"You were brave," Lord Stephen told me later. "It wasn't easy to speak to Alan like that."

"He's always so angry, sir."

"But by asking him to leave his own armory, you were adding insult to injury."

"I just said it. Without thinking."

"Perhaps you and Turold would have done better to walk away," Lord Stephen said. "It's wise to avoid making enemies. Alan was rude to Turold, but the person he's really damaging is himself. Not for the first time either. He attacked Rhys once for very little reason, and broke his right arm. One more thing, and he'll leave my service."

For a while Lord Stephen stared into the spitting fire. "Now the fire's angry," he said, and he sighed.

"We had a cat called Spitfire," I said, "but a peddler stole him. To make a pair of white mittens, Sir John said."

"Yes, making enemies . . ." Lord Stephen said. "Weak kingship fosters enmity. Everyone curses and complains, and then some earls and lords start to think they could do better themselves."

When Lord Stephen said that, I thought of how Sir Pellinore prevented Arthur-in-the-stone and Merlin from riding down the king's highway.

"Enemies within," said Lord Stephen, "and enemies without. Out here in the March, we need more than words from King John. We have strong leaders . . . Hereford and Chester. Mortimer, too — he's the constable at Wigmore. But they need the support of their king."

"Are they coming on the crusade, sir?"

"If they were to turn their backs, the Welsh would soon attack," Lord Stephen replied.

"But why don't the Welsh join the crusades as well?" I said.

"That's a good question," Lord Stephen replied. "I could answer that their hatred of the English is greater than their faith. And I could tell you that Welsh warlords still take slaves, human slaves, from here on the March, and they're not worthy to be Christian knights. And I could say they'd be unreliable allies. They're unruly and don't like taking orders and are always falling out with one another."

the wall hanging

OU SEE THAT SQUARE?" SAID LADY JUDITH, STANDING
on her toes and reaching up as far as she could
with her long right forefinger. "That shows our
betrothal."

I stared up at the blue silk boy and the green silk girl kneeling
in front of their parents.

"How old were you, my lady?" I asked.

"Nine," said Lady Judith.

"Nine!" I exclaimed.

"What's wrong with that?" Lady Judith asked. "The second
stage of childhood begins when you're seven."

"How old was Lord Stephen?"

"Fourteen," said Lady Judith. "Now that one right up there!
Can you see Lord Stephen falling out of the tree? He was eleven,
and he broke his wrist and his right leg. Yes, here he is holding
manor court for the first time. And this is when Piers was plowing
in Fallow Field and turned up a pot full of Roman coins."

"Roman coins!" I cried.

"All in good time," said Lady Judith. "Lord Stephen may show
them to you."

"Who is this lady?" I asked.

"The mother of Coeur-de-Lion and King John. Queen Eleanor
of Aquitaine."

"Lord Stephen has met Queen Eleanor?"

"She's old now," Lady Judith said, "very old, and her years are full of groans. But when Lord Stephen met her, she was still the most beautiful woman alive. Look! She was wearing a red mantle, poppy red, with a silver border embroidered with gold lions."

"Did you meet her too?" I asked.

Lady Judith shook her head. "Coeur-de-Lion was away crusading, and the queen was ruling England. She summoned Lord Stephen with the earls of Chester and Hereford to advise her."

For a while we stood and stared at the enormous wall hanging: The dozens of colored panels were bright as the beds of storm-purple pansies and orange marigolds and cream lilies and red roses in the garden at Caldicot; the wide borders were stitched with little sundials and burning candles.

"So this is the life of Lord Stephen de Holt," announced Lady Judith, flexing her fingers. "Up to today. The seventh day of February in the year 1200. The plain linen at the bottom is for the part still unlived. God grant us both the years to complete the whole hanging."

I looked at Lady Judith, and I know we were both thinking about the crusade and whether Lord Stephen and I will ever come safe home.

"I've been sewing it since we were married," Lady Judith told me, "and that's twenty years ago."

"Do your fingers sometimes get stiff?" I asked.

"All the time. On the worst days, Rowena has to sew on her own."

"Mine ache when I've been writing for a long time."

"Look!" said Lady Judith, and she pointed to the last stitched square. "Do you recognize this?"

I stared at a girl on horseback, with red-gold hair, her cloak on fire, pelting downhill from a castle towards a waiting boy and his horse.

"You see?" Lady Judith said. "You are part of the story already."

three times three

AST SPRING, I WORKED OUT I HAD THREE SORROWS, three fears, and three joys.

I still have, but they're all different.

My first sorrow now is that I realize my mother cannot have even wanted me to be born. I don't belong with her or Lady Alice or Lady Helen or anyone. My second sorrow is that my father is Sir William. He's a murderer and loathsome, and I dread having to meet him again. My third sorrow is Gatty. She and Jankin may never be able to marry, and I wish I could see her sometimes and talk to her.

My first fear is that my mother may not even be alive. But even if she is, she may not want to see me, and that's my second fear. My third is that Alan's right about my Yard-skills not being good enough, and that in the end Lord Stephen will decide not to take me to Jerusalem.

Winnie is my first joy. I like her and I think she likes me, and I'm looking forward to visiting her at Verdon. Second, I'm glad I'm Lord Stephen's squire. He's fair and usually friendly and even thanked me for coming to serve him. My third joy! That's my glorious chestnut warhorse. I'm going to call him Bonamy.

death-pigeons
and delays

ESTERDAY WAS AN UNLUCKY DAY, I'M NOT SURE WHY. Maybe because it was the feast day of Saint Julian the Hospitaller, who mistook his father and mother for two robbers and killed them both. They were certainly unlucky!

Lord Stephen excused me Yard-practice and my lesson with Haket so I could accompany him to the muster at Verdon and meet all the other knights of the Middle March who have taken the Cross. But he had some business to attend to first, so I went up to my room and unwrapped my seeing stone.

It was odd. What I could see and what I could hear didn't exactly fit; or rather, they were two sides of the same story. That has never happened before.

King Arthur is mounted and in company, and at least fifty earls, lords, and knights are riding with him, as well as several hundred men on foot. His brother and steward, Sir Kay, is riding on his left, and Sir Brastias, commander of the North, is on his right. I can see Sir Lamorak and Sir Owain. And Sir Balin of Northumberland, King Bors of Gaul, King Ban of Brittany, and with his gold shield crossed by three grass-green stripes, the Knight of the Black Anvil: They're all with the king.

They're riding up a wide valley, and there's a wood in front of them.

Now a herald blows his trumpet, three short blasts, and King Arthur reins in.

"The dark drumroll of war," says a voice, Merlin's voice, but I can't see Merlin in the stone. It's as if the words are inside Arthur-in-the-stone's head.

And now I can hear voices coming from the wood.

"Not until he's down and dead."

"Our kiss-curl king!"

"Easy meat!"

"England has been lawless for too long," Merlin says. "I've told you that before."

"Down and dead," says a voice in the wood. "Destroyed."

"I can raise one hundred men."

"And I can raise one thousand."

"Last night," says the voice of a young man, "I had a dream. I was right up in the air, staring down at all our castles and manors. They looked as small as chess pieces. Then the south wind spun, it rocked and toppled them. After that, there was a flood. A silver scythe. It picked up all our castles and our manors and carried them away."

There's quiet for a while, and now I see King Arthur's whole army has come to a halt.

"For each man loyal to the crown, there is some Sir Pellinore, ready to take the law into his own hands," Merlin's voice says, "and for each Sir Pellinore, a man intent on treason. Hunt down your enemies wherever they are — King Brandegoris and King Clarivaus, the King of the Hundred Knights, King Lot of Orkney. Oblige them to swear their allegiance; and if they will not, put them to death. A weak king soon fosters enemies."

"There will be a fierce battle," says a dark voice in the wood. "That's what your dream means."

"We'll topple King Arthur."

"And we'll sweep him away."

Now King Arthur's knights shout and separate, they canter away to left and right. There's a wind at their backs, and the linen surcoats over their armor tug and flutter.

Arthur-in-the-stone raises his gold shield, and the scarlet dragon ramping on it roars at whatever is lying in wait for it.

"The dark forest of my life," Arthur says.

"But not alone," says Merlin's voice.

The herald puts his trumpet to his mouth. He gives a long blast and Arthur's knights canter forward, followed by the foot soldiers. Now the king's enemy breaks cover. Hooting and howling, they run out of the trembling wood. . . .

At this moment, there was a loud smacking and cracking on the stone steps up to my room. Hurriedly, I wrapped my obsidian in its cloth, and then there was a clout on the door.

It was Izzie, podgy and pink-faced.

"Why are you making all that noise?" I asked.

Izzie waved a stick and then smacked the wall with it. "It all echoes," she said. "Is this your room?"

"What do you want?"

"Who's that man?" Izzie asked, pointing at my clay tile.

"Izzie!" I said. "What do you want?"

Izzie giggled and put her hand over her mouth. "Lord Stephen's ready to ride to Verdon," she said, and then she giggled again and ran back down the steps, trailing her stick behind her.

"Now," said Lord Stephen as we set off, "this country will be new to you. North through Bryn and Einion."

"Welsh?" I asked.

"The names are Welsh but the land's English. It's east of Offa's Dyke. The muster's at midday and it's seven miles to Verdon, so we must keep moving."

"I'm looking forward to seeing Winnie," I said.

"And I want to know exactly how many Marcher knights have decided to take the Cross," Lord Stephen said.

What I didn't tell Lord Stephen was that I was nervous Sir William might show up. "Adventure and the land oversea burn in his blood," Sir John had told me before I left Caldicot, saying that he wouldn't be surprised if Sir William decided to go crusading one last time.

The first unlucky thing yesterday was that Izzie stopped me from seeing the battle between Arthur and his enemies. And then, while we were riding alongside the graveyard at Bryn, Lord Stephen made an awful choking sound and sneezed.

"God bless you, sir," I said.

"Right next to all these graves," said Lord Stephen, shaking his head. "I couldn't help it."

It wasn't long before the angry dead took their revenge on us. About one mile after we had left Bryn, Lord Stephen's palfrey went very lame; and then, while we were struggling along, we saw two brown-and-white pigeons sitting on the path in front of us.

"The pigeons of Caehowell!" Lord Stephen exclaimed. "First my sneeze, then this lame beast, and now these death-pigeons. A man may choose to ignore one omen, but we can't ignore three. We weren't meant to travel today."

And with that, Lord Stephen patted his palfrey and wheeled him round.

Before long, it began to drizzle; then the rain quickened, and by the time we got back to Holt, we were both drenched. My nose was dripping. My chin and eyelashes. Everything!

"First things first," Lord Stephen said briskly. "I must talk to Rhys about this poor hobbled creature. You go indoors out of this vile weather."

Lord Stephen is never angry or even downcast, so I suppose the four humors must sing in harmony in his body. Johanna once told me at Caldicot that a child is only gloomy or resentful if he's conceived under a sickle moon; then his liver will be perforated with hundreds of tiny holes, like cheese, and he won't want to eat or drink much.

All the same, Lord Stephen wasn't at all pleased this morning. He sent Simon over to Verdon to find out about the muster and explain to Sir Walter why we hadn't come, and Simon returned with the news that only seven knights had turned up. "And five of them," he said, "haven't decided whether or not to take the Cross."

"I'd hoped we'd be sailing to Flanders soon," Lord Stephen told me. "Count Baudouin will be taking the Cross in Bruges with his wife, Countess Marie, and I thought the Marcher knights could do so at the same time. But only seven! We'll just have to wait."

To make matters much worse, Lord Stephen then said: "This delay does mean there'll be time for you to go Gortanore. After your birthday. That'll be best."

19

SON AND MOTHER

AHERE WAS SITTING UNDER THE TABLE. AS SOON AS he saw me, he called out, "Can you sing, Arthur? *Ut, re, mi . . .*"

"I don't want to sing," I said.

I haven't wanted to do anything all day, and above all, I don't want to have to go to Gortanore.

"What are you doing under that table?" I asked.

"Why is a man usually under a table?"

"When he's drunk."

"I'm drunk with sorrow here in my prison." Rahere plucked the fingerboard string of his fiddle, lower and lower. In his light voice, he started to sing:

> "You all know, my earls and barons
> — English, Norman, Poitevin, Gascon —
> I've never had one companion
> So worthless I'd abandon
> Him because of the ransom.
> I'm making no accusation
> But, dear God, I'm still in prison."

"That's a very mournful song," I said.

"Coeur-de-Lion composed it while he was imprisoned by Leopold of Austria."

"I know about that," I said. "He had to wait two winters before he was ransomed. And while he was in prison, his mother cared for his kingdom."

Rahere plucked the top string of his fiddle:

> "If this western world were mine
> From the foreshore to the Rhine
> I would give it all away
> — all its manors, all its farms —
> If the Queen of England
> Would but lie in my arms."

Rahere grinned and laid his fingertips over his sky-blue eye. "That's what they sing-and-say about Queen Eleanor. What about your mother, Arthur? Is she as beautiful as that? Now come on! *Ut, re, mi, fa, sol, la . . .*"

haket's instruction

HEN I OPENED THE CHURCH DOOR, ROWENA WAS standing just inside it, looking as flushed as Tanwen did when I found her with Serle in the kitchen at Caldicot. Her eyes were burning. Then she brushed past me and ran down to the lych-gate.

Haket stepped out of the church-gloom.

"What's wrong with Rowena?" I asked.

"I . . . she was instructing me," Haket said.

"What? In needlework?"

"Ha!" exclaimed Haket. "Of course not."

"What then?"

"In minding my own business," Haket said sharply, and he put his hands on his hips and tugged down his gown.

"I was only asking."

"And if you keep sticking your nose into other people's business —" said Haket, grabbing and twisting my nose, "— it will come off. What happens in confession is secret, as you well know. It's only for the ears of the priest — and God."

"Does God have ears?" I asked.

Haket looks rough-hewn, as if God left off making him halfway through. His cheekbones are like planks and his chin like a sawing block, and his skin's rough as bark. He has a big red mouth.

"That's enough of that," Haket replied, leading the way into his vestry, which is just as damp and chilly as the one at Caldicot. "Let me hear you read. The Book of Exodus, chapter twenty, beginning at the twelfth verse."

"Honor thy father and mother . . ." I began.

My father. How can I? How can I honor him? He's a murderer and he beats Lady Alice. He wounded me in my right shoulder and I think he may have meant to. I do honor my mother, though. I think about her and pray for her each day.

"Arthur!" said Haket keenly. "What's wrong with you today?"

"Thou shalt not murder," I read. "Thou shalt not commit ad . . . adult . . ."

"Adultery," said Haket.

"What's that?"

"Go on."

"Thou shalt not steal. . . ."

When I have my lessons with Oliver, it's often quite easy to distract him because he likes the sound of his own voice. He doesn't mind me arguing with him either, and that way I've found out lots of new things.

But Haket is much more unbending. When I am reading, I have to read. When I'm writing, I have to write. Like Oliver, he won't hear of my using my left hand, and several times he has smacked it.

Haket is nothing like as rude about the Saracens as Oliver; but all the same, he believes they worship a false prophet and are not equal with Christians in the eyes of God.

"Does God have eyes?" I asked. "Is He shaped like a human being?"

But of course Haket refused to change the subject. "In truth, many men who say they're Christian . . ." he began. "Arthur, have you heard how King Richard defeated Saladin, the Saracen leader, at Arsuf?"

"Yes."

"Because of Coeur-de-Lion, we do still have a kingdom of Jerusalem. But although King Richard stood and stared at the gates of Jerusalem itself, he could never enter the Holy City. Do you know why not?"

"Because his men were exhausted."

"Because Christendom is a wasteland."

"What does that mean?"

"A wilderness, Arthur. A wasteland of the spirit. Many men are behaving like animals. Think of the wildmen who imprisoned King Richard at Dürnstein. They guarded him night and day with unsheathed swords."

I thought of the beautiful, horrid man on my clay tile: little lower than the angels, little better than a hideous beast. . . .

"Pay attention!" said Haket. "This is the truth. Many men and women say they're Christian, but do not behave in a Christian manner. Is everyone here at Holt Christian? Is that what you think?"

"I don't know," I faltered.

"All over Europe, people take the law into their own hands," Haket said, "and their law is to threaten and maim, to rape and kill. Until we're Christian not only in word but in deed, how can we enter Jerusalem?"

"But human beings can never be perfect," I said.

"That is the paradox," Haket said, "and I want you to think about it. That's all for this afternoon."

I put my hand on top of the vestry chest and pulled myself up.

"Oh!" I exclaimed. "Look!"

Haket looked.

"Rowena's muffler!" I said. "I'll give it to her."

Haket squeezed the muffler in one of his horny hands. "I'll give it to her myself," he said.

But what was Rowena doing in the vestry? I thought Haket said she'd come to church to make her confession. He can't have been telling me the truth.

21

GUINEVERE

ATE THIS AFTERNOON, I HELPED RHYS TO GROOM Bonamy. He must be three hands taller than Pip, and I had to stand on the mounting block to reach across his back.

"Bonamy!" said Rhys. "What kind of a name is that?"

"French," I replied.

"Poor beast!" said Rhys.

"'Good friend.' That's what it means." I laid my hand on Bonamy's muzzle. "And that's what he'll be when we're crusading," I said.

In the dying light, the star on Bonamy's forehead began to shine, and when I left the stables, he whinnied.

There was still some time before supper, so I looked into my seeing stone. . . .

Her smolder of Welsh gold hair, hanging thickly over her shoulders.

Her eyes, chestnut, with little yellow flecks in them, and her eyebrows, so delicate, like new quills, like skeletons of leaves.

Her wasp waist . . .

Arthur-in-the-stone can scarcely bear to look at Guinevere, sitting with her father, King Leodegrance, on the other side of the great hall. But he cannot bear not to.

"I love her," he tells Merlin.

Merlin slowly shakes his head. "Love can be blind," he says.

This is the same hall where I saw King Uther fall in love with Ygerna, her sloping shoulders and slender arms, her violet eyes; where I saw him feast and hold court and lie on his deathbed, poisoned by his enemies.

"Against your enemies," Merlin says, "God was on your side. You were fighting in the name of Vortigern, Uther Pendragon, and all the kings of Britain who have been and will be. Your enemies are oath-breakers, law-duckers, crown-mockers."

"I swung my sword," says Arthur, "and sheared through one man's helmet, right down to his teeth."

"If a man is weak, his rivals soon pounce on him," Merlin says.

"Then why did you stop me?"

"If you hadn't stopped, God would have grown angry and turned the tide. The battlefield was swimming with brains and blood."

"Many men loyal to the crown died in the fight," the king says.

"There's always a cost," Merlin replies in his deep, dark voice. "But after this, no one will be quite so eager to confront you. It's another thing, though, to win the battle with ourselves."

"We're each our own worst enemy," says Arthur-in-the-stone. "Is that what you mean?"

"I mean Guinevere," says Merlin.

"But I love her."

Merlin waves his spotty hand. "Don't say I haven't warned you," he murmurs.

"I love her and I always will."

"I can see you've made up your mind," Merlin says. "But if you were not so deeply in love, I could find you a wife beautiful and loyal. You would love her, and she would always love you."

spiked

NE OF LORD STEPHEN'S MUSTER OF PEACOCKS WAS standing in front of the armory door, displaying his feathers, and as we walked up to him, he screamed.

"Beautiful creatures, vile tempers!" Lord Stephen said. "Go on with you!"

The peacock held his ground.

"Go on!" Lord Stephen barked, and he poked at the peacock with his stick until it strutted away. "Now, you know about Alan, do you?"

"Sir?"

"You don't! Last night a worm . . . it came out under his right eyeball."

"A tapeworm!"

"His whole eye's on fire. As red as the setting sun. So I've sent him down to see what Agnes can do for him; I told him we can manage for ourselves."

Everything went all right to begin with. First, I invited Lord Stephen to sit on the armory stool, and knelt in front of him, and fitted on his leather boots. Then I wrapped his shins and knees with strips of boiled leather, and over them I strapped his shining greaves.

"Tightly round my calves," Lord Stephen said. "But leave some room round the backs of my knees."

I had more trouble with Lord Stephen's thigh-pieces. They kept slipping out of position, and then Lord Stephen said the right one felt very sharp. Before long, he complained that his right foot felt wet, and when I pulled off his boot, it was swilling with blood.

Lord Stephen wrenched off his right thigh-piece, screwed up his eyes and inspected it.

"I thought so," he said. "Look at this!"

One of the nail-bolts had lost its rounded head.

"Spiked!" said Lord Stephen.

"What shall I do, sir?"

Lord Stephen laughed. "Many men get wounded on the battle-field," he said, "but not so many in their own armories!"

And not so many, I thought, when they cross swords with their own fathers. I'm sure Sir William tricked me, and when I think about having to meet him, the nape of my neck begins to tingle.

Lord Stephen rubbed away some of the blood. "Run and ask Agnes to come up to the hall as soon as she can," he told me. "We're certainly keeping her busy this morning."

"Alan will blame me for being careless," I said.

"It's Alan who was careless," Lord Stephen said sharply. "I expect my armorer to keep my armor in good repair."

Sir William told me once that Lord Stephen would never be strong enough to be a crusader, but I think he was wrong. He is always robust in spirit, even if he is not very manly in body.

the wedding
feast of arthur
and guinevere

UINEVERE AND ARTHUR-IN-THE-STONE: THEY'RE SIT-
ting on top of Tumber Hill.

With Merlin and Ygerna. With a gnashing of
knights and a loop of ladies. A May-month of squires
and a secret of young women. With a stumble-and-swill of people from the common fields, stables, sties, and barns. A cheer of
children . . .

They're sitting on three-legged stools carved from white ivory.
Each has one leopard leg, one antelope leg, and one leg of manticore.

Ringed by a muster of peacocks. Preening popinjays and wobble-
throated pigeons and red-breasted robins, all-promising larks. A
charm of goldfinches . . .

This whole, sweet, green patient world at their feet, face
upward.

Flanked by a pride of lions. Hugging brown bears and misty-
eyed cows, see-yourself monkeys and sheepish sheep. A peep of
chickens . . .

This world's ministry is gathered on top of Tumber Hill for
their wedding feast.

Servants step out of the beech woods, carrying bread baskets and flagons of red and white wine, and they lay them on long tables dressed with damask.

A string of harpers. A fretsaw of fiddlers . . .

Arthur and Guinevere gaze at each other. They seal their love with a kiss.

"I will give each man and woman in my kingdom whatever they ask of me," the young king calls out.

And now a young woman walks right up to them and she begins to sing:

> "Love without heartache, love without fear
> Is fire without flame and flame without heat."

I remember! It's the song the girl sang at Caldicot last Christmas. The snow-skinned girl with bruises under her eyes, her voice as piercing as the North Star.

"*Dulcis amor!*" the girl sings.

"Bittersweet!" all the knights and ladies chorus, the young women and squires. "Sweet bittersweet love."

Again the girl sings:

> "Love without heartache, love without fear
> Is day without sunlight, hive without honey.
> Love without heartache, love without fear
> Is summer without flower, winter without frost.
> *Dulcis amor!*"

"Bittersweet!" sings the great hill choir. "Sweet bittersweet love."

Then, around Arthur and Guinevere, all God's creatures begin to move. They rock and sway and strut and stamp, they leap and lollop and plod and pad, they hop and flutter and fly: grave and gay, each of them, caught up in this world's dance.

24

A Singing Lesson

RE YOU READY?" ASKED RAHERE.

"I am," I replied.

Izzie stopped passing the shuttle through the loom and looked up.

"A voice is a musical instrument," said Rahere, "and you can't play an instrument if you're standing on one leg and twisting your right earlobe. Stop fidgeting!"

"Love without heartache, love without fear," I sang, "is day without sunlight —"

Rahere clapped his hands. "That's all wrong."

"But is it true?" I asked. "Does love have to be like that?"

I don't know why but I suddenly thought of my dream about swinging on my climbing-tree, and how Tom and I competed to impress Winnie, and I was afraid of losing.

Izzie gazed at me with moon-eyes. She keeps doing that and I wish she wouldn't. She is so stupid.

Rahere shook his head like a wet dog. "Listen," he said. "There was a Saracen called Ziryab, a wise singing teacher —"

"A Saracen!"

"— and he wrote down how he taught his pupils. First, they had to sing a long, steady note on each degree of the scale. Listen to this! *Uuu-uuu-uuu-t.*"

"How can you sing a note for that long?"

"You practice," said Rahere. "Singing takes more wind than speaking, and that's why we must do breathing exercises. Now you try."

"*Uuuuuu-t!*" I sang.

"You were forcing the sound," said Rahere. "Wasn't he, Izzie? Sounds must come out of your nose and your head."

"How can I make them do that?"

Rahere gave me such a strange look, half-begging, half-wild. Then, in the top of his head, he sang notes so long and low that they sounded exactly like a nightingale.

"How?" cried Rahere. "You fall in love! You sit at the feet of Ziryab!"

25

The Round Table

 T'S SHAPED LIKE HALF AN EGG. LIKE A HUGE, UPSIDE-down beehive. Or the pale half-moon, lying on her back.

"What is it made from?" asks Arthur-in-the-stone.

"Rock crystal," says King Leodegrance. "One enormous piece."

Arthur touches it with his fingertips, the palms of his hands.

"Like soap," he says. "Mutton fat."

"Adamantine," replies Leodegrance. "Like an iron hand in a velvet glove."

Now Arthur leans out across the massive table. He peers down into its hemisphere. Black spots like tiny tadpoles. Silver stars. Scrapes and swerves. Right down. This world's deep, dark fault lines that could split and shatter it; the sudden shinings and strong knots that brighten and fasten and secure it.

"Your father gave it to me," King Leodegrance says, "when I swore him allegiance. Now, as Guinevere's dowry, I give it to you."

"Nothing could please me as this table pleases me," Arthur replies. "How many men can sit at it?"

"One hundred and fifty," Leodegrance says.

"Each of my knights," says Arthur-in-the-stone, "would have me believe he is the best. But when I sit them at this Round Table, not one of them will have a place above or below any of the others."

"That is wise, Arthur," Merlin says.

"I want all the knights at this table not only to be equal, but to form one fair fellowship. One round of honor. One unbroken ring of trust."

"Is this your quest?" Merlin asks.

"I will build a castle to house this table," Arthur says, "and around the castle a city, around the city a kingdom."

"When Christ and his disciples ate their last supper together," Merlin says, "their table was round. After Judas ran out, one place was empty, and it has been empty ever since. You must leave one place at this Round Table empty—the Perilous Seat for the knight who will achieve the greatest quest of all."

"What quest is that?" Arthur asks.

"The knight who journeys across the dark wasteland, this world's wilderness, and reaches the castle of Carbonek. The knight who kneels before Christ's drinking cup. The quest for the Holy Grail!"

Now, man by man, the king's knights enter the hall. Sir Accolon. Sir Agravain. Balin and Bors. Sir Cador, Sir Dagonet . . . a quarrelsome, bright alphabet!

From north and south, east and west, they come to the table. They walk right round the rim, like a great hoop slowly turning, until they come back to where they began.

"Knights of the kingdom," Arthur calls out in a loud voice. "To those of you who have little land, I will give land. Never injure an innocent man. Never murder a man. Swear this."

"We swear it!" shout all the knights.

"Never betray my trust in you. Never commit treason."

"We swear it!"

"If a man begs you for mercy," Arthur calls out, "be merciful to him. Otherwise you will forfeit your place at this table."

"We swear it!"

"Upon pain of death, help and protect those who are weaker than you—ladies, young women, orphans, poor people."

"We swear it!" all the knights shout.

"Never take the law into your own hands," Arthur calls out. "And never try to rise by pushing another man down. Let your companions at this Round Table be called Kindness and Friendship, Courtesy, Humanity, and Chivalry."

Now each knight kneels in front of Arthur. He swears to be loyal and serve the king.

Sir Lanval . . . Sir Loholt . . . Sir Marholt . . . Sir Melwas . . .

"Beware of him!" whispers Merlin. "He will try to abduct your lovely young wife."

Sir Marrok . . .

"And his wife will turn him into a werewolf."

Sir Nescien . . .

"Stranded on an island spinning round and round in the sea."

Sir Nestor . . .

With his slateshine eyes, Merlin looks deep into the king's eyes. "His own son will kill him," he says.

the kNight with two swords

KEEP WONDERING WHY ROWENA WAS SO FLUSTERED when I found her and Haket together in the church. And what about her muffler?

I just asked her this evening whether she likes Haket, and she flared up like a dying candle.

"That's nothing to do with you!" she cried, and she hurried out of the hall up to the solar.

Later this evening, I looked into my stone. . . .

"There are times when a man likes company," says Arthur-in-the-stone, "and times when he needs to be alone."

His servants bow and leave his pavilion, and at once he lies down on the bed. But he's too tired to sleep.

Now a knight on horseback dashes up to the pavilion. He dismounts and groans.

"What's wrong?" the king asks.

"You can do nothing about it," the knight replies, and he remounts and rides away.

No sooner has Arthur-in-the-stone closed his eyes again than a second knight, with crossed swords on his shield, enters the pavilion.

"Sir Balin!" Arthur says. "Just now, a knight rode in, moaning and groaning. I don't know who he is or what's wrong with him. He rode off in the direction of Castle Meliot."

Sir Balin catches up with the knight and a young woman as they ride through a forest.

"Sir," says Sir Balin. "Who are you?"

"Which man has a name before he has achieved his quest?" sighs the knight.

"You must come with me," Sir Balin says, "and explain yourself to King Arthur."

"I will not," says the knight.

"The last thing I want is to have to force you," Sir Balin says.

"If I come," the knight says, "will you guarantee my safety?"

"Of course," says Sir Balin. "With my own life."

"You wait here," the knight tells the young woman. "I'll come back as soon as I can."

But while Sir Balin and the knight are dismounting outside Arthur's pavilion, the knight howls and falls to the ground. He has been spiked with a spear. The point is sticking out of his chest.

Whoever has wounded the knight is invisible.

"Sir Garlon has killed me," the knight gasps. "Take my horse. Follow my quest. Complete it . . ." The knight begins to choke on his own blood.

Balin cradles the knight's head. "I am a knight of the Round Table. I will avenge you," he says. After a while, he closes the knight's eyes with his left forefinger and carries him back to the young woman in the forest.

"He knew he was in danger," the young woman says sadly. "Against some kinds of evil there's no protection."

"What was his name?"

"Sir Herlews le Berbeus," the young woman replies.

When Sir Balin and the young woman have buried Sir Herlews, they ride on, and the young woman carries the shaft of Garlon's spear with her. That evening they reach a manor house.

"Not long ago," the knight there tells them, "I jousted with a knight who was invisible. He's King Pellam's brother, that's what he told me, but I don't know his name."

"Sir Garlon," the young woman says.

"I couldn't see him," their host continues, "but I could hear his horse's hooves, and I managed to throw him. 'I'll pay you back for this.' That's what Sir Garlon told me. 'And I'll pay back your best friend.'

"Do you know what he did? He stabbed my own son. He jabbed him under his rib cage with a short knife, and he told my son his wound would never heal without a pint of Sir Garlon's own blood."

"You've good reason to find him, then," Sir Balin says. "And so have we."

"King Pellam of Listinoise has announced a feast," our host says, "and it will be held in fifteen days' time. Sir Garlon is his brother, so he's bound to be there. We can ride together."

When they arrive, Sir Balin and the young woman are invited into King Pellam's castle, but their companion is turned away because he has brought no lady.

"You must leave your two swords in your bedroom," King Pellam's servants tell Sir Balin.

"No," says Sir Balin. "In my country a knight always carries at least one weapon with him."

"Not here," say the servants.

"In that case," Sir Balin says, "I will leave at once."

The two servants look at each other.

"Well, then," says one, "leave one sword in your bedroom and wear one to the feast."

Sir Balin and the young woman step into the feasting hall. What a hubbub! Hundreds of knights with their wives, their lovers, their squires.

"Is there a knight here by the name of Garlon?" Sir Balin asks one old knight.

"Can't hear you," says the knight.

"King Pellam's brother?"

The old knight smiles and cups a hand to one ear.

"King Pellam's brother! Sir Garlon!"

"What about him?"

"Is he here?"

"Everyone's here!" The old knight points at a whole group of knights and their ladies. "That one," he says. "With the black face. Sometimes black, sometimes white. Makes himself invisible."

Sir Balin turns to the young woman. "What shall I do?" he says. "If I kill him here, I'll never escape with my life. But if I let him go, he'll strike again; and this may be the last time I set eyes on him."

Before the young woman can reply, Sir Garlon strides up to Sir Balin. "You've been staring at me," he says in a loud voice, and he smacks Sir Balin across the face with the back of his hand. "Have you come to this feast to eat and drink or stare at me?"

"Not to eat and drink," Sir Balin says.

Now Sir Balin steps back and, in one shock of light, he draws his sword, hoists it, and opens Sir Garlon's skull right down to his shoulders.

At once the young woman gives Sir Balin the spear shaft Sir Garlon used to kill her knight; and Sir Balin rams the shaft right into Sir Garlon's stomach.

"Find our companion!" he shouts. "Tell him to take as much blood as he needs to heal his son."

King Pellam himself stalks across the hall and stares down at Sir Garlon.

"You have killed my brother," he mutters, "and you'll pay for that here and now."

"Kill me yourself then," Sir Balin says.

King Pellam pulls his mace out of the rack by the door. He rubs one of its steel spikes between his fingers. Then he swings it and tries to bury it in Sir Balin's brains.

Sir Balin holds up his sword like a steel bar in front of his head. The spiked mace crashes against it, and the sword breaks into a thousand splinters.

Sir Balin runs out of the hall, searching for another weapon, and King Pellam follows him.

Out of the hall into the solar; out of the solar into the kitchen. From the kitchen to the storeroom to the pantry to the staircase. Sir Balin runs along the creaking gallery and turns into a bedroom. . . .

Tapestries . . . a canopied bed . . . a man in the bed: Sir Balin has no eyes for them. He sees a golden table with silver legs. A lance is lying on it, blood trickling from its tip.

Sir Balin snatches it up. And as King Pellam charges into the bedroom, he runs him through his left side with the lance.

Heaven itself howls. The whole world shakes. King Pellam's castle begins to crumble and collapse. Now the bedroom ceiling sags and falls in. The sleeping man is safe under his oak canopy, but Sir Balin and King Pellam are both trapped beneath fallen beams and plaster.

Now Merlin walks into my stone. Merlin! Where has he come from?

The magician stares at the wreck of the room. From the rubble he lifts King Pellam and lays him on the golden table. Then he takes Sir Balin's right wrist and the knight opens his eyes.

"Where is the young woman?" Sir Balin asks.

"Dead," says Merlin. "And so is your companion. Everyone in this castle is dead, except for you and King Pellam and this sleeping man."

"Heaven howled," Sir Balin says dreamily.

"This the lance Longinus used," Merlin says, "when he pierced Christ's side while He hung on the cross. The king will lie in agony and his kingdom will be a suffering wasteland until the day a knight achieves the most difficult of all quests — the quest for the Holy Grail."

"Who is the sleeping man?" Sir Balin asks.

"King Pellam's father," Merlin replies. "The man who wrapped Christ's body in linen and laid him in his own sepulchre."

"Joseph of Arimathea!" Sir Balin exclaims.

"Now!" says Merlin. "You must find two new swords. One is shattered, and the other buried beneath this castle. Then ride back to the court of King Arthur."

"Will you ride with me?" Sir Balin asks.

Merlin shakes his head. "I have work to do," he says.

In my stone, I see Sir Balin riding through the wasteland. Parched fields where grass and wheat have withered. Starving children sit outside huts and hovels, and follow Sir Balin with their slow eyes.

At last Sir Balin leaves King Pellam's kingdom and he comes to a moated castle. I can hear the pulse of music inside it, and a lady comes to the drawbridge.

"I am Lady Dionise and you cannot come across. Not until you've jousted with the island knight. Any man who comes here has to joust."

"I'm weary," says Sir Balin. "And so is my poor horse. We've been riding for eight days."

"Your shield's rather small," Dionise calls out. "I'll lend you a larger one."

Then servants lower the drawbridge and Dionise walks across. She gives Sir Balin a large shield and takes the one with the two crossed swords on it.

"There's the lake," she says. "Row yourself and your horse out to that little island. The scarlet knight is waiting for you."

First, Sir Balin and the scarlet knight joust and throw each other, then they fight with their swords. They slit each other's chain mail until the scarlet knight's arms are bare and Sir Balin's chest is naked and gaudy with wet blood.

"Who are you?" Sir Balin shouts. "The only man I've ever met who can match me."

The scarlet knight lowers his shield and sticks his sword into the blood-stained earth.

"Balan," he pants. "The brother of Balin."

Sir Balin gasps. He topples over sideways, more dead than alive.

Now on all fours, Balan crawls towards him and tugs off his helmet, but Balin's face is masked in blood, and his brother doesn't recognize him.

Balin opens his eyes. "My brother," he murmurs. "You have killed me. I've killed you."

"You're not carrying your own shield," Sir Balan cries. "I didn't recognize you."

"Lady Dionise took it," Sir Balin says in a weak voice. "She said mine was rather small, and so she lent me this one."

Balan growls. "First she trapped me, and now she has trapped you."

While the brothers are talking, Lady Dionise and her servants row across to the little island.

"We came out of the same dark womb," says Balin.

"And we'll lie in the same tomb," Balan says.

"It shall be done," the ladies promise, and they begin to weap.

"And the stone which shadows us," Balin whispers, "let it say we are two brothers who loved each other and killed each other."

Lady Dionise sobs. "I did not know your names," she says.

Then she and her servants comfort Sir Balin and Sir Balan.

"We will send messengers to King Arthur," says Lady Dionise. "Today and tomorrow and each tomorrow: Whoever passes this way will pray for your souls."

love spells

KNOW I'LL GET PUNISHED FOR IT, BUT I SKIPPED MY lesson with Haket this afternoon because I wanted time to think about everything I've seen in my obsidian.

I was walking upstream along the riverbank when I saw Rowena and Izzie sitting on a flat stone with their backs to me, and Rowena was holding something twisted in her right hand.

"Scratch him!" she cackled, and then she scratched whatever it was with her long fingernails. "Squeeze him! Screech him!"

"Haket's heart is as black as his cassock," Izzie said.

"Hell-black," said Rowena fiercely.

Izzie was holding something in her right hand as well, and she bent over it and crooned:

> "Witch-in-the-twig,
> Rider-in-the-broom,
> Tell me, tell me,
> Teach me what to do.
> In the water's womb
> Whirligig!
> Tell me, teach me,
> How to make him love me.
> Make him love me
> And I will love you."

"It's a pity his ears stick out so much," Rowena said.

Izzie giggled.

"You witches!" I exclaimed. "What are you doing?"

The two girls clutched each other and looked up at me with open mouths.

"Nothing!" said Izzie, and she tossed a stick-man into the dark river.

Rowena shook her head and her long, dark hair whipped from side to side. "Go away, Arthur!" she said fiercely.

So Rowena does hate Haket. But why? I'm going to have to find out.

Anyhow, whose ears stick out so much? Surely Izzie wasn't putting a spell on me? She's so stupid.

my birthday

 OMORROW, ASH WEDNESDAY, IS MY BIRTHDAY.

"The first day of Lent," said Lord Stephen. "Very disappointing, Arthur. But we can't change the Church calendar. Ash Wednesday follows Shrove Tuesday, and Shrove Tuesday follows Collop Monday, and they always have done. However! What we're going to do is recognize your birthday eve."

This morning, we all had to make our confessions to Haket, and I felt very uneasy, because I've been thinking about what I heard and saw on the riverbank and I'm sure Haket is forcing Rowena to do something against her will, maybe even giving him her body. If he is, how can I confess to him? And, anyhow, who does he make *his* confessions to?

Shrove Tuesday is a holiday, the first since I came to Holt, and this afternoon many of the people living on the manor gathered in the South Yard. But not Haket, I'm glad to say.

First Anian and Catrin tied little spurs to two cocks, but I don't really like watching them stab each other's eyes and rip each other to pieces. After that, I wrestled with Anian and threw him, although he's two years older than I am. But then Sayer, the kennel-man, threw me, and so did Simon — he's stronger than he looks. All the same, I know I'm stronger than I was last year.

"Arthur!" Rowena called out. "Izzie wants to wrestle with you."

Everyone laughed, and Izzie blushed.

"I won't," I said. "You're both stupid."

"What about Rahere?" Alan said in a sneering voice. "You'd like to wrestle with Arthur, wouldn't you?"

"Certainly not!" said Rahere huffily. "Wrestlers don't jest!"

When we met in the hall for supper, Lord Stephen bowed to me. "Will you sit down, sir?" he said.

Lord Stephen showed me to my place and brought me a little basin of water. He kissed the towel draped over his right forearm, and I washed and dried my hands. Then Lord Stephen served me, and not until I'd eaten the first mouthful of my egg-and-butter pancake was anyone else allowed to start.

After we'd finished our pancakes and boiled chicken stuffed with garlic and apricots — the last meat and butter we'll eat until after Easter — Lord Stephen rang his little handbell, and Gubert carried in a wobbling, striped jelly. It had fourteen layers, and each one was a different color.

"Gubert!" exclaimed Lord Stephen, and he smiled and opened his hands.

"Ah!" sighed Rahere. "The very sight of it . . . turns my insides to jelly."

"Strained saffron, my lady," said Gubert.

"Which?" asked Lady Judith.

"The bottom stripe. Then parsley-juice green, and pink rose petals . . . that violet-blue, that's sunflower. Egg white . . ." Gubert explained each stripe until he'd reached the top layer.

"Poppy," guessed Rowena.

"I know," said Izzie. "Plum skin."

"Or blood," said Lord Stephen.

"Sandalwood red," said Gubert proudly.

"Imported from Venice," Lady Judith announced. "My merchant buys sandalwood and pepper and caraway from Venice."

"Let Arthur sniff!" Lord Stephen said.

I leaned over the jelly, and the sweet confusion of scents and spices swirled inside my head.

"Arthur's smelly!" Rahere said quite fondly.

"You'll bring home lots of spices from the Holy Land, I hope," Lady Judith said. "They cost so much here, when you can get them at all. I've heard the Saracens even serve their meats with sauces of different colors."

After this, everyone shook hands with me and wished me a happy birthday.

"Happy as a clam," Rahere said, and he opened and snapped his mouth several times. "Well! As happy as you can be with ash on your forehead."

"You've been here at Holt for six weeks already," Lord Stephen said. "Now, on Friday I want you to ride over to Gortanore."

"This Friday!" I exclaimed.

"I've arranged for you to stay for one week."

"Do I have to, sir?"

"And in the meantime," said Lord Stephen, "I must somehow make do without my excellent squire."

Then Lord Stephen and Lady Judith stood up. They bid us all a peaceful night and left the hall. Gubert and Anian and Catrin cleared the dishes, and everyone lay down around the fire.

I couldn't sleep, though. I kept thinking about having to go to

Gortanore. . . . I'll be really glad to see Lady Alice. She under-stands and trusts me. But I haven't seen Grace since we talked to each other about being betrothed. The light danced in her eyes, and she said we must be a matter of faith to each other. That's what I wanted too, and I feel so sad. I do want to talk to Grace, but I don't know what to say. But what makes me afraid is having to meet Sir William. I'm not looking forward to that at all.

After a while, I came up here to my room, carrying two can-dles. I began to write this.

I know Lord Stephen and Lady Judith honored me this evening, but I feel so sad. Holt's not my true home. Neither is Caldicot, and I wish it were. It's where I grew up, and I miss everyone, even Serle. It's weeks and weeks already since I saw Gatty, and I don't even know when I'll see her again.

To serve as a squire: That's like being a false son. It lasts for a while, but then it comes to an end. And when it does, where will I belong?

I wish Lord Stephen wasn't so reasonable. He doesn't have to be. He could have said he wanted to keep me here, and refused to let me go to Gortanore.

29

HONOR THY FATHER
AND THY MOTHER

E WAS SITTING ON A GRAVESTONE WHEN I WENT INTO the church for my lesson, and he was still there when I came out again.

"Are you all right?" I asked.

The old man looked up at me with his watery eyes. The skin on his face was almost transparent, and I could see the blue veins stretched over his collarbone.

"Who is?" he replied.

"You. Are you all right?"

"They're here, you know," the old man said in his cracked voice.

"Who?"

"He went first," the old man said. "I buried them."

"Your parents, you mean?"

"I'm listening to them," the old man said. "She does most of the talking. You, boy! You obey the commandment."

I lowered my eyes.

"You think too much," said the old man.

"Who are you, then?" I asked.

The old man looked at me and smiled forlornly. "I can't remember," he said.

"That's Wilf," Rowena told me in the hall. "Haven't you seen him before?" She goggled her eyes and tapped her head. "He's cracked and empty. An old water pot."

the cowherd's son

N MY STONE, I COULD SEE A HANDSOME YOUNG MAN mounted on a mare, with a herdsman standing beside him holding the bridle. Three door-knights were blocking their way.

"Where will I find King Arthur, then?" the herdsman asks.

"Not so fast," one knight replies. "Stable your mare first, and change your clothing."

The herdsman looks at his dirty smock and torn trousers. "All I got," he says. He walks up to Arthur-in-the-stone and bows awkwardly. "Bless you, sire," he says. "When you was married, you promised to give any man what he asked for."

"I did," replies the king.

"Right!" says the poor man. "Will you make my son here a knight?"

"A knight!" exclaims the king, and he looks at the youth, his open, almost flat face, his tousle of fair hair. "You're asking a great deal," he tells the herdsman. "Who are you?"

"The cowherd, sire. Aries."

"And is this your idea?"

"His," says the cowherd. "I got thirteen sons and they're good lads. But this one! He never lifts a finger if he can get away with it. He's always throwing his javelin or loosing arrows. He's even got an old sword."

"What is your name?" Arthur asks the young man.

"Tor, sire," he replies.

"Daylight and nightlight," the cowherd goes on, "he won't give me no peace. He keeps asking to be made a knight."

"Let me see your other sons," Arthur tells Aries.

As soon as Aries comes back into the hall with his other twelve sons, I can see none of them look in the least like Tor. Some have mouse-hair and some dark, and some have eyes set rather close together: One way or another, they all look like their father.

"I will keep my word," the king tells Tor. "Give me your sword."

Tor lifts his smock. "Here, sire," he says.

Tor kneels to the king and Arthur taps him on the shoulder with the naked blade. "I dub you knight," he says. "Sir Tor, be gallant. Be courteous. Be loyal. And if you prove yourself, there will be a place for you at the Round Table."

Sir Tor rises, and at once Merlin steps into my stone. He walks up to the king.

"Will Tor make a good knight?" Arthur asks him.

"He should," says Merlin. "He's the son of a knight and king."

"A knight and king?"

"Listen to me," Merlin says. "This cowherd, Aries, is not his father."

Aries growls.

"No," says Merlin. "Sir Pellinore is."

"Yes," says the cowherd. "And I'm the son of Queen Eleanor!"

"All right!" Merlin tells him. "Fetch your wife. Let's hear what she has to say."

When Aries's wife comes into the hall, she curtsies and smiles.

"Me and my greyhound went out the end of Frigg's Pasture," she says, "to milk my two cows. And this knight rode up."

"Go on, woman," Merlin says.

"Well!" says the woman. "I didn't want to, really. Not really! Well! I didn't even know his name." Then the woman smiles brightly at Tor. "But there!" she says. "Look at my fine son."

"You see?" Merlin says to the cowherd.

Aries doesn't look Merlin or the king in the eye. "First I heard of it," he says in a surly voice.

"I'm not surprised," says Merlin.

"Are you insulting my mother?" Tor demands.

Merlin sighs. "The truth will help you much more than it hurts your mother," he says. "Your mother conceived you before she was betrothed to Aries."

"That's the truth," says Tor's mother.

"And your blood-father is a good man," Merlin tells Tor. "Sir Pellinore. A knight and a king. He will recognize you and provide for your mother."

Tor's mother takes her husband's arm.

Aries sniffs. "Well, then!" he says gruffly.

31

TO GORTANORE

HE THIRD DAY OF MARCH. IN MY WHOLE LIFE, I HAVE
never dreaded anything as much.

"We'll be there in good time," said Sir William's
messenger, Thomas. "Before midday."

The way Thomas clucks and makes sudden jerky movements is
very strange, and so is his habit of tilting his head and peering at
me with one keen eye. He's not chicken-brained, though, and I
know Sir John trusts him.

Just before we reached Gortanore, we came to a little wooden
shelter on the top side of a large meadow, right on the fringe of
a wood.

"Where the wild boar snorts," said Thomas.

Before I could get Thomas to explain himself, a grubby little
woman stepped out of the shelter and blinked in the bright light.

"Maggot," Thomas informed me. "My wife."

"God be with you, Maggot," I said.

Without bothering to hitch up her muddy skirt, and not for
one moment taking her beady eyes off me, Maggot gave me a kind
of bow. Then, still looking at me, she drew Thomas behind the
shelter.

"Exactly the same," she said in a whisper.

At this moment, a lady on horseback came galloping across the meadow towards us. It was Lady Alice, wearing her burnt-orange cloak and raising her reins high in greeting.

"Arthur!" she cried. "Arthur! Come on!"

Then Lady Alice wheeled round. Her wimple billowed behind her, and I galloped after her into Gortanore.

fire=bench warnings

HALF-EXPECTED SIR WILLIAM TO STRIDE OUT OF Gortanore and thwack me over the head with a mace. But as soon as we reined in, Lady Alice panted, "He's not here!"

"Not here?" I shouted, and I led Lady Alice's horse to the block and helped her to dismount.

Lady Alice took my head between her hands, tousled my hair, and kissed me on both cheeks. "He's gone over to Catmole," she said. "You didn't expect that."

"And you know . . . I'm your stepson," I said uncertainly.

"True!" said Lady Alice. "And I can't say I expected that!" Then she narrowed her hazel eyes. "So you're going to obey me, aren't you?"

"Oh!" I said. "I'm so glad to see you. I was afraid of coming."

"I know," said Lady Alice, smiling. "Tom and Grace are waiting in the hall."

"Doesn't he want to meet me?"

"You may be partly right," Lady Alice replied. "It's very painful for you, I know, but it is also difficult for Sir William. No! A messenger rode over from Catmole after breakfast. Three of Sir William's cows are bloated."

"When will he . . ." I began.

"He never tells me," Lady Alice replied.

As soon as we opened the hall door, Tom jumped up from the fire-bench. First we bowed politely and then we hugged each other. But Grace stood up rather stiffly. When I smiled at her, she only half-smiled back; and when I embraced her, she felt like a cat arching its back.

"Welcome to Gortanore!" Lady Alice said brightly. "We've all been looking forward to your visit. You three saw one another in November, I know, but Arthur's a year older now; this whole world's a century older."

"What's it like?" said Tom. "At Holt?"

"Now, then!" said Lady Alice. "There'll be plenty of time for you to talk. But first things first."

"We know already," Grace said quite fiercely.

"On New Year's morning," Lady Alice continued in a calm voice, "your father informed you that he has a second son. Arthur!"

Tom shook his head and grinned at me.

"And on the same morning," said Lady Alice, "at Caldicot, Sir John told Arthur that he and Lady Helen are his foster parents."

"But why did they have to foster him?" Tom asked.

"And then Sir John told Arthur he's actually Sir William's son . . . but not Lady Tilda's son."

"Not Lady Tilda's son?" exclaimed Tom.

"Who is your mother, then?" Grace demanded.

I lowered my eyes.

"So, Arthur," said Lady Alice, "you and Tom are half brothers. And Grace is your half sister."

"I don't want another brother," said Grace loudly. Then she whirled round and walked away.

"Grace!" called Lady Alice.

But Grace walked right out of the hall and left the door open behind her.

Tom shook his head. "Well!" he said, and he blew out his cheeks. "At least you won't have to marry her now."

"Please!" said Lady Alice.

"I don't know what to think about all this," Tom said, frowning. "I need to think what to think."

"Tom!" said Lady Alice. "Go and find Grace, and tell her to go straight to the solar. She's to wait for me there."

"Why is Grace so upset?" I asked Lady Alice as soon as we were alone.

With her thumb and right forefinger, Lady Alice drew one of her brown curls out of her wimple. "Why do you think?" she asked.

"Is it because . . . ?"

"Yes," said Lady Alice. "You hoped to be betrothed to Grace. Didn't you?"

"Yes," I said in a small voice.

"And she wanted to be betrothed to you. With each fingertip and drop of blood in her body."

"Did she?" I whispered.

I remembered how I sat with Grace in my climbing-tree on Tumber Hill and asked her whether it would be all right if we were betrothed. I remembered how my heart leaped when Grace told me that even though we couldn't often see each other, we could still know the other would be faithful and waiting.

"I still wish we could be," I said. "I wish Sir John were my father."

"You're a boy," Lady Alice said quietly, "and your life is changing. It's exciting! You've gone into service with Lord Stephen; you're taking the Cross, and that's a wonderful thing to do. But it's not like that for Grace. Her life today is exactly the same as it was last year, except that now it's without the hope of being betrothed to you."

"But surely you and Sir William will find her someone else."

"Of course," said Lady Alice. "But that's not what she wants. Be patient with her, Arthur! She's not really angry with you; she's hurt. If she's angry with anyone, it's with her father because he has wrecked her dreams. But she can't lose her temper with him, can she?" Lady Alice twisted her curl round her forefinger and slid it back under her wimple. "When I was a girl, I used to confuse love and marriage," she said. "Many young girls do."

The fire whined and sucked; then it shook itself, and we sat down side by side on the fire-bench.

"Now, then," said Lady Alice. "Almost one year ago I entrusted you with my terrible secret."

"I haven't told anyone," I said.

"I told you Sir William murdered a young man."

"Yes."

"And that was all I knew."

"Sir John knows as well," I said. "Or at least he half-knows. And he told me this man was the husband . . . my blood-mother's husband."

Little stinging sparks flew up and out of the fire. Smudges of ash drifted down and settled on our laps.

"All of this happened before I married Sir William. Before I had even met him," Lady Alice said. "The first thing I heard was my husband had murdered a young man. But later I was told this man had accused Sir William of committing adultery with his wife. He shouted at Sir William, in front of God's altar and the congregation. And then someone told me that a village woman and her baby had been sent away from Gortanore."

"You mean . . . ?"

"So of course I was sure the baby must have been Sir William's. But listen, Arthur!" Lady Alice took my hands between hers and squeezed them. "What I never, never knew was that the baby was *you*."

"When did you find out?"

"Only when we came to Caldicot before Christmas, and Sir William and Sir John talked about you. Until that moment, I believed you were Sir John and Lady Helen's son."

"But why did Sir William take me away from my mother?" I asked. "Didn't she want to keep me?"

Lady Alice squeezed my hands again.

"Do you know her?" I demanded.

"Arthur, you know how I care for you. I always have. My own stepson."

"But I want to find her. Do you know her?"

Lady Alice shook her head. "I know where she might be."

"She's alive, then! Is she?"

"Arthur!"

"Please!"

"This is dangerous. The last thing Sir William wants is for you to start digging things up."

"Does he beat you?" I asked.

Lady Alice lowered her eyes. "That's nothing to do with you," she said quietly. "Now be very cautious when you talk to Sir William. Remember, he doesn't suspect you know all this. He doesn't even know that I do."

"How did you find out?"

"That's another story," Lady Alice said. "All Sir William knows is that if ever the truth were told, he would be tried and hanged. King John would take Gortanore and Catmole and the manor in Champagne. So you see, he'll stop at nothing to ensure that what's dead and buried stays dead and buried."

"He's not going to stop me from finding my mother," I said fiercely.

"And remember," said Lady Alice, "Tom and Grace don't know anything either."

"Does anyone else here know that Sir William is my father?" I asked.

Lady Alice looked at me. "If I tell you . . ." she said slowly.

"Who is it?"

At this moment, Tom ambled back into the hall, grinning. "I found her," he announced. "Up a beech tree."

BULGING AND BLOATED

 KNOW A REMEDY FOR A BLOATED COW," I TOLD TOM. "Gatty taught it to me. When a cow's lying on her side, you get up onto her ribs, just above her udders. You leap up and down on her as hard as you can."

Tom smiled happily.

"And it's even better if two people do it at the same time," I said. "The cow's stomach is bursting with air that needs to come out. But she's too weak to force it out herself."

"Disgusting!" said Tom. "I thought you had to stick a knife between her left hipbone and her first rib."

"What's disgusting is the smell down here in this cellar," I said. "Worse than our latrines."

"Fulcold should never have asked us to carry up this barrel," Tom replied. "It's his job, not ours."

"I don't mind," I said. "Sometimes I did yardwork and fieldwork at Caldicot."

Tom shook his head.

"With Gatty," I added.

"You shouldn't," Tom said seriously. Then he put both his hands around his neck and let his tongue loll out of his mouth and bulged his bright blue eyes.

"You could murder a man down here," he said. "These walls are so thick that no one up in the kitchen would hear a sound."

ALL CONTRADICTIONS

OM HAS ALWAYS BEATEN ME AT SWORDPLAY, AND HE can beat Serle too. But when we fought in the Yard this morning, I scored five hits before Tom reached seven. We had to count for ourselves, though. Grace said she had better things to do.

"It's because of me," I said. "I think she's avoiding me."

"You can't help being her half brother," Tom replied.

After our swordplay, Tom and I tilted at the ring with our lances, but I've never been much good at that, and he beat me easily. And after that, we wrestled.

"You're different," said Tom, frowning.

"What do you mean?"

"Stronger."

"I don't know," I said. "I'm practicing hard because Lord Stephen says I'll need all the strength I can build up, but Alan, the armorer, keeps picking on me. He says I'm nothing like strong enough. Not to join the crusade."

"He's probably jealous," said Tom.

"Once, he pinioned me and almost choked me."

"Did you tell Lord Stephen?"

"I don't want him to think that I can't look after myself."

Tom grinned. "I wish I were you," he said. "Have you got your new armor?"

"Not yet," I said. "And I think that's why Alan is angry: My father has chosen Turold, the Ludlow armorer, to make it."

"Is he knitting you a mail-shirt?"

"Yes, and I'm going to have a flat-topped helmet."

"My father says armor costs its own weight in silver."

"It doesn't!" I replied. "He only said that because he's paying for it."

"Who?"

"Sir William."

"He's paying for your armor," said Tom slowly.

"Well! Yes, that's what Lord Stephen told me."

I could see Tom was taken aback. "I'm sorry," I said.

"It's his duty," Tom said thoughtfully. "And your right. But I do wish I were you. I wish my father and I were joining the crusade."

"Why can't you?"

"He says he's too old. He's sixty-five, you know, and almost blind in his left eye. All his bones ache."

"But when he came to see us before Christmas, he was all for going, and stopping the bloody infidels from trampling all over Europe. That's what he said."

"That's him," said Tom. "He's always changing his mind. He's all contradictions. He curses the Saracens and yet he believes they're equal with Christians in the eyes of God. He won't learn to read and write but respects learning. He shouts at Lady Alice and sometimes he thrashes her, but he also worships her."

"Well," I said, "she's loyal and very beautiful."

As soon as Tom and I walked in from the Yard, we all ate dinner together, and Lady Alice told us Sir William sent a message to say he wouldn't be coming back from Catmole until tomorrow. Then she quickly excused herself and left Grace and Tom and me alone.

"I think she means for us to talk," I said.

"What about?" asked Tom.

"There's nothing to talk about," said Grace.

Tom stared down at the crumbs and spots on the table, and Grace kept licking the back of her spoon. And then Tom and I both opened our mouths at the same moment. . . .

"You first!" I said.

"All I know," Tom began, "is what Sir William told us. You're his son. His second son. And then what Lady Alice said this morning: Lady Tilda is our mother, but not yours."

"Which is what I know," I replied.

But of course that's not the whole truth. I know about my mother already being married, and about the murder. And I know Sir William has named me and not Tom as the heir to his manor at Catmole, because Sir John told me so.

"Who is your mother, then?" Grace demanded.

"Don't blame Arthur," said Tom.

"Is it Lady Alice?" Grace asked, and her blue eyes were shining.

"Of course not!" Tom said. "Our father didn't even know her then."

"Then . . . a countess or someone?" Grace asked breathlessly. "You must find out."

"Why?" I asked.

"You must! You would, wouldn't you, Tom?"

Tom scratched his head.

"I'll help you," Grace said.

"He may not want you to," said Tom.

"You do, don't you, Arthur?" Grace asked, and she laid a hand on my arm, then just as quickly took it away again.

At this moment, Tom clutched his stomach. "God's gizzards!" he panted. And without another word, he pushed back the bench and ran out of the hall.

"As usual!" said Grace. And she picked up something and pushed it into her right nostril.

"What's that?" I asked.

"You know! My jasper olive to dissolve the phlegm."

After this, Grace began to comb her hair with her fingers, and I could feel the silence building up between us like a cold wall.

"I know what you're thinking," I said.

"You don't."

"I do," I said, "just as you knew where to find me when we played hide-and-seek. Remember?"

Grace hunched her delicate shoulders.

"We always know," I said.

"What, then?"

"You think I don't care. About us."

Grace said nothing.

"But I do," I said hoarsely.

Grace wouldn't look at me. "You're just saying that," she said.

"No."

"Lady Alice told you to."

"No, Grace," I said. "I just keep thinking."

"What?"

"About everything. How I hoped we'd be betrothed. Lady Alice did, too, because she never realized I was Sir William's son."

Grace stared at me wide-eyed.

"No, she didn't," I said. "Not until last Christmas." And then I reached out and lightly touched Grace's snub nose.

"Don't!" Grace said fiercely. She tried to smack my hand away but I caught her by the wrist.

"Don't!" cried Grace again, struggling and helpless as a fawn.

And then all at once she burst into tears. She threw herself against me and pummeled my chest. She sobbed, and I held her to me, and my face was wet with her tears.

35

BETROTHALS

HIS EVENING, GRACE WAS PRICKLY AGAIN.

First she told me I didn't really mean what I'd said when we talked earlier, and then she told me I'm much better at saying than doing. And then she announced that boys are unfeeling and accused me of already thinking about being betrothed to someone else.

"I'm not!" I said indignantly.

Grace was right, though, and she knew it. I do sometimes think about that, and it would be very strange if I didn't.

"Cecily Quaritch," Grace said unhappily. "Or April de Pavord. Or Hawisa des Bois. Winnie de Verdon . . ."

I gave a start when Grace mentioned Winnie, but I don't think she noticed.

"Yes, Winnie de Verdon," Grace repeated. "It's bound to be one of those."

"What about you?" I asked. "To whom will you be betrothed?"

"No one," Grace replied.

"You'll have to be."

"No," said Grace.

"Not Serle, anyhow," I said slowly.

"Never Serle," Grace said fiercely. "I've told you that before. He's mean. His mouth stinks." Grace grabbed my right arm and shook it. "Please, Arthur! Please talk to Sir John. Tell him bad things about me. You can set him against me, can't you?"

my father

IR WILLIAM SCRUBBED HIS STONY LEFT EYE.

"Blasted itch!" he muttered, more to himself than to me.

Then he sniffed loudly and spat on the rushes.

With his good eye, Sir William inspected me. "I suppose you've been looking forward to this," he said.

"Yes, sir," I said in a small voice.

"So have I," Sir William said. Then he cleared his throat fiercely and raised his mace of a fist. "You liar!" he roared. "Nothing of the kind! You've been dreading it."

I didn't know what to say.

"Tell the truth!" Sir William said, baring his black teeth. "Always tell the truth. That's what I expect of a son."

"Yes, sir."

"Now, then! My brother's told you that you're my son." Sir William paused. "Well? Has he?"

"Yes, sir."

"And you know he and Helen have brought you up since you were a baby."

"Yes, sir."

"And you thought you were their son. . . . What else did John tell you?"

I didn't know whether or not to refer to the manor at Catmole. "I'm not . . . I don't know, sir."

"Don't know?"

"I can't remember."

"There you are!" Sir William bellowed. "Too much reading and writing. They swallow memory. Right! John has honored his part of the bargain, and now I'm honoring mine. How's that arm of yours?"

"Healed, sir," I said.

"Good lad!" Sir William said loudly.

What I wanted to tell Sir William was that he had fought foul and even his brother called it disgraceful. I wanted to hear him apologize. I wanted to hear him tell me he knew how hurtful our meeting must be. But I didn't say anything, and he thumped me on the top of my head. "My part of the bargain," he boomed. "Do you want to know what it is?"

"Yes, sir."

"To talk to you as soon as you were fourteen, in this new century. To recognize you. As my son."

Sir William paused. I knew he was staring at me, and slowly I raised my eyes and tried to look steadily at him. This old man with white bristles sticking out of his nostrils and a ferocious temper and a booming voice. Who shoveled me out of sight to suit himself. This murderer. My own father.

"Do you know what that means?" Sir William asked me.

"I . . . well . . . not really, sir."

"You're my heir. You and Tom. That's what it means. And that's why this is the best day of your life."

With the back of his sleeve, Sir William fiercely toweled his left eye. "Blast it! I'll tear it out!"

"It must be alive," I said. "There's bright blood in it."

Sir William glared at me. "Thank you very much," he said coldly. "If I need a healer, I know where to find one. Where was I, boy?"

"My life," I said miserably. "The best day."

"Yes!" barked Sir William. "I own three manors. Did you know that? Gortanore here, and my manor in Champagne, and then there's Catmole, east from Knighton. One foot in England and one foot in Wales, right on the bank of the Teme. Well, Arthur! I've named you as the heir to Catmole."

"Sir," I said quietly, and I inclined my head.

"Well? What do you think of that?"

"Does Tom know?"

"I'm telling you first," Sir William replied.

"It may upset him," I said.

"For God's sake, boy. What's wrong with you? I tell you you're my heir and you start to fret. Three months ago, you thought you were the second son of a second son. You feared you might never be a squire and never inherit any land. Isn't that so?"

"Yes, sir."

"And now look at you! You're the second son of a first son. Squire to Lord Stephen! On your way to Jerusalem! All this, and then my manor at Catmole to look forward to."

Sir William stuck his left forefinger into one of his nostrils and twisted it.

"Today and tomorrow, Arthur," he said gruffly. "They're what count." He inspected his forefinger and then wiped it on his sleeve. "Troublesome questions that rise like black bubbles in the middle of the night . . . turn your back on them! Do you understand?"

"Yes, sir."

Sir William's right eye glittered. "When people start digging," he said, "they may find their own bones."

Black Bubbles

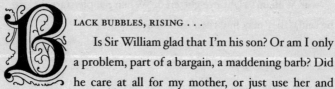LACK BUBBLES, RISING . . .

Is Sir William glad that I'm his son? Or am I only a problem, part of a bargain, a maddening barb? Did he care at all for my mother, or just use her and throw her away? And why couldn't I have stayed with her? Who is she? Where is she?

Lying beside the fire, I thought for a long time about all the questions I couldn't ask Sir William, all the questions our meeting didn't even begin to answer. I felt so sad and lonely. Then I reached for my seeing stone.

A lady is standing in front of King Arthur. She's wearing a dress that falls to her feet in loose folds. It must be made of expensive silk, because — although it's black — it flares crimson and flashes freezing blue.

"Of course you are welcome here at Caerleon," Arthur-in-the-stone tells her. "But who are you?"

"I am not at liberty to tell you," the lady replies.

"Then what shall I call you?"

"You may call me Lady Anna."

Her perfume, orange-blossom — the way she moves, her dress and mantle and their sweet sway — Arthur-in-the-stone cannot look at this woman without beginning to long for her. He knows that she's twice as old as he is, and that he's married to Guinevere. . . . but he leads her to his chamber.

For some while, my seeing stone turns sky-blue as Lady Anna's mantle, and the sky is bright with one hundred moons and one thousand stars, bowing and dipping and very gently shaking.

Now I can see King Arthur again. Sitting alone.

A boy enters the hall and walks straight up to him. "Why are you looking so thoughtful?" he asks.

"I have much to think about," the king replies.

"I know your thoughts as well as you do," the boy says.

"What do you mean?"

"I knew your father, King Uther. Yes, and I know exactly how he tricked your mother when she conceived you. I know how he entrusted you, wrapped in gold cloth, to the hooded man on the day you were born."

"How can you know?" the king asks. "You're not old enough."

"I know more than anyone else about you," says the boy.

"Go away!" the king orders him. "You're wasting my time."

So the boy bows and leaves the hall, and almost at once an extremely old man limps in. He must be almost eighty.

"I'm very glad to see you," says Arthur-in-the-stone. "Just now a younger boy was here, telling me things. . . ."

"As you well know," the old man says, "he was telling you the truth. And he would have told you more, had you allowed him."

"Who are you?" the king asks.

The old man jabs his stick into the rushes. "God is angry with you," he says. "Do you know who Lady Anna really is? You have made love to your own half sister, Morgause."

"Morgause!" cries the king.

"You could not have known," the old man croaks, "but Morgause knew. She's spitting jealous of you, and her husband, King Lot, sent her here to Caerleon to spy on you . . . and make love with you. There's nothing they would not do to ruin you."

"What shall I do?" Arthur asks.

"Morgause will bear you a son. She will call him Mordred. And Mordred will destroy you and your dream, your Round Table."

"Never!" shouts the king, leaping to his feet. "Who are you?"

"Who do you think?" the old man asks. "I am Merlin. And I was that young boy. You have made love to your own half sister, and God will punish you."

"Is there nothing I can do?" Arthur asks.

"You will do much," says Merlin. "When you hear that Morgause has given birth to a boy on May Day and has gone into hiding, you'll send out messengers and have every May-Day child in your kingdom carried to court. You'll set them all adrift in one boat. A cargo of babies! And they'll all be drowned — all except Mordred.

"A fisherman will find him on the foreshore, half-dead, swaddled in seaweed. He and his wife will foster your son until he's fourteen years old, then they'll bring him to your court. Oh yes, Arthur!" says Merlin. "You will do much. But it will all count for nothing."

My Arthur! My namesake whose dream is one fair fellowship.

One ring of trust. Who told all the great men of Britain, "I will root out evil wherever I see it. . . ."

Morgause has tricked you and you have been unfaithful. But can Merlin be right? Is there no forgiveness? And if a son is born in sin, must he be evil?

I never thought you would fail yourself.

38

GRACE'S SONG

"Whatever boys say!
Whatever men sing!

They say they care
And sing how they hope,
They say they fear
And can scarcely sleep
They're so on fire.

Whatever boys say!
Whatever men sing!

They praise our pride,
They praise our fear,
Our bodies, our minds,
And unless we care
They'd rather be dead.

It's just cruel sport,
This praising and pleading.
They quicken our blood,
Loosen our feelings
And mean not one word.

Whatever boys say,
Whatever men sing
Are mouthfuls of air.
They mean not a thing!"

"That's not true," I said.

"It is," said Grace.

"Where did you hear it?"

"From a traveling singer. Inside my heart."

Tom is right. It's not my fault that I'm Grace's half brother —
but I wish she didn't feel so hurt.

the white hart

Y SEEING STONE. MY CLOSE COMPANION.

No! It is more than that. I'm not Arthur-in-the-stone, but I know I'm seeing part of my own story.

"This fellowship!" King Arthur exclaims. "Was there ever a company such as this?"

Guinevere and Merlin and the king stand and look at the hoop of knights, one hundred and forty-nine of them, sitting at the Round Table.

"As keen as swifts," says Merlin.

"What do you mean?" Guinevere asks.

"They'll quarter this green earth and tear the sky into blue ribbons," Merlin says. "Or so they think."

"We shouldn't begin this feast without some sign," Guinevere says.

"She is right," murmurs Merlin, and almost at once a beautiful white hart leaps into the hall. He has ten tines on his antlers.

And now a white scenting-hound bounds in, trailing a leash and, hard on his heels, thirty couple of black running-hounds.

It's too late now for the hart to mislead the hounds by doubling back on its tracks. First it circles the Round Table, then prances down the hall between two of the long trestle tables, dips its branches, and leaps back up the hall again.

But the scenting-hound is getting closer — and now it launches itself. It sinks its teeth into the hart's buttocks and rips away a chunk of flesh.

The white hart gasps and vaults. It crashes into a knight sitting at a refectory table, and as the knight falls, his arms open, he catches the scenting-hound. The hound snarls and wrestles, but it cannot break the knight's grip. He digs his fingers inside its collar, and now he grabs its leash.

The hart, meanwhile, escapes from the hall. He kicks up his heels and slams the door in the face of the black hounds. By the time the door has been opened again, the hounds have lost ground; the white hart may be able to outrun them or deceive them.

The knight gets to his feet, holding the scenting-hound on a tight leash. Without looking up, without even bowing to Arthur-in-the-stone, he strides out of the hall.

"A sign!" exclaims Guinevere. "A wonder!"

"Is this your doing?" the king asks Merlin.

Before Merlin can reply, there is a clatter of hooves, and a lady on a white palfrey trots into the hall and right up to Arthur.

"Sire," she calls out. "Have you seen my white scenting-hound?"

"I have," Arthur replies. "A knight led him out of here no more than two minutes ago."

"He's mine," spits the lady.

"You should look after him better," Guinevere says.

"Are you going to stand by and see me wronged?" the lady yells at Arthur.

"What would you have me do?" the king asks.

Now an armed knight on a charger clops into the hall. Without a word, he grabs the lady and heaves her, screeching, over his shoulder, and rides out of the hall.

"I'm glad to see the back of her," Arthur says. "I've never heard such a vile noise."

"A wounded hart and a stolen hound," says Merlin. "A lady abducted. You can't leave things like this."

"What shall I do?" Arthur asks.

"Call Sir Gawain," Merlin replies. "Your own nephew! It's high time he rode out on his first adventure. Have him follow the white hart and bring him back to this hall, dead or alive. Ask Sir Tor to bring back the scenting-hound and that knight who stole him. And charge his father, Sir Pellinore, to come back with that lady and the knight who abducted her."

"I will," Arthur says eagerly.

"Enable your knights to ride out and right wrongs and tilt at the impossible," Merlin says. "Their fame is your fame."

40

MURDER

E WAS LYING OUTSIDE THE ARMORY DOOR WITH THE point of Lord Stephen's iron mace buried in his skull. His whole face was masked with blood, and his mouth was half-open and twisted.

When Simon and I rode in from Gortanore, everyone was out in the courtyard, standing around him.

"It was Alan!" shouted Rhys. "He came barging right past me, but I didn't think twice. You know how he is. He mounted Floss and rode her out bareback."

"I was sewing in the solar," Rowena said. "I heard him shouting he'd been tricked."

"Alan's always shouting," Sayer said.

"And threatening," added Rowena.

Gubert inspected the dead man's dreadful head wound. "He made a good job of it," he said, quite admiringly.

"It was Alan, then," said Haket. He stooped and with his right forefinger closed the dead man's eyes. Izzie began to weep.

"He had it coming, mind," Rowena said fiercely.

"Why?" Sayer asked.

"He's a Jew. That's why," Rowena replied. "Pawning and that. If he loaned you one penny, you had to give him back two. Inside one year."

"How do you know?" said Gubert.

"Alan told me," Rowena replied.

"What's his name, then?"

"Jacob," said Rowena.

"Where's Lord Stephen?" I asked.

"Over at Verdon. With Lady Judith."

Simon and I walked right up to the dead man. There were dark strings of blood hanging from both his eyeballs and the tip of his nose.

"Jacob the Jew," Haket informed us, and then he rounded on Izzie. "Stop sniveling!" he snapped.

"What shall we do?" I asked.

Haket rubbed his blubbery red mouth. "'Thou shalt not steal,'" he said. "God's fourth commandment. This Jacob was a pawn-broker and a moneylender. He took poor people's possessions and paid them almost nothing for them. Then, when they wanted to buy them back with corn or livestock, he charged them double or three times as much. He was a thief, and thieves deserve to die."

"But he was murdered," Sayer said.

"I reckon we've seen the last of poor Floss," said Rhys.

Haket waves his right fist. "'Thou shalt not murder,'" he said. "God's third commandment. Hear what the Book of Numbers says: 'If one man strikes another with an instrument made of iron, so that he dies, he is a murderer; and the murderer must be put to death.'"

"But Haket," I said desperately. "What shall we do now?"

"He won't lie in our churchyard," Haket said. "Jews aren't Christians. They're animals."

"How can you say that?" I cried, my voice rising. After that, I don't know quite where my voice came from, but I heard myself sounding quite calm again, the same as when I spoke to Alan after he'd shouted at Turold. "You're a hypocrite, Haket. It's you who's not Christian. You're not even merciful."

Everyone looked at Haket to see what he would do.

"This poor man's dead —" I went on.

"He wasn't poor," said Rowena.

"— and all you can do is vilify him. That and preach."

"Have you finished?" said Haket coldly. "How dare you? God will punish you."

"Simon," I said, and I felt as though I were out of breath. "Lord Stephen ought to know. He ought."

"Who do you think you are?" asked Haket between his teeth.

"I know it's a long way, and we've only just got back, but —"

"Dead men can wait," Sayer said. "They got plenty of time."

Simon stretched his arms above his head. "I'll go," he said.

"And I'll ride with you," said Rhys. "It's like a prison, this place."

"Come on, then!" said Simon, and everyone except Haket and Gubert and Rowena headed for the stables.

Haket glared furiously at me, swung on his heel, and stalked away across the Yard.

"Rowena!" he called, without even looking over his shoulder.

I caught Rowena by the arm. "We can't just leave him here," I said. "For the dogs and everything."

"Do it yourself," Rowena said.

"Rowena!"

"I hated him."

"Why?"

"What he did."

"What did he do?"

"Rowena!" Haket shouted for a second time, as if he were bringing a bitch to heel.

"Coming!" Rowena called, and she ran after him.

Suddenly my legs went weak beneath me. I'm glad I said what I did to Haket, but I felt afraid.

"Where can we put him?" I asked Gubert.

"You were brave," said Gubert.

I shook my head and started to shiver.

Gubert bent down. In both arms he picked up Jacob, as if he were an empty barrel. Then he stepped into Alan's armory and gently laid him on the dressing-bench, with the iron spike still buried in his head.

"God have mercy," I murmured.

We shuffled out of the armory and quietly closed the door behind us.

"I think there should be an eleventh commandment," I said.

"Ten's enough for me," Gubert replied.

"'Practice what you preach.'"

Gubert nodded. "Haket's an animal himself."

I shivered again, and then I began to gag. I ran to the latrines, but before I got there I was violently sick.

 144

41

Beheaded

OR A LONG TIME, I COULDN'T GET TO SLEEP BECAUSE
I felt so cold. And then I dreamed I was still in the
armory with Jacob, and he was lying on the dressing-
bench. Then Alan burst in. He kept yelling at me
and jabbing at me with one end of his quarterstaff . . . and then my
dream woke me up. I pulled out my dirty saffron cloth. Lying beside the dozy fire, I cradled my seeing stone.

Sir Gawain is cantering across a heath and Gaheris, his own
younger brother, is riding with him and serving as his squire. I'm
sure it's Gaheris because his hair's so blond that it is almost white,
and he's carrying a blue shield with a white cross on it.

The two brothers ride up to an enormous oak tree. Underneath its branches, two knights on horseback are fighting.

Sir Gawain rides right in between them. "What's all this
about?" he demands.

"We're brothers," one knight replies.

"That's even worse," Sir Gawain says. "What are you fighting for?"

"Earlier today," the first knight says, "a bleeding white hart
raced across this heath. And a long way behind, a whole pack of
black running-hounds was following it. My brother and I said that
whoever runs that hart to earth will win great fame at King
Arthur's court."

"He will," says Sir Gawain.

"I said I'd chase it," the first knight continues, "but my brother argued with me. He said he was the better huntsman. So we're fighting to prove which of us is the better man."

"But brothers shouldn't fight," says Sir Gawain. "Unless you do as I say, I'll take you both on."

"You've lost so much blood you're both worn out," Gaheris says.

"Go to King Arthur's court," Sir Gawain instructs them. "Put yourselves in the king's hands."

"Whom shall we say sent us?" asks the younger knight.

Sir Gawain stares up into the oak, and through the oak at the white sky. "You can say," he says, "'the knight whose quest is the white hart.' Now! What are your names?"

"Sourlouse of the Forest," replies the elder brother.

"I'm Brian of the Forest," the younger brother says.

In the night-gloom of the hall, someone sighed, and then sighed again. I'm not sure who it was, but I think it was Rowena.

I've never felt afraid in the dark before, and I don't know exactly what I was afraid of because Alan must have been miles away, but I still felt glad that Simon and Rahere and Miles and Izzie and Rowena were all sleeping around me.

After a while, it was completely quiet again. All I could hear was hallooing and the sound of galloping hooves, as Sir Gawain and Gaheris chased after the white hart.

Now the two brothers are riding side by side along the bank of a whirling, dark river.

"Can you hear them?" Gaheris calls. "The hounds!"

The brothers spur their horses and gallop even faster.

On the opposite bank is a manor house, and the white hart is swimming across the river towards it. But the current is too strong for most of the hounds. It chops and churns around their heads, and sweeps them far downstream. Only three couple are able to struggle over to the far side.

"If that hart can swim across, so can Kincaled," Sir Gawain shouts. And at once he urges his horse into the racing, deep water, and Gaheris follows him.

Sir Gawain is right! Kincaled's as strong as the hart, and so is Gaheris's horse. They cross the river and ride straight into the manor hall, followed by the three couple of dripping hounds.

There, the great hart turns and faces them. He has ten tines on his antlers, and there is nowhere left for him to go. While the hounds snarl and yelp, and Gaheris soothes and praises the hart, his beauty, his courage, his endurance, Sir Gawain quietly steps round behind him. Now he creeps foward. He raises his sword. He drives it from behind the beast's right shoulder deep into his heart.

At once a knight stalks into the hall, and his sword is drawn. He stares at the hart slumped on the floor and the hounds tearing at him; he scowls at Sir Gawain; and then with two swipes, forehand and backhand, he cuts off the heads of two of the hounds.

"How dare you?" shouts Sir Gawain.

"Dead!" says the knight in a stricken voice. "White of white! My own wife's gift to me."

"They're hounds," growls Sir Gawain. "That's their nature."

The knight kneels beside the hart. "Your death will be costly," he says quietly.

"You'd have done better to avenge yourself on me than on these dumb beasts," says Sir Gawain.

"I've avenged myself on your hounds," says the knight, "and now I'll avenge myself on you."

The knight swipes at Sir Gawain, but Sir Gawain fends him off with his shield and then he thrusts straight at the knight's throat, and the knight trips over and falls on his back.

"Mercy!" he gasps.

Sir Gawain pinions the knight. "You've killed two of my hounds," he says between his teeth, "and you can pay for them with your life."

"I'll make amends," says the knight. "Mercy!"

Now on her soft feet the knight's wife steps up behind Sir Gawain, and he hasn't seen her or even heard her. He unbuckles the knight's helmet so as to strike off his head. He forces the knight onto his knees and whirls his sword. . . .

With a shriek the lady throws herself over her husband and Sir Gawain cuts off her head by mistake.

"My brother!" cries Gaheris. "What have you done?"

Sir Gawain covers his eyes with his left hand.

"You should have spared him," Gaheris sobs. "A knight without mercy is without honor. You will never wash this shame away."

Sir Gawain is so stunned that he scarcely knows what he is doing. He offers the knight his right hand. "Stand up!" he says. "I will spare you. I will show you mercy."

"No, no!" the knight says hoarsely. "Saraide! I loved you more than my own life. Why should I care about mercy now?"

"Dear God!" Sir Gawain says. "I've never regretted anything so much. I had no quarrel with her."

"My wife," says the knight. "Saraide!"

"You are to go to King Arthur's court," Sir Gawain says. "Tell the king how you yielded to the knight whose quest is the white hart. Tell him everything."

"I don't care whether I live or die," the knight says.

"You are to go," repeats Sir Gawain.

"I will," says the knight. "I swear it."

"Now tell me your name," Sir Gawain says, "before we ride our own ways."

"I am Blamoure," the knight replies. "Blamoure of the Marsh."

"Take with you the two hounds you slew," Sir Gawain says. "One in front of you and one behind you."

The colors grew dim, the words faded . . .

What will King Arthur do when he hears that Sir Gawain has beheaded a lady? And how will God punish him?

SIR GAWAIN'S PUNISHMENT

F I WERE YOU," GAHERIS TELLS SIR GAWAIN, "I WOULD sleep in my armor. Not everyone around here will be happy when they hear you've beheaded Sir Blamoure's wife."

At once four armed knights ride into my stone: two of them with axes, one with a bow, and one with a mace.

"Call yourself a knight?" one of them shouts. "We're friends of Blamoure and you're a disgrace."

Another knight licks his lips. "A knight who shows no mercy," he says, "is no longer worthy of being a knight."

Gaheris draws his sword. While two knights engage him, the knight with the mace plays a terrible tune on Sir Gawain's head, and the knight with the bow unleashes an arrow and pierces Sir Gawain's left arm.

Now four ladies-in-waiting ride into the stone. One kneels in front of each knight and begs him to spare the lives of the two brothers.

"Their lives, yes!" the knights tell the ladies. "Their freedom, no."

"Who are you?" Sir Gawain asks.

"Lady Saraide's ladies-in-waiting," the first lady replies.

The four knights lead Sir Gawain and Gaheris out of the hall to a flight of stone steps. It's so dark in the cellar under the

"You have told us how you slew the knight who abducted this lady," Arthur tells Sir Pellinore. "You, too, have achieved your quest."

Sir Pellinore sniffs. "The Yelping Beast is my quest!" he says.

And now I can see Sir Gawain and Gaheris riding into King Arthur's hall. Lady Saraide's head is hanging around Sir Gawain's neck. Her fair hair is so long, it covers his thighs, and her body, dressed in lily silk, is lying over Kincaled's mane.

"Who is she?" King Arthur demands. "I've never seen such a terrible sight."

The king is right! When I saw Jacob lying in the dirt, oozing blood, it was the most gruesome thing I'd ever seen in my life. But isn't this even worse? Why am I seeing these horrible killings?

King Arthur and everyone in his court gaze at Sir Gawain and at the lady's head still hanging around his neck.

"I cannot judge you, Gawain," the king says. "Not for this crime. A jury of ladies must pass judgment on you."

Now Guinevere and many other ladies retire to the far end of the hall and confer in low voices.

"This is your punishment," Guinevere calls out in a loud voice. "For as long as you live, you're to fight for any lady who believes she has been wronged and asks you for help. You must never oppose any woman whomsoever, unless you're fighting on behalf of another. And you must always show mercy to other men."

the jews

ORD STEPHEN HAS INSTRUCTED HAKET TO BURY THE Jew just outside the north wall of our churchyard. Then tomorrow morning, Simon has to ride all the way to Ludlow, to inform the earl that Alan is wanted for murder.

After supper, Lord Stephen talked to me about the Jews. "You hear all kinds of things about them," he said. "Most of those things are bad and few of them are true."

"Haket says they're animals."

Lord Stephen sighed. "I've heard that story, but it's not in the Bible," he said.

"Will you tell me, sir?"

"Well, as you know, Jesus was a Jew. All his friends were Jews. Once, when he was a little boy and playing hide-and-seek, some of his friends hid inside a large oven.

"'Is there anything inside that oven?' Jesus asked the mother of one of his friends.

"'Young goats,' the woman said.

"'All right, then,' said Jesus. 'I'll turn them into goats.'

"Before long," said Lord Stephen, "the woman opened her oven. All the little children had been turned into goats!

"'Jesus!' exclaimed the woman angrily. 'What do you think you're doing?'

"'If you call children goats, they may become goats,' Jesus replied.

"'You change your friends back into children at once!'

"So that's what Jesus did," said Lord Stephen. "No, the Jews aren't animals. Quite the contrary. They're very clever. I met one Jew at court in London who teaches medicine, and in Chester there's a goldsmith who spins gold and silver as if he were a spider. He looks quite like a spider, actually."

"No one liked Jacob," I said.

"True!" said Lord Stephen.

"And Sir John told me the Jews in Norwich were massacred."

"All over the east of England," Lord Stephen replied. "And worst of all in York. That was ten years ago."

"But why, sir?"

"Why do Christians dislike Jews?" Lord Stephen said. "That's a very difficult question. First, because of the crucifixion."

"But it was the Romans —"

"I know," said Lord Stephen. "But the Jewish elders and chief priests resented Jesus. They didn't try to stop the Romans. And there's a second reason. Money!"

"What do you mean, sir?"

"Our Church teaches that Christians should not lend money, because it's sinful. So we get the Jews to do our dirty work and then resent them for it." Lord Stephen smiled faintly. "Anyhow," he said, "I hear you spoke up."

I lowered my eyes.

"You shouldn't have spoken like that to Haket," Lord Stephen said.

"No, sir. But he's so . . ."

"Arthur!" said Lord Stephen, raising a warning finger. "Mind your manners! You must apologize to him."

"Yes, sir."

"Simon tells me it was you who asked him to ride over to Verdon."

"Only because no one else did."

"Quite right!" said Lord Stephen. "Nothing to be ashamed of. How did you get on at Gortanore?"

"Sir," I said. "You told me I must talk to Sir William — because he's my father and it's my duty. But he didn't tell me anything."

"Not about Catmole?"

"Catmole! Yes, he told me about that, but —"

"There you are, then."

"— but he didn't say anything about my mother, and I couldn't even ask any questions."

"No, well . . ."

"Sir, I must find my mother. I must, even though I don't know how. Please allow me to, sir."

"Arthur," said Lord Stephen, "you're my only squire and we're joining the crusade and there's a great deal to do. Do you understand that?"

"Yes, sir."

"You must learn to put first things first."

Because of Jacob and my discussion with Lord Stephen, I haven't even written down what happened before I left Gortanore. I didn't see Sir William again, because he went back to Catmole.

Just before Simon and I set off, Lady Alice took my head between her hands.

"You're thinking about your mother," she said.

"I thought I'd find out about her. Or even meet her. But the only thing I know is that she's alive."

Lady Alice kissed my forehead. "Come back soon," she said.

the yelping Beast

STRANGE BEAST COMES MINCING OUT OF MY SEEING stone, and I know at once who he is. The body of a leopard and the haunches of a lion. The feet of a hart. He's Sir Pellinore's quest, the Yelping Beast! And when he bays, he makes such a racket you'd think there were thirty couple of hounds inside him.

Arthur-in-the-stone stands up and steps aside from the well, but the Yelping Beast ignores him. He lowers his snake-head into the well and, for as long as he drinks, he's completely silent. But then he begins to bay again and, without so much as a backward glance, he lifts his delicate feet and disappears into the forest.

Almost at once, Sir Pellinore rides up from the opposite direction.

"Your Yelping Beast!" cries the king. "I've just seen him."

"I've hunted him for ten years," Sir Pellinore says, "almost eleven, and my poor horse is dying. Let me ride yours."

"Give up your quest," Arthur says. "Give it to me, and within one year I'll capture him."

"Never!" says Sir Pellinore. "This is my adventure, not yours."

"Then what is my quest?"

"You will recognize it. Allow yourself to be lost and you will begin to find it."

Now Sir Pellinore mounts the king's destrier. "Thank you, sire," he calls out in a loud voice.

"I never said you could take him," Arthur protests.

As soon as my seeing stone went dark, I ran down the steps and across to East Yard to check that no knight — or anyone else — had taken Bonamy!

In the gloom he gazed at me and kept pricking his ears, quite puzzled about why I should be disturbing him.

hoouuu!

HE KISSED ME!

No, I can't begin at the end. If we all did that, we'd soon be walking backwards. We'd eat sweets before meat and be wise before we wailed.

I woke to the sound of the hunting horn: three short blasts, then twelve even shorter, and then three long ones. Over and over again Sayer blew, whooping bright notes, summoning us to the hunt.

When I put my nose out of doors, I could feel the early morning chill: the first day of April, undressed and shivering. And it was still cold while Lord Stephen and I rode north with Rhys and Sayer and our pack of running-hounds. When we reined in beside the well at Einion, the hounds wrapped themselves in mist-clouds of their own breath.

Winnie and her father, Sir Walter de Verdon, arrived at our meeting place soon after we did, and the first thing I noticed was Winnie's beautiful white fur mittens.

"Who made them?" I asked.

"My mother bought them from a peddler last summer. And a blue nightcap."

"What did he look like?"

"He had a wart on his nose," Winnie replied.

"That's him!"

"Who?"

"The man who stole Spitfire — Sian's cat! Your mittens are made from her fur."

"That's disgusting!" Winnie exclaimed, and she held out both her hands in front of her and shook them until the mittens fell off.

"You can't do that," I said. "Your hands will get cold."

"I won't wear them!"

"Just never let Sian see them," I said.

Winnie's hair is as red-gold as Queen Guinevere's, and Sir Walter's is the same. He even has gold eyelashes, and the bridge of his nose is spotted with freckles. He and Lady Judith are twins, but Sir Walter seems much more merry and affectionate than his sister.

"I've heard plenty about you, Arthur," he said with a wry smile. "And I'm still glad to meet you!"

"Are we ready, Sayer?" Lord Stephen asked.

"Let's hope for better luck than last time," Sir Walter said. "Nothing but that miserable wolf."

"We cured the skin," Lord Stephen said, "but it still stinks. We sent the right forefoot over to Caldicot for Lady Helen's sore breasts."

"Ready, sir," said Sayer.

"What we want," said Lord Stephen, "are two juicy hares. Hare pie for Easter!"

"Lady Alice rubs her forefingers and toes with hare's foot," I said. "It makes them less stiff."

Then Sayer uncoupled the hounds and raised the ox horn to his lips and blew the call for the quest.

Hou-hou! Hou hou hou hou!

Away went the hounds, opening out like a fan, yelping and yapping! They sprang over the scrubland — retracing their steps, circling, checking — and we all rode after them.

Almost at once, the pack picked up the scent of an old buck, and one of the hounds had him by the throat within a minute.

But soon after that we picked up the scent of another hare — and an agile one. We cheered as our hounds unraveled his tracks, springing first one way and then the other — running straight, zigzagging, leaping right round in circles, sometimes streaming out across the heath ahead of us.

"There he is, look!" shouts Rhys. "Ears up!"

Then Sayer blew such a pattern of bright blasts, quick and short and breathless, that they made the nape of my neck tingle.

When at last the hounds caught Jack-Hare, Sayer waded through the pack and grabbed him, and held him up.

Hoouuu! Hou hou! Hoouuu! Hou hou!

So the horn sang the death-song of the brave hare. And then we all hallooed, and the hounds bayed, but they sounded quite mournful now.

"The prayer of Saint Basil then," Lord Stephen called out. "Lord God, we're all one fellowship, humans and animals. They're our brothers, our sisters, and this earth is their home too. Let us remember they live not only for us but for themselves, and for You. They, too, love the sweetness of this life."

"Amen," we all said. "Amen."

"Strip him, then!" Lord Stephen told Rhys.

"What about the hounds, sir?" asked Sayer.

"Soak their bread with his blood," Lord Stephen said. "They've done well, haven't they? Give them the heart and kidneys as well."

Later, when we were all eating dinner, sitting side by side on the trunk of an elm tree, Winnie told Sayer and Rhys about seeing two hares fighting.

"Two jacks," she said. "Standing up. Cuffing each other."

"I seen them swipe each other with their claws," said Rhys.

"And thump the ground with their back feet," added Sayer. "They kick each other."

"Why, though?" asked Winnie.

Sayer smirked.

"The old story," Rhys said.

"What do you mean?"

"Two males . . . more sometimes. Fighting over one girl."

"They only fight when they're mating," Sayer explained. "I seen fur fly, and one hare blind another."

"I've heard it said," Lord Stephen said, "that hares can change sex."

"They can, sir," Rhys replied. "One March moon, I called them with a piece of grass. You know! Between my thumbs. Well, one hare came so close I knocked it over. That was pregnant all right, but it had testicles."

"You saw that?" Lord Stephen asked.

"I did, sir."

"Last year," I said, "I made up a song about the hare."

"How does it go?" asked Sir Walter.

"Squat-in-the-hedge . . ." I began. "No! That's wrong.

> Cat-of-the-wood and cabbage-patch stag,
> Squat-in-the-hedge and frisker,
> Sit-still and shiver-maker,
> Snuffer, twitching whisker . . ."

"Eight times true, boy," said Rhys.

"I've added some more words now," I said.

> "White-spot and lie-low-by-the-dyke,
> Boxer, little busker,
> Wide-eye, wall-eye,
> Witch, dew-tracker, trickster."

"Nine times true, that is," Rhys said, solemnly nodding.

"You must sing that poem to Rahere, Arthur," said Lord Stephen.

"You've clever!" said Winnie. "Father, Arthur writes because he wants to."

Sir Walter shook his head and smiled.

"And he's going to write about me."

"He is, is he?"

"I never said that," I protested.

Sir Walter stroked Winnie's hair and looked at her fondly. "Young women!" he said, smiling. "They like nothing so much as to be talked about and admired."

"So do boys," said Winnie.

Lord Stephen stood up and began to dust down his straw-colored cloak with the flat of his hands. I couldn't see a speck of dust on it, or else I would have asked him to take it off, and shaken it for him. Then he blinked and smiled, and we all stood up, and the hounds began to bark.

On the way back to Einion, Sir Walter asked me about my warhorse and my Yard-skills. And then he invited me to visit Verdon.

"Winnie's orders!" he said, smiling.

I can't imagine Sir John obeying Sian, willful as she is, and Sir William certainly wouldn't take orders from Grace. He's a kind man, Sir Walter. I wish I had a father like him.

Before long, the woods of Einion wrapped their blue arms around us, and the meadows of Bryn stretched their new green limbs toward us.

"Arthur!" said Winnie, almost under her breath. "You're very clever."

"I wanted to tell you about Gortanore," I said.

"At Verdon you can," Winnie said. "My father likes you."

Then she leant over and grabbed Pip's reins, and I saw she was wearing Spitfire's white mittens again.

"Come here!" she ordered.

"Why?"

Winnie put her right arm round my shoulders. She pulled me towards her, and with her warm lips she kissed my cold left cheek.

46

CAMELOT

"WHERE DO TRUE NAMES COME FROM?" ASKS ARTHUR-in-the-stone.

"Where do flowers come from?" Merlin replies, and he pulls up his dark hood, and then sweeps it off again. "From waiting and secret thought."

"Slowly, then," Arthur says.

"But all at once," Merlin replies. "One man looks for guidance to his own family tree, one woman hovers over a name because she hears its music's meaning, children float twigs, wisewomen divine dreams . . . But these ways are only pointers: They may point to the true name but they do not name it. And then one night, after long listening and only because of it, the name grows out of the dark. It perches in your morning mind, singing like a blackbird."

"Merlin," says the king. "I have listened. I've waited. My castle and court, and the city surrounding us: Their name is Camelot."

the knight with an
unbroken voice

S SOON AS WE'D FINISHED OUR LENTEN STEW, AND
Lord Stephen and Lady Judith had bidden us a safe
night, I brought a candle up to my room.

First I thought about Winnie, and how she
kissed me. . . . She always seems to know exactly what she thinks
and expects people to do as she wants. But whenever we argue she
starts to grin, and I think she's just testing how strong I am.

I'm really glad Sir Walter has invited me to Verdon and hope
Lord Stephen will let me go soon.

After that, I thought about Arthur-in-the-stone. I saw him
on the day he was born, wrapped in gold cloth; I've seen him the
same age as I am, pulling the sword from the stone; I've seen him
grow older than Serle, and marry Guinevere, and be unfaithful
to her . . .

One fair fellowship. One unbroken ring of trust. That's King
Arthur's dream, but he cannot always live up to it himself, and
some of his knights are quarrelsome and murderous.

I pulled my stone from its hiding place and unrolled the dirty
saffron bundle.

"Knights of the Round Table," Arthur-in-the-stone calls out,
"you can see Sir Miles's body lying here. You've heard from his
squire how he was killed. Who is going to avenge him?"

Not a word. No one says anything. But when the king asks his knights for the third time, a boy calls out, "I will! I'll avenge him."

"Who are you?" asks the king.

"Griflet, sire."

"How old?"

"Fourteen, sire. I'm a squire. And if you'll knight me, I'll avenge Sir Miles."

"I can't knight you," Arthur replies. "Your voice hasn't even broken."

"Knight him, Arthur," Queen Guinevere tells him. "He's honorable."

"He's too young."

Merlin stands behind the king. Like his own inner voice: the one Arthur should never ignore.

"You're right," he says quietly. "If Griflet fights the knight who killed Sir Miles, you may never see him alive again. Give him time to grow up, and he'll be loyal to you for as long as he lives."

"Dear God!" the Queen complains. "Are you married to Merlin or to me?"

"All right, then," Arthur tells Griflet. "I will knight you."

At once Griflet drops onto his left knee, and Arthur touches his right shoulder with his sword. "This is my gift to you," he says, "and now you must give one to me."

"Anything, sire."

"Promise me that as soon as you've fought the knight who killed Sir Miles, you'll come straight back to court."

"I promise," says Griflet, and at once he leaves the hall.

Now Griflet canters up to a tree and there's a shield hanging from it. He reverses his spear and rams it so hard against the shield that it falls off the tree, and at once a knight strides towards him.

"What's all this?" he demands.

"We're going to joust," Griflet replies.

The knight shakes his head. "Your voice hasn't broken."

"I'm a knight."

"Nonsense!" says the knight. "I'm much stronger than you."

"Even so," says Griflet, "you killed Sir Miles, and I've sworn to avenge him."

"If you challenge me," the knight says, "I have no choice. But I don't like it. Where do you come from?"

"The court of King Arthur," Griflet replies.

Now Griflet and the knight gallop towards each other. Griflet aims his lance right into the center of the knight's shield, and it shivers and splinters. But the knight's so strong he drives his lance right through Griflet's shield into his shoulder, just above his heart. Griflet and his mount are both thrown to the ground.

"God's bones!" shouts the knight. "I haven't killed him."

At once he dismounts and unfastens Griflet's helmet, and bathes his face with water. And then the knight prays.

"Father," he says, "breathe on this boy. He does not deserve to die."

Now the knight tenderly lifts Griflet onto his own horse and carries him to Arthur's court.

The knights and ladies see Griflet, lying facedown. They see the knight's expression, so sober and downcast.

Merlin takes Griflet into his arms and lays him out on a table, and examines his deep wound.

"He was prepared to die," says the knight.

"And just one inch away from his death," Merlin replies.

"His only fault was his impatience," says the knight. "He wanted to achieve too much too soon."

Merlin looks up. He stares at Guinevere unblinking, and fiercely she glares back at him.

48

EASTER

UR EYES WERE STREAMING AND OUR BOOTS WERE
sopping. But we got to the top of Swansback just
before the sun rose.

Haket surveyed us. His panting, obedient Easter
flock.

"Questors for Christ," he called out, "watch the sun dance!"

I put my hands over my eyes and peeped through my fingers.
For a moment the sun was gold, then it turned purple as an Easter
anemone. And then green. It began to spin.

"Bloodred," sighed Rowena.

"No!" shouted Izzie. "Black as a cormorant's wing."

"White," said Miles.

"Burning white," Lord Stephen said.

They were standing all around me, I knew that, and so were
Lady Judith and Rahere and Simon and Anian and Catrin —
everyone in the household except for Gubert, who stayed behind
to prepare breakfast — but their voices seemed distant.

"Is it leaping?" Haket asked.

"I can't!" cried Rowena. "It's blinding me."

"When you think you cannot," Haket urged her, his voice rising, "that's when you must."

"I can't!" protested Izzie, and I heard her flop down on the wet
grass beside me.

"Can you see Him?" shouted Haket. "The Lamb! Can you see His banner burning white, and its blood cross?"

I don't know whether I could or not. I saw all kinds of shapes, but they kept changing. Seething dark brightnesses!

"Could you see the Lamb, sir?" I asked Lord Stephen, as we walked down from the hilltop.

"Each and every man who chooses to take the Cross has seen the Lamb."

"I mean . . ."

"I know, Arthur." Lord Stephen turned to me and half-smiled. "No! I couldn't. Poor eyesight."

"Rahere and Miles say they did."

"Mmm," Lord Stephen murmured. "Unless their eyes deceived them."

"But do you believe . . ."

"What was it you told me when we talked about the Sleeping King?" Lord Stephen replied swiftly. "Yes: 'It's best to believe unless it's impossible to do so.'"

"We've never done this at Caldicot," I said. "I'm going to tell Oliver. Everyone could climb to the top of Tumber Hill."

After Easter Mass at Caldicot, we have always said the same words before leaving church, words that told the Resurrection, and each year we took different parts. Last year I was one of the Roman soldiers who discovers on Easter morning that Jesus's body has gone from Joseph of Arimathea's tomb, and I had to shout out:

"What? Gone? Not a sign? Not a trace?
Where's the corpse that lay in this place?

172

If Sir Pilate finds out, we'll be in disgrace.
He'll give us a clout!
He'll crown us all with his spiked mace,
And lay us out."

Lady Helen and Ruth and my grandmother Nain were the three Marys told by the angel that the stone has been rolled away from the tomb, and that Jesus has risen from the dead. Tanwen was the angel. Everyone in the manor house had a part in the play, even Sian. She had to curl herself up and keep absolutely still, because she was the huge and heavy stone.

Each time we called out these words in church, I pretended I was really standing beside Jesus's empty tomb, scared as the soldiers, amazed as the three Marys, calm and certain as the angel:

"He is not here, wonder to say.
This is the place in which he lay
And here's the shroud he wore that day
When he was cold.
He is risen and gone on his way
As he foretold."

For dinner, we had hare pie, and before Lord Stephen ate the first mouthful, he showed the palms of both his hands to the hare and said, "Eostre, Eostre, this is your hare. Keep us all in your green care."

"Who is Eostre?" I asked.

"Do you know, Miles?" Lord Stephen said.

"No, sir," said Miles.

"A saint, I suppose," said Lord Stephen. "Anyhow, it's what we always say before we eat hare pie at Easter. I can remember my grandfather saying it."

"Eostre sounds like Easter," I said.

"True," Lord Stephen replied rather thoughtfully.

Not only hare pie. Boiled flounders from the estuary of the river Severn — fresh and unsalted — shin of beef layered with marrow, and then chicken, roasted on the spit. Lent was over at last.

After dinner, Gubert told us that while we were up on Swansback, he'd seen the Easter Hare.

"He came right into my kitchen," he said, grinning. "And this hare, you know what he did?"

"No," we chorused, though of course we all did.

"He laid a nest of eggs, and I'm not saying nowhere."

This was the signal for us to run out of the hall in different directions and begin to search for the nest of eggs, just as we did at Caldicot.

"Wherever you like!" Lord Stephen called out. "Our solar. Our bedrooms. Anywhere."

It was Lady Judith who found the nest, and she turned pink with pleasure.

"Tucked between those sticks," she clucked. "Right under our noses! Well, I never!"

There were fifteen little eggs in the nest — plover's and pigeon's and thrush's and blackbird's — all different colors and sizes. Lady Judith gave one to each of us, including Gubert, and that left her with three.

It is dark now, but when I close my eyes I can still see the sun. Inside the disk, I can see shapes. I can see Jacob's shadow, staggering, and another shape, jerking and twisting.

But Christ is risen! Christ is risen, and in Christ we will all have eternal life.

49

LANCELOT

HE KNIGHTS OF THE ROUND TABLE HOLD THEIR NOSES. The ladies bury their faces in their sleeves as they pass the wounded man, the Knight Without a Name, lying in the chamber that leads to the hall.

A snapped sword blade is sticking through the knight's rotting rib cage. Barbed arrow-tips are embedded in his neck, his stomach.

"If no one here can heal my wounds," the knight says quietly, "I will soon die."

But no one can. Neither Sir Gawain nor Sir Balin, nor Sir Tor or his father King Pellinore. Not the ladies who feel the knight's pain as if it were their own. Not even the healers or teachers at King Arthur's court.

"The only man who can heal me," says the Knight Without a Name, "is the one who swears to avenge me. He must fight every single man loyal to the knight who gave me these wounds."

"No one here can do that," Arthur-in-the-stone tells his knights. "Who knows what that might lead to?"

Now there's a rumpus at the hall door: Nimue has returned to court. The moment Merlin sees her, he sighs and hurries down to meet her. He is almost old and she is almost young. He cannot help himself.

Behind Nimue, there's a young man, and I like the look of him.

His brow is broad and his eyes are like Tom's eyes, blue and amused. His horse is white, he's wearing a white woolen cloak, and the sword slung around his neck has a white scabbard. His shield, though, is blue as lapis lazuli and has three gold lions prancing across it.

Guinevere stiffens beside King Arthur. "Who is that?" she asks.

"We'll soon find out," Arthur replies.

"He looks rather pleased with himself," says Guinevere.

"This young man, sire," Nimue says, "is my foster son. Lancelot!"

"He is welcome here," says Arthur.

"His father was Pant, king of Gwynedd. When his kingdom was under attack, he sent Lancelot to me under the lake, and I brought him up with my own sons, Hector and Lionel."

"Lancelot of the Lake," Guinevere says.

"Will you grant me a wish?" asks Nimue. "It will cost you nothing."

"I hope I can," replies the king.

"Knight Lancelot then," Nimue says, "in this white cloak and white scabbard."

"My new custom here," says Arthur, "is for the king to give a new knight his clothing and his sword."

"If you refuse," Nimue says, "I'll take him to another court."

"Are you threatening me?" Arthur asks.

Nimue says nothing, and I can feel Guinevere stiffen again beside me.

"Arthur," Merlin says quietly, "do as Nimue asks."

"You're besotted with her," Arthur replies.

"Merlin's right," Guinevere says.

"Last time you said he was wrong," says Arthur. "Because of you, I knighted Griflet."

"We're not both wrong," Guinevere says huskily. "A young man as promising as this — you must not allow him to go."

Lancelot kneels before the king. "Pure in mind . . ." he begins, "pure in body . . . I will oppose evil. . . ."

Arthur-in-the-stone listens to Lancelot's voice, unhurried yet eager. And now, with Excalibur, the king gives him the accolade: Three times he taps his right shoulder.

"Go to church," Arthur says. "Make your confession and receive the Sacrament. And when you come back, I'll belt on your sword."

Lancelot bows to the king, glances at Guinevere, and then leaves the hall. But he doesn't go straight to church. He turns aside to the wounded knight lying in the chamber.

"I will heal your wounds," he says.

"You cannot," says the Knight Without a Name. "Not unless you swear to avenge me. To fight every single man loyal to the knight who dealt me these wounds."

"I swear that."

"You are very young," the knight says.

"Better I should die than you," Lancelot says. "You may be one of the finest knights in this kingdom, whereas I've done nothing yet to prove myself."

"If your actions speak as well as your words," says the wounded knight, "you'll have no equal."

Now Lancelot bends over the Knight Without a Name. Very

gently he draws the sword blade from between his ribs, and the knight scarcely feels it. And now Lancelot unhooks the barbed arrow-tips. The wounded knight quivers and closes his eyes.

"Send for a doctor," he murmurs, "to wash and dress my wounds. Lancelot, may you become King Arthur's best knight — his most trusted friend."

Now Lancelot does go to church. He makes his confession and receives the Sacrament, and for a long time he remains on his knees. When at last he returns to the hall, no one is there except Queen Guinevere.

"The king waited," Guinevere tells him, "but you did not return."

"I was in church," Lancelot says.

"He has retired to his rooms."

"What shall I do?" Lancelot asks. "The king said he would belt on my sword."

Guinevere half-smiles, and then she sighs. "I will belt it on myself, then," she says.

Guinevere takes Lancelot by the hand, and he gives a start when he feels the queen's bare skin touching his. I felt the same when we were out hare hunting and Winnie kissed me.

"You've belted on my sword," Lancelot says, "and from now on, wherever I am, I would like to think of myself as your knight."

"I should like you to do that," Guinevere replies.

"I have healed the Knight Without a Name," Lancelot tells the queen, "and now I must avenge him. I must fight each man loyal to the knight who wounded him. Far better I should die than some greater man."

"No," says Guinevere.

"I'm ready to die," Lancelot says. "Who can fully live unless he's ready to die?"

Queen Guinevere bows her head. There are tears in the corners of her eyes.

50

MIRIAM

 HO ARE YOU?" I ASKED.

She looked very frail, like a leaf skeleton. With one puff, I thought, I could have blown her away.

"What's your name?"

"Miriam."

"Where do you live, then?"

"Ludlow."

"Ludlow!" I cried. "How did you get here?"

She had to tilt back her head to look up at me. Her eyes were enormous, liquid, dark moons.

"You seen him," she said.

"Who?"

"Our father."

"Your father?"

"Jacob."

"Jacob!" I exclaimed.

Miriam searched my face. "Dead," she said solemnly. "Is he?"

"Yes," I said very quietly.

Miriam looked at the ground. She scraped it with her left foot.

"Who told you?" I asked.

"No one," said Miriam. She squatted down and crouched into a little scruffy bundle.

"Come with me," I said gently.

I led Miriam down towards the churchyard. The only person there was old Wilf, sitting on his parents' grave, talking to them.

"Over here," I said, and I took Miriam's little hand and walked along the outside of the north wall.

"A madman attacked him. Our armorer, Alan. Just one blow. He felt no pain."

Miriam's whole face was quivering like a flimsy poppy petal. "But . . ." she began, ". . . his prayer shawl."

"What do you mean?"

"At home . . . You can't bury him!"

Then Miriam gave one terrible piercing scream and fell over her father's grave. "*Abba,*" she sobbed. "Our father!"

The hot sun heard her and blinked. The cold stars heard her, and their knuckles cracked.

Miriam stretched herself out over the grave; she dug her fingertips into the loose earth. Then I saw Haket walking up across the glebe land and I knew I had to protect this little creature from ever knowing how people here hated her father. I bent down and scooped her up: a light, damp bundle in my arms.

"Arthur!" shouted Haket. "What's going on?"

I walked as fast as I could — out of the churchyard, up the steep path, and into the castle yard.

"You've been searching for him," I said.

Miriam gazed up at me. "He'll never go away," she said.

"No, he won't," I said.

"I searched everywhere," said Miriam, and she closed her eyes.

"I'm searching too," I whispered. "I'm the same as you."

I carried Miriam straight through the storeroom, past Anian's and Catrin's twitching noses, and up two flights of steps to the solar.

Lord Stephen was very practical. He told Miriam that her father would have been proud of her. He sent me down to Gubert to get some milk and bread. Then he said it was high time Miriam got back to Ludlow.

"How old are you?" he asked.

"Eight, please," said Miriam.

"And your mother gave you permission?"

Miriam opened her dark eyes wide and slowly shook her head.

Lord Stephen has instructed Simon to ride Miriam all the way back to Ludlow tomorrow and to tell her mother that she can have Jacob's body back, if she wishes.

"Christians and Jews and Muslims all bury their dead in different ways," he told me. "We should respect that." Then Lord Stephen looked at me, gave an extremely long sigh, and gently shook his head.

If you didn't know him, you might think Lord Stephen didn't have strong feelings. He does, though. And he cares for other people's feelings as well.

"I think Miriam should sleep up here tonight," he said. "Isn't that a good idea?"

"Oh yes, sir. In case . . ."

"Exactly!" said Lord Stephen. "And why don't you keep her company?"

One candle on the tabletop. One candle, burning. I have been writing those words for a long time, and Miriam hasn't moved or made a single sound.

Her right arm lying across my leg is weightless as thistledown.

where NOTHING
is impossible

IGHT, PLEASE."

  Miriam is the same age as Sian. I remember that when little Luke died, Sian threw her game of knuckle-bones into his grave.

"He may need them." That's what she said. "He's not dead for me."

After Miriam had left for Ludlow with Simon, I felt lonely, so I unwrapped my obsidian. . . .

"Here in Caerleon," says Arthur-in-the-stone, "where England ends and Wales begins. Between worlds. This is where nothing is impossible."

Through the hall door crowd three young men. The one in the middle is supported by the other two. He has his arms around their shoulders. His own shoulders are broad and he has large, handsome features.

And look at his hands! They're large, too, and beautifully cared for. No cracks, no callouses. They're pink and perfect.

And yet this man's wearing a filthy smock and hairy breeches. Who is he?

Once he's standing in front of the king, the young man removes his arms from round his friends' shoulders and stands upright quite easily.

"May God bless you and your fair fellowship, sire," he says.

"What do you want?" Arthur asks.

"Three wishes," the young man replies. "One now and the others in a year's time. My first wish is for you to give me food and drink for the next year."

"Is that all?"

"That's enough."

"I'd never refuse that to friend or enemy," says Arthur. "What is your name?"

"I cannot tell you," the young man replies.

"Cannot or will not?" Arthur asks. "It would be a strange thing if a man didn't know his own name."

Now the king turns to his brother and steward, Sir Kay, and asks him to ensure the young man gets well fed. "Treat him as though he's the son of a knight."

"Certainly not!" Kay replies. "I'm not wasting money. A knight's son should have asked for armor and a warhorse."

"You heard me," Arthur says.

"No name?" says Kay. "All right, I'll give him one. Beaumains! Pretty hands!"

"That's enough," says Arthur.

"Pretty hands," Kay repeats. "Not after he's worked for his keep in the kitchen. He can have a bowl of greasy broth each day, and by the end of the year he'll be as fat as a hog."

At this, Sir Lancelot and several other knights start to protest.

"Foul mouth!"

"Let him be."

"Bite your tongue, Kay."

"He'll prove a better man than you think," Lancelot says. "I'm certain of it."

Kay's mouth curls. Just like Serle. He's never charitable. "You fools!" he exclaims. "You can always judge a man by what he asks for. Come on, you scullion! Where have you been with your pretty pink hands? Praying in a monastery? It's high time you did a proper day's work."

My stone seethes with freezing sparks, as many as the Milky Way. Then it grows warm again, and I can see King Arthur sitting in a second hall. He is surrounded by many knights and ladies, and a pretty young woman is standing in front of him. . . .

"I need your help," she says. "My sister's a prisoner in her own castle. The Knight of the Red Lands is holding her captive."

"I've never heard of him," says Arthur-in-the-stone.

"I have," says Sir Gawain. "I crossed swords with him and scarcely got away with my life."

"Who is she," the king asks, "your sister?"

The young woman half-smiles and puts her fingers to her lips.

"Lady," the king says, "there are plenty of knights here who would do their utmost to rescue your sister. But not if you refuse to tell me who she is."

"In that case," the young woman says, "I will have to go elsewhere."

"Sire," booms Beaumains in his loud voice from the far end of the hall, where he is standing with the other kitchen boys. "I've worked in your kitchen for twelve months."

"What do you want, Beaumains?"

"My second wish. Allow me to help this young woman."

"As you wish," replies the king.

"And my third wish," say Beaumains "is to be knighted. By Sir Lancelot."

"Pismire!" the young woman cries. "Is this the best you can offer? Your greasy kitchen scullion?"

She turns her back on King Arthur and marches out of the hall, straight past the dwarf who has just staggered in, carrying shining armor.

"Beaumains's armor," the dwarf shouts.

"Who are you?" the king asks.

"His servant, Huon," the dwarf replies. "Wherever he goes in this wide world, Beaumains can count on me."

At once Beaumains bows to King Arthur and leaves the hall with the dwarf, and as he does so, he asks Sir Lancelot to joust with him.

"I thought you wanted me to knight you," Lancelot replies.

"I do," says Beaumains, "but only if you think I'm worthy of it."

Outside the walls of Caerleon, the two men gallop toward each other and clash so fiercely that each unseats the other. Lancelot falls clear of his horse, but Beaumains is unable to release one foot from the stirrup. His horse drags him round, bumping his head and shoulders against the ground, until Lancelot is able to grab the reins.

"Are you hurt?" Beaumains asks.

Lancelot smiles. "It's you who are hurt," he replies.

"I'll fight you on foot, then," Beaumains says, and at once he draws his sword.

Beaumains keeps lunging forward, thrusting and thwacking, and

Lancelot can only parry and wait for an opening. Now Beaumains gives Lancelot's helmet a terrible smack with the flat of his blade, and Lancelot reels away as if he were drunk.

"Enough!" he shouts. "Isn't that enough?"

"No!" yells Beaumains. And then he remembers whom he is fighting, and sticks his sword into the turf. "Yes," he says.

"We've no quarrel," says Lancelot.

"But I haven't shown you —"

"You've shown me quite enough," says Lancelot. "It was all I could do to keep you at arm's length."

"Will you knight me, then?" asks Beaumains.

"Only if you tell me your real name."

"I will," says Beaumains, "providing you tell no one else. I am Gareth, Gawain's younger brother. The son of King Lot and Morgause, King Arthur's half sister."

Lancelot smiles and shakes his head. "Just as I thought," he says.

Now Beaumains kneels. He swears oaths to protect people who cannot protect themselves. In turn, Lancelot undertakes to protect him.

Now Sir Lancelot knights Beaumains. He belts on his sword, and the two men embrace.

"With your permission," Beaumains says, "I'll ride after that young woman at once — otherwise I'll never catch her."

Beaumains and Huon chase along a windy ridge. They canter down below the spring line, and all around them are clumps of purple-eyed pansies and rashes of scarlet poppies. There at last they catch up with the young woman.

"You!" she exclaims. "Stained with grease and spotted with wax! Stinking of stale food! I thought I'd seen the last of you."

"Lady . . ." begins Beaumains.

"You ladle-washer!"

"You can say what you like," Beaumains replies.

"You glutinous glob! Who do you think you are?"

"I've promised King Arthur that I'll rescue your sister."

"Pismire!" shouts the young lady. "You won't live long enough for that. The man you're about to meet — you won't even dare look him in the face, not for all the greasy broth in the world!"

52

BATTLE DRESS

HEN I CHOSE BONAMY, LORD STEPHEN TOLD ME
that a warhorse is not only a piece of equipment
but a friend. That's true, I know. When I go
across to the stables, Bonamy always welcomes
me now. He doesn't know how strong he is when he nuzzles me and
sometimes almost knocks me off my feet. But he does know I'll
look after him. And I know that when we go crusading, and I really
need him, he'll be loyal to me.

I think new armor is more than equipment as well. It's battle
dress, and tells you as much about the knight wearing it as the cut,
color, and trimmings of a lady's finest dress tells about her.

As Turold spread out my glistening armor on the table in the
armory, I thought how Gubert and I laid Jacob there just before
Easter. . . .

"Yes," said Turold, "I've made your helmet flat-topped." He
smiled, and the wrinkles in his cheeks bunched and deepened.
"Very effective and very fashionable. But as I told you, you'll have
to wear a leather skullcap with it. Otherwise your young brains will
get buffeted and beaten."

I inspected the insides of the thigh-pieces. "When I was arming Lord Stephen," I said, "the head of one of these nail-bolts came
off. I spiked him."

"You must always look after your armor," Turold said.

"I do. I graze it. In a bag of wet sand."

"Exactly. Piece by piece. And then polish it, oil it, and grease it. Even then, metal can fracture. That's why a knight needs a good armorer."

"Not Alan," I said.

"And it can snap," said Turold. "Now! Try this on. It may pinch in one place and be too loose in another. We'll need to make small adjustments."

First my leather ankle boots and my mail-leggings, clicking and clinking. Then the bolster around my waist, and a new aketon with well-padded shoulders; and over that a wonderful mail-shirt, with leather mittens stitched to it.

"Have you ever seen rivets like these?" Turold asked.

"Never!" I gasped.

Each one has a high head — ridged and pointed — and since there are thousands of them, my whole mail-shirt bristles.

"They look like barleycorn," I said.

Turold clapped his hands, and his sunken eyes gleamed. "Exactly! You're wearing a whole field of it. Sir William's orders!"

"Sir William?"

"He's paying, isn't he? He said welded links weren't good enough. He wanted them all fastened, and these barley-heads are the new design."

I've quite often helped Sir John and Lord Stephen to put on their armor, but wearing my own felt completely different. By the time I'd fitted on my skullcap and my helmet, my armor was so heavy that I couldn't swing my arms or quicken my pace, let alone run. I was in my own tight, hot world, and could only hear half of what Turold was saying. If I were buried alive, I suppose a coffin would feel like that.

"Go on!" shouted Turold. "Walk around the Yard. Find out how it fits."

As soon as Rowena and Izzie saw me, they screamed and came running up. First they pressed their soft fingertips into the barley-heads. Then they looked at their own reflections in the back of my helmet, all bulging and misshapen. And when I took it off, Rowena pointed out the row of tiny stars and crosses engraved around the neck guard.

"I hadn't even noticed them," I said. "What are they for, Turold?"

"You're taking the Cross," said Turold.

"What about the stars, then?"

"Just an armorer's fancy," Turold replied.

"These three in a row," Izzie said, "they look like Orion's belt."

Turold pressed his lips. "As they were meant to," he said.

"Why?" I asked.

"May Orion protect you," Turold said, "and bring you safe home."

After supper this evening, Lord Stephen said, "I've some news, Arthur, and I hope it will please you: I've asked Turold to be my new armorer, and he has accepted. He'll be coming with us when we join the crusade."

53

TREMBLING AND TOTTERING

 TARS AND CROSSES! YES, AND LITTLE BLOBS AND squares and splinters, thousands of tiny shapes scoot around inside my stone like water boatmen. Then somehow they begin to combine into shapes — human beings, animals, buildings . . .

"All right!" says the young woman. "I've insulted you each time you've defeated another knight. I've called you every foul name I know. I've refused to eat with you. Despite all this, you have never once answered back or raised your voice. No matter how much I've humiliated you, you've been courteous to me. Beaumains, you're no kitchen scullion."

"If a man can't put up with a few barbed words," Beaumains replies, "he won't be much of a knight. When your words made me angry, I turned my anger against my opponents — the six thieves, and the two river knights, and the Knight of the Black Lands and his brothers. You helped me to defeat them."

"What is your true name?" the young woman asks.

"A man may be wellborn and he may be humbly born," Beaumains replies. "I would rather people valued me for what I do."

"Forgive me," the young woman says in a soft voice, "all my insults."

"They gave me strength," Beaumains replies. "So think what your support will do."

"You will need all your courage."

"Will you tell me your name?"

"You have proved yourself, and so I will tell you. I am Lynette. My sister, imprisoned by the Knight of the Red Lands, is Lady Lyonesse."

Lynette and Beaumains and his dwarf, Huon, are riding side by side through a pine forest. The bed of needles is springy under their horses' hooves. Soon they emerge onto a bright plain, and not far ahead is a beautiful small castle with strapping horse-chestnut trees and rings of mature oaks. Hundreds of men are camped beneath the castle walls. Smoke is rising from their campfires.

"What's hanging from those trees?" Beaumains asks.

"What you fear," Lynette quietly replies.

Beaumains is horrified. He sees fully armed knights hanging by the neck from the lower branches of many of the trees. Their shields are slung over their shoulders. Their swords and gold spurs are hanging from their heels.

"This is Castle Perilous, my sister's castle," Lynette says, "and each of these men tried to rescue her from the Knight of the Red Lands."

For a while Beaumains stares at the grove of corpses. And now he counts them.

"Thirty-nine," he says.

"And you'll be the next," says Lynette, "unless you're stronger than they are."

Now Beaumains sees a huge horn, made from the tusk of an elephant, hanging from a sycamore tree.

"Don't touch it!" cries Lynette. "Throughout the morning, the Knight of the Red Lands grows stronger, and at noon he'll have the strength of seven men."

"I'm not going to wait," says Beaumains. "I can overcome him, however strong he is."

Beaumains raises the horn and blows it, and at once many knights and squires hurry out of tents, and up in the castle, white faces are framed in the little windows, eyes watch through dark arrow slits.

"There!" says Lynette, pointing to a high window.

Beaumains looks up and sees a lady dressed in white.

"Lady Lyonesse," says Lynette.

"In her name I will fight," Beaumains shouts. "I will rescue her!"

As if she has heard Beaumains's vow, Lady Lyonesse curtsies to him.

Now Beaumains hears the thumping of hooves. A knight rides right up to him.

"You can stop looking at her!" the knight bawls. "Look at me!"

The knight's armor is bloodred. His shield is red and his sword is red. And his horse is wearing boiled leather covered with scarlet cloth.

"My sister has no love for you," Lynette says.

"You cannot force her to love you," says Beaumains.

"I can force your words back into your mouth," replies the Red Knight. "And these hanged men are my witnesses."

"You disgrace each man who calls himself a knight," Beaumains says.

"Have you finished?" asks the Red Knight, and he bares his teeth.

The two knights gallop towards each other, and I can hear metal squeaking and chirruping; leather groaning; the *crump-crump, crump-crump* of the horses' hooves. They drive their lances right into the middle of the other's shield: The two horses collide and their saddle straps snap, and the two knights are jolted over their horses' necks.

Slowly Beaumains stirs. He sits up, and the Red Knight gets to his knees. Now each man helps the other to his feet and draws his sword.

They cut and carve and chop until they're both completely out of breath. Beaumains's right arm is naked and the Red Knight's neck and left shoulder are naked. Their thighs and knees are unguarded. They stand facing each other, trembling and tottering.

All morning they fight. The Red Knight is as strong as seven men, and Beaumains matches him. They fight all afternoon. Wearily the Red Knight tries to shake the stars out of his head. Beaumains closes his eyes and he can scarcely open them again.

And now, without a word, the two knights sit down side by side.

Maybe it's the chill wind, or the cold water that squires bring to them, or maybe it's their own deep wells — but before long, both look revived, and Beaumains glances up.

Lady Lyonesse is still there, far-off and white and waiting. And when she sees Beaumains, she raises both arms and leans forward smiling: She reaches right out of the dark frame.

The sight of her gives Beaumains new strength. He swipes, he hacks, he slashes, until at last the Red Knight's fingers loosen and his sword falls from his hand.

At once Beaumains swings his sword like a scythe and cracks the Red Knight on the side of his neck. The Red Knight collapses, and Beaumains pinions him and unstraps his helmet.

"Mercy!" mutters the Red Knight.

"Why?" barks Beaumains. "You showed none to these hanging knights."

He looks at the ring of knights and squires surrounding him.

"This Red Knight deserves to die," he says, "but I will spare him. He must lift this siege of Castle Perilous at once and release Lady Lyonesse. She does not love him, and he does not deserve her love. Then he must ride to King Arthur's court and submit to the king's will." Beaumains glares down at the Red Knight.

"I swear to do all this," the Red Knight croaks.

There was a clatter in my little room. I leaped up at once, ready for whatever was coming through the door. But it was only my tile, which had slipped from the place where I'd propped it up.

My seeing stone didn't wait for me, though. By the time I looked into it again, Beaumains had been unarmed and his wounds dressed. He was outside the castle's lowered portcullis, looking in, and Lady Lyonesse was on the other side, standing in the shadows.

"I thought I had won your love with my blood," Beaumains says. "Almost all the blood in my body."

"You cannot buy love any more than you can demand it," Lady Lyonesse says. "Be patient! I know the dangers you have faced for me."

"Then why is your portcullis closed?" Beaumains growls. "I deserve better."

"Come back in twelve months," Lady Lyonesse says softly. "Trust me. I will wait for you."

Beaumains mounts his horse, and he and his dwarf, Huon, plod away from Castle Perilous. He is bone-weary. Heart-weary. After a while, they come to a lake, and Beaumains dismounts and lays his head on his shield. Half the night he lies wallowing and writhing.

Just before dawn, Beaumains does fall asleep at last. At once a dark shape steals up to Huon, clamps a hand over his mouth, picks him up, squealing and kicking, and lopes away.

As soon as my stone fills up with light again, I can see Huon standing in a small room with a knight in black, Lady Lyonesse, and her sister Lynette.

"Where am I?" Huon demands.

"In my castle," replies the black knight.

"Who are you?"

"He's my brother, Gringamour," Lady Lyonesse tells Huon. "I asked him to capture you. We'll let you go if you answer my questions."

"What questions?" Huon repeats.

"Where was your master born?" Lyonesse asks. "Who is his father? His mother? What is his real name?"

Huon grins. "Is that all?" he says. "I'll tell you the truth. My master was born in Orkney. He's the son of a king and queen."

"I knew it," says Lyonesse.

"The son of King Lot and Queen Morgause. His name is Gareth. Now let me go."

"All in good time," says Lyonesse.

"When he finds out you've captured me," Huon says, rolling his eyes, "he'll tear this castle to pieces."

"Who are you to threaten me?" Sir Gringamour asks.

Huon wails, but Lady Lyonesse, Lynette, and Sir Gringamour turn their backs and lock the door behind them.

"Huon was telling us the truth about who his master is," Lynette tells her sister. "I called Sir Gareth by every stinking name I know, but he never once answered me back. He's the most patient, well-bred man I've ever met."

While they're at dinner, the three of them are interrupted by a terrible racket — a knight shouting and smacking his shield against the wall right under the hall window.

"You thief!" he yells. "Give me back my servant, Huon, or I'll tear this castle to pieces."

Sir Gringamour leans out of the window. "Learn some manners, Gareth!" he shouts. "We're eating dinner."

"No," says Lady Lyonesse. "Let Gareth have Huon. And I . . . I will have Gareth."

Lynette claps her hands and laughs.

"I love him and I long to talk to him," Lady Lyonesse says, "but he mustn't know who I am."

"I will bring Sir Gareth here, then," Gringamour says, "and I'll set Huon free."

"He has seen me only at a distance," Lyonesse says to her sister, "and then only in shadow, through a portcullis. I'll wear my cornflower dress and my silver-green wimple, and he won't recognize me."

As soon as Sir Gareth sets eyes on Lyonesse, he feels flushed; and each time she smiles at him or speaks to him, his blood begins to seethe.

"Jesus, son of Mary," he says to himself, "I've never seen such a woman. If only Lady Lyonesse were as beautiful as she is."

All evening Sir Gareth and Sir Gringamour and Lady Lyonesse and Lynette, talk and play drafts. They play chess and sing and dance.

"Dear God!" whispers Gareth, "I've no appetite. My mouth has gone all dry. If she looks at me like that one more time, I'll go mad."

Lady Lyonesse turns to Sir Gringamour, and he smiles and nods. And now she comes and sits beside Gareth. She pulls away her wimple, and her long dark hair waterfalls down her back.

"Do you recognize me?" she asks softly.

"I dare not," Beaumains says, never for one moment taking his eyes off her.

"Who dares, wins," says Lyonesse, and her voice is trembling. She slips both her hands inside Beaumains's large right hand.

"Lyonesse!" cries Beaumains. "Lady of Castle Perilous."

"I love you for what you have done," Lyonesse says. "I love you for who you are."

"Lady," says Gareth in a hushed voice, "I will love you for as long as I've breath in my body."

"Your kitchen knight!" says Lynette, laughing and crying. "King Arthur's own nephew."

"We must go to court," Gareth says, "and ask King Arthur's permission to marry. He will feel the force of our love."

Lyonesse gazes at Gareth. She takes his large hands between her own.

"In the morning," she says quietly.

at the crossing-places

"LOST AND FOUND," SAID A DARK, DEEP VOICE.

"Merlin!" I cried. "I was just thinking about you."

"Ah!" said Merlin.

"Can you fly into people's thoughts?"

Merlin smiled gently. "You think I can do anything," he said.

Merlin does know magic. Last Christmas he jumped forty-seven feet when we had our leaping contest. I saw him do that with my own eyes. "The salmon-leap," he called it. Joan and Brian said they saw him flying on New Year's Eve, and once he just disappeared while we were on top of Tumber Hill.

Not only this. Merlin gave me the seeing stone. And he's the hooded man inside it who told the earls, lords, and knights that Arthur-in-the-stone is the trueborn king of all Britain.

Merlin gazed at me. "Well?" he asked.

"What I was thinking was that, since the day Arthur-in-the-stone was crowned, you've always been at his side. What kind of king would Arthur be without you?"

Merlin closed his eyes. "There comes a time," he said in a melancholy voice.

"Oh Merlin!" I cried. "I'm so pleased to see you." With both hands I grasped his cloak — the same old one he always wears, earth-brown with grey patches. "I haven't seen anyone from Caldicot. Not since January. Not for four months."

"I saw Gatty yesterday," Merlin said. "I told her I would see you."

"What did she say?"

"Say? What did you expect her to say?"

"I don't know," I mumbled. "Something."

"Mmm!" Merlin murmured. "When something's too deep for saying, is it worth saying anything?"

"I haven't seen her for so long," I said. "Gatty walked all the way here, you know, and she slept up a tree. What are you doing here at Holt?"

Merlin stared at me solemnly, and then he opened the palms of his hands. "I'm passing," he said.

Merlin is nothing like so good at telling as asking. He's like a deep well: If you stop winding the handle, the water doesn't come up! But, sitting in the sunlight, on the same flat rock where Rowena and Izzie chanted their love spells, I did find out that Nain has lost her only tooth, and Sian thinks she saw Spitfire in the hay barn, though she can't have done, and Lankin's wrist wound is healing. Merlin told me Joan will have to appear in front of Lord Stephen again at the next manor court, this time for not working on my father's land for an extra day, and he said Howell and Ruth were married in March, and Oliver still means to take me to Wenlock Priory to see how the monks paint their manuscripts.

"Oliver told me your mother was a nun," I said. "And your father — he said . . . he said he was a demon."

Merlin sighed and edged one toe into the water. "Is that what you think?" he asked.

"He told me terrible things about you."

"Because he's afraid of me," Merlin replied.

"The more I know about you the less I know about you," I said.

After all this, Merlin finally told me the most important news of all. Last week — last Wednesday, on the ninth day of the month — Tanwen gave birth to a baby son.

Tanwen's son. Serle's son. Illegitimate.

But he won't be given away and he won't be lied to. He won't be unwanted. He will know who his own mother is and have her love.

"Will they stay at Caldicot?" I asked Merlin.

"I don't suppose Sir John will force her to leave," Merlin replied. "Is that what you mean?"

"Serle thought he would," I said.

"Now, Arthur," said Merlin. "What about you?"

"You remember we talked about crossing-places," I said, "and you told me they're never quite sure of themselves? Fords and bridges and foreshore. The place where England ends and Wales begins. Midnight and New Year's Eve. You said they're places and times where changes can happen."

"Did I?" said Merlin, looking rather pleased.

"And in my seeing stone, I heard you tell King Uther that his newborn son was a child of the crossing-places."

"Really!" murmured Merlin, closing his eyes.

"Merlin!" I cried. "I'm between my child-self and my man-self.

My squire-self and knight-self. Between Caldicot and Gortanore . . .
Between my life here and the world of the stone."

Merlin stared into the dark water. It seemed scarcely to be
moving, though it was running fast. It looked like a mirror,
slateshine, the same as Merlin's eyes.

"I'm at the crossing-places," I said.

"On a quest," Merlin replied, "is there anywhere else to be?"

55

TRAITORS

FTER MERLIN LEFT, I WISHED SO MUCH I COULD SEE
everyone at Caldicot.

I wished I could go walking up the Little Lark
with Gatty, and listen to Nain tell us all a story, and
play the Saxon-and-Viking game with Sian. I even wished I could
see Serle.

I thought I'd have found out much more about my mother
by now.

I wish I had a home. A real home.

When Haket dismissed me from my lesson this afternoon,
I saw Rowena wandering down the far side of the churchyard.
She pretended not to see me, and I'm sure she was waiting to
see Haket. But why? Rowena's afraid of him, I can see that, but
I still haven't managed to find out what's going on between
them.

It was raining quite steadily, and there was no one in the hall,
so I came up to my room. I unwrapped my obsidian, and at once I
saw Merlin talking to Arthur-in-the-stone.

"Wherever you go, take Excalibur with you," he says. "Wear it
by day and wear it when you sleep — the sword and the scabbard.
The day will come when a woman you trust with your life will try
to steal it from you."

Now King Arthur leaves Camelot and goes out hunting with Sir Accolon and Sir Urien, the husband of his sister Morgan. It's getting dark as they come to a lake and see a barge moored to the bank. From bow to stern, its gunwales are draped with colored silks.

As soon as they step aboard, one hundred flaming torches light themselves. Then twelve beautiful young women step forward and lead them to a table covered with white linen.

They eat, they drink, they yawn, and the young women conduct them to their beds. . . .

But now! Now Sir Accolon and Sir Urien have disappeared, I don't know where, and Arthur-in-the-stone is sitting on the floor in a gloomy prison cell with twenty other knights. He's not wearing his sword.

"Some of us have been here for seven years," one knight says. "Some even longer."

"On account of Sir Damas."

"That piece of scum."

"He won't allow his own brother, Ontzlake, his share of the inheritance — his own manor."

"Ontzlake has challenged him."

"And Damas has refused to fight. Unless someone will fight on his behalf."

"Who'd fight for him?"

"No one here."

"And that's why Damas won't let us go."

"On condition that I get my sword and scabbard back, and Sir

Damas releases you all," the king calls out, "I will fight on behalf of Sir Damas."

Now the scene in my seeing stone is changing again. First it fades, then somehow breaks into dozens, hundreds, of tiny colored pieces dancing a jig, like the spots of sunlight under our copper beech. And now they all come together again.

Sir Accolon is sitting beside a wall, and a dwarf walks up to him, holding a sword as long as he is tall.

"Your lover, Morgan le Fay, greets you," says the dwarf. "She says you'll have to fight against a knight tomorrow morning, and so she's sending you Excalibur, King Arthur's sword. You're to show no mercy. She wants to see that knight's severed head."

"So!" says Sir Accolon. "The barge, the torches, and the young women were all her doing?"

"Of course," says the dwarf. Then he bows and leaves. At once a knight on crutches swings towards Sir Accolon.

"Sir Ontzlake," says Accolon, "last night you gave me lodging when I was lost. Let me repay you."

"I can't fight," says Ontzlake, "not until these thigh wounds heal, and tomorrow I must honor my challenge to my brother, Sir Damas."

Sir Accolon grasps Excalibur. "I will fight for you," he says.

The very moment Accolon says this, the scene in my stone changes again, and I can see Arthur-in-the-stone standing outside Sir Damas's castle, surrounded by the twenty prisoner-knights. Some are whey-faced, some haggard, and they reel around in the light. "Freedom!" they shout. "Freedom! Freedom!"

A young woman rides up and hands the king a sword. "Your own loving sister Morgan le Fay owns the barge you boarded last night. While you slept, she looked after your sword."

Arthur-in-the-stone inspects the sword and scabbard. He is in terrible danger.

Many people are gathering outside Sir Damas's castle. Among them I can see Merlin's apprentice, dark-eyed Nimue, whom the king favored by knighting her foster son, Lancelot.

Before long, Sir Accolon rides up, and neither he nor Arthur-in-the-stone recognize each other. Three times they splinter their lances without unseating each other. But when they gallop for the fourth time, they each ram their lance into the center of the other's shield. They're both jolted backwards and hit the ground with a terrible clatter.

As soon as they cross swords, Arthur knows something is wrong. His sword looks and feels like Excalibur; but its edge only grazes Accolon's gauntlet, while Accolon's shears right through the king's mail-shirt. His rib cage is gashed.

Like a wild boar or a stag at bay, Arthur-in-the-stone launches himself at Accolon. He smashes his sword into the side of Accolon's helmet, and the sword snaps. It breaks off at the crossguards, and the king is left holding the pommel in his right hand.

Furious, Accolon glares at King Arthur through the slit of his helmet. "You won't last long," he gloats. "Submit!"

"Never!" the king says. "I'd rather die with honor than live in shame."

With his shield he pushes Accolon back three steps and boxes his left ear-guard with his steel pommel.

 210

Accolon bares his teeth and grins. He whirls his sword so fast it looks like a silver halo, and then his grasp loosens. Excalibur flies out of his right hand.

Nimue smiles, tight-lipped. Around her everyone is shouting and waving, but she is intent. This is all her doing. I can feel her power. She takes a deep breath and flexes her fingers, then locks them inside her left fist.

Accolon and the king lurch after the sword, and the king gets to it first. Excalibur!

One stroke's enough! He smacks Accolon's helmet and Accolon topples over sideways.

"No," says Accolon in a husky voice. "I will not submit."

"Who are you?" Arthur demands. "Tell me here and now or I'll cut your throat."

"Accolon. Accolon of Gaul. I am a knight of King Arthur's Round Table."

"Who gave you this sword, then?" the king asks in a low voice.

"Morgan le Fay," replies Accolon. "She lent it to me so I can fight the man she most hates — her own brother, King Arthur."

"Why does she hate him?"

"She's jealous of him: his power. The loyalty he inspires. She's promised me that if I kill him, she'll do away with her husband, Urien, and marry me. She says we'll rule together. She says I'll be king of Britain."

"So you are ready to kill your own king," Arthur says.

Accolon stares up at Arthur-in-the-stone through his helmet-slit; his eyes are misty. "I am dying," he says in a faraway voice. "Who are you? What court? What is your name?"

"Accolon . . . I am Arthur. Your king."

"Dear God!" cries Accolon, and he struggles to sit up, but he's too weak. "My king! Have mercy on me!"

"Mercy?" the king says. "Yes, I'll forgive you for fighting and wounding me, because I can see you didn't know who I was. But you agreed to kill me. You are a traitor."

"Mercy!" croaks Accolon, and then he begins to choke.

"You are nothing but Morgan's puppet. You're under her spell, just as I was when she stole my sword." Arthur's voice rises in anger and sorrow. "Morgan!" he cries. "Morgan! I have loved you. I would have trusted you with my life."

Around them crowd all the knights and ladies and people who work on Sir Damas's manor. The king has lost so much blood that he's light-headed; he totters around like a drunkard.

"Sir Damas," he says, "you're not worthy to be called a knight. Give Ontzlake the manor that is already his. If a single man in my kingdom comes to me complaining of you, I will have you put to death. But you," says King Arthur, and he leans on Sir Ontzlake's shoulder, "I hope you will come to court. There'll be a place for you at the Round Table."

"I swear to serve you," Sir Ontzlake says. "And yet I would have fought you, but for these wounds."

"I wish you had," the king replies. "My wounds would not have been so grievous. Morgan, my own sister, stole my sword. She used my own power against me."

Beside the king, Sir Accolon sighs. His eyelids flutter and settle. Very lightly, he crosses the bridge from life to death.

"Lay him out on his shield," Arthur tells Sir Ontzlake, "and have him carried to my sister. Tell her I'm sending him as a gift. Tell her I have Excalibur and my scabbard."

The king closes his eyes. He's giddy, twisting in air. "Take me to an abbey," he says, "where nuns can search my wounds with leeches — a peaceful place where I can rest and recover."

56

STOLEN

S HE HERE?" MORGAN ASKS. "MY BROTHER?"

"He's sleeping at last," a nun says. "I'll take you to him."

"You can leave me with him."

"But . . ."

"I'll sit beside him until he wakes."

King Arthur is holding Excalibur in his right hand, but his scabbard is lying on the floor beside the bed. Morgan looks at him. Her dark eyes are on fire. Now she stoops, quietly picks up the scabbard, and steals out of his room, silent as the first soft rain.

But we can sense things even when we're asleep, and wake already knowing.

"She's your own sister," a nun explains, "and none of us here dared to disobey her. She said she'd sit beside you."

The king's wounds are still seeping water and blood, his bones are aching. But he rides after Morgan.

Between boulders, hunched over a rocky lake, Morgan reins in and brandishes the scabbard.

"Arthur will never see this again," she shouts, and she heaves the scabbard into the lifeless water. Its gold casing, inlaid with emeralds and rubies, is so heavy that it sinks at once.

When the king rides up to the lake, he reins in as if he can sense that his scabbard is hidden in its dark heart. The rocks and boulders cluster around him, as if they want to squeeze the life out of him.

And one strange, rearing boulder seems to be staring at him and scowling: more rock than woman and palfrey. More heartless than rock.

A SONG WITHOUT
A VOICE

RACE IS WRONG. BOYS ARE NOT AS DIFFERENT FROM girls as she supposes. It's not true that I think love is just a cruel sport like hart hunting or hare hunting. I have strong feelings too.

When I had my second singing lesson with Rahere, he taught me a riddle-song about a cherry without a stone and a dove without a bone and a rosebush without flower or leaf. I've changed all the words into a kind of reply to the poem Grace told me just before I left Gortanore, and I'm going to write it out onto a new piece of parchment. The next time Simon rides over to Gortanore, he can give it to her:

> I have a half sister
> Who lives at Gortanore,
> And the little I give her
> She can make more.
>
> I'll send her a song
> Without a voice,
> And send her a lover
> With no face.

I'll send her a name
Lacking a squire,
I'll send my half sister
Hope and fear and fire.

How can there be a song
Without a voice?
And how can a lover
Have no face?

How can a name
Lack a squire?
Why send your half sister
Hope and fear and fire?

When a song is unheard
It has no voice,
And when a lover is ignored
He has no face.

A name lacks a squire
Until he knows his quest.
Hope and fear and fire, Grace:
They're beating in my chest.

58

BURNED ALIVE

ORGAN IS SO ANGRY AT SIR ACCOLON'S DEATH THAT
she wants to kill King Arthur.

"Your sister Morgan has sent me here to
Camelot," the young woman tells the king. "She
begs you to forgive her, and promises to give you back your scabbard. With love, Morgan sends you this cloak."

Its color is very strange. It is pearly and silver-grey, like an oyster. You think you can see through it, but you can't. And embedded in it are hundreds of tiny, winking orange seeds.

"She had it made for you," the young woman says.

Sir Ontzlake is standing quite close to the king. "Sire," he asks, "can you trust her?"

"I'll ask Merlin."

"He's not here," says Nimue. "But we'll soon find out. Let this young lady try the cloak on first."

"I won't do that," the young woman says quickly.

"Why not?" asks Arthur.

"I can't wear a cloak made for my king."

"You may," Arthur tells her.

"No!" protests the young woman.

"Put it on her, then!" the king instructs Sir Ontzlake.

At once the tiny winking seeds burst into leaping orange flames. The young woman screams: But the more she struggles, the tighter the cloak becomes. She is burned alive.

I screwed up my eyes and turned my stone over. I buried it in its saffron wrapping.

59

Degrees of Magic

HAVE BEEN THINKING ABOUT MAGIC.

The first degree isn't really magic at all. It's conjuring —the kind of tricks people do at Ludlow Fair — and conjuring is trickery.

Merlin told me once that many things seem miraculous until we understand them, and that's true of the second degree of magic. Herbs can heal us, provided we pick them on the right days, and drugs can change the way we look. But until we know their properties and powers, they seem magical.

The third degree is when a person concentrates and finds a force inside himself or within an object, and releases it.

This is what happened when Arthur-in-the-stone pulled the sword from the stone. He stared at the sword — he stared into the sword — until nothing else in the world existed. There was no room for doubt or disbelief.

I think it's like this with my seeing stone too. Sometimes when I look into it, it shows me nothing, because my mind and heart are already too busy. To see anything in it, I have to come somehow empty and ready.

Some people use words and sounds when they practice the third degree. When Merlin told Sir John he knew a charm to make second sons vanish, I think he was just teasing me. And I doubt whether it can be true, as Nain claims, that there are words that can swallow sound. All the same, I know some words are magical. Charms and prayers, maybe: the way they sound.

If words can be used to help and to heal, they must also be able to hurt. There's no good without evil, not since Adam and Eve ran howling out of Eden. Haket says God allows evil to enable each of us to win clear drops of virtue from it.

And then there's the fourth degree: God's magic. When Jesus fed a whole crowd with five loaves and two fishes . . . and when He raised Lazarus . . .

"How dare you?" Oliver shouted at Merlin once. "You heretic! How dare you call the Christian mysteries magic? Do I have to explain them?"

"You can explain them?" says Merlin, smiling.

Oliver puffed himself up. "And it's high time you listened," he said.

"Divine magic surpasses human understanding," Merlin said. "Even yours, Oliver."

"Get away from me!" exclaimed Oliver, waving his pudgy hands. "You poisonous loaf!"

"If you can explain divine magic," Merlin said, "you're really saying God is so small that He can fit inside your brain."

I wish Merlin were still here, so I could discuss all this with him.

60

MERLIN, ROCKFAST

CAN HEAR PEOPLE GATHERING DOWN IN THE COURTYARD, although the sun's not yet up. First the quiet river of voices. Someone coughing. Robert's chuckle now, like water pouring over a weir. I'd recognize that anywhere. I can hear Haket. The haymaker's prayer. The same words Oliver always says on this first day of June.

So with our magic words we wake and quicken the year. We say it green and sing it ripe. And Lord Stephen and I will be able to take the Cross at last.

But Merlin has gone. In my stone he has gone. He was always at the king's side, strange and familiar, and now he is not.

"If you know what is going to happen," Arthur-in-the-stone says to Merlin, "stop it from happening. You know magic?"

Merlin blinks. "I cannot," he says.

The king stares at Merlin.

He is Arthur's cornerstone.

Because of him, Arthur is king.

"Not because of me," Merlin says. "Because of who you are." Gently he smiles. "But Arthur!" he says. "What kind of king?"

"Will I see you again?" Arthur says.

Merlin bows to the king slowly and deeply. He takes Nimue's hand, and leads her down the length of the hall — away, out of sight.

My seeing stone follows them. Merlin is watching Nimue. He can scarcely stop himself from touching her.

"Teach me," says Nimue. Her voice is as eager and clean as wind over the hill.

One by one Merlin teaches her his magic skills. He is besotted. Blind. Or worse — not blind, but unwilling to save himself.

And day by day Nimue wearies of Merlin's attentions. She's half-stifled by his infatuation. She makes him swear not to give her a drug or put her under any kind of spell. She keeps wondering how to get rid of him.

Merlin and Nimue are walking towards a hill. It's almost the same shape as Tumber Hill — the steep rise, the level ridge. At the bottom there's a massive rock: larger than Haket's church — as large as a cathedral.

"It is more than it is," the magician murmurs.

"More than it is?" Nimue asks.

Merlin closes his eyes:

> "The head of the wonder
> Is the cave of making
> Under the grey rock
> And green hill, quaking."

"What do you mean?" cries Nimue. "What wonder?"

"Time cannot touch it," Merlin says,

"I dare not!" Nimue cries. "You go in. You tell me."

Merlin looks at Nimue.

He knows.

He cradles his head between his hands. He voices the magic sounds. He opens the dark passage and walks in under the rock.

At once Nimue clenches her fists white. Sound by sound, syllable by syllable, she repeats what she has just heard. She turns Merlin's own magic against him.

He is helpless. Bated. He is unmade. Merlin is trapped under the grey cathedral rock.

GOD'S GRISTLE!

R WRESTLING MATCHES," LORD STEPHEN DICTATED. "Wrestling matches. Have you got that?"

"Yes, sir," said Miles.

"Our shepherd of Caldicot is a good wrestler," I said.

Lord Stephen glared at me. "We can't both talk at the same time," he said. "Where was I, Miles?"

"No shepherd is to leave his fold after nightfall, or to go to fairs, markets, or wrestling matches . . ."

". . . markets or wrestling matches," Lord Stephen repeated, "without asking his lord's permission and ensuring that another dependable man will look after his flock for him. Otherwise it is his fault. . . . Have you got that?"

"Yes, sir," said Miles.

"Now then. I want to say something about markings. I'm going to stamp out all the sheep stealing and cattle rustling in this part of the March."

There was a knock at the solar door.

"Teeth!" exclaimed Lord Stephen. "We came in here to get some peace."

"I'm sorry to bother you, sir," said Simon. "Daw has ridden over from Verdon."

"Daw?" I repeated.

"Sir Walter's messenger," Simon replied.

"That's not a name."

"It is," said Miles. "*D, a, w.* Short for 'David.'"

"Manners!" said Lord Stephen sharply. "I'll see Daw later."

"He wants to see Arthur as well, sir."

Lord Stephen clicked his tongue and sighed noisily. "All right! Show him in."

Daw brought exciting news. Sir Walter and Lady Anne have invited me to visit Verdon for the midsummer solstice, provided it won't inconvenience Lord Stephen.

"You'd like to go, I suppose," Lord Stephen said, plucking his lower lip.

"I would," I said, "But not if —"

"Yes, yes," said Lord Stephen. "Well! You've been working hard here, haven't you?" Lord Stephen turned to Daw. "Petition approved," he said. "Arthur will ride over on the day before Midsummer Eve."

No sooner had Daw left the solar than there was another knock on the door.

"God's gristle!" complained Lord Stephen.

"I'm very sorry, sir," Simon said, "but another messenger's come in. From Champagne."

"Champagne!" exclaimed Lord Stephen, standing up. "From Milon, it must be. It's no use, Miles. We'll have to try again later." Lord Stephen turned to me. "You'd better stay here," he said. "News of our crusade!"

"Who is Milon, sir?"

"Milon de Provins," Lord Stephen replied. "One of the great men of Champagne. His father was the marshal, and Milon was one of the very first to take the Cross. When the friar Fulk preached the crusade here last December —"

"I remember him," I said eagerly. "He kept punching the pulpit. 'Drive out and kill the Turks!' he shouted. 'Recapture Jerusalem!' Half the people in church were weeping."

Lord Stephen blinked at me several times. "As I was saying, when Fulk came over from Neuilly, Milon de Provins came with him. He stayed here with us. First with us and then with the earl of Chester."

"Was it Milon who persuaded you, sir?"

"I persuaded myself," Lord Stephen said.

Milon's messenger spoke little English, so he and Lord Stephen used French.

"We're invited to Champagne," Lord Stephen announced. "Milon has invited us so that we can meet Count Thibaud. He's leading the crusade. And we'll be meeting many other crusaders as well. . . ."

While Lord Stephen and Milon's messenger were still talking, Simon knocked on the solar door for the third time. This time he just smiled mournfully.

"Who it is now?" Lord Stephen asked. "Saint Gabriel himself?"

"A messenger from the king, sir," said Simon.

"I see," said Lord Stephen. "Well! You'd better send him in. I'll talk with Milon's messenger again before supper."

As soon as the king's messenger walked in, I recognized him. He was the man who insulted Sir John, and complained about our food, and cursed half the night, and had to run out to the latrine five times.

"Not you again!" he said to me. "What are you doing here?"

Lord Stephen cleared his throat.

"I beg your pardon," the messenger said, and in his right hand he raised his red wax disk, stamped with a mounted knight brandishing a sword.

"What's your message?" Lord Stephen asked rather testily. "Nothing good, I suppose."

"King John greets his loyal earls, lords, and knights who are the strength and health of his kingdom, and brings you news of peace. He has made peace with Philip, king of France, and they have signed a treaty at Le Goulet. King Philip recognizes King John's right to all the lands his father and brother held in Normandy and Maine, Anjou, and Touraine and in the south."

"And in return?" asks Lord Stephen.

"King John acknowledges Philip as his overlord. He agrees to pay Philip a duty of twenty thousand marks."

"I see," said Lord Stephen, pursing his lips. "So the lands King Henry and Coeur-de-Lion held for free, our new king has to pay for. Or rather, we have to pay for."

"It's the price of peace," the messenger replied.

"It's the cost of weakness," Lord Stephen said. "And it's going to hurt every man, woman, and child in England."

I don't like the king's messenger. He looks down his nose at us here on the March, as if we were all half-wild. And he smells sour.

When I told Rahere about his visit to Caldicot, and then about the new tax and how it will hurt everyone, he raised his pipe, the large one, and made it fart loudly.

First Rahere looked at me with his blue, then with his green eye.

"Five times, was it?" he said, grinning.

"Six, actually," I said. "He got caught short again the next morning."

"Well, then," said Rahere, "we'd better introduce him to our latrine."

As soon as it grew dark, Rahere and I left the hall and hurried out across the courtyard. We grasped the wooden frame of the latrine and dragged it back three steps behind the stinking pit.

Rahere burbled with laughter. "The horrible, hairy hellhole of Holt!" he exclaimed. "The huge, hungry, humming stinkhorn."

Sure enough, in the middle of the night, the messenger woke us all up with his groaning and cursing. First he kept doubling up, then he hurried out of the hall. Rahere and I followed him.

It was so dark, and he was in such haste, that the messenger never saw the pit. He went in right up to his neck, and Rahere and I let him splash for a while before we fished him out. By the time he had squelched down to the river, cursing, the messenger had roused all the dogs and geese. And after he'd hammered at the locked door and yelled at us all, absolutely everyone was awake, even Lord Stephen and Lady Judith.

When Rahere came out of the solar this morning, he pretended to fall into my arms. "Sshh . . ." he murmured. "Sshh . . . IT!"

Lord Stephen was just as angry with me. "How dare you treat any visitor like that?" he demanded. "You're my squire, aren't you? Aren't you?"

"Yes, sir."

"Yes, and today's Saint Blandina's Day."

"Sir?"

"Just a little slave girl. The Romans tied her in a net and threw her to a raging bull. Then they tortured her, but all she would say was, 'I am a Christian, and we do nothing vile.' Nothing vile! Is that true of you, Arthur?"

"No, sir."

"No, it is not. I've a good mind not to let you go to Verdon."

I had to apologize to the messenger, but my only real regret is that I've made Lord Stephen so angry.

A soft, sweet, hay-thick wind has put its mouth to my window, and a lark keeps lacing me with his glittering song. But this room's chill, and I have to stay here all day.

Down in the courtyard, poor Rahere is mucking out the latrine. That's the worst job of all.

there comes a time

HILE I WAS IMPRISONED FOR THE WHOLE DAY IN MY room, I thought about Merlin.

When he came here last week, he seemed more melancholy than usual. And when I asked him what kind of king Arthur-in-the-stone would be without his advice, all he said was, "There comes a time."

What did he mean?

Did he mean there comes a time when each of us has to make his own choices and decisions? Or that each human being comes to an end of his time on earth?

In my stone, Nimue has trapped Merlin inside the rock, but surely that doesn't mean anything has happened to Merlin of Caldicot.

Why did Merlin come to see me, though? I keep thinking of the things he said:

"When something's too deep for saying . . ."

"I'm passing. . . ."

And all the things about crossing-places . . .

Has Merlin come to his own crossing-place?

There's only one way I can find out. I'll ask Lord Stephen whether Simon can ride over to Caldicot with some questions for Merlin, and tell him it's urgent. I've been here almost five months and never asked him a favor before.

the GolD RiNG

T FITS MY FOURTH FINGER. BUT I CAN'T WEAR IT. IT'S LIKE my seeing stone: No one must know about it.

While I was out in South Yard with Turold, practicing at the pel, Thomas galloped in from Gortanore with a message for Lord Stephen. When I went up to the hall, Thomas was still there, on his own.

He peered at me sideways. "I've got something for you."

"What?"

"Where can we —"

"Up in my room," I said. "No one comes up there."

Thomas kept clucking all the way up the stone steps. By the time we got to the top, he was breathing heavily. He sat down on the floor and started to unlace his right boot.

"Only way to be sure," he said.

Then Thomas reached inside the toe and pulled out a little screw of cotton, mouse-grey.

"Open it!" he said.

Inside the grey cotton was a wrapping of cream silk, soft and floppy as the mutton-fat soap Lady Helen makes. And inside the cream silk was a gold ring.

The top of the ring is almost square and flat, and engraved with a tiny portrait of baby Jesus in His mother's arms. She's holding Him so safe that black storms could shout and the earth itself could shake and He would still be all right. Jesus is reaching out toward His mother, I think He's giving her something, and she looks so patient and tender, so motherly.

I stared at Thomas.

"Your mother's," he said.

"My mother's!"

"It was hers."

"My mother's!"

"Maggot's looked after it. Kept it safe for you."

I turned the ring over and over. I closed my palm and squeezed it, and quickly it warmed to the heat of my own blood, as the best gold does.

"You want to find her —" Thomas said.

"You know her?" I asked breathlessly.

"I didn't say that," muttered Thomas. And twice he jerked his head from side to side. "The ring's for you. And if you do want to find her — well, we can help you, maybe. No promises, mind." Thomas smiled, sharp as a knife's edge. "Don't tell no one," he said. "Understand?"

"I won't," I gulped.

Thomas shook his head fiercely and clucked. "If anyone finds out . . ."

My mother's ring! The first link in my search. I will find her. I know I will.

When I was born, my mother was living on Sir William's manor. So did he give it to her?

Thomas told me Maggot has looked after the ring. When did my mother give it to her? Is she sending me a message?

What are the questions I have to ask if I'm to win the true answers? Unending, warm, bright ring: What are you telling me?

the voice inside
the rock

IR CAN PULL A VOICE TO PIECES. ROCK CAN MAKE IT repeat itself and sound more and more hollow.

In my warm right hand I held my obsidian. So firm and four-cornered, its rough underside covered with little lumps and grooves and white pocks, its glossy face like the eye of a dark pond. I know exactly how my seeing stone looks, and yet I scarcely know it at all. Each time I look into it, it surprises me.

I can see the hill shaped like Tumber Hill. The rock-prison. A knight is riding toward it.

And now I hear the terrible noises inside the rock. Howling. Sobbing, dry sobbing. But which are the cries, and which are their echoes?

The knight reins in and listens very carefully. He's uncertain whether this is a rock with a voice, or whether someone — maybe more than one person — is trapped inside the rock.

Now the knight sees what could be a passageway, blocked by a massive boulder. But not even one hundred men could move that.

Stormy howling — wild sobbing. The knight backs away a little and stares up at the rock.

"Is there anyone there?" he shouts. And then: "Where are you?"

Are-you-are . . . ooo . . . The grey rock gives his own sounds back to the knight. And now the utter silence is as dismaying as all the cries were before.

"I am Bagdemagus," the knight calls out. "Is anyone there?"

"Merlin!" booms the voice inside the rock

A little swirl of wind picks up the word, giddies it, and whirls it up into the bright morning.

"Bagdemagus," booms the voice inside the rock. "You cannot help me. No one can help me except for the one who has trapped me."

That's true for Merlin, I know, because Nimue has trapped him with magic, but it's not true for me. I don't have to be helped by the people who have wounded me — Serle, Sir William. I can help myself. My own efforts can set me free.

Slowly Sir Bagdemagus rides away from the rock.

I have hidden my gold ring. It is under the short floorboard in this room, right next to my seeing stone.

65

ErEC AND ENID

ORD STEPHEN SAYS I CAN SEND A MESSAGE TO MERLIN when Simon next rides to Caldicot, but today he's gone to Ludlow and tomorrow he's riding to Gortanore.

"Is it about me, sir?" I asked.

"I don't know why you should think that," said Lord Stephen.

Lord Stephen has decided to let me go to Verdon after all. "We don't want to disappoint Winnie," he said with a half-smile. "You can ride over next Tuesday. Lady Judith will accompany you."

It is very strange. During my lesson today, I read Haket the Gospel chapter about the wedding feast in Cana, when Jesus turned six stone jars of water into good wine. And when I looked into my stone this evening, the first thing I saw was a bridegroom and bride leaving their wedding feast. What happens in my life and what happens inside the stone are often connected like sounds and echoes — or like my left and right eye, which overlap but can each see more than the other. What I see in the stone sometimes seems like a promise, sometimes like a warning.

The bridegroom is leading his beautiful young wife along in a narrow town street carpeted with reeds and rushes and fresh mint. Flowered silks are hanging out of all the upper windows. The wedding party is following a man holding high an orange banner. All the bell ringers are busy. . . .

Now I can see a bedroom. It's festooned with boughs of fruit trees — apple and pear and cherry and quince — but all the leaves are dry and curled, and although the sun's high in the sky and glaring fiercely at the bride and bridegroom through the leaded windowpanes, they're still lying on the bed. They're mother-naked!

The beautiful young woman stares at her sleeping husband. Tears are streaming down her cheeks. "Look what I've done to you," she whispers. "Have you forgotten you're a knight?" She wipes her eyes. "It's a disaster!"

The man suddenly sits up. "What's a disaster?" he asks.

"I didn't say anything."

"Enid! What's a disaster?"

"You were dreaming. You imagined it."

"And these tears," says the young man, laying one forefinger gently under his wife's right eye. "Did I imagine them?"

Now Enid clings to her husband. "Erec," she sobs, "they're all laughing at you. Your friends. Your whole household. 'Soft, completely soft . . . a slugabed . . . not a shred of honor left . . .' I keep overhearing them," the young woman says. "They think I've stolen you and ensnared you. 'It's all her fault. She's a love-witch.'"

Erec leaps out of bed. "All right!" he says. "Get up! Get dressed! Put on your finest gown, the one Queen Guinevere gave you. Put on your purple riding cloak."

"Are you sending me away?" Enid asks timidly.

"Do as I say," Erec replies.

Now I can see Erec and Enid riding away down the narrow street that led them to their marriage bed. Erec is mounted on a Gascon bay and Enid on a dappled palfrey.

"They're putting us to the test," Erec tells Enid, "and we'll prove they're all wrong. We will ride together, but you must not help me. Whomsoever you see, and whatsoever you think is going to happen, you're not to say one word unless I speak to you first. Do you understand that?"

Enid takes Erec's hand and nods.

"Ride ahead of me!" Erec instructs his young wife. "You're not to turn round and look at me."

All at once, slapping their horses' necks and bawling, three mounted men spring from my stone. Out of an ash copse, they come careering down the track towards Erec and Enid.

Enid twists round in her saddle. "Erec!" she calls. "Erec!"

"No!" shouts Erec.

At once he spurs his bay and surges past Enid. He kills two of the robbers, each with a single stroke. The third he unhorses, and the man hits the ground with a horrible grunt.

"This once I'll forgive you," Erec tells his wife, "but you mustn't speak to me again."

The day deepens. Waves of dark clouds rush in from the west, in too much of a hurry to shed their rain, and Enid keeps glancing over her left shoulder.

"We're being followed," she says to herself. "I know we are. I must disobey him."

Enid reins in. "Forgive me!" she says very quietly.

"What now?"

"Shapes in the wood. Over there. We're being followed."

"Enid!" protests Erec. "Have you no respect for me? Not one ounce?"

Now five dark shadows turn themselves into five mounted men. Side by side four of them gallop towards Erec, and the fifth rams right into Enid's palfrey.

But Sir Erec is fully armed, while the mounted men are not. He whirls his sword around his head until it looks like ten swords, and the four men wheel away and escape into the dark woods. The fifth man throws himself on the ground and begs for mercy.

"You would have molested my wife," Erec shouts, "and now you won't even stand and fight."

In disgust, Erec turns his back on the groveling man. He rounds up his handsome horse, and he and Enid ride on.

The anxious moon rises and floats. The bleeding sun quickly sinks. Venus first, then Orion — and now, hundreds of stars, like all the tiny glittering crosses spangling Enid's beautiful dress.

Husband and wife slowly plod up to an old chestnut tree. They've been riding all day, and Enid is so tired she can scarcely sit upright in her saddle.

"We'll have to shelter here," Erec says. "You sleep, and I'll watch over you."

But Enid shakes her head. She gestures to Erec to lie down and tenderly lays her purple cloak over him. For a while she sits with her back to the twisted trunk and gazes at her sleeping husband. "Did I really doubt you?" she whispers to herself. "You've fought three robbers single-handed and killed them. You've driven off five men. How could I have doubted you?" Enid is so tired that only her strong will keeps her awake. "I'll obey you, Erec," she whispers, "but I'll have you need me. I'll have you need me even if you don't recognize it."

I'm not certain, but I think I must have fallen asleep myself while Enid was watching over Erec, because suddenly it was dark in my room, and nearby an owl was hooting. In the stone I could see a handsome hall, lit with hundreds of flickering candles, and a servant pouring wine from an earthenware jar.

Erec and the host are sitting at one end of a long table and Enid is at the other, and they're listening to a young woman playing the harp. Her fingers are long and very nimble.

"Your wife has been very quiet all evening," the host says to Erec. "I'll cheer her up."

But as soon as he sits down next to Enid, the host sings a different tune. "So far as I can see," he says quietly, "that man's not worthy of you. You're very beautiful, and he's a boor. The moment I saw you, I desired you, Enid, and desire leads to love."

Enid sits very still. She doesn't look at the host.

"He hasn't said a word to you all evening," the host says. "Now listen to me. If you want to stay here as my mistress . . ."

Enid presses her fingernails into the palm of her right hand. "I'm not that kind of woman," she says. "I'd sooner burn on a hawthorn pyre. I'd rather my ashes were scattered to the four winds than be unfaithful to my husband."

"I see," says the host, and he twists the lobe of his left ear. "So persuasion won't work."

Enid glances at the host. She sees the evil in his eyes; she can feel it on the back of her own neck.

"Listen carefully," the host whispers. "I'm giving you this choice: Either you agree to stay here with me, or I'll signal to my men and they'll pinion your husband and cut off his head. In this hall. Not only that — I'll make you watch them."

Enid rubs her lips together and smiles at her host, and I think she's forcing herself to say words she does not mean. "I was testing the strength of your feelings," she whispers. "But you can't kill my husband when he's defenseless. It's true, he's tired of me. I'm tired of him. Send your men to our chamber very early in the morning. Erec may try to fight them, but they'll overpower him."

The host looks at Enid like a wolf.

"And after that," says Enid, "you can do what you want with him. I don't care."

The host stands up and stretches. He embraces Erec and wishes him a peaceful night.

"I commend you to God," he says.

At this moment, I heard a clattering at the bottom of the stone steps. Quickly, I wrapped my stone and hid it under the joist, and went to the door.

Anian was climbing the steps, banging a metal ladle against the wall.

"What are you making that noise for?" I asked. "You're as bad as Izzie. She came up here once, smacking the wall with a stick."

Anian leered up at me. "Did she now?" he said.

"What do you want, anyhow?"

"Supper," said Anian. "Lord Stephen says you're keeping everyone waiting."

wild edric

INNIE WAS WAITING ON THE DRAWBRIDGE FOR LADY
Judith and me. Her red-gold hair was tied back at
the neck, as it was when I first saw her, and she
was wearing a gold hairpin behind each ear.

First she greeted and kissed her aunt, then she turned to me. "I
told you!" she exclaimed. "I knew Lord Stephen would let you
come to Verdon. Follow me."

The water in the moat was spangled with water lilies. There
were clusters of iris on the far bank, and the manor walls were
draped with honeysuckle, all its flowers shining in the sunlight.

Lady Anne is almost as spirited as Winnie. Her eyes are
cornflower-bright, and she's very quick with words and often com-
pletes other people's sentences. Some people stump around as if
their bodies are too heavy for them, but Lady Anne moves as if
hers is too light and she can only just stop it from flying away.

"You're very welcome," she said, with a gay smile, "very, very
welcome. We want you to see everything — absolutely everything,
don't we, Winnie. As if you were at home."

Lady Anne doesn't look like Winnie, though, except for her
snub nose. Her hair is covered with a wimple.

"It's as yellow as a crocodile," Winnie told me. But I've never
seen one, and neither has she.

"Crocodiles are bright yellow," Winnie said, "and they have horrible teeth and claws."

Tomorrow is Saint John's Eve. Before supper, Winnie and I helped Edie, Lady Anne's chamber-servant, to decorate the hall. Not with boughs of fruit trees, like Erec and Enid's bedroom, but with strings of marigold and midsummer-men, birch branches and wiry hanks of fennel. At least that's what I call it, but everyone at Verdon calls it spignel.

As soon as we had eaten, Lady Anne said: "Now, Arthur! When someone visits Verdon for the first time, we always, always welcome him — him or her — with a story. Isn't that right, Judith? And this is the story for Saint John's Eve. Have you heard about Wild Edric?"

I shook my head and Winnie squealed. "I'm going to sit next to you," she announced.

"He lived in Clun Forest," Lady Judith told me.

"Where we went hare hunting," Winnie added. "He looked like the wildman on your tile."

"A wild boar of a man," said Lady Anne enthusiastically. "A man with an appetite! One summer day, Edric went hunting with his page, just the two of them, and he strayed so deep into the forest that he didn't know where he was. As it was getting dark, he rode up to a wall — a high stone wall, right in the middle of the forest. There was a little wrought-iron gate let into it, and Edric peered through . . ."

Next to me, Winnie began to rock gently, and then to hum-and-sing:

"Mmm . . . mmm . . . acadam merlaster . . .
sam o thrat glista . . . mmm . . . mmm . . ."

"A circle of young women were singing and dancing," said Lady Anne. "They were wearing white linen dresses, and they were taller than Englishwomen. Even you, Judith! But those fairy women! How light they were on their dancing feet.

"The longer Edric looked, the more hungry he grew. Especially for that one, the lovely one with ear-jewels. She seemed to know Edric was there. Three times she turned and looked straight at him.

"Edric couldn't bear it," said Lady Anne. "He grasped the gate with both hands, but of course he couldn't tear apart the iron bars. So then he shouldered it and burst the lock. He rushed over to the girls and snatched up the one with the ear-jewels. He tossed her over his shoulder."

Lady Anne smiled and sipped at her tumbler of wine. "Well," she said, "somehow or other, Wild Edric found his way home."

"Lydbury North," Sir Walter told me. "That was his manor."

"Only three miles away," Lady Judith added.

"He didn't let go of the girl," Lady Anne continued, "not for one moment. And she wouldn't say a word. Nothing! Not for three days and nights. But on the fourth day, as soon as she woke up . . .

"'Edric! Edric, I will be your wife. I will take you as my husband, and you will prosper. But if ever you speak ill of my sisters, or blame them for anything, I will leave you at once.'

"Well, Edric and the fairy woman were married. And do you

know, Arthur, when King William heard about her — her strange, precarious beauty — he summoned her to court so he could see her for himself.

"To begin with, Edric and his wife got on well enough, and they had a son. Alnod. But the fairy woman was a silent creature, and sometimes she had a desperate, lost look.

"One evening, Edric rode in late — very, very late — after hunting. He was so hungry he could have eaten a haunch of raw venison. He could have eaten the bark off the trees. But when he hurried into the hall, there was no supper awaiting him on the table. Not even a plate and spoon. Not even any ale.

"Angrily, Edric shouted at his wife's chamber-servant to fetch his wife, but even then she didn't come to the hall for some time.

"'Where have you been?' Wild Edric shouted. 'With your sisters, I suppose? This is their fault.'

"Right in front of Edric," Lady Anne went on, "the fairy woman vanished. As if she were made of air. That was the last time Edric saw her, though he often searched for the place where he found her. And almost at once, things began to go very badly for him. He lost one manor to the Normans. Then he was besieged in his castle at Wigmore. He ended up in prison and in chains.

"But people still see him. Around here they do . . . flying north and east on his white horse, with his wife beside him."

"I can see him in your words," I said.

"Out of the forest and over the hills," Lady Anne cried. "They're dressed in green, and their phantom hounds are rushing behind them."

For one moment, Winnie laid her warm fingers on my left wrist, then she took them away again.

"Has that story been written?" I asked.

"Arthur writes everything," Winnie said.

Lady Anne smiled. "I think we should remember everything we need to know," she said.

"That's what Nain, my grandmother, says," I replied. "But isn't there more knowledge in the world than we can remember?"

"There's too much," said Sir Walter. "That's the trouble."

"I wish I'd learned to read," Lady Judith said.

"No," said Sir Walter. "If people spend their lives inside books, they'll read a great deal they don't really need to know."

"Instead of thinking for themselves!" added Lady Anne. "Now, Winnie, I want you to play the harp for Arthur."

Winnie got up from the table and walked over to the harp in the corner of the hall. Her fingers are not all that long but they're nimble, and she's very proud of her pretty fingernails.

"Like filberts," she told me once.

"You mean hazelnuts?"

"Exactly," said Winnie.

I liked watching Winnie, leaning forward with her arms around the harp, but she hasn't been learning for very long. She could play some chords but couldn't pick out a melody.

"Very good," said Sir Walter fondly.

"You must learn melodies, Winnie," said Lady Judith.

"Quite right!" Sir Walter said. "I want you to play so well that, listening to you, a man will never notice he's growing old."

"I'm not going to marry an old man," Winnie objected.

"No, no," said Sir Walter, and he flapped both hands rather hopelessly, as if he would only know what he meant when he heard what he'd said.

"Time to sleep," said Lady Anne. "Winnie and Arthur, I want you to pick the wort in the morning. Before the dew's off the flowers."

love's disobedience

I COULDN'T GET TO SLEEP. IN THE MIDDLE OF THE NIGHT I unwrapped my stone.

"Wake up!" whispers Enid. "Erec! Wake up!"

Enid tells her husband of their host's intentions. Quickly they dress and creep out of their chamber through the hall. They saddle their horses and leave the sleeping castle.

Dawn breaks. The sun quickens and rises, and Enid reins in. She sits very still in the saddle and frowns. "Can you hear what I hear?" she asks.

"I've told you before," Erec replies. "You're not to speak to me unless I speak to you first."

Enid dismounts. She kneels and puts one ear to the ground. "Hooves galloping!" she cries. "Our host is following us. Not even you can fight one hundred men."

"You do not love me, Enid," Erec says. "How will others ever have faith in me if you do not trust me?"

The host leads the charge. He splits Erec's shield and drives his lance between Erec's chest and his right shoulder. But Erec's aim is no less accurate. His lance pierces the host's stomach and comes out through his back.

The host collapses in his saddle like a sack of onions, and his charger trots round in a circle and then pulls up.

The host stares at Erec with bulging eyes. "God's price!" he croaks. He thrashes the air with his right hand. Now he tells his followers to allow Erec and Enid to go in peace.

On they go, but Erec is badly wounded. And when Enid turns round, she sees her husband hanging upside down with his head bumping on the ground.

Enid dismounts. She releases Erec's foot from the stirrup and lays his head in her lap. Over and again she kisses his blue lips. Her tears shine on his cheeks. "He's dead and it's my fault. I've murdered my own husband."

Enid starts to sob. "I should never have told him what people were saying about him."

Gently Enid lays Erec's head on the ground and now she draws his sword from its scabbard. She's very pale, and breathing in little gasps and stabs. She plants the pommel on the ground and places the point against her stomach, and leans into it.

"Stop!" shouts a voice, and a knight gallops right up to Enid. He grasps the sword and sheathes it in the scabbard strapped to Erec's wrist; and now he stoops and feels Erec's cold forehead.

"Stone-dead!" he announces. "So who are you? His wife or his mistress?"

Enid closes her eyes. "Both," she whispers.

"Is that so?"

"Let me die."

"Tut!" exclaims the knight. "The death of a knight is a pity, but yours would be a tragedy. I've a better idea."

Enid settles beside Erec, graceful as a swan. She grasps his right shoulder and her purple cloak half-covers him.

"I'm Count Oringle," the knight tells her, "and my castle's at

Limors. First, we'll carry your husband back to my castle and give him a Christian burial. And then, lovely lady, I think you should marry again."

Count Oringle's no better than the host who threatened to pinion Erec and lop off his head. In fact, he's even worse. He's debauched. He is actually making advances to Enid in front of her own dead husband.

Enid isn't scared, though. There's a sharp stone in her heart: She aches all over.

"Let me die," she says again.

Now I can see Count Oringle's hall. At the far end, Erec is lying on a table raised on wooden blocks, and Enid and Count Oringle are standing beside him.

"Right!" says the count. "A dead man can wait! Time's for the living, and it's high time we were married."

Enid looks at Oringle with eyes of stone.

"Chaplain!" calls the count. "Say your words. Pronounce us man and wife."

The chaplain recites the sacred words and now Count Oringle puts his mouth to Enid's ear. "You were poor, my lady," he whispers, "and now you're rich. You were a nobody and now you're a countess."

"I wish I were dead," says Enid. "I won't eat or drink. I'll fast until I die."

"We'll see about that," says the count.

"In no way will I satisfy you," Enid says.

The count claps his hands, and servants bring in steaming dishes: pike and perch and salmon and trout. The count himself arranges little pieces on Enid's plate.

Enid won't touch it, though. Not one mouthful.

"If you refuse to eat the next course," the count tells her, "you'll get what you deserve."

But Enid ignores the count's threats. She refuses all the grilled and stewed meats.

At once the count stands up and smacks Enid across the face.

"Sir!" protests the chaplain. "You can't expect her to eat in front of her dead husband."

All down the table Count Oringle can hear his household protesting. He listens and smiles. "This woman's mine," he says. "I'll do exactly as I like with her."

Erec's fingertips, they're beginning to twitch. His eyelids, they're flickering. He's alive! Erec's alive! Now he opens one eye. Both eyes. Several times he blinks. He must be working out where he is and why he's lying on his back on a cold stone slab.

Here come more servants, carrying slices of date, ginger waffles, and sweet cheese tart.

"This is your last chance, Countess Enid!" shouts Oringle. "Either you eat or I'll force your little mouth open and stuff your gullet."

Erec feels for his sword. It is still strapped to his wrist. He fingers the pommel, he grasps it. And now in one movement he unsheathes it and swings himself down from the raised table.

The count's household all leap to their feet. The long benches topple over backwards. Men yell, women shriek, and Erec staggers straight towards the count. He swings his sword and swipes the side of the count's head with the flat of the blade. He beats his brains into a pancake.

All the count's household are punching and scratching one another, fighting to get through the hall doors.

"He's a devil!"

"A demon!"

"The dead man's after us!"

Away they go now, Erec and Enid — away they gallop, on one horse. Erec wraps his arms tight around his wife. He presses his heart against her.

"Our journey's over," he whispers. "I'll test you no further."

"I only disobeyed you because I love you," says Enid.

"I know how you love me. And I love you. Every knight and lady at Camelot will hear of our adventure."

"How could I have doubted you?" whispers Enid.

The light in my stone shivered, it faded; the stone grew cold, as if there were no life in it. . . .

Enid was meek yet stubborn. It's just as she said: Erec needed her. They needed each other.

Not all women are like that. Lady Judith's not meek. She speaks her mind. She argues. So does Winnie! It's a good thing Erec wasn't married to her.

I think Erec's friends were right in a way. Because of his passion, he turned his back on his duties as a knight. Overseeing his estate. Serving at court. Protecting the defenseless. And fighting in the field, as Lord Stephen and I are going to do. But if he has to be away from home so often and for so long, how can a man be a true knight without dishonoring his marriage? And how can a loving husband ever be a good knight?

golden eyes in the gloom

OU WANTED TO TELL ME," WINNIE BEGAN, "AND IT was important."

"What?"

"About Gortanore. When we went hare hunting."

I swallowed, and stared at my damp bundle of golden Saint-John's-wort.

"Come on!" said Winnie.

"You know Sir William's my father?"

"And Grace is your half sister. That's why you can't be betrothed."

"But my mother —"

"Who is she?"

"I don't know. I don't even know how to find out."

"Ask Sir William, then," said Winnie, and she laughed.

"I can't. When we met and talked, as father and son, he kept barking and shouting at me. He raised his fist."

"But she's your own mother."

"I am going to find out," I said. "I am."

"Everyone needs to know who their own mother is," Winnie said indignantly. "We have to know. I'm going to help you."

"How?"

"I don't know. Yes, I do. My father can find out. He will if I ask him."

"That's much too dangerous."

"Why?" asked Winnie.

"I can't tell you everything. Sir William warned me not to start digging things up, and I know he'll do everything he can to stop people from finding out the whole story. If they did, he'd be hanged!"

"Really?" exclaimed Winnie.

"And Lady Alice and Tom and Grace would have to leave Gortanore."

"I know," said Winnie brightly. "I can talk to Tom. He'll help us."

"No!" I said in alarm. "He doesn't even know Sir William has named me as his heir."

"Instead of him, you mean?"

"Tom will inherit two manors and I will have the third. But we haven't even talked about it yet."

I could feel my mother's ring in my pocket and I kept wondering whether to show it to Winnie. I wanted to so much. But I could hear Thomas, warning me — I could see him drawing his fingers across his throat.

"Do you know what Sir William said?" I asked Winnie. "'When people start digging, they may find their own bones.'"

"That's a black threat," said Winnie fiercely, and then she shivered. "I'm glad my father's not like that. Come on! We'd better take this wort back to the hall."

This evening, Winnie and I built a little stone chamber on the scrubland beyond the archery butts, and stowed all the wort into it. Its golden eyes shone in the gloom. And then the people who live on Sir Walter's manor made a cocoon around it of hawthorn cuttings and beech branches, and set light to them. The wood spat — the flames danced.

Sir Walter rubbed his hands. "So you didn't step on any," he said.

"What if we had?" I asked.

"On Saint John's Eve?" said Sir Walter. And then he called out, "Judith! Arthur's asking what would happen if he stepped on Saint-John's-wort."

Lady Judith advanced on us. "Our parents said," she told me, "that the ground could open and a horseman rise under us. He gallops you all night until you're far from home, and then he vanishes."

"Well, I'm still here," I said, grinning. "Do you believe that, my lady?"

"Why shouldn't I?" Lady Judith replied. "Saint-John's-wort is the most magical plant of all. It drives away all kinds of evil. Dark elves. Demons. Witches."

"What I think," said Sir Walter, "is that it's wise to respect the old beliefs. That prayer Lord Stephen said after we caught the hare: 'We're one fellowship . . .' Do you remember? Humans and animals, plants and trees as well. We're all one fellowship. We can use them as we need them, but we must respect them with the old words and the old customs."

"That's what Nain says," I told Sir Walter. "She's Welsh and thinks that when trees whisper and sigh, they're the voices of the dead."

In the firelight, Sir Walter took my right elbow and squeezed it warmly. I like the way he listens to me.

"Winnie!" Sir Walter called. "Come over here! As soon as

you wake up, I want you and Arthur to lift all the wort out of the chamber."

"I know," said Winnie.

"And put a good handful beside each outside door."

"The hall door, the kitchen door, the door to the armory," Winnie recited, "the doors to the stables and each cow stall . . ."

"What would I do without you?" murmured Sir Walter, and he quietly withdrew into the darkness.

"He knows I know," said Winnie, tossing her head, "but that doesn't stop him telling me."

"You will be sure to save plenty of wort for me?" Lady Anne said. "Winnie?"

"Yes, mother."

"Lady Helen uses it for melancholy," I said.

"So do we," Lady Anne said. "And nerves. And to kill pain. All kinds of things."

Lady Anne and Sir Walter and Lady Judith stepped into the hall, and Winnie tugged on my left sleeve.

"Arthur!" she whispered.

"What?"

In the darkness, I could see her eyes shining.

"What is it?"

Winnie looked at me forever. Then, all at once, she laid her hands on my shoulders, leaned forward, and kissed me right on my mouth.

"Winnie!" called Lady Anne.

"Coming!" Winnie shouted. "If you tell anyone," she whispered in my ear, "I'll vanish for a year and a day!"

"Where are you?" Lady Anne called again.

"Hurry up, Arthur!" Winnie said loudly. And then she skipped into the hall.

"Now!" said Lady Anne. "I've saved this sprig." She gave the glistening flower to Winnie. "Put it under your pillow, and when you dream, you'll see the man you're going to marry."

fires and head guests

HEN I STARED DEEP INTO THE SAINT JOHN'S EVE fire tonight, I could see a flame-giant, wilder by far than Edric. I saw the gardens of paradise and scathing, hissing demons. Oringle's hot eyes, and the pure white flame of love.

It's often like this. Even when I stare into a hearth fire, it's somehow like staring into myself. I can see good and evil. I'm a battleground, dragged this way, dragged that way — a wishbone, unable to break.

I'm not mad! At least, I don't think I am.

Anyhow, Nain told me that madness and knowledge are twin sisters, and sometimes we have to think wild thoughts before we truly understand.

"Cader Idris," she said.

"What's that?"

"The mountain. If you climb that and stay on top until midnight, you'll turn mad or become a great poet."

70

BLOODSTONE

EFORE LADY JUDITH AND I LEFT VERDON, I ASKED
Winnie whether she had put the sprig of wort under
her pillow.

"What if I did?" she replied.

"Whom did you see?" I asked.

Winnie lowered her eyes. "No one," she said in a loud voice,
and then she began to blush.

Is it possible that Winnie and I could be betrothed? I do like her.
She makes me feel like I've never felt before. But I know she likes
Tom, too, and I'm going away, for two years or even longer. Would
she wait? And, anyhow, who will decide for me now? Will it be Sir
William or Sir John and Lady Helen? Or can I choose for myself?

Lord Stephen welcomed us back to Holt with a tight smile. He
told me he wanted to hear about everything, but then he withdrew
to the solar with Lady Judith. I stayed down in the hall, and was
just telling Miles and Rowena and Rahere about Wild Edric, when
Lord Stephen and Lady Judith reappeared.

"Arthur," said Lady Judith, "will you go and get Haket? I'll find
Gubert and Izzie."

As soon as we'd assembled, Lord Stephen began. "This affects
us all, so we should all hear it." He laced his fingers over his stomach and flexed his thumbs. "I had a visitor today," he said in a

clipped voice. "From Ludlow. Jacob's wife. I thought she'd come for him, to carry his body home. But it wasn't that."

Lord Stephen screwed up his eyes and blinked, but he was watching us all very closely. He went over to the square oak box beside the fire and took something out. Then he opened his hand, and lying on his palm was a knob of apple-green crystal. It was as large as a walnut.

Rowena drew in her breath sharply.

"Lady Judith's bloodstone," Lord Stephen said. "Her life stone. She used to wear it round her neck. But last June," said Lord Stephen, turning to me, "Lady Judith lost it. It disappeared."

Lord Stephen showed me the crystal. It had brown spots inside it, and dark red veins.

"So why did Jacob's wife come to see me?" he asked.

I looked at Haket. He was scraping the back of his hand against his rough chin. And then, all at once, Rowena gulped and began to weep. Lord Stephen ignored her.

"She came to give me this stone," Lord Stephen went on. "But how did this woman, this Jewess in Ludlow, come to have Lady Judith's bloodstone?" Lord Stephen looked at the rafters. "I'll tell you," he said very sharply. "Jacob bought it. He bought it here. That's what he told his wife, and she came to give it back because we buried Jacob just outside our own graveyard." Lord Stephen sniffed and cleared his throat. "So who sold the stone to Jacob? That's the question."

"I didn't mean to," Rowena cried, and she buried her face in her hands.

Lord Stephen waited patiently.

"It was for my mother," sobbed Rowena. Her whole body was shaking. "She hurt so much. I was going to buy medicines."

"You could have asked me for help," Lord Stephen said. "We could have made your mother's dying less hard."

"I didn't dare ask," Rowena sobbed. "I confessed it. I did!"

"I see," Lord Stephen said slowly. And then he bent down and put his face close to Haket's. "Rowena confessed her sin," he said in a low voice, "to you and to God, and you used it against her. Is that it?"

"No," said Haket.

"It is!" Rowena said fiercely.

"I've been watching you," Lord Stephen told Haket, "and I suspected as much. What did you say to Rowena? That unless she did as you wanted, you'd tell Lady Judith about the bloodstone?"

Haket clenched his teeth. He stood up and I thought he was going to strike Lord Stephen.

"Yes," said Lord Stephen calmly, "and Rowena believed you. She didn't realize that if you did that, you would be incriminating yourself. You took most of the money, didn't you? And you've been taking advantage of Rowena."

Haket sat down again, heavily. All the fight had gone out of him.

"Who is most to blame?" Lord Stephen asked himself. "What's the right punishment?"

Outside the hall, I could hear two birds squabbling and someone yelling. But inside, there was not a sound.

Lord Stephen stared at Rowena. "I suppose you know the punishment for theft from your own mistress?" he said mildly. Then he turned to Haket and screwed up his face. "As for you . . ." he began in disgust. Lord Stephen flapped his hands. "Get out!" he snapped. "All of you."

I still don't know what Lord Stephen is going to do about Haket and Rowena, and neither does anyone else. It is dark and long past time for supper, and he and Lady Judith are still up in the solar, talking.

While I was away at Verdon, Simon did ride over to Caldicot and he took my message for Merlin, but this evening he told me he was unable to find him, or even to find out where he was. Sir John explained that Merlin's often away, and half the time he doesn't know where he has gone. This is exactly what I feared.

Once Merlin told me about an island. He said we're looking for it all our lives, without knowing it. But although we don't know what it looks like, we'll recognize it the moment we see it. On this island, Merlin says, there's a house of glass, and as soon as you step into it, you become invisible. So you can see the world, but the world can't see you.

I think that, when his time comes, Merlin will go and live in that house of glass. But because of everything I've seen in my stone, I am afraid I may never see him again.

pockets of silver
and gold

N MY STONE, I CAN SEE A MAN IS LYING ON THE BANK OF a stream with his cloak folded under his head. His horse is unsaddled and rolling on his back beside him. Around them the grass is thick with daisies, speedwell, and clover, and the stream gurgles like a baby.

But all this only mocks the man's unhappiness. "No love," he says. "No land. I serve King Arthur, but he ignores me. The knights who say they admire me haven't lifted a finger to help me."

Now the man turns his head and looks downstream: Two young women wearing dark-purple dresses are walking towards him. One is carrying a golden bowl, the other a towel.

At once the man scrambles to his feet.

"Sir Lanval?" one of the young women says. "My mistress has sent us for you."

"Look!" says the other woman. "Over there! Her tent."

I've never seen such a tent. The cloth glistens: It looks as if it has been cut from a rainbow. The poles are wrapped in gold foil. Even the slender ropes are woven from gold thread.

A most lovely lady steps towards Lanval. She's wearing white ermine. Much of her it covers, but much is uncovered. Her skin's smooth as silk, whiter than hawthorn blossom.

"Sir Lanval," the lady begins, "I've been looking for you all my life. I want to love you more than any other man. Are you worthy of that?"

Lanval's blood rushes to his face. "There's nothing you can ask of me that I will not do," he declares.

"All right!" replies the lady. "After you leave this tent, you can have whatever you wish for, and as often as you wish for it. However much gold and silver you spend or give away, I'll make sure you still have enough. But if you tell anyone at all about me, you'll lose my love at once and forever. You'll never see me again."

Now Lanval takes the lady into his arms and he kisses her. More than once.

"You must go now," the lady tells him. "Whenever you want to talk to me, I'll be beside you and will grant your wish. Only you will be able to see me or hear my voice."

Lanval dips his hands into the golden bowl and dries them on the towel. Once more he embraces his lady, and now he leaves the rainbow tent.

Sir Lanval's in no hurry: He wants time to think. "I was so unhappy," he says to himself. "Did all this happen, or was it a dream while I was lying on the riverbank?"

Several times he looks over his shoulder, but of course the tent is no longer there.

"I wish," says Lanval, "I wish I had some proof."

At once he's aware that someone is riding just behind him. "This proof!" says the lady, and she's smiling.

Lanval exclaims and reaches out. But the lady vanishes.

Now Lanval gallops for joy! He rides back towards the court at

Carlisle, and when he returns to his lodging, he finds his right pocket is stuffed with silver.

"Try the other pocket," says a voice at his elbow.

So Sir Lanval puts a hand into his left pocket. It is full of gold!

Now I can see Sir Lanval walking through city streets, and he's giving a coin to each beggar. He's at the prison gates, purchasing the freedom of all the men he believes to be innocent. I can see him buying tunics, hoods, and stout shoes for the singers and jugglers: sitting with his guests at the head of a well-stocked table . . .

And now I can see a garden in Camelot, with many knights and ladies taking their ease. But not Sir Lancelot — I don't know where he is. Sir Owain is walking with Lionors along a row of box bushes cut into the shapes of lions and camels and crocodiles, and Sir Cador and Moronoe are looking at little fish nosing and squirting around a pond, and Sir Brian is strolling with Ettard beside one of the little canals dividing the garden. And they are all talking about love's joy, love's suffering.

But Sir Lanval is sitting on his own. The one person he would like to be able to talk about, he cannot even mention.

Queen Guinevere herself approaches him, and Lanval stands up.

"Every man here except for you is twinned with a lady, and every lady is twinned with a man," Guinevere says. "You must be very fond of your own company."

"It's not that," says Lanval.

The queen takes Lanval's arm and they sit down side by side. "Tell me what you'd like most," she murmurs.

Lanval stiffens. He says nothing.

"Maybe you can have it."

Still Lanval says nothing.

"Have you no time for young women?"

"I love a lady," Lanval replies, "and she loves me. She's a better woman than you are, and more beautiful."

"I see," the queen says coldly. She stands up. "You'll regret saying that, Lanval."

Sir Lanval regrets it already. He fears he will never see his love again.

Now Guinevere returns to her chamber, and by the time King Arthur comes to her, after a day's hunting, she is lying in bed. Her eyes are swimming with tears.

"Sir Lanval asked me for my love," she says, "and when I refused him, he insulted me. He has humiliated me and wronged you. I won't get up again until you right this wrong."

"Lanval can defend himself in court," says Arthur-in-the-stone. "If he's found guilty, he'll swing or burn."

In court, the king accuses Lanval of asking Guinevere for her love, and at once he denies it. Many of the knights in court exchange quick glances. They know how the queen is.

"Did you say," the king asks Lanval, "that the lady you love is a better woman than the queen, and more beautiful?"

"I admit it," Lanval replies. "And I bitterly regret it. Now I'll never see her again."

"My earls, lords, and knights," says King Arthur, "what is your verdict?"

"Whether or not Lanval asked the queen for her love cannot be proved or disproved," Sir Gawain says. "If he did, he's a traitor."

"By boasting," says Sir Gareth, "Lanval has angered the queen."

"By angering her, is he dishonoring the king?" asks Sir Brian of the Isles.

"Without seeing his lady, we cannot say whether or not Lanval was telling the truth," argues Sir Gawain.

"If Lanval can prove the truth of his words," says the king, "I will pardon him. But if not, I will banish him."

Sir Lanval cannot prove it, though. He can no longer call on his lady. But just as the king's earls, lords, and knights are about to reach a decision, two young women ride into court. They're dressed in the same tight-fitting, mulberry dresses as the young women who carried the golden bowl and the towel, but Lanval doesn't recognize them.

The young women walk up to Arthur-in-the-stone. "Sire," says one, "will you prepare one of your chambers? Hang it with silk curtains. Open the windows."

"Our mistress is coming here to Carlisle," says the other young woman. "She wants to speak to you. She may wish to stay."

"Sir Kay," says the king, "show these ladies to the upper rooms."

Now the knights begin to debate again. I can hear them arguing whether these two young women have anything to do with the case; whether to wait until their mistress arrives.

A woman on horseback enters the town, alone. She's wearing a silk cloak, golden brown streaked with bloodred, the color of beech leaves just before they fall. Her hair is gold thread, her skin smooth as silk, whiter than hawthorn blossom. On her wrist, a sparrow hawk perches.

As she rides into the courtyard, all the people there turn and stare at her. In no haste, she dismounts, then enters the hall and walks towards the king. How can any human being be so beautiful? First, everyone gazes in wonder, then they laugh for pure joy.

Lanval can scarcely breathe. "If only you'll forgive me," he whispers, "I don't care what this court does with me."

The lady lets her cloak slip from her shoulders. She's wearing a white tunic and a shift so loosely laced you can glimpse her sides.

"Sire," she says to Arthur-in-the-stone, "I am the lady your knight Lanval loves, and I love him. He stands accused in this court, but it would be unjust to punish him. Your queen misunderstood him — Lanval never asked her for her love. As for his boast . . . Your earls and lords and knights must decide whether I can acquit him."

All around him, the king can hear voices urging him to forgive Lanval and set him free. He cannot hear a single dissenter.

"Let it be as the court recommends," the king calls out. "Lanval! You are free."

An upper room in the court is open and prepared, but the lady will not stay. She thanks the king, bows, and leaves the hall. In the Yard, she mounts her white palfrey.

Now I can see Lanval walking over to the far gateway. He steps up onto the marble mounting block, the one used by fully armed men.

The lady trots across the yard. Smiling, she turns to Lanval, and with one great shout and a standing leap, Sir Lanval mounts her palfrey behind her.

"At once and forever!" cries the lady, and she spurs on her palfrey. "To Avalon!"

surprises,
like spices

ORD STEPHEN HAS ORDERED HAKET TO LEAVE HOLT.
He says he never wants to see his shadow again.

Haket shouted at Lord Stephen and told him
he had no right to take the law into his own hands,
and a priest could only be tried according to canon law, not in a lay
court. He said he'd talk to the bishop of Hereford himself, and
bring a lawsuit against Lord Stephen. And he kept tightening and
loosening his fists and licking his lips.

Lord Stephen replied very soberly, but he was just as definite
as when he came to our manor court at Caldicot and sentenced
Lankin to lose his thieving right hand. He said he certainly had
the right to decide who should serve as parish priest at Holt. He
said Haket had abused his position by blackmailing and seduc-
ing a young woman, and that he'd be extremely unwise to press
matters further, since even a Church court would be bound to rule
against him — and, in all likelihood, call for his excommunication.

"The punishment for blackmail is most unpleasant," Lord
Stephen observed. "And for seduction, even more so. The testicles!
A priest is required to be strictly celibate. I'm giving you another
chance, Haket, but not here. Leave Holt at once, or I'll make accu-
sations against you."

"You can't accuse me without accusing Rowena," Haket said nastily.

"Once," said Lord Stephen, "I saw a fish so rotten, so revolting, it glowed in the dark. You are disgusting, Haket!" Lord Stephen waved his hand dismissively.

Haket licked his lips again. And then, large as he is, he slouched, and almost slunk out of the solar.

Lord Stephen hasn't told me yet, but I suppose Miles will give me my lessons now. He's the only person here who can read and write better than I can. But it can't be long before we leave for Champagne to take the Cross, and before that I have to help bring home the harvest as well as visit Wenlock Priory. I do wish I could see Winnie again — I keep thinking about her.

As for Rowena: Lord Stephen and Lady Judith have decided to forgive her, because she has never offended before and because she stole the bloodstone not out of greed, but to pay for medicines for her mother. But instead of serving Lady Judith with Izzie, she has to help Gubert in the kitchen. Lord Stephen made it quite clear that if she's accused of stealing again, he will also charge her with stealing the crystal.

I was down on the riverbank very late this afternoon, trying to measure the length of my shadow and divide it by my true height, when I saw Simon ride in with a young woman and a baby.

Tanwen and her son! Serle's son. My nephew.

So Serle was right and Merlin was wrong. Serle said Sir John would never allow Tanwen to stay at Caldicot once her baby had been born, because the baby wouldn't belong in the manor or in the village either. But I'd no idea they'd be coming to Holt.

"Surprises," said Lord Stephen, blinking and smiling, "They're like spices. They make our daily bread more tasty."

"What will she do here?" I asked.

"Serve Lady Judith," Lord Stephen replied.

"You mean . . . instead of Rowena?"

Lord Stephen's eyes gleamed. "God moves in a mysterious way," he said.

The baby is called Christopher, but Tanwen calls him Kester. He doesn't look like Serle. He hasn't got Serle's thin, curling lips, and I hope he won't have his sharp tongue either.

"White fire," said Tanwen. "You've got my Welsh white fire, haven't you, Kester? Haven't you?"

One moment she talks to him as if she expects him to reply, the next she coos as if he were a dove. Kester looks plump and pink, and he's got strong lungs. He's already nine weeks old — nine weeks and four days — so I hope he'll live. Tanwen says Serle will ride over to see them once each month.

I think Tanwen was pleased to see me, and I was certainly glad to see her. I asked her at once about Gatty and Jankin, and whether Lankin's stump is still healing. I told her I wanted to know everything: how many calves Brice sired this spring, and whether Howell and Ruth still laugh so much now that they're married, and who lit the fire on Saint John's Eve, and whether Martha still has a warm eye for Macsen, and . . .

"*Gogoniant!*" said Tanwen. "Glory be! I've only just got here, and the first thing I have to do is feed you, isn't it, Kester?"

It is difficult to think of Kester as my nephew, or even as a person. He is just a baby.

Tanwen embraced me. "You've grown," she said. "Gatty and Sir John and Sian and everyone, they're all glad you're coming to Caldicot."

"Am I?" I exclaimed, and I hugged Tanwen for a second time.

"After the harvest's home! Simon told us."

she-devil

 ORGAN LE FAY GLARES DOWN AT URIEN, HER SLEEP-
ing husband.

"Loyal to Arthur," she whispers. "Loyal to the king is disloyal to me."

Morgan's servant is standing outside the chamber.

"Go and get his sword," Morgan whispers. "I'll be waiting in the solar."

But Morgan's servant doesn't go to the armory. She hurries to the little room where Owain is sleeping and tugs his shoulder.

"Your mother has sent me to get your father's sword," she says. "She is going to murder him."

"Go and get it," Owain says. "I'll prevent her."

At once Owain hurries up to his sleeping father's room.

Now the servant brings back the sword from the armory. Her hands are shaking as she gives it to Morgan.

Morgan unsheaths the sword. Very quietly she creeps back into the dark chamber, right up to Urien's bed. Her black eyes, they're snarling!

At once Owain steps up beside her. He throws his arms around her. His mother wrestles like a wild beast in a net — like a black fiend pierced by an arrow of God's light.

"My son!" Morgan whispers.

"Were you not my mother . . ." Owain growls.

"Mercy! It was madness. A devil was inside me. I didn't know what I was doing."

"I'm the son of a she-devil," says Owain.

"Never again! I swear it!" Morgan says. "Owain, protect me. Never breathe a single word about this."

the right questions

ANWEN WAS BORN AT CALDICOT, AND IT HAS ALWAYS been her home. Now it is not. I know how that feels.

Last night, Kester kept grizzling, and each time I fell asleep he woke me again. So in the end I sat up with Tanwen while she tried to feed them. She told me about Caldicot, but I kept yawning.

Sir John has accused Cleg of knowingly selling short measures of wheat, and I hope the manor court finds him guilty. He's a cheat. If he'd come to court last June, and Lord Stephen had been able to question him, Lankin would never have been found guilty.

Macsen may be betrothed to Martha this Hallowe'en, and one of Sian's molar teeth is loose, and Oliver surprised everyone by telling a joke about a naked nun and a blind man, but it wasn't very funny and Tanwen said she couldn't even remember it. . . . And Tempest and Storm put up a doe and chased her into Pike Forest, but they didn't come back all night, and when they did, Sir John gave them both a good thrashing . . . and the copper beech and Tumber Hill are the same as always, and Tanwen says that even with all the sorrow and the pain, even with having to leave Caldicot, giving birth to her baby son is still the most wonderful thing that's happened in her life. . . .

"Wake up, Arthur!" said Tanwen. "Come on, boy! I'm not your pillow."

I stretched and gave a yawn, as wide as the world, and lifted my head from Tanwen's warm lap. Piers's cock was crowing!

One of the squares in Lady Judith's wall hanging shows Piers standing beside his plow and holding a pot. This afternoon, I asked Lord Stephen whether he would show it to me.

"Yes, I did promise you," Lord Stephen said. "Here it is."

Then he tipped up the pot and emptied more than one hundred silver and bronze Roman coins onto the solar table.

Gently, I picked up a coin: delicate as a flake of flint, no larger than the pad of my forefinger. On one side, there was a man's head, wreathed, but I couldn't read the letters around the rim, because the coin was quite worn. On the other side were two tiny men facing each other, wearing helmets and holding spears as tall as they were. I picked up a second coin: just a little wafer, grey-brown with a greenish tinge . . .

"Who did this pot belong to?" I cried. A young mother, I wondered. Or a thief? Or a priest? A woman about to murder her own husband? Who hid these coins? And why?

I thought if only I could ask exactly the right questions — who and why and how and when and where? — the coins might start to wink and tell me their story.

On the tabletop, I began to arrange them in a loop: silver and bronze — bronze, then silver — silver, then bronze.

"What are you doing?" Lord Stephen asked.

"Making a necklace," I said.

Lord Stephen smiled.

"What were they like?" I asked. "Here in Holt."

Lord Stephen blinked. "The question is," he said, "does human nature always stay the same?"

iNNer voice

 CAN THINK BETTER WHEN I AM OUT OF DOORS.

Up in my climbing-tree on Tumber Hill, between earth and sky. Sitting on the flat stone in the middle of the river. Around the stables.

Once the door has been bolted for the night, Lord Stephen doesn't allow anyone to leave, except to go to the latrine, but last night I went out all the same. Winnie and my mother and Tanwen and her baby, all were tugging inside my heart. I wanted to be on my own and think about them, one by one.

The still night air smelled so sweet. The lolloping moon was harvest heavy. And Bonamy and Pip both grunted and then stamped as soon as they recognized me.

I couldn't think clearly, though. I kept worrying how Lord Stephen would be certain to hear about my disobedience, because he always finds out about everything, and how I'd be punished. Probably with extra Yard-practice. Perhaps with the cane.

But is disobedience always wrong? By speaking up and saving Erec, Enid proved how much she loved him. But Wild Edric disobeyed his wife because he was selfish. And Lanval knew he'd lose his lady if he talked about her, but he still couldn't stop himself.

Half my life is choosing: this way or that way, honorable or not, impulsive or thoughtful, and each choice has its own consequence.

I may never see Merlin again, but I can go on learning from

the stone he gave me, just as much as I'm learning here as Lord Stephen's squire.

But whom can Arthur-in-the-stone learn from?

A baby wrapped in gold, a boy pulling the sword from the stone, a king naming the knights of the Round Table: King Arthur has always had Merlin at his side.

But now Merlin is imprisoned under the rock. He cannot help anyone because he will not help himself.

King Arthur is very strong, but he is surrounded by enemies and dangers. Sometimes he must feel half-naked. Inside his head he can still hear Merlin's voice, but he knows the time has come to listen to his own voice.

76

HARVESTING

HOMAS RODE IN," LORD STEPHEN SAID.

"Thomas!" I exclaimed.

"Is that such a surprise?"

"No, but —"

"I've been busy since dawn receiving rents from each household in this manor and arranging which days people will work my land. And as if that's not enough, Thomas says Sir William wants me to release you." Lord Stephen clucked irritably. "He wants you to help him harvest at Catmole."

"But I can't."

"No, you can't. You're my squire, and I need you here."

"Yes, sir."

"Your father. He's unreasonable!" Lord Stephen's eyes gleamed. "I told him your first duty is to me. And I wished him a merry Christmas."

"Sir!" I exclaimed, and I laughed. "Did Thomas want to talk to me as well?"

"He did, as it happens," Lord Stephen replied. "I told him he'd have to find you himself."

"He didn't, though."

"Well, it can't have been anything important then, can it?"

Why did Thomas want to see me? Was it about my mother? Anyhow, I want to see him. I want to ask him and Maggot to help me.

That's what I wrote on the eve of Lammas, ten days ago, and since then I've been so busy with the harvest that there hasn't been time to write another word, or even to look into my seeing stone. I've been out in the fields, reaping and binding and stoking, or else fast asleep in the hall.

My forearms and the backs of my hands are puffy with nettle stings and crisscrossed with thistle and barley-beard scratches. My whole body prickles, and I've inhaled so much husk dust I keep sneezing.

This afternoon I worked with Anian and Rowena and two villagers — Robert, who never stops chuckling, and Donnet, who's as strong as the other four of us put together. We reaped and bound the last two acres on the other side of the river.

The oat stalks were almost greasy. Like tallow. A thousand thousand swaying tapers.

Just as I was about to scythe the outmost strip, Donnet yelled, "No! That's the mare's, that strip."

"Which mare?"

"I don't know, do I. We never cut that. That's the mare's."

Everyone at Holt seems to have heard of the mare, but the only person who knows anything about her is Miles. "She comes from the north," he said, "and trumpets like the north wind, and she has eight legs."

Anian's face was on fire. Rowena's whole body was smoldering.

"Come on!" said Donnet. "One more effort."

Slowly we walked to the bottom end of the field. We shouldered the bound sheaves, and one by one, we set them up in stooks to ripen.

On our way back across the ford, I sat down in the water. So did Anian. But when I tried to splash Rowena, she tossed her head. Since Haket left and Lord Stephen sent her down to work in the kitchen, she has been quite angry with everyone.

"I'm wet enough already," Donnet said, and Robert just went on quietly chuckling to himself.

Half the people in the manor had already gathered in Clunside Field, and when we'd set down our scythes, Gubert gave us cider and lumps of cheese. Then Sayer began to prod Izzie with his pitchfork, and Izzie said Gubert was the son of a purple plum . . . and Gubert kept twitting Catrin, and Catrin lay on her back while Simon poured cider straight into her mouth and all over her face . . . and all the while we milled around the last uncut sheaf, as we did around the fire on Saint John's Eve at Verdon, when Winnie kissed me.

At last Lord Stephen came out into the field with Lady Judith, and she was carrying a linen bag.

"Well?" asked Lord Stephen. "Who's going to cut the last sheaf?"

I could hear a lark trilling halfway between me and heaven.

"You, Sayer," Lord Stephen said. "Was it you last year?"

"The year before, sir," said Sayer. "That's why my wife died."

"I remember," said Lord Stephen. "Who cut it last year, then?"

"Alan," replied half a dozen voices.

"Ah yes!" Lord Stephen said thoughtfully.

"If I throw my scythe at it," Donnet said, "that might cut itself. Stand clear, you!" Then Donnet picked up his scythe and hurled it at the barley, but it only quivered and swayed.

The barley whiskers were Welsh gold. Almost as red as Winnie's hair. And that lark: It was like an auger, drilling into my skull.

Surely, I thought. Surely I can. I'm Arthur de Caldicot, and I'm going to take the Cross. Surely I can make my own luck.

"I will," I heard myself say. "I'll cut it."

"That's the boy!"

"Go on, Arthur!"

"Good luck!"

I could hear voices around me, encouraging me, warning me. Then I picked up Donnet's scythe and grasped the barley. With one stroke I severed all the stalks. At once there as a shout, and then Donnet quickly bound the sheaf, and Lady Judith opened her bag and pulled out a linen shift and a woolen kirtle and a battered old straw hat.

She gave them to Donnet and Robert, and they dressed the sheaf while everyone encouraged them.

"Dressing a woman!" Donnet complained, grinning. "That's unnatural."

"A maiden," said Lady Judith. "With long hair."

"Like Winnie's, almost," I said to Lady Judith.

Lady Judith smiled. "You and your Winnie," she said.

"What? Winnie again?" Donnet said loudly. "It's been nothing but Winnie, Winnie, all day long."

"That's not true," I protested, and several people began to laugh.

"If things get any worse," Tanwen called out, "we'll have to wrap Arthur in water lilies."

"That's right," said Agnes. "They'll cool his blood."

When Donnet and Robert had dressed the corn-maiden to everyone's satisfaction, they presented her to Gubert.

"Keep her in the kitchen!" Lord Stephen told him. "Then she'll give us a good harvest again next year. Now, Sayer!"

Sayer was holding a black-faced ewe on a very short tether. She had a blob of green dye on the top of her head, and around her neck was wound a tawny woolen scarf.

Lord Stephen untied the scarf. "This is for Arthur," he announced, and everyone hurrahed. "He cut the last sheaf, and that's always risky. But he'll be all right. He'd better be. He's my squire!" Then Lord Stephen looked around at all his villagers — all the poor people living in his manor. "You've all worked hard," he said, "and you deserve your reward. Tomorrow you can glean, here and in Otherside."

"What about the fodder, sir?" Rhys asked.

"I was coming to that," said Lord Stephen. "On the day after, everyone's to pick stubble for my horses and carry it up to the stables to mix with the hay. On the third morning, you can take as much stubble as you need for thatching and bedding. All the corn will be ripe in ten days, God willing, and then we'll bring it home. We'll feast all night."

At this, almost everyone yelped and barked and clapped.

"But now . . ." began Lord Stephen, and he screwed up his eyes. "You know what to do." Before he had even finished speaking, he let go of the ewe, and she scuttled across Clunside and away across the grazing land and down to the river, followed by a pack of scrambling, shouting villagers.

First, the ewe sidestepped Simon and then she squirmed out of

Abel's grasp, leaving him holding two handfuls of wool. Then Rowena tripped and fell face-first into the river. After that, the ewe suddenly doubled back and ran right round the chasing pack and straight up to old Wilf, who fell over backward, clasping the ewe tightly in his arms.

"Fair and square!" exclaimed Lord Stephen, laughing. "She's Wilf's! He won't let go of her until he sees his Maker."

"Fair and square, but dark and round!" Rahere said mysteriously, and then he began to warble:

> "What would you do with a ewe?
> Would you milk or wear or kill her?
> Tell me now, tell me true:
> Would you boil or smoke or grill her?"

Lord Stephen smiled faintly, then waved Rahere away as if he were a noisy bluebottle.

"We're going to have to manage without you," Lord Stephen told me.

"Why, sir?"

"Because in seven days' time the priest at Caldicot —"

"Oliver?"

"— Oliver, is coming over to take you to Wenlock Priory. You and Miles, to see the scribes at work."

"We were going to go last December," I said.

"I heard about that," said Lord Stephen. "Well, better late than never! After that, how would you like to ride over to Caldicot?"

"Oh!" I cried. "Thank you, sir."

"And not long after that we'll be leaving for Champagne."

"When?" I asked.

"When Milon names the date," Lord Stephen replied. "We should hear any day now."

the GReen knight

 Y STONE FLARED LIKE A DYING CANDLE, LIKE SUN-light swiping one of the little glass windows in the solar. Rose-gold first: then silver, freezing and blue. It's beginning to snow. How strange to see sky-feathers in my stone, when today the sun never blinked and I baked a hen's egg on the flat stone in the middle of the river.

I can see Arthur-in-the-stone, entering the great hall at Camelot with Guinevere. The whole company rises to greet them.

Sir Erec, Sir Fergus, and Sir Gawain. Sir Helain, Sir Ither, Sir Joram, and Sir Kay. Side by side and shoulder to shoulder, each knight is as high and as low as all his peers. The Round Table shines like a water lily.

"You know my rule," the king calls out. "It's New Year's Eve and I won't eat one mouthful of this feast until I see or hear of some marvel. Something to sharpen the appetite!"

Now the trumpeters try to raise the hall rafters, and the pipers point the way to love, the drummers pound their stretched skins. Together they play this New Year's promise and its resolution.

But now there's a loud banging and the hall's dark mouth swings open. A huge knight rides in.

He's as large as a troll and green! Completely green. His skin, his surcoat and tunic and boots, they're grass-green and willow-green, first-dawn, rosemary.

He's wearing a silken cloak, and now he's so close I can see it's embroidered with hundreds of birds and butterflies — all of them green. No sword or spear. No shield. In his left hand he's holding a branch of holly, and in his right hand a battle-ax.

The green blade is more than three feet long. The spike's inlaid with gold studs.

The Green Knight slowly rolls his bloodshot eyes, so that everyone in the hall has to meet his gaze or avoid it. He clears his throat and spits on the rushes. "Who's the kingpin here?" he demands in a deep voice.

Arthur-in-the-stone stands up. "I am Arthur," he says. "You're welcome here. Will you sit at our feast?"

"Heaven help me!" booms the Green Knight. "I'm not staying that long. But I've heard your court is the bravest, the very best on this middle-earth, so I thought I'd come and see for myself. I haven't come to pick a fight." The Green Knight glares around him. "Anyhow, there's no one here worth fighting. I could beat all these beardless boys with my eyes shut. No, I come in peace. You can see this holly. All I hope is that you'll play a Yuletide game."

"Name it!" the king says.

"I'll name it, but who dares play it?" the Green Knight asks. "Which man here dare exchange blows with me? I'll give him this ax and he can strike me once, if he promises to stand and take my blow. Not today! No! A year and a day from now."

No one says anything at all. The Green Knight laughs, a hard, biting laugh. "I see," he says. "And this is King Arthur's court?"

The king looks at his knights and not one of them meets his gaze.

"What are you all made of?" the Green Knight demands. "Sawdust? Feathers?"

Arthur half-rises from his chair and leans on the edge of the table until his wrists stretch tight. "No one here is scared by you," he says. "I'll strike you myself. Give me your ax!"

Now Sir Gawain leaps to his feet. "Never!" he shouts. "That's not fitting."

The Green Knight smiles and swings down out of his saddle. He's a whole head taller than anyone else in the hall. "That's more like it," he growls.

"Sire," Sir Gawain says to the King, "give me this quest. I'll strike the blow."

"Cut off his head," Arthur says. "That'll keep him quiet!"

"Tell me your name," the Green Knight says, his eyebrows bristling, "so I know I can trust you."

"Gawain."

"Very good!" says the Green Knight, his voice deep inside his throat.

"But where will I find you?" Sir Gawain asks. "I don't even know your name."

"All in good time," the Green Knight replies. "Strike me first, and then I'll tell you!"

Now the Green Knight leans right forward. I can see the nape of his neck.

Sir Gawain places his left foot a little in front of his right. He grips the huge ax, and with a shout cuts off the Green Knight's head.

The head rolls over the hall floor, right up to Guinevere's feet.

But the Green Knight's body doesn't fall over. No! It strides after its own head and bends down and picks it up.

Now the Green Knight mounts his horse and holds up the head by the hair. He turns it to face Sir Gawain, and the head slowly clears its throat.

"I am the Knight of the Green Chapel. Keep your word, Gawain! Come to the Green Chapel on New Year's morning."

Now the head chuckles, and its bloodshot eyes glare at Sir Gawain. And with that, the Green Knight rides out of the hall.

My whole stone is sparkling. Hoarfrost! Thick, white hoarfrost. Each grass blade, each twig: The whole world is wearing dazzling, spiky armor.

Now I can see Sir Gawain again, one year later, and he's riding Kincaled north through wild hill country. They're making their way into a freezing forest. Tangled trees. Gruff rocks and hillocks of long-haired moss.

A ragged army of sparrows hops from branch to branch ahead of Sir Gawain, peeping and squeaking, and now he crosses a quagmire to the base of a waterfall. It's curtained with icicles, but water's still cascading into the pool.

Sir Gawain dismounts and kneels on the bone-hard ground.

"It's Christmas Eve," he says. "Mary, Mother of Jesus, show me where in the morning I can hear Mass."

For a while Sir Gawain stares into the seething pool and the freezing air hanging over it. He sighs and crosses himself. And as soon as he remounts and takes Kincaled's reins, he sees the outline of a castle through the trees.

High white walls. Towers and turrets. Peep windows, parapets, clusters of pinnacles. They look as if they've been cut out of parchment and fastened to the pale blue sky.

Sir Gawain rides up to the moat, and a man looks down from a parapet.

"God's greetings!" Sir Gawain calls. "Will you ask your lord to give me shelter?"

Before long, the same man lets down the drawbridge, and Sir Gawain rides into the castle courtyard. One servant leads Kincaled away, two more take Sir Gawain's helmet, sword, and shield, and a fourth leads him to his room, to disarm and wash and put on fresh clothing — a maroon mantle, lined with ermine.

When Sir Gawain enters the hall, he sees the lord of the castle standing in front of a blazing fire, rubbing his large red hands. He's a large, well-built man, and his beaver beard looks like a spade. His face is fiery.

Sir Gawain walks up to him and embraces him.

"You're most welcome," says the lord. "All the more so on Christmas Eve."

Near to the fire, there's a trestle table covered with a pressed linen cloth and laid with a napkin and a saltcellar, a silver spoon, and a knife.

"You must be ravenous," the host says. "We've eaten already. We eat early here, up in this wilderness."

First, a bowl of fish broth. Now, grilled trout and salmon baked in fine pastry, both of them served with tasty sauces.

"A feast!" says Sir Gawain.

"Fast, more like!" replies his host. "We'll feast tomorrow. Eat up now!"

Once Sir Gawain has eaten, his host asks him where he has come from.

"The court of King Arthur," Sir Gawain replies.

"King Arthur!" exclaims the host. "King by blood and king by deed! The best of young men!"

"He is," Sir Gawain says.

"You've ridden all that way? Two hundred miles! What was your business there?"

"I serve the king. I'm his nephew."

"You!" bellows the host, and he thumps the table so hard the saltcellar jumps in alarm. "King Arthur's nephew?"

"I'm a knight of his Round Table."

The host explodes with delight. He waves his arms in the air, and the salmon and trout stare at him with bulging eyes. "A knight of the Round Table," he chuckles. "Think of that! A knight of the Round Table at our humble Christmas feast. You do us great honor."

Sir Gawain shakes his head.

"Will you tell me your name now," the host asks, "or can I guess it?"

"Gawain."

The host leaps to his feet and gazes at the rafters. "God be praised!" he calls out. "Sir Gawain here, in my uncouth castle!"

At this moment, two ladies enter the hall. The host's wife is extremely beautiful, even more so than Guinevere, and I can see Sir Gawain thinks so too. She has laughing grey eyes and a broad brow, and the most lovely full lips.

The other lady is three times as old, maybe even older. Her skin's as wrinkled as parched barley, and it's grey.

"Just in time!" the host exclaims. "Do you know who this is?"

Sir Gawain and the two ladies greet one another, and the host's wife asks, "What brings you here, so far from court, on Christmas Eve?"

"I've no choice," replies Sir Gawain. "I gave my word to go to a place I don't even know how to find. On New Year's morning. Have you ever heard of the Green Chapel? The Green Knight?"

The host leans back and laughs. "The Green Chapel!" he bellows. "That's only a couple of miles away."

Sir Gawain stares at his host, amazed.

"You're exhausted," the host says, "and no wonder. You need food and drink and sleep, and plenty of them. I'll tell you what. On the last three days of the year I always go hunting, but you stay here. Sleep late, and when you rise my wife will keep you company."

The host's young wife smiles at Sir Gawain.

"Not only that!" the host exclaims. "Let's make a bargain. Whatever I win out in the forest, I'll give to you. And whatever you win, here in the castle, you must give to me. How about that?"

"Gladly," says Sir Gawain.

At once a servant steps forward and pours more wine. Christmas Eve grows old and yawns. Two servants with flaming brands lead Sir Gawain away to his own room.

a love letter

RAN UP THE STONE STEPS, THREE AT A TIME. I HURLED myself onto the window ledge in the evening sunlight, and broke the wax seal, and unrolled the little square of parchment:

Winnie to Arthur
on the fifteenth day of August

To my well-beloved friend

I greet you and send you God's blessing. I am not skilled at writing like you because you write everything and this is the first letter I have written so can you read my words.

You know I placed the sprig under my pillow. I did see the person, Arthur. If I agreed, I wonder whether you would agree. What do your head and heart say. You will inherit Catmole so I can speak to my father and he likes you I know.

If you want to know how I am, I am heartsick and I will be till you write to me. Please let me know when you are leaving.

May the Blessed Virgin Mary keep you safe. Written at Verdon

BY YOUR LOVING WINNIE

79

A WORLD INSIDE
OUR WORLD

LMOST AS SOON AS I'D READ WINNIE'S LETTER, MILON'S messenger arrived from Champagne. Then Oliver rode in from Caldicot, and early yesterday morning we left for Wenlock, so I don't know when I'll be able to reply to Winnie's letter.

Anyhow, what am I going to say?

Would I agree?

It's all a tangle. I won't know exactly what I'm going to write until I'm holding my quill and fingering the piece of parchment. Then my head and heart will start to speak my words to me.

"It's all agreed," Lord Stephen told me later in the evening. "We'll leave for Soissons one month from today: the seventeenth day of September. Milon will arrange for us to meet Count Thibaud — and that's when we'll take the Cross."

The most important thing in my whole life. The day when I dedicate myself. My own crossing-place.

"Before that, there's our harvest to bring home," Lord Stephen went on, "and the extra precautions in case any Welshmen do show their faces, and your visit now in Wenlock, and then Caldicot, and we must plan all the day stages of our journey, and attend to our horses and armor, and our clothing."

"How long will we be away, sir?"

"No more than six weeks," Lord Stephen replied. "But from

now until the day we leave, you'll find each day passes more quickly than the previous one."

Oliver and Miles and I were in the saddle for most of the day, and Oliver kept beaming at me and gently sighing to himself. He's just the same as ever.

"What about your reading and writing?" Oliver asked. "You are practicing each day?"

"I was."

"What does that mean?"

"With Haket."

"Ah, yes!" said Oliver. "Disgraceful! There's always a rotten apple somewhere in the barrel, and it has to be dug out. What about the girl?"

"Rowena," I said. "She's all right now. She's helping Gubert in the kitchen."

"Anyhow," Oliver went on, "why can't you read with Miles?"

"We're going to," I said. "Aren't we, Miles? But first there was the harvest, and now —"

"The only time is now," Oliver said. "The person who thinks he can put things off until tomorrow will never reach the gates of paradise."

"I'm not putting things off," I said indignantly. "I'm riding with you to Wenlock so I can learn about writing and painting."

Oliver patted his stomach and beamed at me. "Very true, dear boy," he said. "And about time too."

I do like Oliver. I like arguing with him, and although I often disagree with what he says, he always makes me think. By the time we rode into the priory, he had delivered his opinion on a hundred subjects, and we'd talked about the Saracens, whom Oliver despises, and about Merlin. I know Oliver says he is a heretic, but all the same, I think he still misses him.

Before I knew Sir John had arranged for me to be Lord Stephen's squire, I was worried in case he meant me to be a priest or a schoolman, or even a monk.

I'm glad he didn't. For most of the day, monks here at Wenlock are not allowed to talk to one another, and they have to get up in the middle of the night to sing Matins. I sometimes feel lonely at Holt, but it would be much worse if I were a novice monk. I wouldn't be able to see Winnie.

The old monk in the cell next to mine has stopped me from getting to sleep. First he kept snorting like a wild boar, and then I think a nightmare must have ridden him, because he started to yell. He's quiet now, but I'm wide awake, and I've been pretending to be a novice here at Wenlock:

> We're allowed to speak
> between None and the supper bell
> if we need to,
>
> but slowly each monk grows
> to love
> his own silence.
>
> I talk to Winnie half the time
> in my head
> but I can't always

hear her answers.
The prior says time will be my friend.

You can never hear all the words
read during supper in the refectory,
but tonight
there was not much chewing
and the wind stopped whistling.

Darius sealed Daniel in the lair
but an angel came in the blue hour
and shut the lions' mouths.

Most nights there are sudden yelps
in the cells near mine,
horrid mutterings and gasps.

I am excused Matins
because, the prior says,
green bones need growing time.

Little Brother of the Watches,
speak to me.

Miles has visited this priory several times before, and in the
scriptorium this morning, old Brother Austin and Brother Gerard
treated him like a friend. In fact, Brother Gerard embraced him,
and Miles's long white face turned quite pink!

I don't know why Miles didn't become a monk. He doesn't think he'll ever get married, and his books are his best friends. His beard hair is silky and he's so light-footed I never hear him until he's standing beside me.

The moment you climb up to the scriptorium, which is quite warm because it's above the kitchen, it's like entering a world inside our world, with its own language and methods, even with its own time.

Or rather, you leave time outside the door. If you're a scribe, each stage takes just as long as it must take. And if you try to rush it, you will wreck everything. I often get impatient, so I don't think I would have made a good scribe.

"Is it true two novices work with you?" I asked the brothers.

Brother Austin shook his head, and I noticed that it's somehow too large for his body. "It was true," he said. "We've still got Greg — he's doing the dirty work — but Crispin's in the infirmary."

Brother Austin and Brother Gerard caught each other's eye.

"More than one month now," Brother Gerard said. "It's was dreams first. The devil got inside him and howled. And now he's wasting. Just wasting!"

"Betony," said Oliver. "The only cure."

"We've tried that," said Brother Austin. "And jasper."

"Take it to bed with you," Oliver said. "Hold it tight and it should drive out the dark ones."

Brother Austin sighed. "We need him here," he said, "but he's halfway to God. His skin's like goat parchment."

He pointed at a goat's pelt stretched on a hoop-frame to dry. It was grey, brownish grey.

"You see these pegs?" said Miles. "You turn them each day to stretch the skin while it's drying."

"Is that when it tears?" I asked. "The parchment I write on always has holes in it."

"That was Crispin's job," said Brother Gerard. "Checking for tears and stitching them up. You have to do that while the skin's still damp."

"Look at this piece!" complained Brother Austin, pointing to a second frame. "Like a slice of cheese after the mice have got at it."

"Another trouble with goat," added Brother Gerard, "is that it's so thin: It curls easily. Very poor parchment, really."

"But some vellum —" Miles began.

"Vellum?" I asked.

"Any kind of parchment," Miles said. "Some vellum is almost furry, and some almost shines . . . some's thin, and some too thick to fold. . . . At Holt I have one piece with ghost-branches inside it —"

"Deerskin," said Brother Gerard at once. "That's the blood that was inside the skin when the beast died."

"Some pieces have ridges," said Miles.

"They do," said Brother Austin. "Where the backbone has run under the skin."

Soaking the skin in lime and water and scraping away all the hair and stretching the skin on a frame and shaving it . . . rubbing it all over with pumice-bread . . . sewing together the gatherings . . . ruling the pages with a scraper but being very careful not to cut right through them: all this and more before you even begin to cut your quills and make your inks and blacken them.

"Two inkhorns," said Brother Gerard. "One for black, one for red. Black for the text, red for headings and initials."

"And red-letter days," Brother Austin said, smiling.

"I love making ink," I said. "It's a kind of magic. Ink is the words' blood."

We had to leave the scriptorium for Terce and then for Sext, and after that there was dinner. Brother Almund is so short he could only just peer over the reading-desk, and he read so quietly I could scarcely hear him.

When we returned to the scriptorium, Brother Austin led us to a sloping desk with an unfinished page on it, its weights dangling over the edges.

"Now, Arthur!" said Brother Austin. "Sit down!"

The burnished gold leaf and vermilion and blue of the initial *A*! The height of the writing-space matching the width of the page! The words, purplish. The lettering, so simple and stately, but a little larger at the bottom of the page than at the top . . .

"All this to the glory of God!" said Oliver grandly. "Truly, the art of the scribe is a sacrament!"

"Read the words!" Brother Austin told me.

"*A*," I began. "Arthur!"

Arthur? I looked up and saw the monks and Miles were smiling.

"Arthur," I read, "you need a chair with high arms and a back-rest, and a footstool. You need a knife to shape your quill, and don't forget to scrape out the fuzzy part on the inside. You need pumice-bread or a boat's tooth to polish the parchment, so that the ink does not run. . . ."

Oliver puffed himself up and sighed rather noisily. I could tell he thought the monks had been wasting their time, and their precious parchment, but at least he didn't say anything.

"I copied it very early this morning," Brother Gerard said. "We are lost to the world here, and sometimes the world forgets us. But take this with you, and you'll remember us."

"I will!" I cried. "I write words each day, and now it will all be different. And when Lord Stephen and I join the crusade, and have to fight, I'll remember the peace in this scriptorium."

"*Deo gratias!*" announced Brother Austin. "Come on, or we'll be late for None."

"And if we are," Brother Gerard added, grinning from ear to ear, "Prior Humbert will castrate us!"

Late this afternoon, Lady Marie de Meulan arrived here with three servants, and they're staying in the prior's own lodgings.

Brother Gerard told me that she writes story-poems that are recited in courts and castles all over England. The first time she came to Wenlock, she recited one about two lovers and it wasn't really Christian at all.

Lady Marie is French, and quite tall and lean, and she has piercing blue eyes. She seems rather proud and expects people to defer to her, but Brother Gerard says she's kind and she has already visited Crispin in the infirmary.

This evening, I saw her on her own in the prior's garden. She

stretched out her right hand and held it very still, and then —
chook! chook! chook! — a nightingale flew out of a willow bush and
nestled into it.

She isn't a saint, is she?

I heard the bell toll the second hour, and now all the monks
have come back from Matins, flip-flopping down the passage to
their own cells.

Quite soon, the choir of birds will be clearing their throats and
singing their own sweet offices. Makers of light!

Is there a prayer for sleep? Words that dawdle and begin to forget themselves?

the green belt

IR GAWAIN'S HOST, THE LORD OF THE CASTLE, PUTS TWO
fingers in his mouth and whistles, and at once a servant walks in, bearing a boar's head on a platter.

"My winnings!" says the host. "He's yours, Gawain."

Sir Gawain strokes the boar's head and grasps its sharp tusks.

"He ripped three of my dogs — stem to stern. We kept shoot-
ing arrows at him, but his hide was tough as oak bark. He was
snorting and foaming, but I buried my sword in his chest."

"Praise be to God!" Gawain exclaims.

"Now what about you?" growls the host, and his bushy eyebrows bristle. "Yesterday you gave me one kiss. What have you got
for me today?"

Sir Gawain steps up to his host and puts his arms around his
neck and kisses him twice, once on the left cheek and once on the
right.

"Really?" booms the host. "And where did you get those from?"

"That's not part of our bargain," Sir Gawain replies.

The host smiles and rubs his beard. "If you go on like this," he
says, "you'll soon be a rich man!"

Dark again. One moment my stone's quick with laughter and
colors, the next silent and dark as a starless December night. But
why? Why does it sometimes die? Is it because of me?

For some time all I could see was myself.

I can make my right ear twitch without touching it. And I used to scare Sian with my demon-faces, but I can't touch my blobby nose with the tip of my tongue like she can.

I cradled my stone in my right hand. I kept it warm. I wanted so much to see . . .

Footsteps first. Very soft. Then a latch lifting; a creak. The host's wife peeps round the door, and now she creeps into Sir Gawain's bedroom and gently sits down on the edge of his bed.

Sir Gawain opens one eye and quickly closes it again.

"Good morning!" says the lady, bending down and kissing Gawain on his right cheek. "How careless of you! You left the door unbolted."

"Was I wrong to trust you?"

"Of course not! You're among friends here."

"I feel quite helpless lying on my back," says Sir Gawain. "Let me get dressed, and then we can talk all morning."

The lady tosses her head and the opals in her hairnet flash. "I've trapped you, and every woman in the kingdom would envy me," she says.

"I'm not worthy of such attention."

"You're so strong and honorable, always in good spirits. No woman could hope for a better husband."

"You've already chosen a better man," Sir Gawain says.

The lady gives a small sigh. "The best stories of all," she says, "tell of love and battle. Don't you agree? Of men who risk all for love, and the women who challenge and reward them."

"The love of battle," Sir Gawain agrees, "and the battle of love."

"Exactly!" exclaims the lady. "But you've never once told me about love. Not one loving word."

"My lady," says Sir Gawain, "it's I who should learn from you. You could teach a whole army of fellows like me."

The lady tucks up Sir Gawain and kisses him on his left cheek. "Your last morning here," she sighs. "Will you give me something to remember you by? A glove, maybe?"

"Lady," says Sir Gawain, "I'd give you the moon for a sister, but I've nothing with me — nothing worthy of you."

"I know, then," says the lady, and she unties her green silk belt, hemmed with gold, and slides it off.

"No!" says Sir Gawain.

"Why not? It looks valueless, I know, but whoever wears it can never be wounded."

Sir Gawain gazes at the silk belt.

"For my sake," says the lady very softly, and she inches back Sir Gawain's sheet and slips the belt under it. "It has circled me, now let it circle you. But promise not to tell my husband."

The lady stands up, and now she bends right over Sir Gawain and kisses him on the mouth. Her grey eyes flicker.

"I'll give you my winnings first," says Sir Gawain. He steps up to his host and puts his arms round his neck and kisses him three times: on his right cheek, his left cheek, and then on his mouth.

"My heaven!" exclaims the host. "Where do they all come from? And what did they cost?"

"I've kept my part of the bargain," Sir Gawain says. "Now what about yours?"

"Bah!" trumpets the host. He whistles, and at once a servant brings in a tawny pelt. "You see? Nothing but a mangy fox. May the devil take him!"

Now the host's wife and the old lady enter the hall. Music and candlelight, wine from Aquitaine. Sir Gawain thanks his host over and again for all his kindness.

"So! In the morning you must ride to the Green Chapel," the host says, and he combs his matted hair with his left hand. "My gate-watchman will point the way. Sleep well, my friend."

But Sir Gawain doesn't sleep well. He lies awake half the night, thinking about his meeting with the Green Knight. The New Year is still dawning as he strides out to the stable, dressed and fully armed. He's wearing the lady's green belt hemmed with gold, and it's tied with a double knot.

The wind's from the north and the sky is lumpy. A few snowflakes go whirling round the courtyard.

"May little Lord Jesus watch over the good people in this castle," Sir Gawain says. "And may He save me when I meet the Green Knight."

"You see that high peak?" the gate-watchman says. "The one half-shrouded. Head for that, and when you come to a stream, follow it down. Past a rock pile, and you'll come to a clearing. You won't miss the Green Chapel."

Sir Gawain mounts, almost lost in the great puffs of steam Kincaled is blowing from his nostrils.

"I wouldn't be in your shoes," the watchman says, "not for nothing. If I were you, I'd head off while you can. I won't tell nobody."

Sir Gawain smiles ruefully. He thanks the watchman and follows his directions until he reaches the little clearing, and on the banks of the boiling stream, a green mound. A burial barrow!

Sir Gawain dismounts. He walks right round the barrow. It's quite hollow, with an entrance at either end.

"Is this it?" he says to himself. "The Green Chapel? I've never seen such a God-forsaken place."

All at once there's a clatter on the other side of the stream. The Green Knight is running down the scree, and when he reaches the bottom, he stabs his battle-ax into the ground and vaults right across the stream.

"So!" booms the Green Knight. "You've kept your word. New Year's greetings to you."

Sir Gawain pulls off his helmet. "One stroke," he says.

The Green Knight glares at Sir Gawain and wipes his mouth with the back of one hand.

"One will be enough," he says.

Sir Gawain stares at the Green Knight's ax. The blade's even longer than the one he brought with him to King Arthur's court. It's at least four feet long.

"Wait here!" says the Green Knight. He walks over to an outcrop of rock and hones his ax on it. Now he coughs. That horrible hacking cough he had before. "Are you ready?" he asks.

Sir Gawain slowly drops his head, and at once the Green

Knight swings his ax. But Sir Gawain glances sideways and hunches his shoulders, and the Green Knight checks his stroke.

"You flinched!" he shouts.

"It won't happen again," Sir Gawain says. "But I can't put my head back on."

At once the Green Knight swings his ax over his head again. But for a second time, he checks his stroke.

"Ah!" he growls. "I see you're ready at last."

"Strike me!" says Sir Gawain in a low voice.

"The knighthood King Arthur gave you — let it save you if it can!"

"Strike!" says Sir Gawain hoarsely. "Or have you scared yourself?"

For a third time, the Green Knight hoists his shining ax. He swings it and brings it down — and just nicks Sir Gawain's neck.

At once Sir Gawain leaps away, yelling. He draws his sword. But the Green Knight? He just jabs his ax-point into the ground and begins to chuckle.

"Sheath your sword, man," he says. "You've kept your word."

Sir Gawain frowns.

"My first stroke. It didn't harm you, did it? I should hope not. On the first day, you kept your promise and gave me all your winnings. Then you gave me my wife's two kisses. But the third day! Gawain, you deceived me, and that's why I've nicked your neck. That belt is mine! My wife made it for me, and I sent her to your bedroom to test you."

All the blood in Sir Gawain's body rushes to his face. He unties the belt and hurls it at the Green Knight's feet. "Curses on my cowardice!" he shouts.

"You're too harsh on yourself," the Green Knight says. "You kept my belt out of love of your life. Not out of lust! Not out of greed! Who can blame you for that?"

Sir Gawain stares at the drops of blood in the snow, and he fingers his neck.

"No man can be quite perfect," the Green Knight says. "Not even you. Let me tell you: That old lady, she's Morgan le Fay, King Arthur's half sister. She hates him and his court, and spits at the name of Queen Guinevere. With her magic, Morgan turned me green. It was she who sent me to test the courage of the Round Table. Come back to my castle now until Yuletide's over — everyone will be glad to see you."

"I must return to Camelot," Sir Gawain replied. "But will you tell me your name?"

"Bertilak," the Green Knight replies. "Sir Bertilak of the High Peak. Now! Take this belt! You've earned it, and whenever you look at it, you'll remember . . ."

"Your wife maddened me," Sir Gawain says. "She made my blood whirl. I'll remember my failure."

The Green Knight laughs. "I don't suppose King Arthur or the knights of the Round Table will see things like that," he says in his deep voice. "I believe they'll want to wear green belts as well, as a sign of the honor you've brought to them all."

White flakes whirl around them, Sir Gawain and the Green Knight. And now the wind neighs, the snow thickens. . . .

Arthur-in-the-stone and Sir Ontzlake, Sir Palomides, Sir Quercus, Sir Roland . . . they're all waiting to welcome Sir Gawain back to Camelot, and to honor him.

In my stone cell, at Wenlock, I flexed my muscles. I'm a squire. I'm ready. I'm ready to take the Cross and turn towards Jerusalem. I'm a knight-in-waiting and ready to prove myself.

inside the story

 HE NEXT EVENING, MARIE DE MEULAN DID RECITE A story, in Prior Humbert's lodgings. It was about two lovers and the lady's husband. The lovers can never meet — their houses are separated by a high stone wall — but each night they go to their bedroom windows and whisper to each other. But one night the lady's husband wakes up and asks her what she's doing, and his wife says she's listening to the song of the nightingale: the greatest heart's joy in this world.

Then the husband snares the nightingale. He wrings its neck and throws it at his wife, and spatters her breast with blood.

The lady knows she'll never be able to whisper again to the man she loves. She sends him the dead nightingale, and he understands — he knows it's the lady's own broken heart. The lover lays the bird in a little gold casket and carries it with him wherever he goes.

By the time Lady Marie had finished, half the lay brothers and guestmasters were sniffing and dabbing their eyes.

"Jealousy," observed Prior Humbert. "The old destroyer."

"What else could the husband do?" asked one lay brother. "Stand by and allow his wife to make love to another man?"

"No love without suffering," another called out.

Then Oliver stood up. "How can there be?" he demanded.

"How can there be love without suffering when Christ Himself suffered for His love of us?"

"Well said!" exclaimed Prior Humbert.

"No," said our guestmaster. "I don't agree with that. Haven't you heard of a marriage made in heaven?"

Lady Marie looked round with her keen blue eyes. I could see she was devouring every word of the debate, and I wondered whether she could make a new story out of it. Then she thanked the prior and all of us for listening so attentively, and she and her servants retired for the night.

I was on my way to the scriptorium this morning when Lady Marie suddenly came out of the chapter house, and she was on her own.

"God's blessings!" she said.

"Lady!" I replied.

"What's your name?"

"Arthur."

"Arthur . . . I saw you liked my poem."

"I did!" I exclaimed. "Everyone did."

"They're a soft lot," Lady Marie said. "But at least they're not jealous."

"I've never met anyone who makes her own stories," I said.

"I build them from old Breton ones," Lady Marie replied. "I reshape them, like clay. So that they say what I want them to say."

"About love and suffering?"

"That, yes, and about jealousy, as Prior Humbert said. But also about women — their spirit and daring, their frustration." Marie de Meulan considered me. "You like words," she said.

"I do."

"And stories."

"Yes."

"More than sermons?"

"Some sermons have stories inside them," I said.

"Very good!" said Lady Marie. "The best ones always do. Well, Arthur! You can make a story."

With that, Marie de Meulan smiled and turned back into the chapter house, and for a moment, her long gown fluttered against my legs.

I am! I am writing a story, though it's not a poem. The story of my life and how it's changing. The story of my namesake, inside my seeing stone.

In a way each of us is a story, and all the stories we hear become parts of our own story. . . .

I can see it plain now. With these words, their red and black blood, I'm telling a story about a lady who told me a story about telling a story inside this story of my own life.

WORDS FOR WINNIE

FTER WE RODE BACK FROM WENLOCK, AND BEFORE I
set out for Caldicot, I wrote this:

Arthur to Winnie
on the twenty-fifth day of August

To my dear friend

I can read your letter, Winnie, and I hear your voice
each time I read your words. I hoped I was the person.

I think I would agree if everyone does. First speak to
your father. I am not sure who will decide for me, but I will
try to discover while I am at Caldicot. Sir William, certainly, but I hope Sir John and Lady Helen will also.

I dressed this piece of parchment for you. It is lamb-
skin. Simon says he will put these words between your
hands as soon as he can, but I wish I could.

We leave for Champagne in three weeks. May Saint
Winifred keep you safe. Written at Holt in haste, by candlelight.

BY YOUR LOVING ARTHUR

RETURN TO CALDICOT

HE MOMENT I SAW TUMBER HILL, I COULD SEE MYSELF up on the crown again, playing hide-and-seek with Sian, climbing my climbing-tree, dancing round the New Year bonfire, sitting and talking with Merlin . . .

Then I saw her. She stepped out into the sunlight from behind the knotty trunk of an oak, her fair hair sizzling.

"Gatty!" I shouted, and I swung out of the saddle.

When Gatty came to Holt, she was a crock of mucus. Her eyelids were orange and her lower lip was raw, and she was so worn out she could scarcely speak.

But now!

"Gatty!" I cried. "You're taller. And, well . . ."

Gatty lowered her eyes and her eyelashes swept her cheeks.

"You walked all this way," I said, "and you slept in a tree. Lady Judith said you were like a bear cub."

"And she's an eagle and all," Gatty said.

I hadn't planned to, and I'm not sure how to arrange it, but I heard myself saying, "You remember what we said? About going to Ludlow?"

Gatty looked at me. The way she does. Half-hopeful, half-wistful.

"This time we will, Gatty! Ludlow Fair!"

While we were still talking, Serle rode up and interrupted us.

That's exactly what he did when I was saying goodbye to Gatty last January, and the strange thing is we were talking about Ludlow Fair then as well.

"I thought so," Serle said loudly, looking down at me. "Laying plans?"

"Serle!" I exclaimed, and I grinned and grabbed his right knee. "I haven't even arrived yet. I haven't seen anybody."

"I'm off," Gatty said. "Got to get some wood."

"I'll see you, Gatty," I said. "We will, this time."

"Will what?" Serle asked.

"Nothing."

Serle hasn't changed much since January. Now he knows I'm not his blood-brother and he'll inherit Caldicot, all of it, I thought we could get on, but he keeps finding new reasons to be sour, and whatever I say only seems to make things worse.

"I've got a chestnut colt," I said. "A destrier! He's wonderful. I wanted to ride him over to show you, but Lord Stephen wouldn't let me."

"Of course he wouldn't!"

"I thought he might. I mean, Sir John paid for him."

"Thank you for reminding me," Serle said.

As Serle and I were riding up toward Hum's cottage, I saw Merlin stepping into the church. I know I did!

"Merlin!" I yelled. "Merlin!"

I spurred Pip and cantered up to the church.

But Merlin wasn't there. He wasn't anywhere. Just like that time when we were sitting on top of Tumber Hill and he disappeared while I was talking to him.

"What was all that about?" Serle asked when he'd caught up with me.

"You heard," I said. "I saw him."

"You couldn't have. No one's seen him for weeks and weeks."

"I do. Every day."

"What's that supposed to mean?" Serle asked.

What Merlin said to me at Holt and what I've seen in my stone make me think his time really has come. But I don't think he has gone into the earth, or thin air, or into the minds of schoolmen at Oxford. No, not even to an island of glass. I think Merlin's still here, a wise old spirit, hovering, and it's just we can't see him unless he wants us to.

Last night, Sian insisted on sleeping next to me, and she woke me up this morning by clinging to my back.

"Let me go!" I said.

Sian dug her fingernails into me.

"I'm mother-naked! Let me get dressed."

I shook Sian off me and scrambled to my feet. Then I threw her up and caught her, and she squealed with excitement.

"I love you, Arthur," she said fiercely.

When Serle and I talked again this morning, I thought he would want to hear about Tanwen and Kester.

"No," he said.

"But —"

"Just because you see them the whole time, that doesn't mean you know everything."

"I know but . . . Tanwen does like Lady Judith, and Kester . . ."

"Shut up, Arthur!" Serle said angrily.

"Tanwen told me you'd ride over every month. She wants to see you."

Serle said nothing.

"Will you come before we leave for Champagne?"

"And that's another thing," Serle said. "I've no idea why you're joining the crusade — and neither has Sir John. No one else from the Middle March is going."

"That's not true," I said. "Sir Josquin des Bois."

"Two knights, then," Serle exclaimed scornfully.

"And hundreds from other parts of England," I said hotly, "and thousands from Picardy and Flanders and Champagne and France."

"While you're away," said Serle, smiling with his thin lips, "lining your pockets with gold, you're shirking your duties here. That's what my father thinks. He says you're as bad as Sir William: He's been away in Champagne now for a full month."

"Running his manor," I said indignantly. And as soon as I said it, I realized that's the first time in my life I've spoken up for Sir William.

"When the Welshmen show up, who'll defend Holt?" Serle's piggy eyes gleamed. "We will! We'll have to. Sir John and I and Sir Walter de Verdon and everyone else. You think you're so brave, battering the brains of a few infidels and entering the golden gates of Jerusalem, but your real duty, your real responsibility, is here at home."

I didn't tell Serle what I thought. I didn't tell him how this would be the turning point of my whole life. I didn't say that, anyhow, I don't really belong anywhere in the Middle March — not at

Caldicot, not at Gortanore, not even for all that much longer at Holt.

"So you and Lord Stephen do exactly as you please," Serle continued, "and then expect us to defend your backs. There's no justice in that."

"It's you who's unjust, Serle," I replied. "You know you are."

Oliver was right! Nain has lost her last tooth. But that hasn't stopped her from having a mouthful of opinions.

"You don't need teeth to have teeth," she told me. "White fire! I always said that girl was no good."

"It wasn't only her fault, Nain."

"Pah!" exclaimed Nain.

"But Kester," I said. "He's a bundle!"

Nain gargled. "That baby! He's wrecked his mother's life and poisoned Serle's. That brother of yours, he's sour as a crab apple."

"He's not my brother," I objected.

"Just as well," said Nain.

"But wasn't I like Kester?" I asked. "I mean, my father and my mother, they weren't married."

"Don't think of it!" said Nain.

The truth is I do think about it often. Did my birth wreck my mother's life? Where is she now? How can I find her?

I haven't seen Sir John and Lady Helen for six months, and after I'd climbed Tumber Hill, we sat and talked in their chamber. To begin with, we were quite awkward. But then we began to laugh, and they asked me all sorts of questions about my life at Holt.

"You've got a warm eye for Lord Stephen's niece," Sir John said, smiling. "That's what we've heard."

"Well . . ." I began, and I could feel myself flushing. "I do like her."

"What about Winnie?" Lady Helen asked. "How does she feel?"

"Sir," I said, "when I get betrothed, who'll decide for me? Sir William, I know, but will you as well?"

"Mmm!" said Sir John. "I'm not sure I know."

Then Lady Helen smiled at me; she clapped her hands.

"Anyhow," said Sir John, "come home safe first from your great crusade."

"You're not against that, sir?"

"Against what?"

"Lord Stephen and me. Going on crusade."

"Of course not. What gave you that idea?"

"Nothing!" I said.

After that, I told Sir John and Lady Helen how I keep thinking about my mother. "I must find her," I said.

"I understand," said Sir John. "We've always tried to make the right choice for you, haven't we, Helen? Do you remember I told you once that what one wants to do and what is right are not always the same thing?"

"When I wanted to go into service with Sir William," I said.

"Exactly," Sir John said drily.

"I didn't know then. About everything."

"No," said Sir John. "Now, what Lady Helen and I think is that searching for your mother would be very dangerous."

"Because Sir William doesn't want me to dig anything up."

"What hurts Sir William is bound to hurt you as well," Sir John replied. "Of course you want to find out — but the price would be too heavy. For Lady Alice and Tom and Grace. For us all."

"But I must find out!" I said desperately.

I looked at Lady Helen, and the corners of her mouth were twitching. She stood up and wrapped her arms round me.

"Arthur," she said huskily. "You told me I'd always be your mother. And I called you my crusader son."

"I've loved you as a son," I said quietly, "and you have loved me like a mother."

Lady Helen sniffed. "But that's not enough?"

"Where there's love, there's duty," Sir John said. "Isn't that right?"

"Yes, sir."

"So what is your duty to Lady Helen and to me?"

Up here in my writing-room, the floor is covered with bird droppings and little drifts of white flakes. And when I put my hand into the gap between the blocks of dressed stone where I used to hide my seeing stone, I pulled out a whole cluster of snails. Somewhere, something's ticking! I smell the friendly thatch-scent and yawn. It's almost as if I've never been away.

love's snare

OVE WITHOUT FEAR," SIR LANCELOT SAYS, "IS FLAME without heat."

I've heard those words before. At the wedding feast of King Arthur and Guinevere. And here, last Christmas! The song of the snow-white girl with dark pouches under her eyes.

Guinevere's right hand, her long fingers, are stretched across Sir Lancelot's open palm.

"What are we to do?" she whispers.

"Have we any choice?" Sir Lancelot asks.

"It's true!" Guinevere says, and she is breathless. "We're helpless. We're caught in love's snare."

"This is God's gift," Sir Lancelot says. "We must accept it with all its joys and terrors."

Guinevere slowly shakes her head. "A woman may be ready to sin and to suffer," she says, "but unready to allow her husband to suffer."

"Where there is love there's suffering," Sir Lancelot replies.

"But I am Arthur's queen."

"He is my king."

"But his quest!" says Guinevere. "His dream." Fearfully she clutches Sir Lancelot's hand, and he closes it like a vice around her fingers. "Around the table my own father gave him. One fair fellowship. One round of honor. One unbroken ring of trust. If what I do in any way dishonors him . . ."

"How can our love be wrong, if no one knows?" Sir Lancelot asks. "Heaven help troublemakers and gossipmongers."

"I am torn," says Guinevere. She is fearful and in pain.

Lancelot comes close to her. On her cheek she feels his warm breath, and she can hear the stamping of her own blood.

"The song of the nightingale," the queen murmurs, and she closes her eyes.

the Nightingale's Reply

 LIVER TOLD ME AT WENLOCK THAT THE GREEK WORD for a nightingale is *philomela,* a lover of song. But lovers seem to think it means the opposite: a singer of love.

In Lady Marie's story, the song of the nightingale was the song of the wife's own loving heart. And when Queen Guinevere heard the nightingale, she allowed Sir Lancelot to kiss her.

Poor nightingale! Everyone blames his song, but it's not his fault, is it?

> What if the young girls do as they please
> Or if young men grow hot and strong?
> You can't blame that on my song.
>
> Or if a man gets on his knees
> And sighs and begs? Just like some dove!
> What if a girl gives all her love?
>
> *Chook! chook!* As if that is my fault!
> I'll tell you who should get the blame
> For love's joys and tearing pain.
>
> You should! You all know right from wrong.
> I won't keep quiet, I won't lie low.
> The choice is yours: Say yes or no.

86

SOFT-SWORD

IR JOHN DISLIKES THE NEW KING EVEN MORE THAN he did before I left Caldicot.

"Soft-sword!" he said in disgust. "That's what people are calling him. That treaty he made in May with King Philip, agreeing to pay him twenty thousand marks: His brother would never have stood for it."

"Then why has he, sir?"

"Because he's soft," retorted Sir John, "and we have to pay for it. Our kings may rule by the will of God, but just look at them! Coeur-de-Lion despised England. His men may have loved him and his enemies admired him, but he was wolf-cruel. And as for our king's great-great-grandfather —"

"William the Bastard?"

"He was as porky as a pig's bladder," said Sir John. "They didn't bury him in time, and his body blew up and burst."

ludlow fair

 HAVE TO FIND HER," I SAID. "I MUST."

Pip half-stumbled and indignantly swished his long tail. He didn't like having to carry us both.

"I'd hunt for my mother," said Gatty, "if she was still alive and I didn't know who she was."

"Because Sir John doesn't want me to," I said, "it doesn't mean I can't."

"That's not his mother," Gatty observed.

"I know I have a duty to him," I said, as much to myself as to Gatty, "but I keep wondering . . . If I were to ride over to Gortanore . . . Sir William's away!"

The sun kept winking at us as we rode down the track through high, waving trees, and there was time for everything! Time to talk, and time not to . . . time to dismount beside a little stream and feed each other with little lumps of cheese and bread I'd begged off Slim . . . time to splash each other and shout and laugh . . . time to find out about everyone.

"There are fifty-nine people living in Caldicot," I told Gatty as we remounted, "and before we reach Ludlow I want to hear about each of them."

Gatty laid one warm hand on my back. "My brother died," she said quietly.

"Not Dusty!"

"He started laughing, and laughed until he choked, and no one could stop him."

"Oh Gatty!" I cried. "When?"

"They didn't tell you," she said.

"No. They must have wanted to let you."

Gatty didn't reply. She just took hold of my shirt, and as we jogged along, tugged it a little.

"Little Dusty!" I said. "You were everything to him. . . . You know, when Luke died, Oliver told us dead children become angels in heaven."

Later, Merlin told me Oliver was completely wrong and didn't know what he was talking about, but I didn't tell Gatty that.

Gatty sniffed. "Ruth's pregnant," she said.

"Already!"

"Five months married, five months gone. I reckon that'll come on Christmas Eve."

"What about Lankin, then?" I asked.

"Just sits," replied Gatty. "Half the day he's hot as any stew, that's what Jankin says. Takes his clothes off and just sits. Naked as a needle."

I turned round and looked at Gatty over my shoulder. "He can't last long," I said.

"You said that."

"I hope he won't! It's not fair on you and Jankin."

Gatty didn't reply.

"Well? Is it?"

"Nothing's not fair," said Gatty.

"He and Hum should make things up once and for all, and then you can be betrothed."

Ludlow Fair!

First we led Pip into a pen where there were dozens of other saddled horses, and I was glad then that I hadn't brought Bonamy over from Holt. He's so strong and handsome, and someone might have tried to steal him. We paid the keeper a farthing to feed Pip and look after him, and then we joined the crowd.

I did tell Gatty there would be lots of people, but she didn't realize there would be hundreds and hundreds. One thousand, even.

Stall holders bawling for attention! Bargaining! Blasts of laughter! The braying and neighing and snorting of all the animals in their pens. And everywhere, people jostling . . .

You can't walk in a straight line because people get in your way. You have to keep stepping sideways and using your elbows, and after a while, walking feels more like wading. Some of the time Gatty and I had to hold hands so we didn't lose each other.

We watched a man playing three pipes at the same time, one in his mouth and one in each nostril. And then we paid to see a woman put a dwarf in a coffin and cover the coffin with black sacking and saw the coffin in half. Everyone gasped, but somehow the dwarf had tied himself in a knot at one end. And after that, we paid to see the woman with three breasts, but it wasn't worth it.

"I've only got two-and-a-half pence," I said.

"Don't matter!" Gatty said joyfully.

"Sweethearts!" shouted a man, and he grabbed my elbow.

"What?"

"Sweethearts, are you?"

"No! No, we're not."

"Pastry hearts! Mincemeat tarts!"

"We're not hungry," I said.

"I am and all," said Gatty.

So I bought two chewets, but they were stuffed with gristle and sharp little bits of bone.

While Gatty and I were walking under the castle wall, we had a shock. We saw Johanna, the wisewoman.

"Quick!" I said, spinning Gatty round. "Before she sees us."

"What's she doing here?"

"Selling her medicines," I replied. "Some of them are true, like the ones she gives to people at Caldicot, but some are bogus. Tanwen told me."

"Why do people buy them, then?"

"They're buying hope," I said. "Hope is easy to sell."

After that, I kept thinking I'd seen someone I knew: the peddler who stole Spitfire, and Haket, wearing a hood, selling relics. But then I really did see Miriam, hand in hand with a friend: the dark moons of her eyes, her solemn little face. I wanted to find out how she was, but by the time I'd told Gatty about her, she had skipped away again.

We stayed at the fair until the sun was quite low, and before we left, I bought a long, violet ribbon with my last farthing.

"To tie up your hair," I told Gatty. "Or wind round your field hat. Or you can wear it like a belt."

Gatty looked at me. Unblinking and grave.

"We going upstream?" she asked.

"Upstream?"

"Like you promised."

"Gatty!" I said. "We can't do that as well. Not this time. I've got to leave the day after tomorrow."

Gatty slowly lowered her eyes. Then she lowered her head.

"We will next time. Come on! We ought to be going."

Gatty wound the ribbon round her left wrist. Round and round. Then she looked up again and tried to smile, and at once she broke into tears.

"Oh no!" I said helplessly.

Gatty rubbed her eyes against the violet ribbon, then fiercely shook her head.

On the long journey back to Caldicot, we didn't say very much. Not that we had nothing to say, but our hearts were heavy. Some of the time, Gatty put her arms round my waist and rested her head on my back.

If she were the daughter of a knight: Lord Stephen, or Sir Josquin, or Sir Walter . . . Or even the other way round: if I were the son of a miller or bowyer . . . And if I hadn't met Winnie . . .

I do hope Gatty and Jankin will be betrothed. But sometimes I think how she deserves better, and how unfair things are, and I wish — well, I don't think Jankin's really worthy of her.

"Will Hum beat you?" I asked.

"Don't matter."

"Not with the whip?"

"What about you?" asked Gatty.

"I don't know," I said. "Sir John would have while I lived here. Maybe he'll tell Lord Stephen."

In the dark, we dismounted and walked up to the stables.

"You've got your ribbon?" I asked.

"Mmm," murmured Gatty.

I pulled Gatty to me and she laid her warm cheek against mine.

A dog barked. Cleg's, probably. Or maybe Wat's. Sitting up here, in my writing-room, I can hear the same dog barking again now.

"I keep thinking," Gatty said. "I can't say it exactly."

"About us?"

"Best things," said Gatty. "They don't never get lost."

88

Risks

OU HELP US AND WE'LL HELP YOU," MAGGOT SAID.

"To find her?"

"Maybe."

I didn't tell anyone what I was going to do, but soon after we left Caldicot I told Daw I could easily find my way back to Holt and sent him home. Then I rode to Gortanore. I knew Sir William was away, so I thought I might be able to find out more about my mother. But I didn't know that Lady Alice and Tom and Grace would be away too. They have gone to Verdon.

"Did she give you the ring?" I asked. "Herself?"

Thomas clucked. "Not so fast," he said.

"I will," I said. "I will help you. But how can I? I'm only a squire."

"Not yet," said Thomas.

"When Sir William's gone," said Maggot.

"You mean . . . when he's dead?"

"And you're at Catmole."

"If you'll bring us over," Thomas said.

"To Catmole? But what about Lady Alice?"

"That's as may be," Thomas said. "What we need is your word, Arthur."

"Your promise," said Maggot.

"But why can't you stay here?"

"Maybe we can and maybe we can't," Thomas replied. "We're taking a risk even talking to you."

Maggot sniffed and drew a finger across her throat.

"I promise then," I said. "I promise to help you."

"Right!" said Thomas, and he nodded at Maggot. "We won't forget that, will we, Maggot?"

"The ring, did she give it to you?"

Maggot nodded.

"When?"

"When we told her."

"What?"

"About you."

"She knows about me?" I exclaimed.

"Maggot told her," said Thomas.

"When?"

Maggot scratched her head. Something fell out of it, and she crushed it under her left foot. "When was that, Tom?"

"When we was over," Thomas said. "May or thereabouts."

"Over where?" I asked.

Maggot's face narrowed. It was nothing but shifty eyes and a gap-toothed smile.

Thomas shook his head. "Too risky," he said.

My heart was bursting. "Did she . . . did she want you to give me the ring? I mean, was it for me? What did she say? Is it a message?"

"One at a time," said Thomas.

"But —"

Thomas looked intently at me with his one good eye. "Your

mother," he said, "she gave Maggot the ring so's she could give it to you."

"She did! Then what does it mean?"

"She don't know whether you want to see her."

"Want to!" I yelled. "Of course I do!"

"You do now," Thomas said, "but that all depends."

"What do you mean?"

"On what you don't know."

"I know she was living here when I was born," I cried. "I know she was a village woman. I don't mind who she is."

"We'll see about that," Thomas said.

"Who gave her the ring? Sir William?"

Thomas nodded.

"Then he did!" I said breathlessly. "He did care for her."

"I didn't say that, did I, Maggot?"

"Please!"

"That's enough for now," Thomas said.

I can't really remember what happened during the next hour. I know Thomas and Maggot left me on my own, and I kept walking round and round Sir William's hall, sobbing. I know my whole body was hot and cold, as though I'd caught a terrible fever. I know that, before I left Gortanore, I begged them to tell me more.

"I promise," I said. "I do promise to help you."

"Poor soul!" said Thomas. "She didn't even know you were alive. Not until we told her. When they took you away, they let her think you were sickly and died."

"And she thought they done away with you, and all," Maggot said. "I told her you grown up in a fine household."

"Can I see her?" I asked hoarsely. "Please! Where is she?"

Thomas clucked again. "That's not for us to say."

"You said you'd help me."

"What I'll do," said Thomas, "is take her a message. That's a risk, mind. I'll tell her you want to see her and you don't care."

"She's my mother!" I cried.

"She's afraid," Maggot said.

"Not of me."

"Partly that," said Thomas. "And Sir William."

"He won't know," I said fiercely.

Thomas stared at me and slowly narrowed his eyes.

"I'm going away," I said, "I have to. But only for six weeks. Will you tell her?"

the scarlet sleeve

T LAST!" EXCLAIMED LADY JUDITH. "YOU'RE VERY LATE
back, Arthur."

"I'm sorry, my lady."

"We were beginning to wonder whether we'd
got the wrong day."

"No."

"No! Well, it's much too late to hear everything now. Lord
Stephen has already retired. You can tell us tomorrow."

"Yes, Lady Judith."

Lady Judith looked round the hall. "God's grace!" she said.
"May He save us all from the dangers of the night." Then she stared
at me. She knows there's something I haven't explained.

Before long, I crept up here to my room. There are so many
things I wish I'd asked Thomas and Maggot. "Exactly the same."
That's what I heard Maggot whisper when I went to Gortanore
last March, and I want to know whether she meant I actually look
like my mother. I didn't even ask her that.

I took my gold ring out of its silken bed, and for a long time I
cradled it. Little Jesus giving His mother . . . what? A stone? An
apple? His own heart? Her long fingers contain Him and set Him
free. Both at the same time.

Then I unwrapped my seeing stone, and at once I saw Queen
Guinevere talking to Sir Bors.

"Fie on him!" Guinevere exclaims.

"I'm sure there's an explanation, my lady," Sir Bors replies.

"You're telling me Sir Lancelot was wearing a lady's sleeve? Fastened to his helmet?"

"He tricked us all," says Sir Bors.

"He's false," says the queen. "He's unworthy, and I'm glad you did wound him."

Sir Bors knits his brows.

"I don't care if his wound is the end of him."

"Lady," says Sir Bors. "Lancelot is my friend. You mustn't speak of him like that."

"I'll say what I want!" cries the queen. "What did it look like? The sleeve?"

"It was scarlet," Sir Bors replies, "embroidered with large pearls."

The queen tosses her hair into flames. "Lancelot!" she cries. "He's so puffed up! Anyhow, you bettered him."

"No, my lady," Sir Bors replies. "I did not. He unhorsed thirty men. He made us all submit."

"I suppose it belonged to Elaine of Astolat," the queen says. "I keep hearing how Lancelot adores her."

"I don't believe that," Sir Bors replies. "He loves each lady as much as he loves the others."

"Pah!" spits Guinevere, and she turns her back on Sir Bors and walks out of her solar into a room overlooking the river Thames. Arthur-in-the-stone is standing beside a window.

A slender boat swathed in thick, black silk is riding gently on the russet-and-silver water. There's one oarsman standing near the stern, and his oars leave whorls of silver in the boat's wake.

"Sir Kay!" calls the king. "Sir Brandiles! Come down with me. I want to know what this is about."

"I'm coming too," Guinevere says.

The oarsman steers his little boat alongside the landing stage. And there, lying within it, is the body of a pale-skinned young woman. She's covered with cloth of gold up to her waist, and lying on a bed of silk cushions — arum and lavender, sage and yew.

"Who is she?" Sir Kay asks the boatman.

The boatman doesn't reply.

"She's holding a letter," says the queen.

Now the king steps down into the boat and bends over the young woman. She is almost smiling. Gently he looses the letter from her tight, cold grip:

> Knight of knights! Sir Lancelot! I longed to win
> you, but death has won me. I loved you.
> I loved you so wildly I could no longer endure
> my own feelings, and my name was Elaine of Astolat.
>
> Let any woman who has ever loved a man listen
> to me. Pray for me, and have Masses said for me:
> This is my last wish. Sweet Lord Jesus, I
> tried to obey your commandments, and I died a virgin.
>
> Pray for my soul, Sir Lancelot. Knight of knights!

The little boat rocks and gently bumps against the landing-stage. The king and queen and the two knights gaze down at Elaine. So fair, so white.

"Sir Kay," says the king. "Send for Sir Lancelot."

My seeing stone. For a while it is stars trembling: It is tears and silent dark water . . .

"I had no wish to be the cause of her death," Sir Lancelot says, "and I owe her much. She nursed me night and day when I was wounded."

"You wore her sleeve," Guinevere says.

"I wore her sleeve," says Sir Lancelot, "and I've never done as much for any other woman."

"Why? Why did you?" Guinevere demands.

"As a disguise at the Winchester tournament. I borrowed her brother's shield, because he'd only just been made a knight, so I knew no one would recognize it. And I wore her scarlet sleeve because people know I never wear a lady's colors."

"Is that why?" Guinevere asks.

"And to please her," Lancelot replies. "She was a good, sweet girl, but she loved me too much."

"If you'd been even kinder," Guinevere says, "you might have saved her life."

"My lady," says Sir Lancelot, "it would have made no difference at all. She wanted to be my wife, that or my lover. Nothing else would satisfy her. And I did do more: I told her to love and marry another knight, and offered her an income of one thousand pounds each year."

"But she loved you," says Guinevere.

"My lady," said Sir Lancelot, "I've no wish to be compelled to love. Love must well up in the heart; it cannot be forced."

"That is the truth," says Arthur-in-the-stone. "A man must be free to love whomsoever he pleases. If he's forced into something, he'll only grow bitter. Sir Lancelot! You must arrange for Elaine's funeral."

"I will, sire," says Sir Lancelot. He bends his head to King Arthur, and now he leaves the hall, followed by the queen.

"When I heard about that sleeve, I was so angry with you," the queen says.

"Without cause," Sir Lancelot says.

"And jealous."

"Not for the first time."

"Will you forgive me?"

"Where there is love . . ." Sir Lancelot replies.

Lightly he lays his hand on Guinevere's sleeve.

90

ADAM AND EVE
AND ARTHUR

LOSE THE DOOR!" SAID LORD STEPHEN. "I WANT TO
talk to you."

"About my mother, sir?"

"Your mother? Why your mother?"

"I thought —"

Lord Stephen's eyes gleamed. "What's wrong with you,
Arthur?" he asked. "You look like an anxious cub."

"Nothing, sir."

"Will the bowyer rode in yesterday."

"From Caldicot?"

"Yes, Arthur, he brought this letter from Sir John. Oliver wrote
it for him, and I suppose you know what it's about?"

"Ludlow, sir?" I said in a small voice.

"Ludlow!" said Lord Stephen, and he gave a deep sigh. "Arthur!
One moment you acquit yourself honorably, even bravely . . . You
cut that last sheaf, and I haven't forgotten how you took charge
when Jacob was murdered. But at other times! What do you think
you were doing? What's her name? That girl?"

"Gatty, sir."

"Gatty, yes. Going to Ludlow Fair with a village girl. Without
permission."

"I promised her, sir. Before I left Caldicot. But then there
wasn't enough time."

"I see," Lord Stephen said drily. "And Sir John had given you permission, I suppose."

"No sir," I said, and I lowered my eyes.

"Of course he hadn't! You were his page, not a village boy." Lord Stephen's eyes gleamed. "Well!" he said. "Adam and Eve in the garden and now you, Arthur! Disobedient! What about this Gatty, then?"

"She's my friend, sir," I said. "I know she's a village girl, but we've always been friends."

"She was love-dumb for you when she came over here. That's what Lady Judith told me."

"No, sir," I protested. "She wants to be betrothed to Jankin."

"I'm glad to hear it," said Lord Stephen. "Sir John also said you asked who'll decide for you when you're betrothed."

"Yes, sir."

"He says you mentioned my niece several times."

"Not several times," I mumbled.

"Winnie," said Lord Stephen, and he ran the tops of his stumpy fingers across the wall hanging. "Yes, I can see why. And I can see the sense of it." Lord Stephen offered me a smile and then took it away again. "Not that anyone has asked my opinion! Anyhow, all this must wait until we get back. I'm not proposing to punish you this time, Arthur, for going to Ludlow, but you're my squire. I depend on you to be dutiful and obedient."

"Yes, sir," I said, and at once I thought about my visit to Gortanore.

"I know you went out to the stables one night not so long ago, and you know I forbid that. And now Ludlow! This is your last warning. One more thing, and you can stay here. I'll leave you behind. You do understand?"

"Yes, sir."

"All right," said Lord Stephen. "Now we've got two days and that's all. Go and check your armor with Turold, and talk to Rhys about feed for the horses. Then lay out your clothes. And stow them in your saddlebags."

"I can't wait!" I said.

When I ran down the steps from the solar, I found Rowena and Izzie in the hall, and Izzie was sobbing.

"The stupid thing!" said Rowena. "She says you won't come back."

"Of course I will," I said. "In six weeks."

Izzie looked up. Her face was blotched with pink spots. "I didn't say that," she gulped. "It's what my dream told me."

"Well, I'm coming back, anyhow," I told her.

Silly Izzie, always giggling or weeping, always out of breath! She lives inside her dreams:

> Witch-in-the-twig,
> Rider-in-the-broom . . .
> Tell me, teach me
> How to make him love me.
> Make him love me
> And I will love you.

That spell I heard her singing down by the river. It really was about me!

◆ ◆ ◆

Two days have passed since I began to write this, and we leave in the morning.

Tanwen helped me pack my saddlebags. I've decided to leave my ring here, safe in the hiding place under the short floorboard. But when I wake up, I'll put in my seeing stone. It's my dark well. My shining mirror. I must take it with me.

"I told Serle about you and Kester," I said to Tanwen. "At least, I tried to."

"Is he coming, then?" Tanwen asked.

"I'm sure he will. I said you want him to."

"Who said so?" Tanwen demanded.

"You do, don't you?"

"I don't know," Tanwen replied unhappily.

"Kester's happy, anyhow," I said. "He's got his mother. And you like Lady Judith."

Tanwen closed her eyes. The corners of her mouth quivered.

"I thought you did."

"I do, I do," Tanwen said softly. But when she opened her eyes, they were full of pain.

Lord Stephen never takes unnecessary risks. He has hired seven extra men from the constable at Wigmore Castle to guard Holt while we are away. They arrived the day before yesterday, and are billeted in the empty barn on the far side of South Yard.

When Gubert complained about having to feed them all, Lord Stephen was quite angry.

"What do you expect me to do?" he barked. "This is a frontier, Gubert! We have enemies on the other side."

"Yes, sir."

"And if I leave this place unguarded, the Welsh will walk in and grill you for breakfast."

Gubert smiled sheepishly.

"There are women here, and children. Lady Judith! Rowena and Catrin in your own kitchen."

"Yes, sir."

One of the constable's men is called Gib, and he helped last week with a hanging: a man who murdered a woman in Hereford. No one knew where he had come from, and he wouldn't say his name.

"Bitter as a sloe," Gib said. "The last thing he did was curse us, not cry for God's mercy."

After the hanging, the three hangmen drew lots for the murderer's possessions.

"His clothes," said Gib, "and a knife. I got his mare."

"Can I see?" I asked.

"She's got the mange!" said Gib, and he led me into the stables.

"Floss!" I cried. "Floss! You've come home!"

Floss eyed me and blinked and neighed, and I threw my arms around her neck.

As soon as I told Lord Stephen, he went down to talk to Gib, and then he came up here to my room. "There's no doubt about it," he said. "Blackberry eyes. A black chin beard. A bitter tongue. It must have been Alan."

I tried to see Alan in my mind. But all I could see was little Miriam.

"Now in my position, Arthur," Lord Stephen said, "what would you do about Floss?"

"Give her some medicine," I said.

Lord Stephen smiled. "Yes, that would be a good start. But to whom does Floss belong?"

"You, sir. She's yours."

"But as we're just going away . . . Wouldn't it be better to leave her with Gib?"

"Yes, I see, sir," I said.

This afternoon, Thomas rode in from Gortanore, but the first I heard about it was after he had gone.

"It was about you, Arthur," Lord Stephen said, very definitely.

"Stephen!" Lady Judith called from somewhere up the stone steps. "Can you please come up now?"

"One thing after another," Lord Stephen snapped. "You'd think I was going away for a whole year."

Does Lord Stephen know, then, about my visit to Gortanore? Has he found out?

"One more thing . . ." he said.

think of me

UST BEFORE LORD STEPHEN AND I LEFT HOLT, A HORSE-
man came galloping up the causeway. It was Daw, and
he had a letter for me:

Winnie to Arthur
this seventeenth day of September

To my well-beloved friend

Grace is here and she says you are not to be trusted.
You keep playing with words and breaking your promises.

You are not wellborn and I know this is true though it
is not your fault. Grace says you are the same as Tanwen's
son your mother is only a poor woman so a knight's daughter can never be betrothed to you.

From your letter, I cannot believe you really wish to be
in any case. Your words are all roundabout and not at all
about true love.

Tom was stung by three bees. I have rubbed him with
juice of plantain so he feels better.

May Saint Hildegard keep you safe. Think of me. Written at Verdon

BY YOUR TROUBLED WINNIE

There was scarcely a moment to read Winnie's letter before we left, and no time at all to reply. And now, I won't be able to for six weeks.

Oh Winnie! Don't believe everything Grace says. She's upset and angry because we can't be betrothed. And even if I am the son of a village woman, I was brought up in Sir John's household, wasn't I? And now I'm a squire.

Winnie, I did say you should speak to your father, didn't I? What am I to do?

92

TO LONÒON

N THE EVENING BEFORE WE LEFT HOLT, LORD STEPHEN told me Thomas's message was about me, and I was afraid he'd found out about my visit to Gortanore. It can't have been that, though, because he hasn't mentioned it at all.

I was going to write that Lord Stephen embraced Lady Judith. But really, it was the other way round. Lady Judith opened her arms and Lord Stephen fell into them. He only comes up to her shoulders.

Lord Stephen told me this evening that he met Lady Judith only once before they were betrothed, and their parents never even asked them whether they liked each other.

They didn't much, he said. But now I think they love each other. They're quite fond and playful, and always asking each other's opinion, and I've never heard them quarrel.

"When two people quarrel," Lady Judith told me once, "truth is always the loser."

"I don't understand," I said.

"They exaggerate," she said. "They let their feelings get in the way of their reason."

So Sir Lancelot isn't completely right. It's true you can't oblige two people to love each other. But sometimes a boy and a girl may become betrothed without really knowing or liking each other and then grow into love. Just as plants, stiff and straight-backed to begin with, sometimes burst into wonderful blossoms.

England is so large! It is one thing to hear about places and journeys from a peddler or a messenger, or to visit them in my seeing stone, but quite another to travel out of the March for myself.

It took us six full days to ride to London, and my legs and bottom are quite sore. Not only that. My tailbone is aching more than it has done all year.

All the same, I felt proud to be riding Bonamy. He's so alert, and keeps pricking up his ears, and wherever we stopped, people praised his chest and his silk coat, and tried to touch his silver-white star for luck. It's the first time I've ridden him away from Holt, and I did as Rhodri told me, and kept reassuring him.

"You oat-guzzler!" I said. "You London destrier! You channel-crosser! My fast friend!"

London is quite disgusting. It's as packed and noisy as Ludlow Fair but much, much larger, and it smells terrible. Not like the stink that comes from latrines, but something far worse, sour and rotten. After I'd been in London for an hour, I felt as though I'd shrunk as small as a thumb boy and been crammed inside a bad egg.

Everywhere there are chapmen and pickpockets and filthy urchins, friars, easy women, mounted messengers, mongrels, and yowling cats.

It's always noisy here, whereas in the March you can often hear the silence. It's quite thick. It enfolds you. Each sound, especially at night, is sharp and bright as a white stitch on black cloth.

I went with Lord Stephen to see Westminster, where Arthur-in-the-stone was crowned and the whole church echoed with shouts and cries.

"*Vivat! Vivat! Arthurus rex!*"

The archbishop held the crown over my head. . . . The two dragons on my scepter, one with a ruby eye, one with a diamond . . .

And Merlin! Merlin called out in his commanding voice: "Arthur, the trueborn king of all Britain . . ."

"Arthur!" said Lord Stephen. "Where are you?"

I drew in my breath.

"Here and elsewhere?"

"Yes, sir."

"That's how it is in a place like this," Lord Stephen said. "We leave today behind. We're in a world of spirits and memories. Implorings."

Lord Stephen gingerly lowered himself to his knees, and I knelt down beside him.

"Dear Lord," he said, "accompany us, your two servants, Stephen and Arthur. Bless Rhys and Turold, our loyal men. Give faith to those we love, and give us courage, far from our March, to welcome the unknown."

"Amen," I said.

As we were walking out of the church, Lord Stephen turned to me. "Difficult days," he said. "For you."

I didn't reply.

"Winnie, is it?"

"Yes, sir," I whispered.

"She's such a headstrong creature," said Lord Stephen.

"Yes, sir."

"Let her have her say," Lord Stephen said. "She's testing you."

How does Lord Stephen know? He hasn't seen Winnie's horrible letter.

I wish I weren't here, in London. I wish we weren't riding south tomorrow to Sandwich and the English Channel. If only it were a whistling, bright morning, and I were galloping to Verdon.

perceval and blanchefleur

 BOY CARRYING THREE JAVELINS IS STANDING OUT-
side a billowing pavilion. On one side it is gold, on
the other vermilion, and on the top there is an eagle
with outstretched wings.

"My mother told me a church is the most lovely thing there is,"
the boy says, "so this must be your house, God. I'll go in and pray."

Inside the pavilion, a girl is lying asleep on a bed of rushes and
tiny white flowers. Her hair is so fair it is almost white.

The boy tiptoes up to her, and the girl opens her misty blue
eyes.

"God's greetings!" says the boy. "Please kiss me!"

"Kiss you?" exclaims the girl, and at once she sits up.

"My mother said I should greet you with a kiss."

The girl looks puzzled. "Your mother?"

"That's what she said, yes."

"No," the girl says, frowning. "I won't kiss you. Certainly not!
Who are you, anyhow?"

"Perceval," the boy replies. "From Wales."

The girl looks at him: his coarse shirt and hooded deerskin tunic, his hairy shoes. "Where are you going?" she asks.

"Five men came crashing through our forest," Perceval says eagerly, "and I thought they were angels. They were so bright. But
they said no, they were knights."

The girl shakes her head at how simple and ignorant Perceval is.

"They were carrying spears longer than these javelins. You don't throw them, though. You charge with them, and they're called lances. The men were wearing iron, and I asked them if they were made like that, and they said no, and I said I was glad hinds and stags don't wear metal, otherwise I'd never be able to kill them."

"You've never seen a knight before?" the girl asks.

"My mother and I live alone in the middle of the forest," Perceval says. "We never meet anyone, and my mother hoped I'd never even hear about men who are knights."

"She sounds as strange as you are," says the girl.

"But then the five knights in the forest told me about King Arthur and how he makes knights," Perceval says, "and I want to be a knight too. So I'm going to find him, whatever the cost. Now please kiss me!"

"No!" says the girl.

"But my mother said I should," Perceval says, and he puts his arms around the girl and kisses her on the lips.

"Mmmm!" he exclaims. And now he kisses her again — seven more times!

The girl throws herself back on the bed in vexation, and Perceval sees she's wearing an emerald ring.

"My mother said I could take your ring if you offered it to me, but no more than that," he says.

The girl frowns again and tightens her right hand into a fist. "You'll have to rip it off my finger then," she said.

"All right," says Perceval. "I'll try not to hurt you." Then he opens the girl's fist, pulls off her ring, and puts it on his own little finger.

"I'm feeling rather hungry," Perceval says. "Have you anything to eat?"

He lifts a fresh white cloth and uncovers three little pies.

"Don't you dare touch them!" the girl storms.

"But I'm hungry," says Perceval. "One for me and one for you and that still leaves one over."

Perceval quickly eats the pie and smacks his lips.

"Thank you," he says, "for this tasty pie, and for the eight kisses and the green ring. I'd better be off now. God save you!"

"He hasn't saved me from you," the girl replies.

"God save you and bless you!" Perceval says, most politely. "Now aren't you going to bless me as well?"

"Never!" the girl says in a loud voice. "You've shamed me. You don't know anything about girls or kissing. You don't know anything!"

"But my mother," Perceval says, looking worried, "she says a boy who shames a girl shames himself. What is your name, please?"

The girl tightens her pretty lips.

"I will name you then," Perceval says. "White as white snowdrops, white as chamomile and hipperty-haw. You are White Flower."

The girl gazes at Perceval in wonder. "That is my name," she says slowly. "Blanchefleur."

"Please don't cry," says Perceval gently. "I'll look after your ring with my life, and I'll repay you for it. You'll see."

the sea

NEVER KNEW IT WOULD BE LIKE THIS.

In the dark, what was it? Hand-clap, screech, the whistle of ripping cloth. The west wind blowing through the copper beech at Caldicot. Thunder prowling round the far horizon. Or a giant trumpeting and clearing his throat.

Salt on my upper lip when I licked it. The smell of tar and slime and sodden ropes. Rotting fish.

But this morning!

The whole world of the sea was bucking and prancing and flashing. The white sky seemed to be fizzing and somehow lifting into itself.

I walked along the beach beyond the stone jetties and watched the waves. The really big ones leaned forward and hung right over themselves, and I could see inside them before they collapsed. Then they burst into foam. Seething and spitting, they rushed up to my feet, and little pebbles hopped inside them like midges.

For a long time I kept watch, and I thought the sea was a huge army on the move against England, growling and jostling and silver. I thought it was tender as a new mother. . . .

The pebbles here are like frozen sea tears. Charcoal, dawn-green, hoarfrost, purple-veined, and fawn. My pockets are sticky and heavy with them.

the GiANt
oN the mouNt

OOR PEOPLE!" CRIES THE MESSENGER. "PEOPLE WHOSE
only weapons are nets and sickles and knives. For
seven years the giant has helped himself to their
children. He murders them and eats them."

Arthur-in-the-stone stands up.

"There's only a handful left. And now he's grabbed our duchess
while she was out riding, the wife of your own cousin. Sir Howell
couldn't stop him. No one could. A whole troop followed them
back to the Mount, but none of them dared go anywhere near him."

"Shame on them!" shouts the king.

"You are our king," the messenger says. "Put an end to this out-
rage. Protect your people!"

"As I have sworn to do," Arthur says. "Where is this Mount?"

"Beside the sea," replies the messenger, "where Normandy and
Brittany meet."

"Sir Kay!" the king calls out. "Sir Bedivere! We've got work to do."

Now, in my stone, I can see three horsemen cantering through
the shadows to the foot of the Mount. The sun is setting over it.

"I'll climb up and spy things out," Arthur tells his brother and
Sir Bedivere. "You keep watch here."

At first the slope is very steep, and Arthur has to find finger-
and toeholds. But halfway up it eases, and on a little level there's a

bonfire and an earthy bundle sitting on the ground: an old woman rocking to and fro beside a newly dug grave.

"Sshh!" she whispers. "If he hears you, he'll roar down and rip you to pieces."

Far below, Arthur can hear the sea, slicing and slitting and tearing at herself.

"What are you doing here?" the woman asks. "You must be mad."

Arthur stares at the grave. The raw earth.

The old woman sniffs. "With these hands," she says, "I scraped it all out. I buried her."

"Who?"

"The duchess."

"Dear God!" the king whispers.

The bundle grabs his right arm. "Who are you?"

"I've come with a message for the giant from King Arthur."

"Pff! He doesn't give a fig for kings, or anyone else. Though if you'd brought Queen Guinevere . . . he'd lap her up like a bowlful of cream. He'd rather have her than half of France."

"King Arthur," the king repeats.

"He's already murdered fifteen kings," the old woman growls. "He plaited his cloak from their beards. If you must talk to him, do it while he's busy eating his supper."

The giant is lolling beside a fire on top of the Mount, wearing nothing but a baggy pair of drawers. He's tearing at a man's leg with his teeth.

Across the fire, three young women are turning spits, and four babies are threaded on each of them.

I can hear the king sobbing. "You filth! You ghastly, grisly —
Let the devil destroy you!"

The giant snorts and throws away the man's leg.

"Babies!" howls Arthur.

The giant reaches out for his iron club. All at once he rolls over
and up, and whacks Arthur's shield right out of his hand.

With his sword the king slashes at the giant's midriff. The giant roars. He hurls away his club as if it were some stick, and grabs
Arthur, and crushes his ribs.

The three young women are screaming; they're calling on
Christ to save the king.

Arthur and the giant teeter and topple. On the ground they
wrestle. The giant's on top, then Arthur's on top: Locked together,
they start to roll down the side of the Mount. Down and over the
little ledge, down again.

The giant reaches for Arthur's throat. Arthur reaches for his
dagger. He has it. He has it! He jerks and works his right arm half-
free; he drives the dagger right into the giant's chest.

The giant howls. Arthur can smell his vile breath. He gives a
deep sigh and his body slackens, but still the king cannot loose
himself from his embrace.

Down they roll, down until every bone in their bodies is
bruised. Down to the foreshore, where Sir Kay and Sir Bedivere
are waiting.

Each man grabs one of the dead giant's arms and pulls it away
from the king. Sir Kay and Sir Bedivere unwrap Arthur and pull
him to his feet.

For a while the three of them look up at the Mount, at the

wisp of smoke curling from the ledge, the white plume up on the crest.

"May Heaven swallow it!" says Arthur-in-the-stone.

"Amen," Sir Kay and Sir Bedivere reply.

"Climb up!" the king tells them. "Both of you. Comfort the old woman and the three young ones. And bring me back my shield and Excalibur. There's treasure up there, rubies and emeralds. We'll share it amongst the poor people — servants, shepherds, cowherds, and fishermen — each woman who has lost her own sweet child."

"We'll bring it all down, sir," Sir Bedivere says.

"All I want for myself is the giant's iron club," Arthur says. "That and his plaited coat. And I will have a church built here, in the name of Saint Michael, guardian of fighting Christian men."

My stone grew dark. It lay heavy between my hands. My whole body was aching.

When I fight the cruel Saracens, when I hear them howling, will I be able to be brave?

the saracen's blessing

HE WEST WIND OPENED ITS MOUTH AND BELLOWED; waves hurled themselves at the jetty. We had to wait in Sandwich for three days before we could set sail.

On the first day of October, we left as the sun rose away to port. Ahead of us the sea was brown as newly turned earth in the misty autumn sunshine. The huge clouds rolling across the horizon were like spirit galleys.

At one moment the water seemed to be tugging our groaning boat apart, but the next, it buoyed us up and carried us on its back as if we were riding on a sleigh over snow. And all the while, the canvas sail kept whirring and flapping, as though there were a strange sea monster aboard, ravenous for wind.

Two of the shipmen trimmed and fed the sail while the third man steered. I was afraid, and my teeth began to chatter when the waves slopped over the gunwales, and it was impossible to stand without holding on to something.

Bonamy was tethered to the mast and he was nervous as well. He kept rolling his eyes, and when he felt his hooves slipping, he tugged and whinnied fiercely, and I was unable to reassure him.

The shipmen just laughed, though, and told me it takes everyone time to find their sea legs . . . but even after we had disembarked, I kept swaying around inside my own head and missing my footing.

After the crossing, we traveled south and east through Picardy during every daylight hour. On the first evening, we reached the abbey at Saint Omer after dark, and we stayed the second night in a pilgrims' tavern, I can't remember where. Then we rode to Coucy and stayed in the manor where the Lord Enguerrand told us he plans to build a large castle. We crossed into Champagne yesterday and reached Soissons soon after noon.

If Winnie wants to know what Picardy is like, I'll tell her the landscape is flatter and more dusty than in the March. The track through some manors was lined on both sides with tall poplar trees: Their leaves tremble and gossip, and you can't be sure whether they're pale green or silver.

But the real difference is that almost no one speaks English here.

On the second day, we were short of water, and Rhys said our horses were thirsty as well, so Lord Stephen sent me out into a large field to see what I could get from five villagers. But when I asked for "ale" and "water," they just shook their heads.

I pointed to my mouth and threw back my head and slurped. That did it!

"De la bière. Vous voulez de la bière. De la bière!"

All around me, the warm air swarmed with strange syllables. And then one women brought me a gourd.

"Bee-air . . ." I said carefully, and everyone laughed. The woman gestured me to drink, and when I'd done so, she held out her hand as if she expected me to kiss it. Then she sucked her lips noisily, and the men slapped their thighs.

I didn't notice that Lord Stephen had ridden up behind me.

"You seem to be doing very well for yourself," he called out. "Are we going to get anything?"

In front of the church at Coucy there are steps, and sloping away from them a little square where people buy and sell. In the sunlight, the marl was glossy, almost silver.

In the middle of the square, there was a cot, and a long-limbed man was lying on it, propped up on cushions. The moment I saw him, I grew quite breathless, because he looked like Jesus come back to earth: his white skullcap and straggly black hair, and the huge dark pools of his eyes. His skin was sallow — sallow, but pearly grey.

Three women with floating hair and flowing dresses were looking after him — adjusting his cushions, shading his eyes, gently talking to him. We dismounted, and Lord Stephen talked to one of them.

"She says the man is dying," Lord Stephen said. "They've brought him out to die. Into the marketplace. That's what he wants."

Lord Stephen and I both crossed ourselves.

"Who is he?" I asked.

"Salman," said Lord Stephen. "She says his name is Salman. A Saracen."

"A Saracen!" I yelped.

The woman put her fingers to her lips, then smiled forgivingly.

I could hear Oliver's voice in my ear: "You can be sure hell's mouth is wide and waiting. . . . They worship a false prophet. . . . Saracens are infidels."

Then I realized the Saracen was looking straight at me. He smiled and said something.

"He says he hopes Allah always goes with us," Lord Stephen said. "He says he has a son much your age." The Saracen coughed into a scrap of cloth, and I saw that he was spitting blood.

"A son of your age," Lord Stephen repeated.

"Where?"

"In Granada. Near Granada."

"Where's that?"

"In the south of Spain."

Lord Stephen and the young woman talked quietly for a while.

"She says he's a trader. A good trader and a fine storyteller! He has come here several times before, and now he will die here."

The man said something softly.

"He thanks us for pausing on our journey, and asks us to pray for his soul. He says he feels fortunate to have met us."

"Fortunate!" I said, "He makes me feel fortunate. Meeting him."

"Yes, Arthur," Lord Stephen replied. "Both of us. Blessed are the dead who die in the Lord."

The man smiled faintly and murmured to the young woman.

"He says," Lord Stephen told me, "that wherever you turn, there is the face of Allah."

Here in Soissons, we're staying in another abbey. Before I went to Wenlock, I'd never been inside one, and now I've stayed in four! What I like most here are the bells. They're not tethered but swing freely, so they all sound at the same time, and the air quivers.

This afternoon, we went to meet Milon de Provins in his large town house. Lord Stephen says he's extremely rich and owns three large estates and as much land as the earl of Hereford. His father was the marshal of Champagne and almost as powerful as the count.

Milon isn't a big man, though he's taller than Lord Stephen, but he's strong as a fist, strong and friendly. He knows what he thinks, he laughs, but not overmuch, and speaks dreadful English.

He caught me grinning and playfully punched me. "You titch me," he said. "You titch me. *Oui*?"

Milon was very glad to see Lord Stephen and told him Count Thibaud will be able to lead a crusade numbering more than thirty thousand men.

"But no much English," Milon said.

"Not yet," replied Lord Stephen.

"You *ambassadeur*," Milon said to me.

"My father," I told Milon, "Sir William de Gortanore, he's a crusader."

That's the second time I have spoken up for Sir William, and I know Lord Stephen was looking at me.

"He served Coeur-de-Lion and King Philip," I explained.

"*Tel père, tel fils!*" Milon replied.

"Like father, like son," Lord Stephen translated, and he raised his eyebrows.

Milon told us that in three days' time he and Count Thibaud and Lord Geoffroy, the marshal of Champagne, will be meeting to lay plans.

"To discuss where the crusade should head for," Lord Stephen explained to me later.

"But —"

"I know what you're going to say," Lord Stephen said. "Jerusalem!

Yes, of course that's our destination. But that doesn't mean we'll go straight there. One way of fighting a monster is to bleed his gut."

"But where then, sir?"

"As I was saying, that's what has to be discussed — that, and where all the ships are to be built, and when the crusade is to begin. Crucial decisions! I know you! If you had your way, we'd set off tomorrow and sail straight to Acre and the kingdom of Jerusalem."

Milon says he has arranged for us to be received by Count Thibaud the day after tomorrow, at noon, and that is when we will take the Cross.

"And before that," Lord Stephen said, "I must teach you the words to say when you make your vow. You know, Thibaud is only nine years older than you. Young enough, really . . ."

Lord Stephen tailed off . . . What was he thinking? That Count Thibaud is young enough to be my brother? Young enough to be his own son? Tonight, in this chill cell, I've thought about the father I've never had. My crusader-father.

The sounds of the bells lapped around me and washed me. I thought of the gentle Saracen trader with eyes like Jesus, and of his son waiting in Spain.

97

TAKING THE CROSS

WELVE LARGE TORCHES WERE BURNING IN THE courtyard.

"But why?" I asked. "In broad daylight."

Without breaking his pace, Lord Stephen turned and gave me a warning look, but that didn't stop me from thinking the count is wasting a great deal of tallow and tow, and instead of paying his chandler for buckets of fat, he could have been feeding the beggars crowding the steps outside his courtyard gate.

When we entered the hall, a servant bowed and led us to a large lead basin attached to the wall, and poured water over our hands, and presented us with a shaggy towel.

"We're not eating here, are we?" I said. "I washed my hands this morning."

"Arthur!" said Lord Stephen under his breath, and he blinked disapprovingly.

"It's all so strange, sir," I said.

The hall floor was covered not with rushes but woven mats, and over them were colored rugs decorated with circles and stars and crosses, and there was the most enormous fireplace you could step into, almost as large as my writing-room at Caldicot, with logs it would take four men to carry. On the long walls, two huge tapestries faced each other; one was a knight killing a dragon, the other showed four men riding down a dusty track towards a distant city. Looking at it was somehow like looking at ourselves on our way here.

At the far end of the hall, there was a throng of knights, bishops, friars, courtiers, and servants, and I could see quite a number of squires.

Milon came forward and greeted us, and as we walked down the hall, I noticed a number of the knights and squires were wearing squares of white cloth on their chests or on their caps, each with a scarlet cross stitched on to it.

A whole group of squires turned and looked at me, and one of them said something. Then another pulled out his ears sideways, and they all laughed.

Lord Stephen took my arm. "Do you remember?" he began. "I, Arthur . . ."

"Yes, sir. I think so."

The vow I've thought about all this year! The moment I've been waiting for so long. I am ready. I know I am. I have come to my crossing-place.

Count Thibaud and Countess Blanche were sitting side by side on a wooden dais. I've heard that everyone likes him, except his enemies. He does look rather odd, though, because he has already lost most of his fair hair, though he's only twenty-three, and you can see his brains behind his forehead. But there are lights in his eyes, and he keeps half-smiling.

The countess has the same sallow skin as the Saracen trader at Coucy, and she's the daughter of the king of Navarre. Thibaud married her in June last year, and Milon told us she's already pregnant with their second child. She has brown eyes and sits like a statue.

"You are ready?" Milon asked me quietly. "The squire he prepare the way."

I looked at Lord Stephen, and he nodded, so I stepped up onto the creaking platform and dropped onto my right knee. Then the count opened his large hands, and I put mine between his. . . . Inside my chest, my heart was banging.

Fulk at Caldicot, punching our pulpit with his fists and urging us all to take the Cross . . . practicing my Yard-skills against Alan, when he almost choked me . . . riding to Quabbs and choosing my wonderful Bonamy . . . being fitted out by Turold in my shining armor — sometimes, inside one breath, one moment, there's time enough to remember dozens of other moments. . . .

But how can that be? Time can't change speed. It must be our sense of it that changes — we quicken or slow it with the levers of our thoughts and feelings.

"I, Arthur," I began in quite a steady voice, "son of Sir William de Gortanore, squire to Lord Stephen de Holt, swear by Almighty God . . ."

All at once, I was aware of the silence widening around me.

". . . that I will serve Count Thibaud of Champagne and be loyal to him, wheresoever he leads me. I acknowledge him as my true and only lord. I swear this by my squirehood. Let everyone bear witness!"

As soon as I said these words, everyone in the hall shouted, "We bear witness! We bear witness!"

"My lord," I said in a clear voice. "I am your man."

I felt Count Thibaud's hands tighten round mine, warm and quite bony. I looked up at him. His grey eyes were very serious, and we held each other's gaze.

"Arthur de Caldicot," he said slowly.

My heart was so full. My mouth was dry. There were so many things I would have liked to ask and say, but instead I felt Count Thibaud firmly raising me by my wrists.

I bowed and backed down from the dais, and at once a grinning friar with no teeth fastened a scarlet cross to my tunic with a few stitches, and then I was passed from hand to hand through the throng. All the knights and the courtiers, the squires as well, they shook both my hands and laughed and slapped me on the back, and said things in French.

And then the silence widened again. I could see Lord Stephen kneeling. . . .

Three Norman knights and their squires took the Cross after Lord Stephen, then two from Picardy, and then Count Thibaud stood up.

"Make no mistake," he called out, first in French and then in good English, "God wills this crusade!"

Everyone in the hall stamped and shouted; I heard myself shouting.

"You have taken the Cross, and it's your duty to urge other men — knights, squires, foot soldiers, rich and poor — to join this crusade. Why? God wills it!"

Again, everyone in the hall clapped and shouted.

"And the Holy Father wills it. Pope Innocent! To exterminate the pagans, to kill them or drive them out of Jerusalem, every single one of them. Some people say the pagans are ready to share Jerusalem with us. We can never agree to that. They're the enemies of God!"

But what about Salman, the Saracen trader? Surely he wasn't an enemy of God? And Ziryab, the wise singing teacher, and the Saracens who have written about the stars and medicines? If they're learned, how can they be so misguided, and enemies of God?

"If you choose me to be your leader, expect no easy decisions," said the count. "Expect the right ones."

The way he spoke was not nearly as passionate as the friar Fulk, but his warm resolve stirred and moved everyone. "In the watches of the night, you may have doubts. My manor! My wife and children! Have I done the right thing? Doubt," said Count Thibaud, "is only human. But you know the Holy Father will pardon each of you for your sins, without penance. The way to heaven will be open for you."

All around me, people were getting down onto their knees, crossing themselves and murmuring, "God be praised! God wills it!"

Lord Stephen put a hand on my shoulder. "I do wonder," he said quietly, "why all these people are really here. Fervor? A sense of duty? Or is it the chance of rich pickings? A chance to escape, maybe. Or the love of adventure? Well, when the crusade begins, I'm sure we'll soon find out."

"No right-thinking man wishes for war," Count Thibaud continued. "But as Saint Augustine has taught us, to keep the peace can be wrong. God commands good Christians to fight, and strip the pagans of their sins. We fight the Saracens for their own good.

Can anything be worse than for a man to sin without even realizing it?" The count raised his arms. "Let nothing delay us," he said. "Go home now! Settle your affairs! Within one year, we will begin our pilgrimage. Our quest for Jerusalem!"

After Count Thibaud had finished speaking, all the knights and squires who had taken the Cross went to the chancellery, so that our names could be pricked on the crusade muster. And then, as we walked out through the courtyard, eight men began to sing a crusader song, and Lord Stephen and I stopped to listen:

> "Each man who goes with Count Thibaud
> Need have no further fear of hell.
> Paradise will house his soul
> and he will drink at heaven's well.
>
> Christians are few, few as sheep,
> There are more Saracens than stars.
> Wives, lovers, and children, weep!
> Ay! Let Jerusalem be ours!"

Lord Stephen looked up at one of the flaming torches. "You were asking me about these," he said. "What would you say, Arthur, makes a man powerful?"

"His birth," I replied.

"You can be born powerful and still forfeit that power."

"His men, then," I said. "His followers. The loyalty he commands."

"Yes," said Lord Stephen, "and what keeps a man loyal?"

"If his lord is just," I said, "and generous to him."

"Generous?" Lord Stephen asked.

"With gifts and praise. And feasts. If he opens his palm."

"Aha!" said Lord Stephen, smiling. "If his money goes up in flames!"

awkward beasts,
and butterflies

OU'RE NOT GOING TO LIKE THIS," LORD STEPHEN TOLD
me. "Not to begin with."

"What is it, sir?"

Lord Stephen sat down on the bench beside me.
"Neither do I, entirely. Great challenges are awkward beasts; they
always cause hardship."

"What challenge, sir?"

"Now! You remember Count Thibaud told us to go home and
settle our affairs?"

"Yes, sir."

"Yes," and Lord Stephen slowly, and then he gently blew at two
ice-blue butterflies fluttering right in front of us. "Well. As you
know, the count and Milon and the marshal and the bishop of
Troyes, they've all been talking . . ."

"Yes, sir."

" . . . and the upshot is, they're sending six envoys to Venice.
To ask the Doge to build the crusade ships. To negotiate a price."

I've never heard Lord Stephen take so long to get to the
point — as if he were drawing a bow and taking aim very, very
carefully.

"Milon will be going. And so will the marshal, Lord Geoffroy
himself. He'll be the leader, and the envoys will have charters and
the power to make decisions. That's the idea, but it will have to

be agreed next month in Compiègne with Count Baudouin and Count Louis. . . ."

"Yes, sir."

"Well, Arthur, the fact is, they've asked me to go with them."

I stared at Lord Stephen, aghast, and he smiled apologetically.

"And you, of course. As English observers."

"To Venice?"

"Compiègne first, and then Venice."

"But we can't."

Lord Stephen rubbed his right hand across his eyes and nose. "When you'd just come to Holt, last January, I told you this crusade would be the greatest adventure of our lives. Do you remember that?"

"Yes, sir."

"Well, it has begun."

"But —"

"There is no 'but,'" Lord Stephen said. "There's only 'and, and and, and, and.' God has chosen us for this journey. It's a great honor and we must accept it."

"How long will it take, sir?" I asked bleakly.

"Venice? I don't know. I've never been there. South through Champagne and Burgundy and Savoy, then over the Alps, and east to Venice. It all depends on when we leave. October . . . November . . . December . . . Well, Arthur, we should certainly be home to celebrate Easter."

"Easter!" I cried.

"I know," said Lord Stephen. "I can see the difficulties, yours and my own. I must explain to my poor wife to begin with — and we'd better bring her back some good spices from Venice! And then I must send a message to the constable at Wigmore about the castle guards, and organize the management of the manor — all this and much more, with winter about to come. But this is how life is, Arthur. Uncomfortable. Often unexpected. And what are we to do about it? I think we must always expect change. We must somehow try to be ready for it, and even welcome it."

"Yes, sir."

"After all, you wouldn't really like it if you always knew what was about to happen. Would you?"

"No, sir."

"Winnie! Is that it?"

"Partly, sir."

"It won't hurt her, not hearing from you at once."

"But she says . . ."

"What does she say?"

"I'm not wellborn. She says I can never be betrothed to a knight's daughter."

"Nonsense!" Lord Stephen said cheerfully. "And you can tell her I say so. Write her a letter. You can use the messenger I send to England."

"Thank you, sir."

Almost one year ago, I pulled Grace up into my climbing-tree, and we talked about being betrothed. We believed we would be. But first I found out that that's impossible, because she's my half sister, and now Winnie is upset with me. It's all so difficult. The only girl I can really rely on is Gatty.

"You and Winnie," Lord Stephen said. "Yes! Would you like me to tell Sir Walter and Lady Anne what I hope? Would that help, do you think?"

"Oh yes, sir."

"And now your mother," Lord Stephen went on. "You're anxious about her."

"I am, sir."

But I couldn't tell Lord Stephen about my discussion with Thomas and Maggot, and how Thomas promised to take a message to my mother, saying how much I want to see her — saying I was going away, but only for six weeks. I couldn't tell him about her golden ring, and how I won't even see it now for months and months.

"I can't say I wholly agree with Sir John and Lady Helen," said Lord Stephen. "In his letter, Sir John said that searching for your mother would be too costly. Not just for you, but for people you care about. Your own mother, Lady Alice, and Tom and Grace." Lord Stephen hesitated. "It is dangerous, certainly. But after you came back from Gortanore — from your first visit to Gortanore, Arthur . . ."

"Oh!" I gasped. "You knew, sir!"

For a moment, Lord Stephen covered his eyes, and then he half-smiled. "After you came back, you told me you had to find your mother."

"Yes, sir," I said in a low voice.

"I agree with you. Your mother is your mother! You should find her, and that's what Lady Alice thinks as well."

"Lady Alice!"

"She came over and talked to me while you were at Verdon," Lord Stephen said.

"About my mother?"

"Yes."

"Does Thomas know?"

Lord Stephen looked puzzled. "Thomas? Why should he?"

"I just thought . . ." I began.

"Well, Arthur, what I can tell you is your mother is alive. She's alive and strong."

Tears were pricking the backs of my eyes.

"Your mother," said Lord Stephen, "I keep calling her your mother. Do you know her name?"

I shook my head miserably.

"Don't look so stricken!" said Lord Stephen, and he leaned towards me and smiled encouragingly. "Mair," he said gently.

"Mair," I repeated. Her sweet name. I listened to it like a deep secret; I put my whole self around it, and it shook me.

Lord Stephen put a pudgy hand on my shoulder.

"She's living at Catmole," he said, "in your father's manor. She's a poor woman, you know."

"It doesn't matter."

"Anyhow, Arthur, I think I can promise . . . yes, Lady Alice and I promise to try to arrange a meeting when we do get home."

"Oh!" I cried.

I stood up then, and Lord Stephen stood up, and he embraced me.

The two blue butterflies trembled and sipped from a red rose, then they danced on air around each other.

Lord Stephen blinked — at least ten times. "Provided —" he said.

"Yes, sir."

"Provided Sir William is facing the wrong way."

NAKED BRAVERY

OU," MILON SAID, AND HE POINTED AT ME. "BRAVEE!"
Then Milon raised his eyebrows and opened his mouth, but no words came out. So he gave up trying to speak in English altogether.

"Milon says he was out in this courtyard," Lord Stephen translated, "thinking about the crusade . . . and then he heard all the hubbub, so he walked over to that gate to see what was going on."

"It just happened," I said.

"Just happened, did it!" exclaimed Lord Stephen, smiling.

"I mean, I didn't think it out."

"Quite extraordinary!"

Milon looked me straight in the eye.

"You don't have to think to be brave — that's what Milon says. Bravery's something deeper than thought. It's an instinct. A few people have it; most don't."

"I don't usually," I said.

"You saw this man with a knife. It was Milon's own farrier, Jehan, but you weren't to know that. Milon says Jehan stabbed the man in the stomach, and then he rounded on the woman with his knife, and she was screaming. Is that right?"

"I think so, sir."

"No one on the steps lifted a finger. But you, Arthur, you

leaped across, unarmed, and threw yourself at Jehan, and knocked him down."

"Well, yes."

"You wrestled with him and pinioned him. You gripped his right wrist."

"He would have cut my throat, otherwise."

"I expect he would," said Lord Stephen.

"He did slice me here, sir," I said, and I showed Lord Stephen the deep cut down the inside of my left arm from above my elbow to my wrist.

"Dear God!" exclaimed Lord Stephen. "At least it's clotted."

"Bravee!" Milon repeated, and then he spoke in French again.

"Milon says you held this lout down until three of his constables forced him to drop his knife."

"The man he stabbed," I asked, "is he all right?"

"Dead," said Milon.

"No!" I cried. "What about the woman?"

"You saved her life."

"Why were they fighting, sir?" I asked.

Milon shrugged. "Two man woman," he replied.

Now Milon spoke more slowly and gravely to Lord Stephen, and Lord Stephen dovetailed his hands over his stomach.

"Milon says that if you're as good at your Yard-skills as your wrestling and your modesty . . ."

"I'm not really, sir," I said.

"No, well, we won't tell him that," said Lord Stephen.

"Thank you, sir."

Milon laughed and punched me on my right shoulder, the one Sir William wounded.

"You," he said. "Knight."

"No, sir."

"*Oui.*"

"No, sir. I'm Lord Stephen's squire."

"What Milon is trying to tell you," Lord Stephen said, "is that he knows naked bravery when he sees it. He admires you for your courage, and so do I."

"Thank you, sir."

Lord Stephen's face was somehow shining. "And Milon says, Arthur, that after we've been to Venice, when we all muster next year to begin this great crusade . . ."

"Yes, sir?"

"Before we set sail —"

"What, sir?"

"Milon says you may kneel to him. He will be proud to knight you."

the holy GRail

OUND THE RIM ARE WORDS WRITTEN IN GOLD: THIS IS THE SEAT OF SIR SAGRAMOUR . . . THIS IS THE SEAT OF SIR TAULAT . . . SIR URRY . . . SIR VAUX . . .

So the ring of the Round Table is almost complete. One fair fellowship, for all its flaws and feuds. One hundred and forty-nine men, still waiting for the knight who will sit in the Perilous Seat and achieve the quest for the Holy Grail.

The eight hall doors of Camelot swing and slam. The shutters of all the little windows rattle and close by themselves. The Round Table darkens. . . .

Servants scramble to light tapers and candles, and when there's light in the hall again, I see an old man dressed entirely in white standing inside the great door. Beside him there's a young knight, very young, no more than fourteen or fifteen, dressed entirely in poppy red.

"This young man," the old man calls out, "is descended from Joseph of Arimathea, who laid Jesus in His own tomb and then sailed to Britain. You have been waiting for him. Of all the great marvels this court will accomplish, he will achieve the greatest."

Now the old man leads the young one across the hall and round the Round Table. He lifts the white cloth from the table's rim:

At once there's a crack of thunder. Inside Camelot. The blast bounces round and round the walls. All the candles and torches are blown out.

Nothing but dark and cold, and all the knights and ladies of Camelot are shouting and wailing. As if it were Doomsday, and they were all teetering on the brink of purgatory.

One sunbeam, one pillar of light, flows into the hall. It glides towards them, rises, stands right over the Round Table.

The beam is so bright that the king can see all his knights more clearly than in broad daylight — more sharply than he has ever seen them before.

The king longs to shout for joy. Shout and sing. But he cannot utter a single word.

And now, through the great door, into this hush, floats the Holy Grail. It is covered with thick white silk, and I cannot see who is carrying it . . . I cannot see anyone at all carrying it.

Frankincense . . . myrrh . . . the air in the hall thickens and sweetens.

The Holy Grail! At Camelot. Slowly it circles the Round Table. Its redeeming promise enters each man and woman in the hall.

And now, all at once, the Grail sweeps away and out through the great door, as if it were borne on a draft of air. Over the Round Table, the bright beam gently fades, and as all the doors and shutters swing open once more, each knight and lady in the hall finds, steaming on the table right under their noses, the food they love best.

For Guinevere, venison . . . for Sir Lancelot, jugged hare . . . for Sir Gawain, grouse . . . and for the king, wild boar . . .

"Here in Camelot," King Arthur calls out, "we have seen the greatest marvel. Let this Pentecost feast begin!"

"The Holy Grail!" shouts Sir Gawain. "We've been shown it, but we have not seen it. We've been shown all we must try to achieve."

"Wait!" the king orders Sir Gawain.

But Sir Gawain will not wait. "Is there any knight in this hall," he asks, "who does not long to see the Holy Grail uncovered? I will leave Camelot tomorrow to search for it, and I will not come back for a year and a day, longer if need be. I know I must search for it, whether or not I achieve it."

"Gawain!" shouts the king. "No Christian king has ever had such a round of honor, such a ring of trust, as I have here at this Round Table."

But Sir Agravain . . . Sir Banin . . . Sir Cador . . . one by one, many of the king's knights stand and vow to search for the Holy Grail.

Down looks the king, down, deep into the rock crystal, with all its knots and scrapes and swerves, all its darkness and shining.

One by one they swear: Sir Vaux . . . Sir Wigalois . . . Sir Exander . . . Sir Yder . . .

"My lord," Guinevere says to him, "do not let them go."

"I love them as much as my own life," says Arthur-in-the-stone. "I cannot stop them."

"The king is right," Sir Lancelot says. "This is the finest fellow-ship ever seen together, anywhere. But to quest for the Holy Grail is the greatest of all honors. It would be a disgrace not to, now that we've been shown it here at Camelot."

"Do not let Lancelot go," Guinevere begs.

"After you all leave Camelot," the king tells Sir Gawain, "we will never meet together again — not in this world."

All around him, the ladies of Camelot are troubled and fearful.

"If you go," Laudine tells Sir Owain, "I will go with you."

"I am your rib," Lyonesse tells Sir Gareth.

Enid says nothing. She gazes at Sir Erec.

"On earth everything changes," says Arthur-in-the-stone. "And everything must change. But knowing you must die on your quests, many of you, is it wrong to grieve?"

Now many of the ladies are openly sobbing.

"Tomorrow," the king calls out, "let us all meet in the water meadows. Here at Camelot. Let us meet and joust and feast. So that as long as men have tongues, they will remember. They will say that, once upon a time . . ."

Sir Galahad rises from the Perilous Seat. He holds up his shield, white with a scarlet cross. . . .

I cannot see straight. The knights and ladies, the Round Table and the hall itself are nothing but streaks and gashes, white and scarlet and gold.

And my seeing stone: It is wet and shining.

101

A GRAIL OF SUNLIGHT

 AST NIGHT, LYING UNDER MY SHEEPSKIN, I THOUGHT about everything: becoming a knight and Winnie and our winter journey. I thought about my mother and the manor at Catmole.

One day I'll inherit it, that's what Sir William says. But what is it like? Will I ever really see it, or must I imagine it?

Catmole, Catmole. I kept saying the word to myself over and again, and the letters began to seethe like the stars in my seeing stone — the stars in the night sky when I try to count them.

Cometale . . . mot . . . malecot, elmcoat . . . comelat!

That was when I realized. I sat up, I filled my lungs with cool October air, and I yelled!

Catmole. I'll remake it. My pillar. My cloud of dust and, within it, a grail of sunlight. After Venice, after the crusade: my own March Camelot.

WORD LIST

ACANTHUS an herbaceous plant with an elegant, spiny leaf, often represented on stone and wood carvings, and as a decoration of illumination borders

ADAMANTINE steel-like, unbreakable (adamant was believed to be a kind of rock or mineral and to have magical powers)

AFFER a low-value horse, good for chores

AKETON a quilted garment of buckram that reached to the knees and was worn under a coat of mail

AUGER a tool for boring holes

BLOODSTONE a precious stone streaked or spotted with red; also known as heliotrope

BOWYER a person who makes (or sells) bows

BRACER a leather guard for the wrist, used in archery

CAERLEON a Roman legionary fort on the border of England and Wales where King Arthur regularly holds court

CANON LAW the decrees of the Church regulating Church matters

CANTLE the crown of the head

CHANCELLERY the office of the count's clerks

CHANDLER a maker of candles

CHAPMEN merchants or peddlers

CLOTH OF GOLD a cloth partly or wholly woven from gold thread

CLUNSIDE a field at the manor of Holt

COLLOPS small slices of meat

COURSER a war-horse

CROSSGUARD a metal bar located between the pommel and the blade of a sword, and standing at right angles to them

CRUPPER a horse's hindquarters

DEO GRATIAS (LATIN) Thanks be to God

DESTRIER a warhorse

DOCK the solid, fleshy part of an animal's tail

DOGE the elected chief magistrate and leader of the city of Venice while it was a Republic

EXCOMMUNICATION a sentence of exclusion from the communion of the Church, including the Sacraments

FARRIER a person who shoes horses

FARTHING a coin valued at one quarter of a penny

FOLIO the size of a sheet of parchment or paper when it is folded once

GOGONIANT! (WELCH) Glory be!

GREAVES metal shin guards

GULES in heraldry, the color red

HART a male deer (especially a red deer)

HIPPERTY-HAW (SHROPSHIRE DIALECT) hawthorn

JADING the practice of stopping a horse (sometimes with substances and their smells, sometimes with magic) so that it will not move an inch

JASPER a brightly colored precious stone (most valuable when green) with a wax-like luster

JASPER OLIVE a precious stone the size and shape of an olive

JOUST a war-game in which two mounted men try to unseat each other using lances

LAMMAS DAY August 1, the day on which harvesting began and the bread baked with new corn was brought to church and blessed

LANCET WINDOW a tall and narrow window, pointed at the top

THE LAND OVERSEA the name for the territory, including Palestine and the Nile Delta, over which Christians and Muslims fought during the crusades

LAY BROTHER a man who has taken the habit and vows of a religious order but is mostly employed in manual labor

LITTLE LARK a stream that flows through the manor of Caldicot

MANTICORE either a werewolf or a wild beast with a triple row of teeth in both the upper and lower jaws (from the Persian *mardkhora*)

THE MARCH OR MARCHES the borderland between England and Wales

MARK two thirds of a pound sterling

MARL clay

MATINS, TERCE, SEXT, NONE sets of prayers said or sung at 2 A.M., 9 A.M., midday, and 3 P.M. In all, monks attended seven services during each twenty-four-hour period: Matins/Lauds, Prime, Terce, Sext, None, Vespers, and Compline

MIDDEN a dunghill

MIDSUMMER-MEN a plant with purple-pink and purple-red flowers used in magic and medicine; also known as orpine

NOVICE in religious orders, a person under probation, prior to taking monastic vows

OBSIDIAN volcanic glass, usually black, believed by some cultures to have magical powers

OCTAVO the size of a piece of parchment or paper when each leaf is one-eighth of the whole sheet (i.e., when it has been folded three times)

PALFREY a saddle horse for day-to-day riding

PARRY to ward off or deflect the thrust of a sword

PAVILION a large tent with a peaked top

PEL a wooden post against which squires practiced swordplay

PIGEONS OF CAEHOWELL pigeons superstitiously believed to predict someone's death; Caehowell is a farm in the county of Shropshire

PISMIRE! an exclamation that someone or something smells of urine, like an ant-hill

PORTCULLIS a heavy iron grating lowered to bar the gateway to a castle

PUMICE-BREAD powdered glass, flour, and brewer's yeast made into loaves, baked, and then cut into small chunks for use in the scriptorium

QUARTO the size of a piece of parchment or paper when it is folded twice, so as to form four leaves

RECKLING the smallest or weakest animal in a litter

RED-LETTER DAY a letter written in red ink, used in church calendars to indicate saints' days or festivals

REEVE the overseer (or steward) of a manor

RUNE a letter (or character) of an alphabet said to have magical powers

SCREE a steep slope of loose stone

SHAWM an oboe-like instrument that came to Europe from the Near East in the twelfth century

SOLAR a withdrawing room, where one can be alone

SPRING-LINE the dividing line between an elevated hillside and a valley basin

STOOKS bundles of grain

SUMPTER a packhorse

VELLUM the best kind of parchment, made from the skin of a calf, lamb, or kid

WIMPLE a cloth covering for a woman's head arranged so that only her face is exposed

WITHERS on a horse, the highest part of the back, between the shoulder blades

ABOUT the AUThOR

Kevin Crossley-Holland grew up in the English countryside at the foot of a high hill. While an undergraduate at Oxford University, he fell in love with the Middle Ages and Anglo-Saxon poetry—a passion now reflected in his many highly praised collections and retellings of medieval stories and myths. In 1985, he received the Carnegie Medal for his novel *Storm*, while *The Seeing Stone*, the first book in his Arthur trilogy, won the Guardian Children's Fiction Prize and was shortlisted for the Whitbread Award and the *Los Angeles Times* Book Prize. It was also named an ALA Notable Book for Older Readers. The Arthur trilogy, which concludes with *King of the Middle March*, has won worldwide acclaim and is being published in twenty-one languages. It has already sold more than a million copies.

Kevin and his wife, Linda, live on the coast of the North Sea in Norfolk, England.

Follow Arthur's adventures to their triumphant conclusion.

"Outstanding…brings alive the world of the Middle Ages."
—*USA Today*